THE LAST DRAGON OF OZ

WHITNEY L. SPRADLING

Midnight Tide
PUBLISHING

The Last Dragon of Oz

Copyright © 2025 by Whitney L. Spradling

First Edition

ISBN 978-1-964655-26-0 (paperback), 978-1-964655-45-1 (hardback)

Published by Midnight Tide Publishing | Midnight Tide Publishing

Edited by Brenna Bailey-Davies | Bookmarten Editorial

Cover by The Cover Cauldron | The Cover Cauldron

Hardback Cover Art by Dezaray | oblivionsdream

Early Praise for The Last Dragon of Oz

Last Dragon of Oz is a spicy and thoroughly entertaining twist on a favorite childhood tale [...] If you enjoy reverse harem and dragons, this book is a must have!

-Catie O'Niell author of Love and Other Alien Concepts

I love the world that Whitney has brought to life in this. It is a fantastic mix of whimsy with a proper dark and gritty undertone.

-M. Vixen author of The Druid's Bindings

CONTENT WARNING

This book contains adult themes that may not be appropriate for all audiences.

These themes include:
    graphic sexual scenes
    language
    alcohol use
    torture
    cancer of parent
    death of a parent
    mention of an eating disorder
    violence
    murder
    child abuse
    death
    abuse of a parent

The Trevor Project

If you or someone you know is part of the LGBTQ+ community and needs help, please contact the Trevor Project. The Trevor Project is the leading suicide prevention and crisis intervention nonprofit organization for LGBTQ+ young people.

Text 'START' to 678-678
or
Call 1-866-488-7386

You are not alone. Help is available.

For those without a voice.

PROLOGUE
DACIANA

I SKIP THROUGH THE HALLS OF MY HOME, MY BRAIDED pigtails bouncing behind me. It's my time to visit Mama, and I always love hearing her stories. As soon as I push inside her room, I know something is different. The curtains are drawn, darkening the room, and there are more medicine bottles on the nightstand than usual. The ceiling lights have been dimmed, and the air feels heavier, more somber, as if it's pressing down all around me.

Mama opens her eyes slowly and blinks at the brightness filtering in from the hallway lights. I close the door behind me and sit on the edge of her bed, taking her hand in both of mine. Her skin is papery, and every knob and bump of her bones is more prominent.

"Hi, Mama," I say with a weary smile. The atmosphere here is so different than usual. It's lacking the warmth and love that normally fills the bedroom when I visit.

Her smile trembles slightly. "Hello, baby. How has your day been?" Her voice is weak, and it sounds like she's straining to speak loud enough to be heard.

"It was okay. I got in a fight with Sophia. She's so mean to me."

Mama gasps a small breathless laugh. "She's the closest thing you have to a sister. You need to keep her near. Now more than ever."

"What does that mean, Mama?"

Mama's sad smile makes my stomach squirm. But her silence is what sends fear racing through my veins.

"Will you tell me a story, Mama?" I whisper, grasping her hand a little tighter.

"I don't think I can, baby. I'm too tired today." She watches my face fall, and she swallows. Mama bends her head down and attempts to reach behind her neck with shaking arms. "Help me with this," she says breathily, indicating the necklace hanging down her chest.

I help lift the golden chain over her head, dropping it in her open palm. The bumble bee charm dangling on the end wavers with her tremors as she holds it out. "Baby, I want you to take this." She lies back, breathing heavily, like that small action took everything out of her.

I hesitate before I take the necklace. Daddy gave it to her when they got married. He has always called Mama his favorite bee, because her name is Beatrice, and she loves bees. I've never seen her not wear it. Why is she giving it to me now? I take it in my hand, the metal still warm from being against her body.

"I'm so proud of you, baby," Mama says, her voice breaking. "I love you so much. Don't ever forget that."

Something isn't right. Mama is usually so sunny, so happy, even when she's sick. But she seems so sad today.

"Mama, are you okay?" I ask, my voice small and sounding younger than my eleven years.

"Yes, baby. I'm fine. I just wanted to tell you how much I love you."

"I love you too, Mama."

"I need to rest. Give me a kiss before you go?"

I lean down and press my lips to Mama's forehead. Her skin is so dry and warm. Too dry and warm. "I can see you tomorrow?"

Something passes through her eyes, but I'm too young to understand what it means. "Of course, baby."

As her eyes close, a sudden urgency floods me, making me grab her bony shoulders. "Promise? Promise I'll see you tomorrow?"

Mama's smile is small but warm. "I promise, baby," she whispers.

THE NEXT DAY, there are too many people standing outside Mama's door. They're all talking in hushed tones, the words *cancer* and *what a shame* the most common. Their expressions long and forlorn, a few wipe tears from their faces. My stomach drops to my feet, making nausea churn in my belly as I weasel my way between them.

When I step into Mama's room, the world seems to squeeze down on me. Mama lies in her bed, but her skin is too pale and she's too still. Her doctor is packing up his bag, placing all her medicine bottles inside of it. Daddy stands on the other side of the bed, staring at Mama with an expression of such heartbreak that I know without a doubt what has happened.

"Mama?" I whisper, taking a step closer to the bed. "Mama?"

Someone tries to grab my arm, but I yank it away and rush forward. Daddy notices me, and he yells at someone to grab me, to make sure I don't see this. But it's too late.

Mama is gone.

"Mama?" I choke out, falling to my knees next to the bed. My chest aches as the tears build and bubble up. They spring from my eyes and fall down my face like a waterfall. My heart cracks open and I suddenly feel so very alone in a room full of people.

Someone grabs me around my waist and picks me up. They carry me away, and I kick and scream. I tear at their arms with my nails and slam my head back into theirs. They drop me with a curse. I land on my knees, but this time, I don't move closer to the bed. Because I remember what Mama said last night. She promised me I'd see her tomorrow.

And she lied.

I climb to my feet and push through the crowd of people.

Someone says my name. It sounds like my maid, but I'm small and faster than them. I run through my home, not seeing the familiar sights as I careen around corners and skid on the hardwood floor in my socks. In my room, I lock my bedroom door and stare blankly at the wall covered in posters of my favorite band.

Mama lied to me. She knew she wouldn't see me again. That's why she gave me the necklace. I grab the bee charm and yank. The chain cuts into the back of my neck and burns like a sunburn when it snaps. I look at the bee in the palm of my hand and my lip curls in anger.

"You lied to me," I whisper, tears streaming down my face. "You left me and you broke your promise."

In a fit of rage, I throw the necklace. I don't see where it lands through the angry tears that blur my vision. With the comforting weight of Mama's necklace no longer around my neck, I crumple to the floor and break.

1

DACIANA

Social media fucking sucks.

It's just a bunch of people lying. Lying to themselves. Lying to everyone else. Lying about how happy they are and how perfect their life is. And I'm no different.

I bark a humorless laugh as I hit post and watch as the newest picture of me and Sophia appears on my feed. We look happy. Not a care in the world. Makeup and hair perfect. Drinks in our hand. Dresses sexy and expensive.

But it's all smoke and mirrors. Behind the eyeshadow and mascara is endless sadness. Under the lipstick and blush are frowns and tears. The beauty and perfectionism are shields hiding the self-doubt, fear of failure, and the ever-present gaping wound of abandonment.

I mean, take me for example. One glance at all the name brand dresses in my massive walk-in closet, not to mention the entire shelf of jewelry, and you'd think I should be the happiest girl alive. Right?

Wrong.

Trauma is a bitch. And no matter how much I try to fight her, she always returns in full force. All the money in the world won't make my past magically go away.

I sigh and drop my phone to the bed, falling back onto the pile of pink and white pillows, idly twisting the sapphire studded ring around my finger. There is also no point in reminiscing on the past. That only leads to pain.

My gaze lands on the easel positioned in front of the big bay window overlooking the gardens. A blank canvas waits, bright and beckoning, to be slathered in paints and turned into anything. The only limit is my imagination.

I haven't picked up a paintbrush in months, though. And when I do think about painting, the images in my mind are dark and scary. Nothing like the floral paintings I typically create. Maybe if I just go with my instincts, I'll get the shadowy images out of my head. Maybe I need to dust off my mind and open the space for more bright and lovely subjects.

I purposely put my easel in front of the windows for the inspiration the gardens usually give me. They're huge. It was my mother's favorite place to spend time. Even though she's gone, my dad has made sure the gardeners have kept up the grounds in her memory. Gravel paths wind through the flora. Trees with weeping branches trail fingers on the path. A white marble fountain in the center sprays droplets of water into the air.

Roses of every color, size, and variety bloom in neat, organized rows, perfuming the air with their rich aroma. Hyacinth and hydrangea, tulips and peonies, flowers I don't even know the name of. They all sprout from the ground in patterns and designs that please the eye. My moms favorite spot was the corner where wildflowers grow dramatically. Hidden amongst the riot of color is the reason my mom loved that area so much: the beehive.

Bees. I raise my hand to my neck, fingers searching for something that hasn't been there for fifteen years.

With a sigh, I drag my gaze to the blank canvas and snag a charcoal pencil from the cup in my paint bag. Without giving it any thought, I let my hand do whatever it wants, giving in to the dark urges inside my mind. The sketch begins to take form, dark lines that slowly come together to create an image. I still have no idea what it is when movement outside draws my gaze from the canvas.

At first glance, I think a cat wandered into the yard. But . . . No. That can't be. I rub my eyes and lean forward, practically pressing my face to the glass. A tail swishes in the grass and golden eyes blink. That's not a cat.

There is a baby dragon in my yard. Which is impossible because magic has been gone from our world for centuries. But that is definitely a baby dragon.

I look around, seeing no gardeners in sight. My gaze returns to the impossible, and before I know what I'm doing, I'm standing from the stool and rushing from my room, almost as if I'm possessed and someone else is controlling my movements. My bare toes grip the carpet in the hallway that thankfully dampens the sound of my feet thumping on the floor. I skid past the servants stairwell and grab the doorknob to stop myself. This will be the fastest way to the gardens.

The stairs and hallway beyond are empty as I tear through them. This is the most I've run in a very long time, and my lungs are already burning. The outside door looms ahead and I push through it into the warm summer air. I bypass the garden, not wanting to run barefoot on the gravel. As it is, a rock jams into my heel and I limp the rest of the way around the border hedges.

I slow as I come to the back, not wanting to scare it. Part of me hopes I was seeing things, despite what that might mean for my mental health. But as I approach the back of the garden, the breath that rushes in and out of my lungs completely stops. I wasn't seeing things. A baby dragon blinks up at me, tail lined with tiny blue-green spikes swishing through the grass behind it. Its watermelon-sized body is covered in emerald-green scales that glisten in the sunlight. Frail-looking wings flutter on its back, so small and incongruous. Its little face is overtaken by the large ears protruding from its head, almost wing-like in appearance. In other words, it's adorable. It also shouldn't exist.

I stand frozen in place, my mind emptying of all thought as I blink back at the dragon.

It takes a step forward. Then another. I stand still, unsure what to do. Its little mouth opens, empty of teeth, and small croaking sounds come out. It cocks its head to the side and sits, tail still swishing. Body on autopilot, I slowly kneel in the grass. The fronds tickle my knees, and I ignore the fact that there are probably bugs crawling around me. My hand shakes as I reach out, palm up. My chest aches with the need to breathe, but I'm too scared. If I breathe, the dragon might startle. Or the image might shatter and I'll be proven crazy.

The baby dragon approaches and sniffs my hand, its warm breath brushing across my palm. Without warning, it ducks its head and rubs the side of its face on my hand. A soft trilling sound comes from its chest, like it's purring.

"What the hell?" I mutter to myself. "This is a dream. I'm dreaming. There is no way I'm touching a real-life fucking dragon."

The baby dragon chuffs, as if laughing at what I just said, and it jumps forward into my space. Startled, I fall backward onto my ass, and the dragon climbs onto my lap. Big eyes stare at me, vertical black pupils slashing through the shimmering gold.

"Um, hi?" I say, lifting my arms into the air to make sure it knows I'm not going to hurt it. I doubt this little thing could harm me, but better safe than sorry.

The dragon walks in circles on my lap before flopping down and laying its head on my legs. It wraps its tail around its body, curling it over its nose. I stare at it, eyes growing wider and wider.

"Umm, excuse me?" I ask, gently poking the scaly side. "You can't lie there."

It opens one eye and looks at me then closes it, completely ignoring what I said. A noise behind me causes me to whip my head in that direction, jostling the baby dragon taking a nap on my legs. A gardener pushes a wheelbarrow of dirt toward me. He hasn't noticed the dragon yet, and something tells me I can't let him see it.

This world has been without magic for so long, most people don't believe it ever existed. However, this dragon lying here proves that magic does indeed exist. If people find out about this creature, what would they do? I can imagine them running tests and experiments on it, trying to figure out how it exists. What if they hurt it? It's just a baby.

I don't give myself time to think through any repercussions of my actions. With my heart in my throat, I snatch up the dragon and dart between the hedges. It wakes with a jolt and a warbled yowl. "Hush," I whisper. "Unless you want to be caught." I hiss as my bare feet land on the gravel pathway. "Motherfucker," I gasp, gingerly trying to run, crouched, with a baby dragon in my arms. *What in the actual fuck am I doing right now?*

By the time I make it to the house, my arms are shaking. I'm terrible at math, but I'm guessing this thing weighs at least ten pounds. When was the last time I lifted something heavy? Thankfully, the servants hallway and stairwell are empty. But when I open the door into the hallway where my bedroom is, I have to jump back and close the door quickly. Breathing heavily, I press my ear to the door. The muffled voices of my dad and stepmom are barely audible.

"Have you seen Daciana?" my dad asks. "I wanted to talk to her before the party tonight."

"I have not. But I don't make it a priority to keep track of your daughter." My stepmom's haughty voice makes me grimace. I fucking hate that woman.

My dad sighs, and their footsteps softly thump down the hall and disappear. I wait another few minutes, the dragon staring at me questioningly, before I slip out and run to my bedroom. I lock the door behind me before setting the dragon on my bed, shaking out my arms to get the feeling to return to them.

We stare at each other, some sort of supernatural staring contest that I'm bound to lose because I don't have magic. I shake my head and my legs give out. I plop onto the floor, never breaking eye contact with the creature on my bed. A fucking dragon. A magical creature. I don't even know what to do or think.

Girasole has been without magic for centuries. As the stories go, the Parcae—the Fates—created the barrier that locked all magic in a separate realm. The residents of Girasole are supposedly still fae. Many of us *feel* a connection with nature that can't really be explained. The older generations insist there is still a spark buried so deep inside of us, it's impossible to reach. But life is . . . normal. Ordinary. Dull. Magicless.

And somehow in this magicless world, a dragon has appeared.

I swallow, my throat clicking in the heavy silence of my room. "So . . . are you a boy or a girl?"

The dragon cocks its head and blinks slowly.

Right. It can't talk. Yes or no answers, then. "Are you a boy?" My breath catches as the dragon nods. "Yes? You're a boy?" Another nod. "Okay. Well, that's a start. Do you have a name?" This time he shakes his head from side to side. "No. Okay. Should I name you?"

He chuffs, warm air blowing from his nose, and he lays his head on the edge of the bed, staring at me expectantly.

"Right. Umm . . . Brutus?" I ask. The dragon recoils, top lip pulling back. If he had teeth, they would be showing. "No. Okay. Brutus is out. How about Major?"

This time, the dragon actually sticks his tongue out and gags.

"I'll take that as a no," I drawl, staring at the dramatic creature. "Jupiter? Toro? Axe? Mack?" I fire off a bunch of names that the dragon vigorously shakes his head at. "This is impossible. I'm trying to think of something big and strong. Something that suits a dragon."

His tongue flops out of his mouth again and he shakes his head.

"You don't want something like that?" I study his scales, the green shimmering in the lamplight. "Emerald?"

He cocks his head to the side and I hold my breath. Then he shakes it, and I deflate.

"Tiny? Mouse? Squeak? Twig?" I try, throwing out random names that don't sound strong, and stop on Twig when his head pops up. "Twig?" I swear he smiles as he nods. "Not a very scary name."

The dragon's tail swishes angrily behind him, and he lowers his eyelids until he's glaring at me.

"Okay, okay," I say, holding up my arms in surrender. "Sorry. Twig it is."

Apparently content now that he has a suitable name—at least suitable in his mind—he curls up on my pillow and promptly falls asleep. I stare for a moment, watching his tiny back rise and fall with rapid breaths. How big do dragons get? I can't imagine he'll stay this small forever, and there is no way I can keep him hidden once he starts getting bigger. What am I going to do with him?

Already, I know I won't be able to turn him in. I should never have named him. Isn't that what people say? Once you name a stray, you become attached to it? He's so cute and innocent. How could I ever turn him in and risk him being hurt? I sigh and let my head smack into my palms. What the hell am I going to do?

"Daciana!"

I freeze just past my dad's office door. My heart lurches into my throat and I swallow, attempting to shove it back down. He doesn't know, does he? There is no way he can know I have a magical creature hidden in my room. Unless he happened to watch the security footage. Fuck! I didn't even think of that.

I step backward until I can peek inside his office, pasting on my best fake smile. "Yes?"

"Come here for a second. We need to talk about tonight."

Relief punches through me so fast, I almost fall to the floor. Taking a seat in the leather wingback chair in front of my dad's large mahogany desk, I force myself to act normal. My dad finishes signing some paperwork and leans back in his chair.

Lorenzo DeRosa is a massive man. Despite magic not existing in our world, the presence that surrounds my dad is almost palpable. He's powerful, strong, and determined. These things have helped him raise our family to its current status. We've been sitting pretty at the top of the Camorra, the Girasole mafia, for ten years now.

"Tonight is an important night," he begins, shuffling papers around his desk. Piles of papers and weapons litter the top. I get my disorganization from him, unlike my mom, who was strict about cleaning. His green eyes meet mine and he runs a hand through his close-cropped brown hair. "The Santiagos will be here, and I've been working my ass off to make an alliance with them. I know they've been meeting with the Morellis, and I refuse to let those bastards gain the upper hand." He punctuates his sentence by banging a fist on his desk. "Fucking Morellis," he mutters. "I can't get a single moment of peace without them trying to take me down. And I still haven't gotten my payback on them."

"Yes, I'm well aware of the situation. If the Santiagos side with the Morellis, things will get ugly." At my words, my dad nods, giving me an appraising look. He has done his best to teach me everything there is to know about the Camorra. Not only to keep me safe but to give him a leg up in an organization that is strictly male run. No one suspects me to be anything but a pretty princess who has nothing in her head but thoughts of money, booze, and sex. They're not wrong. That is a big part of what I think about, but men talk around pretty girls. And that information goes straight to my dad. Despite how long I've been doing this, and how well he's taught me, my dad always seems surprised that I know what's going on.

"The Santiago heir will also be here," he says, trailing off suggestively.

I raise one manicured brow and smirk, hiding the stab of betrayal I always experience during these talks. "You want me to fuck him?" I ask, going straight for the kill.

My dad grimaces and shakes his head. "Do you have to be so crass?"

"I mean, that's what you want me to do, right?" I ask,

shrugging. What else would he want me to do? The fact that my dad has no qualms about whoring out his only daughter to gain the upper hand in the Camorra is something I've long since gotten used to. At least, I pretend I have.

"I was trying to suggest it a little more . . . *tactfully*. You don't have to come straight out and say it." He shakes his head and leans forward, steepling his fingers on his desk. "I don't care what you do with the boy. Just get me whatever information you can."

A flutter of excitement erupts in my belly. Julian Santiago is supposedly exceptional in bed. Tonight looks promising indeed. I smile wickedly at my dad, taking delight in making him squirm. "Guys always spill more secrets after mind blowing orgasms. Don't worry. I'll get you what you need."

He pins me with a flat stare before sighing and shaking his head. "Just keep it to yourself. I really don't want to know what you're doing. The rumors are bad enough." The way he says that, like he isn't the reason I do what I do, is like a fist squeezing my heart.

"I see you found Daciana," a smooth, cultured voice says.

I shove down the disappointment in my dad, and instead embrace the anger that rises at the sound of that voice. Instead of turning around, I remain facing my dad, mainly because I don't want to see my stepmom's perfectly made-up face. But also because I know it will piss her off if I don't acknowledge her. My dad smiles, making my stomach roll uncomfortably. He knows exactly what my thoughts are about her, but he doesn't even try to pretend he cares about what I feel.

Melanie is a grade-A bitch.

Not only did my dad marry her two months after my mom's death, but Melanie has made it her job to make my life as miserable as possible. Every opportunity she has, she does her best to take me down a peg or two. It was worse when I was younger. As I've gotten older, I've learned to shrug off her hateful remarks. Although, the barbs have already bitten deep into my bones. I'm not sure I'll ever be able to get over all her words.

"I did find her." My dad turns back to me. "And now that I've reminded you of the importance of tonight, I want to give you this." He opens a drawer and pulls out a black velvet box that he slides across the desk.

A smile spreads across my face. "What is it?" I tug it closer and pop open the lid. A stunning necklace sits nestled in black satin, the rose gold of the metal popping against the dark fabric. Diamonds stud the entire length, with a diamond half the size of my fist dangling right in the center. The light catches the gemstones and they throw sparkling rainbows onto the ceiling. "Thank you, Daddy! It's gorgeous!"

As excited as I am to have more shiny jewelry, the reason behind the gift makes it feel less heartfelt. Every piece I own has been gifted to me by my dad when he asks me to do something like this. It started to feel like bribery long ago.

He leans back in his chair with a fond smile. "I'm sure you have a dress that will match, right?"

Behind me, Melanie snorts. "If she doesn't, I'm sure you'll buy her another necklace that matches better," she mutters so only I can hear.

I ignore her words and stand to walk around the desk. I throw my arms around my dad and give him a kiss on the cheek. "I love it. And of course I have the perfect dress for it."

"Good." He smiles warmly at me before turning his attention to Melanie. "Now that I've talked with Daciana, I need to talk to you as well."

I have no desire to hear this conversation so I quickly leave, necklace in hand, and head toward the kitchen. The baby dragon in my room is probably hungry, and I'm sure I need to feed it something.

As with every time I interact with my dad, I reflect on our relationship. I really do love my dad. He protects me, makes sure I'm safe and cared for. He knows how I feel about his marriage to Melanie, and we just opt to ignore that elephant in the room. He has always spoiled me, even when I was a child, but he started doing it more when I was old enough to help him with the Camorra.

I'll never tell him that no number of gemstones or clothing will make up for the fact that my mom is dead and the woman he married two months after her death is a bitch and a half. He wouldn't understand where I'm coming from. To him, it's all about perception. He needed someone to fill my mom's spot. Even though he married my mom for love, and I'm positive she was his soulmate, he can't be seen as weak. So he married Melanie.

And if I try to tell him his bribes for sleeping with sons of the Camorra no longer feel like thoughtful gifts, he'd laugh and tell me it's my job as a woman to do what's necessary. I know that's why he hasn't arranged a marriage for me yet. I'm too useful being single, and my reputation as a slut works to his advantage.

Growing up, Melanie knew this would be my responsibility, and she took great pleasure in the snide comments she would make about my weight. She did it so often, it was no surprise I developed an eating disorder when I was younger. Luckily, I was able to fight my way out of that by sheer willpower and wanting to throw a giant middle finger in Melanie's direction. Of course, some things are easier to overcome than others. I still struggle with image thanks to Melanie.

Forcing thoughts of the bitch from my mind, I push into the kitchen. I grab a piece of chicken thawing on the counter and stare at it, grimacing at the slimy, squishy texture. Do dragons prefer their chicken raw or cooked? I glance around but see no cooked chicken, so he'll have to deal with uncooked for the time being. With my stolen chicken in hand, I make my way back to my room and the dragon hiding in it.

2

DACIANA

I stand in my closet holding the necklace my dad gave me and lift it up to my dresses. It would look good with a few of them, I just have to decide which one. Something cool and smooth brushes my leg and I jump, barely containing a screech. When I look down, I see Twig snuffling around my closet.

"Which one should I wear?" I ask him, holding up two options. I swear it's like he actually contemplates my question before cocking his head to the right. "This one it is then," I say, hanging up the dress I was holding in my left hand. With a little snort, I shake my head. "Letting a dragon dress me. What the fuck is happening?"

I sit at my vanity and begin curling my hair and doing my makeup. I'm only halfway through when I hear a crash from my closet. Jumping to my feet, I dash inside only to find Twig with one of my red heels in his mouth, surrounded by a pile of other shoes he knocked off the low shelf.

"No!" I screech. "Drop it!"

Twig drops the shoe, a trail of dragon saliva connecting the shoe to his mouth. He looks at me with big sad golden eyes. His wings and ears droop, making him look utterly pathetic.

Instantly, my anger cools like snow falling on hot embers. "I didn't mean to yell," I say, bending to pick up the heel. It's slobbery, and I grimace as my fingers slide through the saliva. Those were my favorite pair, and now the velvet material is probably ruined for good. Lovely. "You can't chew on my shoes, Twig." I glance at the slimy one in my hand and sigh. "Fine. You might as well keep this one." I toss it back to him, wiping my hand on a random towel strewn on my floor. Twig catches the heel midair, and his tail swishes happily back and forth. "No others, though. Okay?"

He nods, red heel dangling from his mouth as he settles on the floor to gnaw gummily on the expensive footwear. Shaking my head, I return to the vanity and finish my makeup. After shimmying into my dress, I study my reflection in the floor-length mirror. The tight cream-colored mini is probably the shortest dress I own. I won't be able to sit or bend over without giving everyone a show. It's covered in gold sparkles that shimmer with each move I make, reminding me of Twig's eyes. The bell sleeves are sheer and cuffed at the wrists, with the excess fabric hanging over my hands. I turn and look over my shoulder to check the back. The rouching running from top to bottom makes my ass look phenomenal. And the V-neck is the perfect cut to display my new necklace right between my breasts.

I sweep soft blond waves from my shoulders and clasp the necklace, along with a rose gold choker, around my neck. After adding a few diamond bracelets and earrings, I'm ready to go. I grab my cream-colored heels with matching gold sparkles from my closet and tighten the diamond straps around my ankles.

"No other shoes, remember?" I remind Twig before I leave. "Stay in my room, don't eat anything, and be quiet. I'll bring you more food when I come back." Whether that's tonight or tomorrow remains to be seen. I take a deep breath and don my proverbial mask, strengthening my resolve for what I know is coming.

I can already hear the sounds of the party by the main staircase. This one is going to be the wildest yet, if my dad is trying to impress the Santiago family. I subtly tug the hem of my dress as I descend the stairs, even though it barely budges. My dad is greeting someone at the door, his boisterous laugh echoing off the high ceilings. Melanie stands by his side, clinging to his arm and simpering whenever he looks at her.

I sneak past, not wanting to get stuck greeting people as they come in, and head for the ballroom. Guards line the corridor, each one dressed in black with multiple guns strapped to their bodies. My dad has spared no expense for this party and he's not playing with security either. Glittering lights cast a soft white glow on the ballroom floor and twine up the marble columns. More twinkle in the potted plants spaced evenly along the edges of the room.

The bar at one end of the space is packed, as always. Free liquor is too tempting for most to ignore. Lighted glass shelves display the largest variety of alcohol I've ever seen. At the other end of the ballroom, a band plays on a raised dais, the music calm and smooth for now. The more the liquor flows, the more rowdy and suggestive the music becomes. There isn't much dancing yet, but people are gathered on the dance floor in small groups, talking, laughing, and spilling all the tea since the last time we've all been together.

I make my way across the floor, the clicking of my heels lost in the sounds of music, laughter, and talking. At the bar, I squeeze my way through, elbowing people if they refuse to move. It's my house, and I'll get my drinks whenever the fuck I want without waiting in line.

"Daci, what would you like?" Theo asks. He's my favorite bartender because he never skimps on the booze, and my drinks are always strong as fuck.

"I'll take an espresso martini."

With my drink in hand, I head to the balcony and the predetermined meeting spot with my cousin. Sophia and I grew up together, and for twenty-six years we've attended the same schools, went to all the same parties, and dealt with all of the violence that came our family's way together. We're trauma bonded in more than one way. And despite how much I love her and trust her, I will never be able to tell her about Twig. Family loyalty is drilled into us from the very beginning. And her loyalty to me will only go so far. A dragon in my bedroom is something she would have to tell her dad. The secrets we're forced to keep are the wedge that prevents us from truly being best friends.

"Daci!" She crashes into me, almost making me spill my drink. "You look amazing. And that necklace!"

I take a sip of my incredibly strong martini and run a finger over the diamond resting in my cleavage. "I know, right? My dad just gave it to me. I love that dress by the way! You're gonna let me borrow it someday, right?" I ask, ogling the black lace dress that's just as short as mine. Little scraps of black fabric under the lace barely cover her, and her brown hair is curled and thrown over one shoulder.

The first hour of the party passes in a blur as Sophia and I toss back drinks and talk about the snobby bitches in the ballroom. As much as I love these parties, I need to be solidly drunk before I can even pretend to like those girls with their cheap dresses, poorly dyed hair, and ugly jewelry. Scavengers, all of them. I never claim I'm not fake, but those girls are the worst. They'd do anything to crawl into mine and Sophia's circle, and not for our friendship. Everyone wants a chance at my dad.

That is the main reason I never had any friends growing up, besides Sophia. I could never trust anyone because they only wanted to get close to me for information. Any time I came home and asked if I could have a playdate, my dad would say no. It crushed me every time. And despite how much it hurt, I didn't learn my lesson until well after my mom died. Then I had to learn how to be fake as fuck just so I could go out and put on a show.

I shove aside the ever-present loneliness and focus on the ballroom. Commotion draws my attention from my third martini. All the girls have turned toward the entrance, staring hungrily, practically drooling.

Sophia elbows me, sticky syrup and alcohol splashing onto my fingers from my martini. "Daci, look!"

"What the fuck, Soph! I spilled my drink." I fling my hand, spraying droplets of espresso martini everywhere.

"Who cares about your drink? Julian's here."

I whip my head in the direction all the girls are looking, martini forgotten. Julian Santiago saunters across the ballroom, a smirk gracing his face. A lock of brown hair falls forward across his brow, and his dark eyes smolder as they scan the crowd of women simpering for him.

"The best sex I've ever had," Sophia says, licking her lips.

"You slept with him? When?"

"The last Valentino party. You were sick, and your dad decided to stay home."

"The best ever, huh?" I ask, already plotting. She's not the first person I've heard say that.

"Oh for sure. I think about it all the time."

Julian heads straight for the bar. His gaze meets mine once and he winks, before disappearing in the crowd. I can kill two birds with one stone tonight. My lips twitch in a small smile at the prospect.

"He's mine tonight," I warn Sophia. "Keep your claws off him."

She cackles and clinks her glass against mine. "Sure thing, sis."

Before I know what's happening, Julian emerges from the crowd around the bar and heads straight for me, two shot glasses topped with limes in his hands.

"Oh shit, Daci. He must have the same thought as you," Sophia whispers fiercely. "I'm going to go find my own conquest for the night. Have fun." She sings her last words and wiggles her fingers at me as a goodbye.

I refrain from snorting. He's probably following his dad's orders, same as me. Sleep with the DeRosa princess, get whatever information you can out of her by any means necessary. But whatever his reasoning, I have my own. Not including my dad's orders.

"Daciana DeRosa in the flesh," he says, bowing slightly, keeping the shots upright. "They weren't lying when they said you were pretty."

"Is that the best you can do?" I raise one brow, hands on my hips. "Doesn't bode well for tonight."

He smirks, a look that probably has girls falling at his feet most of the time. While cute, it just looks pompous to me. Up close, his brown eyes are dull and uninspiring. His dark hair is slicked back from his face, showcasing his slightly too large forehead. He's nothing special, but then again, I can't see what's under his clothing. I'm scared he's no different than all the others, though.

"You wound me, and we haven't even had a drink yet."

I hold out my hand and wiggle my fingers. "Well then, hand it over." Although a tequila shot isn't what I would call a drink.

His fingers brush mine when I take the glass, and I down it like water, not even needing the lime. I bite the inside of my cheek to keep from laughing at his sour expression as he drinks his.

"Wanna dance?" he asks, slightly out of breath from his shot. His gaze travels over my body in a way I'm used to. It does nothing for me, though, and I hope this isn't a sign of what's to come tonight.

My head is light, my body vibrating with the need to move. The alcohol loosens my muscles and my inhibition. This is what I love about these parties—when the alcohol numbs my mind enough for me to actually let go and enjoy myself. I brush past Julian with a coy smile. The game is on, and I'm good at playing it. I snag his free hand in mine and tug him to the dance floor.

We spend the next couple of hours dancing and flirting. Sweat drips down my back and between my breasts. I regret wearing my hair down; the underlayer is damp and my neck is hot. Julian's hands rove over my body, and I sway against his, enticing and teasing. Even though I'm not really attracted to him, my hormones know I'm grinding against a guy, and it doesn't take long for desire to burn to life in my belly.

It always amazes me how these parties end up turning into a rave. The men all disappear into the offices or library. Secret meetings and clandestine plans being made. The women gather in the parlor for a drink and gossip. And their children find themselves drunk on the dance floor, dancing in a way that might as well be an orgy.

I know the moment I've got Julian in the palm of my hand. I rub my hips against his, feeling his dick harden behind his nice dress pants. When I dart my tongue out to lick my bottom lip, his eyes hungrily track the movement. Lowering my gaze to his mouth seals the deal. Julian leans down and claims my lips. It's not a horrible kiss, but it's also not the best I've ever had. There are no fireworks or butterflies. He's a little too . . . desperate, in my opinion. But I can work with that.

I stand on my tiptoes and deepen the kiss. His body presses tight to mine and I let a little moan slip past my lips. Julian's fingers on my ass tighten, and I feel his dick twitch against my hips. A flutter of excitement spreads through me as I grind against him. When I break away, his eyes are dark and lust shimmers in their depths.

I lace my fingers with his and pull him off the dance floor into the hallway. I throw him teasing smiles over my shoulder as I lead him up the grand stairs into an empty spare bedroom on the second floor. The lock clicks and I waste no time slowly tugging the sleeves of my dress over my shoulders. Julian watches my every move like a hawk, his obvious erection tenting the front of his pants.

The dress hits the floor in a glittery puddle, and I step backward until my legs hit the bed. His eyes darken as they travel over my naked body. My skin pebbles, and it's not all from the chill in the room. His gaze feels heavy, almost suffocating.

"Well," I ask, my voice throaty and low. "What are you waiting for?" The nerves I've been feeling all night swell, and I do my best to ignore them.

Julian's clothes land on the floor in a flurry of movement and I slip further up the bed, letting my gaze travel over his body in return. He is definitely the most impressive of the guys I've slept with, and I can't help the flutter in my belly. A mix of excitement, nerves, and hope.

Julian climbs on top of me and kisses me again. I try to focus on the feel of his skin against mine, his tongue in my mouth, the scent of his soap and hair product. But when his fingers slide through my core, my focus narrows to that. *What if it's the same as every other time?*

Julian, for all the hype I've heard about him, is only okay with his fingers. He rubs my clit like he's trying to rub it off, and it borders on painful—and not in a good way. Not a good sign. I lift my hips in an attempt to get him to move his focus from my clit, but it doesn't work.

"Enough teasing," I say breathlessly, faking it every step of the way. I grab his hips and tug him on top of me.

Julian goes straight for the target then. He quickly slides on a condom before pushing his cock inside, rolling his hips to ease it in as I fake my moaning and panting. As he pumps his hips, the excitement that had been growing inside of me all night slowly evaporates like mist under the sun. It's not that he's not equipped, because he is, but he falls flat. Nothing he does gives me what I need. After a few moments of Julian thrusting and grunting, and me pretending to enjoy it, I lose my patience.

"Let me on top," I say, shoving against his shoulders.

Julian grins and rolls over, placing his hand under his head like an arrogant bastard. I barely refrain from rolling my eyes. Straddling his waist, I slide onto his cock, moaning for extra emphasis. As I roll my hips, I can't help but think of how pointless this is. Julian isn't even touching me. I'm the only one doing any work and it's obvious to me that it's not going to end in fireworks. At least for me.

Why do I keep insisting on doing this? I should know better by now. After so many years of this bullshit, nothing is going to change. Suddenly fed up and annoyed, I stop.

Julian gapes at me as I stand then shimmy back into my dress.

"What are you doing?" he asks, propping himself up on his elbows.

I force a wicked smile to my face and brush my hair over my shoulder. "It's obvious you're not good enough to get me off, and I don't feel like faking it tonight. Later!" I wave and turn around, my smile dropping the second he can't see my face.

Outside in the hallway, I lean against the closed door, my heels dangling from my fingertips, and I squeeze my eyes shut against the burn of tears. Inside the bedroom, I hear the bed squeaking and Julian moving around as he gets dressed. Not wanting to get caught by him, I hurry upstairs to my bathroom and lock myself inside.

I don't give myself time to think. Falling into my routine, I climb into the shower and let the hot water rain over me. As if on autopilot, my hand reaches for the vibrator and it only takes me a few seconds to get off. The rush of endorphins from my orgasm doesn't last though. Right on its heels are the unrelenting thoughts that I'm broken. A sob crawls up my throat and I drop to the bottom of the shower, curling my knees to my chest. My tears mix with the water falling down my cheeks.

I had so much hope for tonight. I hoped tonight would be the night I *finally* got off with a guy. But yet again, I was wrong. There is something broken within me. Not once have I ever had an orgasm unless I've given it to myself. I don't know why I keep trying, it's obviously never going to happen. And each time I try and fail, the letdown gets harder and harder to ignore.

By the time I get my crying under control, the water has gone cold. I quickly dry off and go to my room with a towel wrapped around my head. Distantly, I can still hear the sounds of the party downstairs, but I tune them out. I probably fucked up big time tonight. Not only did I not get any information for my dad, but I left the son of the Santiago family with blue balls. Fuck it. I can't bring myself to care right now.

The worry of that quickly fades as I step into my room and find utter chaos.

"What the fuck?" I screech, quickly shutting the door behind me.

My makeup is everywhere, tubes and containers open. The sheets are off the bed and in a puddle on the floor. My paints have been scattered throughout the room, a few tubes open and staining the white carpet yellow, blue, and purple. My gaze tracks around the room. It looks like someone tried to rob me. But then I notice the lump tangled in the gauzy white curtains.

"Twig?" I ask, slowly approaching.

He looks at me through the sheer fabric, big golden eyes filled with fear. I approach slowly and grimace. He's covered in paint. Smears of bright colors streak his green scales.

"Is that . . ." I bend down, getting a closer look, and gently remove the tangled curtains from his body. "Yep. That's blush." Faint pink powder shimmers around his mouth. "Did you eat my blush? That can't be healthy."

A little whimper comes from his tiny body and my heart breaks. He looks utterly pathetic. I scoop him into my arms, grunting slightly as I try to avoid the paint.

"Let's get you cleaned up."

The bathroom once again fills with steam. I set Twig in the water and grab a fresh loofah from under the sink. When I turn back around, a smile spreads across my face.

Twig found the rubber duck Sophia gave me as a joke that I set on the edge of the tub for fun. He's currently chasing it through the water, tail swishing like a rudder, wings acting as fins.

I stop him long enough to wash off the paint and blush, then sit on the floor—well out of the splash zone—and let Twig play.

He flounces, splashes, and makes general chaos. By the time the water has gone cold, there is more of it on the floor than in the tub. The cleaning lady is going to have her work cut out for her— and be thoroughly confused as to what I did in here to make such a mess.

"Okay, Twig," I say, unplugging the drain. "It's time to get out." I pick him up and place him on the floor, the bathmat squishing wetly under his feet.

I turn my back for three seconds to grab a towel from the shelf, and when I turn back to wrap it around Twig, he's gone. I glance around, frantically searching for him, but the bathroom is empty. The door to the hall is cracked and little wet dragon prints lead right through it. How the hell did he get the door open?

"No," I whisper. "No, no, no."

My heart kicks into full gear as I dart into the hall, looking both ways, but I see no baby dragon. "Twig!" I whisper-shriek, afraid of drawing attention to myself.

Wet footprints lead down the hall, away from my bedroom, and I follow them. They are quickly drying, the water on his feet disappearing the farther he goes. I hold my breath, too scared to breathe in fear that someone will hear and come looking for me. The footprints round a corner and I skid to a stop.

Twig sits in a potted plant down the hall. I rush forward and he hops out, scattering dirt as he does so.

"Oh," I say, grimacing at the dragon poop in the potted plant. "I see. I never even thought about that." I look around but find nothing to use as a pooper scooper.

A door closes somewhere in the house, and I jump. We can't just stand here. Someone will find us for sure. I'll just have to leave it there. Let the housekeepers find it and wonder what the hell shit in the plant.

"Let's go, Twig. It's late." I scoop him in my arms and head back toward my room. "Tomorrow, I'll figure out what to do with you." Twig lays his head on my arm, mouth opening in a yawn. I smile. He's cute, even if he is trouble.

3

DACIANA

I wake the next morning extra warm. A slight weight radiates heat and makes it even harder to wake up. When I finally pry my eyes open, I find Twig curled next to me, his head resting on my chest.

A strange sensation in my heart takes me aback. I didn't think of the long-term impact of taking in this dragon. I didn't think past the sudden moment of fear when I thought someone was going to discover him. Now that I've had this little guy for a night, I already feel a sense of responsibility toward him. Not only that, but he seems to have wormed into my heart. That quickly.

I run my fingers over the top of his head. His scales are cool despite the heat he puts off. Smooth and silky, almost glass-like. My touch makes him stir. His tail twitches and he yawns, his tongue flopping out of his mouth momentarily.

"Wake up, little guy. We have a lot to do today."

He cracks one eye open, golden and sleepy, before closing it again. I poke the side of his neck, and a quiet rumble comes from his chest. Twig moves his head from me, tucking it against his body and covering his eyes with his tail.

"Not a morning dragon, huh? Ever hear of the saying 'Early bird gets the worm?' Or maybe I should say early dragon."

I slide out of bed and let him sleep while I get ready for the day, tossing around a few ideas of what to do with my new pet. It would be impossible to keep him. He won't stay this small for long, and there is no way I could hide a full-grown dragon. But the thought of getting rid of him makes me pause. My heart hurts at the idea of giving him away, but I don't think I have any other choice.

When I'm dressed in a simple sundress of blue and white checks, my blond hair in a high ponytail on top of my head, I grab the largest bag I own, a bright red leather one with a faint sparkly shimmer in the material.

"Okay, Twig. I let you sleep in. But it's time to get up."

He ignores me, standing long enough to turn his back toward me then lying back down.

I huff. "Seriously? Come on. I'll get you breakfast," I say coyly.

His head pops up and I smile. Food is the way to any man's heart, and apparently dragons are no different.

I set the bag on the bed. "I know you're not going to like this, but I need you to get in here. And stay there. I can't risk anyone seeing you. I'm scared they'd hurt you if they found out about you. Who knows what kind of experiments they'd run on a magical creature."

Twig studies me with his head cocked to the side, his golden eyes appearing suddenly so much older and wiser. Then he turns his gaze to the bag before climbing inside.

"Thank you. I promise I'll make this as fast as possible."

The car I asked for is waiting out front, and I climb in the backseat. "Where to, Miss Daciana?"

"The hippy district." I set the bag next to me and peer inside. Twig is curled at the bottom, his expression annoyed and angry. I pat the side of the bag reassuringly, then make sure the driver isn't watching as I slide five pieces of bacon inside. I barely contain a giggle as Twig practically inhales them. The sound of crunching is loud in the silence, and I wince, hoping the driver can't hear it.

The hippy district is on the outskirts of the city. The people who keep shops there don't seem to realize magic is gone. Or at least, they pretend it still exists. Oracles, soothsayers, and wise women have set up their businesses. Along with little shops containing all natural products—shampoos, soaps, laundry detergent, plants, crystals, and food. It's a little too crunchy for me, but it's not unusual for me to ask for a ride there. I found a shampoo that I absolutely love in one of those shops. But that is not the reason I'm going there today. I'm hoping a visit with a wisewoman can help me with my little dragon problem.

The driver pulls over in front of the shop I usually visit and turns off the car, reaching for his seatbelt.

"Oh, um, I don't need you to come with me today," I say quickly. Shit. Why hadn't I thought of a way to get rid of my bodyguard? "We never run into trouble in this area. I'll call when I'm ready to be picked up." Before he can say anything, I hop out of the car and dash toward the shop door.

I step inside, the bell tinkling overhead, and I glance over my shoulder. The stupid guard is sitting in the car watching. I chew on my bottom lip and think about how I can ditch him. I've gotten good at this over the years, so the guards are all hesitant to let me out of their sight.

"Good morning. May I help you find anything today?"

I spin around and find a young girl standing in front of me wearing a nametag. "Hi, Mable. Do you have a bathroom I could use?"

She smiles and points to the back of the store. "Down that hallway and to the right."

I hurry down the hall, and sure enough, there is a back exit. Making sure Mable isn't watching, I slip outside into a small alley. "Not much longer, Twig," I mutter under my breath and quickly make my way down the alley. When I'm sure I've put enough distance between me and my bodyguard, I step out on the main street and head toward my goal destination: a flower shop run by a wisewoman Sophia swears is the real deal.

The flower shop is cute. Green vines crawl up the sides, and big blooming flowers of pink and white drop petals onto the ground. Inside, it's hot. Sticky. I'm glad my hair is in a ponytail on top of my head. Flowers and plants take up every available surface, and pots hang from the ceiling nestled in white woven hangers. It smells like dirt and nature. Thick and heady.

As I wind through the maze of tables, scanning the shop for

the owner, Shari, I spot her bending over a flower, white hair tied up in a messy bun on her head. Her gnarled fingers gently prune away dead leaves, and I grimace. That has to be painful.

"Excuse me," I say, stopping next to her. "Would it be possible to have a minute of your time?"

She stands with her hands on her lower back, pain crinkling her features as she straightens. The sharp staccato of popping bones echoes in the silence. "Hello, dear. You have a question for me?"

"Yes. I . . ." I stop, glancing around. The shop is empty, but I still feel like someone could walk in and overhear at any moment. "Is there somewhere we can talk privately?"

She studies me with an ancient gaze that sees far too much. "Of course. Sally, I'm heading to the back," she calls over her shoulder.

I jump when a woman pops up behind a large green bush, shears in her hands, and nods. Good thing I didn't say anything. I follow Shari through the flowers to the back room where there are . . . that's right, more flowers.

Shari lowers herself to a chair and motions toward another. "Have a seat. What's your name again?"

"Oh, Daciana DeRosa," I say, blushing faintly at my lack of manners. I may be snobby and spoiled, but I do know how to treat my elders.

Her eyes widen, no doubt recognizing my name. Everyone does. Typically, the recognition is followed by fear. My dad has made a name for himself. Shari, however, only nods for me to continue.

"I found something," I say slowly. "Something that shouldn't exist, and I have no idea what to do. I was hoping you might have an idea?"

"Well, let's see it then," she says, clapping her hands together. Something about her sets me at ease. Whether it's her kind brown eyes, the same color as the soil in the pots around us, or her matter of fact way of speaking.

I set my bag on my legs and open it. Twig pops his head out immediately, nostrils flaring as he scents the air around him.

"Oh!" Shari says, startling backward before leaning forward again for a better look. "Oh."

"It's a dragon," I say stupidly. Of course she can see it's a dragon. "I found him in my yard. I didn't know what to do."

Twig hops from the bag and heads straight to a potted plant, climbing inside. The sound of liquid hitting the soil meets my ears and I jump to my feet.

"Twig! Don't pee in her plants!"

Shari laughs delightedly. "Oh he's fine. Dragon urine is a great fertilizer."

My gaze shoots to her, shocked. She bends down and holds out her hand, clicking her tongue. Twig bounds to her, knocking the plant over in his haste to reach her. She scoops him up and he melts under her attention.

"Despite all the time I've spent in Oz, I see a dragon for the first time in Girasole," she breathes, rubbing under his chin and making him trill happily.

"I'm sorry. What?"

"My grandson's mother is from Oz. I've visited on occasion. Of course, that was before—" She cuts off, shaking her head.

I don't know what to say, so I stare at her with my mouth hanging open. My mind whirls at a speed it has never whirled before.

Oz is . . . Oz is basically a myth. It doesn't exist. Just like . . . just like the dragon in Shari's lap doesn't exist.

Shari sighs and pats Twig's head. "Oz is real. Magic is real. And before the Parcae created the barrier between Oz and Girasole, magic was very much a part of our everyday lives. Of course, that was long before I was even born." She smiles sadly at Twig and runs her gnarled fingers over the scales on his back. "It is possible to visit Oz, but there are few people who can get past the barrier. Being a direct blood relative of Oz residents is the only way."

I swallow thickly, my mouth dry and desperate for moisture. "And your grandson can do it?" It's so hard to wrap my mind around. I thought Oz was a legend. The idea that someone from Girasole can step foot into Oz seems like an impossibility. But as I stare at Twig preening under Shari's touch, I guess I shouldn't be surprised.

"Thirty-two years ago, my son met a woman and he fell in love," Shari continues. "They had a son, my grandson, and upon his birth, his mother told my son she was leaving, and leaving my grandson with him. You see, she is one of the Parcae."

My eyes widen in shock. The Parcae are the Fates of Oz, the magical beings that created the barrier. Nona, the youngest of the three Fates, is the Spinner of the Thread of Life. Morta is the Cutter of the Thread of Life. And Decima, the Measurer of the Thread of Life.

Shari chuckles. "Yes, that was our reaction exactly. But it turns out she wasn't lying. Nona gave birth to my grandson and returned to Oz. My grandson has been able to traverse the barrier freely, due to the nature of his parentage. I have on occasion gone with him."

Oz. Parcae. Dragons and magic. What the hell is happening? I must be dreaming. My throat clicks as I swallow, attempting to gather moisture back into my mouth. My mom used to tell me stories of Oz, passed down from her grandmother's grandmother. Finding out now that it's all real . . . Well, overwhelming is an understatement. My mind tries to wander, searching for some kind of reasonable explanation for all of this, but Shari isn't finished.

"If a dragon has appeared in our world," Shari continues, oblivious to my inner turmoil. "I'd say it's a sign. I'd suggest asking Nona what it means."

I rear back in my seat. "You mean, go to Oz? Talk to a Parcae? That's insane." My voice comes out as a high-pitched squeak, and I clear my throat in an attempt to sound normal again.

She smiles. "It's actually quite wonderful." She digs through her dress pocket and pulls out a pad of paper and a pen. After scribbling on it, she passes it to me.

On it is a name and phone number. "Nicolai Morelli." I read out loud. "Nicolai?" I screech, losing all control at attempting to keep my voice normal.

"That is my grandson. He'll be able to get you through the barrier and arrange a meeting with Nona."

I laugh, but it's more of a disbelieving bark. Nicolai Morelli, the Tin Man as everyone calls him. Vicious, heartless, cruel. She wants me to find him. And let him take me to Oz. The son of my father's biggest enemy?

I'm not dreaming. This is a nightmare.

4
NICOLAI

The gunshot echoes around me, and I only wait long enough to see the body fall to the ground before I tuck the weapon into the holster at my thigh and walk away. I ignore the screams and cries from the two women who collapse next to the body. His wife and daughter, I believe. I fucking hate the sound of crying.

As I pass Mattie and Leith, I give them a nod to follow me, signaling I'm done here. But before I can go far, Mattie's shout draws me to a stop.

"She's got the gun!" he yells, pulling his own from his pants and aiming behind me.

I whirl around, hand on the grip of my gun, but before I can pull it, the wife fires. The bullet tears through my calf like liquid fire. It's not the first time I've been shot, but it still stings like a bitch.

"Motherfucker," I growl, taking the weight off my left leg.

The woman stands in front of me stunned for a moment, giving Mattie time to charge her. He wraps her in his arms and wrestles the gun away.

"That was a bad idea," he says quietly, looking over her shoulder at me.

Her daughter sobs behind them, hunched over her dad's still body. She's shaking so hard, I'm surprised she hasn't fallen over. Her mom gathers her wits and glares at me.

"I should have aimed higher," she spits.

"You're right, you should have," I say quietly. She's too soft. She never would have survived long as a wife in the Camorra. I did her a favor tonight. But she can't get away with shooting me.

I ignore the pain in my leg as I step closer to her. She squirms in Mattie's grip, trying to get loose, but he holds her too tight. He looks at me, and he doesn't need to use words to convey what he wants to say. We've been through so much together, I can read it all in his brown eyes. *Don't kill her in front of her daughter.* I grimace but relent. Although I'm not sure why. I just murdered her father in front of her, what's one more death to add to her trauma?

Instead, I aim the gun at the woman's calf and pull the trigger. An eye for an eye and all that. Mattie lets her collapse to the ground, and I once again tune out the screams as I turn around.

Leith watches quietly as we walk past, ensuring they don't pull anything else, but I already know they won't. That little stunt was the extent of her backbone.

We quickly leave the empty parking garage, ensuring we stay well out of the line of sight of the security cameras. Not that it would matter. My dad owns every inch of the south side of Girasole. But I know how much he hates having to scrub footage, so I always do my best to remain hidden.

Mattie and Leith keep quiet, but I don't miss the surreptitious glances they shoot my way. No doubt they're worried about the wound in my leg, but they know better than to say anything, especially when I'm in the kind of mood I'm now in.

Tonight was supposed to be an easy hit. In and out. Then we could head to La Notte Brothers for a drink before doing it all over again tomorrow. Complications like what just happened always piss me off. I hate when plans go awry. I hate not being in control. And I really fucking hate getting shot.

Neither of my friends say a word even in my car when I grit my teeth each time I have to hit the clutch to shift. They stay silent when I park, climb out, and angrily stalk to the back door of La Notte Brothers. And when I march through the backroom to the door that opens right by our preferred table, they follow without a question.

Some of my anger seeps away when Carmelo, the bartender, brings our drinks without us having to ask. He eyes my leg briefly but wisely keeps his mouth shut. That first drop of whiskey on my tongue eases more of my anger, and my shoulders just start to relax when Mattie opens his mouth.

"You should probably have your leg taken care of." He doesn't look at me as he speaks, as if he thinks my glare could kill him.

I don't say anything but I stretch out my leg, grimacing at the pain that lances through my calf and the small puddle of blood already pooling on the wooden floor. Carmelo will not be happy about that. But fuck him. Most people are afraid to approach us, but seeing me pissy and bleeding will keep away the braver of them.

I close my eyes and tip my drink back, savoring the smoky burn of the whiskey as it slides down my throat. Just a couple more drinks and my leg won't hurt anymore anyway. Not that it really matters. I heal faster than most people, and my dad has a stock of medicine from Oz if I end up really needing it.

Mattie sighs and shakes his head before giving Leith a knowing look. "Bastard could be dying, and he'd refuse to get help."

Leith smirks and signs, "You know better than to try and help him. Just let him do his thing."

I ignore them and signal for another whiskey. They mean well, but when I'm in a mood, everything pisses me off. Just as Carmelo sets a glass on the table, my phone buzzes. I pull it out of my pocket, grunting when I jostle my leg too much. As I read the message, my brow furrows.

> Hi. I know this is a horrible idea, but I need
> help, and your grandmother said to ask you.

"What's up?" Mattie asks, noticing my reaction to the text.

I shake my head. "I have no idea. Probably a scam of some

sort." I close out of the message without answering. A minute later, I get another text.

> Please don't be a dick.

I snort but quickly send a reply.

> who the fuck is this?

> Are you gonna be a dick?

> depends. who is this?

> . . .

The little bubble pops up to indicate the person is writing, then it disappears. It appears again before disappearing once more. I tap my phone impatiently, about ready to turn the damn thing off. But the person finally sends a message through.

> It's Daciana DeRosa

I jerk back in shock, mouth falling open. "What the fuck?"

"Don't keep us in the dark, bro," Leith signs, his movements swift with agitation.

Mattie grins, tapping his hands on the table. "Spill it, Nico."

"The DeRosa princess is asking me for help." I glance up to see both of my friends' faces go slack with shock. Leith blinks at me like he doesn't understand what I just said, and Mattie leans forward.

"You're fucking kidding," Mattie says, holding out his hand for my phone.

I toss it to him and take another drink of my whiskey as he reads then passes my phone to Leith.

"Well, what are you going to do?" Mattie asks, sitting back with a grin.

I groan. This is the last fucking thing I want to deal with. The DeRosas have been my father's target for years. Ever since Lorenzo DeRosa climbed to the top of the Camorra, my dad has been gunning for them. The day he found out DeRosa took out the previous Camorra boss was a bad day in the Morelli household.

"There is no way I can help her, even if I wanted to." I shake my head, thinking through everything. "My dad would murder me."

Mattie tips his head side to side. "If he finds out."

I glare at him. "Why the hell would I help her?"

"Why not?"

"Could be fun," Leith signs.

"Fun? Are you guys insane? It's the fucking DeRosa princess. Just her texting me could start a war." I look back and forth between them, utterly flabbergasted.

"We're already at war." Mattie snags my phone and quickly types in my password.

I attempt to launch across the table, but when pain shoots through my leg I collapse onto my chair with a groan. "Don't fucking do it," I growl.

Mattie jumps up out of the way and his fingers fly over the screen. I grind my teeth, debating the best way to deal with him. I don't pull rank very often, but I will if I have to. Mattie tosses my phone back to me, and I curse when I see what he sent.

> Meet me tomorrow night. Gormond Park. 9 PM.

"Are you fucking serious, Mattie?" I shake my head, too pissed to even think of what to say.

Mattie grins and shrugs. "Can't hurt to see what she wants."

"What if it's a trap?" Leith signs. "The DeRosas haven't gotten their payback on your family yet. This could be a setup."

Mattie snorts. "Lorenzo wouldn't risk his daughter like that. No. This screams Daciana. The conniving, slutty princess. She probably just wants a quick fuck. I'd be more than willing to take one for the team." He grins wickedly and rubs his hands together.

I grit my teeth. "You're a fucking idiot, Matteo. And I won't hesitate to throw you under the bus when shit hits the fan."

I'm too pissed to even react to the pain in my leg when I push to my feet and stalk out the door. They can find their own way home tonight. I need to cool my head before I deal with Mattie again. The fucking idiot.

The next evening, I pull up to Gormond Park, silently cursing Mattie the entire time. At least he picked the most neutral spot in the city. Not that it will matter when it comes to my dad and Lorenzo DeRosa. Those two are intent on destroying each other, fuck whoever else gets hurt in the process.

"Do you see her?" Mattie asks, leaning forward between the two front seats.

"No. Hopefully she chickens out," I mutter. "You could have at least narrowed a location in the park. This place is huge."

Mattie shrugs. "I was in a hurry."

"I'd head to the center of the park," Leith signs. "She'd probably feel the most comfortable being hidden as deep in the park as she can get."

I watch him closely from the corner of my eye to catch everything. Leith doesn't talk. When I met him in Oz as a child, I thought he was stupid. It didn't help that the bitch that calls me her son doted on him. As kids, Leith and I hated each other. My dad took him in and we were raised together. I learned sign language strictly as a way to insult him.

Everything changed when I learned his reason for not talking.

We've been brothers ever since. And when Mattie came along a few years later, we taught him sign as well.

I pull into a spot near the pond at the center of the park and we hop out. Mattie and Leith sit on a bench and start bickering about something I couldn't care less about. I check the time. Nine exactly. I don't see her. And I don't hear a car. Heaving a sigh, I pace back and forth, checking the time every five seconds.

"I'm giving her until 9:05," I say.

"Oh come on," Mattie drawls. "Lighten up for once in your life."

I flip him off and continue pacing, even though my leg twinges every time I put weight on it. I distract myself by checking for my gun and knife. "Make sure you guys stay on your guard."

"Yeah, yeah, yeah," Mattie says, idly scrolling on his phone, clearly not on his guard. It would serve him right to get shot tonight.

When I check my phone again, it's 9:06. I'm about to head back to my car when I notice someone walking toward us. Leith hits Mattie in the chest to get his attention, and they both sit up, hands hovering over their weapons.

Daciana DeRosa strides straight to me and my brothers, shoulders pulled back and chin lifted. The fucking bitch looks down her nose at us as she comes to a stop and places a hand on her hip. Her black jeans are skintight, and her black belly shirt shows off a sliver of her pale skin. In the streetlight, her blond hair almost shines like silver. I've always wondered where her pale skin and blond hair come from. She doesn't look Girasolen.

"I'm impressed you came," Mattie says, looking her up and down with a grin. He takes a small step forward and gives her a small bow. "Matteo Rossi, at your service, your highness."

I barely hold back a snort and see Leith shaking his head with a smile. Daciana narrows her eyes and somehow lifts her chin even higher. She completely ignores him and turns toward me. Mattie's mouth drops open in shock. He's not used to being ignored like that.

"Thank you for meeting me," she says primly. Her words are clipped, but her voice shivers over me.

"What do you want?" I ask gruffly, crossing my arms over my

chest and widening my stance. I can sense a fight coming, even if it won't be a physical one.

"I found something," she says, shifting slightly and tightening her grip on the red bag on her shoulder. "I went to a wisewoman for advice, and it just so happened to be your grandmother."

I nod. Grandma Shari is one of the best wisewomen in the hippy district. But if she's handing my number out to Morelli rivals, I'll have to have a talk with her.

"She told me you'd be able to help," Daciana continues.

I raise one pierced eyebrow, getting impatient with the talking. She seems to pick up on that and skips to the chase. Her nose scrunches as she kneels in the grass, but she sets the bag on the ground and lets the straps fall open.

"Holy . . ." Mattie breathes, eyes going impossibly wide.

Leith steps closer, craning his neck to see inside.

And me? My blood runs cold as a little snout pokes out from the bag and big golden eyes blink curiously.

"I found a dragon," Daciana says quietly, and quite unnecessarily.

Mattie whips his head toward me. "Nico," he says, his voice low and urgent.

Leith takes a step toward me.

I take a step backward. Away from the dragon. Away from the DeRosa princess. Away from my fate.

5
DACIANA

Even in the darkness, I watch the Tin Man's face drain of color. He takes a step back. Then another. I'm so focused on his reaction that I don't notice the other two approaching me.

"Dragon?"

I whip my head in the direction of the voice and immediately stiffen at how close he is. Twig peers up at the man, and I grab the bag and stand to be on more even footing. His skin is a warm shade of brown, rather than the darker tan of most people in Girasole, and half of his locs are pulled back. Matteo Rossi. The Scarecrow.

I protectively wrap Twig and the bag in my arms, turning away slightly. He catches my motions and grins.

"Don't worry, princess. I won't hurt it. I just never thought I'd see a real dragon." His dark eyes sparkle when he throws a disarming smile at me. "Can I touch it?"

I study him for a second before nodding slowly. "His name is Twig." I kneel again and set the bag on the ground. Twig pops his head out the top and his tongue flops from the side of his mouth.

The Scarecrow's face lights up, making him look impossibly childlike, and he kneels and holds out a hand. Twig leans closer and sniffs his fingers before bopping his nose into the Scarecrow's palm. "This is so surreal," he whispers, looking up at the other man.

The Lion has been standing still, gaze bouncing between the dragon and the Tin Man, who is still standing back looking extremely pale. At the Scarecrow's words, the Lion kneels too and gently pats Twig's head. Twig twists and nips at his fingers gummily, making the man smile.

Okay. This isn't going too horribly, but the person I need to help me is staring at me and Twig like we've murdered his puppy. I suck in a breath and stand, leaving Twig on the ground to play with the other two.

"So?" I ask, placing my hands on my hips. In my peripheral vision, I see the others glance at him with a mix of curious and concerned expressions.

The Tin Man visibly gathers himself, straightening his shoulders and lifting his chin. "What do you need from me?" His voice is rough, like he just swallowed sandpaper.

"I need to go to Oz. Your grandmother said Nona would be able to help me figure out what to do with Twig." I glance at the dragon in question and my heart squeezes. His little wings flap uselessly against his back and his tail swishes in the bottom of the bag happily. Why is he so cute?

When I mention Nona, the Scarecrow and Lion both turn their gazes toward the Tin Man, who grimaces. I hold my breath, not sure what I'll do if he says no.

"I'll think about it," he finally says, jerking his head to the side, indicating the others should follow him.

"What?" I screech. "You'll think about it?"

He doesn't even look at me. "That's what I said."

I shake off my shock and stomp forward, stopping in front of him to force him to look at me. "You'll think about it?" I repeat. "I have a fucking baby dragon. This thing has already ruined one of my shoes and my makeup. He shit in a potted plant in my house and pissed in another one at your grandmother's shop. I can't fucking keep him!" Even as I say it, my heart thunders. I can't keep him, but I sure want to.

The Tin Man doesn't even acknowledge my outburst. He steps around me without batting an eye.

I grab his arm to stop him, and his muscles tense under my

hand. "He won't stay this small forever. Soon he'll be bigger than my fucking house. How the hell do I explain that?"

His gaze drops to my hand grasping him tightly, and his lip curls in a mix of anger and disgust. When he lifts his gaze back to me, the pure hatred shining in his dark eyes sucks the breath from my lungs. I release him as if I've been burned.

"Not my problem," he growls, words laced with anger.

I stare open-mouthed as he walks back to his car. No words. I have absolutely no words as he climbs into the front seat.

The Lion walks past me with a small apologetic smile, and the Scarecrow stops briefly at my side.

"Don't worry, princess. I'll convince him to help." He winks at me before joining his friends.

My heart sinks when they pull away. What the fuck do I do now? My body is on autopilot as I gather up Twig and walk toward the front of the park. Without the Tin Man's help, I have no way to get to Oz. If I don't go to Oz, Twig will be discovered. If he's discovered, they'll take him away. Probably cut him open to study him or run awful experiments on him.

I won't let that happen. If I have to, I'll go back to Shari and tell her what happened. Maybe she'll be able to convince the Tin Man to help me. If not, I know how to be a pest. I'll bother him until he helps just to get me to leave him alone.

"Don't worry, Twig," I say, patting the side of the bag. "I won't let anyone hurt you. I'll find a way to get you back to Oz."

When I wake the next morning, Twig isn't in bed with me. He slept by my side all night, a mini space heater that kept me from needing a blanket. A scratching sound by the door draws my attention, and I find Twig dancing from side to side on his feet, his talons occasionally tapping on the door.

I sit up and slip on a pair of sandals. "Is that your potty dance?"

He nods and I grin, picking up the bag and scooping him into it.

"Okay then. Let's get you outside."

I take the route to the garden I did the other day, staying out of the main hallways. There are a few more servants around this time, and I brace myself before pushing into the kitchen. It's morning, and I'm sure the kitchen is busy.

I slip inside and duck my head, making my way through the flurry of activity. Hopefully they are all too busy to notice or bother with me. It's already hot in here with the stove and ovens going, and by the time I step outside, the cool morning air chills my heated skin. I shiver but ignore it, darting through the grass to the garden.

The back corner with the wildflowers is the perfect place to drop Twig and let him do his thing. The flowers are always wild and untamed, growing tall and obscuring even the beehive in its midst.

Immediately, Twig disappears and I hear him scurrying through the flowers. After a few minutes, his tail pops up from the curtain of flora, and I watch it travel between them. When he pops his head out, a purple flower dangles from his mouth, and he quickly chomps it down, using his tongue to make sure not a piece of it falls to the ground.

"Hungry?"

His head bobs quickly up and down, and I scoop him back into the bag and head toward the kitchen. Inside, I glance around and spot a plate piled high with bacon. I grab a handful of it, and I'm shoving it into the bag when someone catches me.

"Miss Daciana?" a small voice says next to me. "Wha' are ye doin'?"

Guiltily, I turn my head and find Mara, one of my maids, staring at the handful of bacon just above the bag. I smile but my mind empties, and I can't think of a single thing to say to get me out of this situation.

She grins at me. "Did ye find a stray dog? Yer da will ne'er allow ye ta keep it. But . . ." She darts away to a cupboard, pulling down a large clear container, then heading toward the fridge. When she comes back, she hands me the container. "This should keep it fed 'til ye find someone ta take it. I won't say a word."

"Thank you, Mara."

She bobs a curtsy and returns to work. I quickly make my way upstairs and into my room. I set the bag on the floor and let Twig climb out while I take the lid off the container. Leftovers from last night's dinner. Roast beef. Green beans. Carrots and peas. Along with the bacon I stole, Twig has a veritable feast. He digs in, and I check my phone. My heart stops when I see a message from the Tin Man.

> tomorrow. 7 am. the field.

This is it. He must be agreeing to help me. The Field. A massive grassy area in Girasole. Rumor abounds about the Field and people tend to avoid it. An air surrounds the place, an otherworldly feeling that you can't shake when you get near. One rumor claims it was where Oz used to be. Before they put a barrier around themselves, keeping themselves safe from the wickedness of the rest of the world. People say this is the access point. This is where you go if you want to get into Oz. Of course, no one knows where exactly in the Field, or how exactly to make it work, but that's what they say. If the Tin Man wants to meet there, then that must mean I'm going to Oz. My phone buzzes again, and I look down.

> pack light. im not carrying your shit for you.
> don't be late.

I roll my eyes. Bastard. But I get up and pull out my favorite name brand backpack. It's white with gold stitching and gold zippers. I throw in comfortable clothes, because I have no idea what type of clothing I'll need in Oz. Leggings, stretchy jeans, sport bras, tanks, and loose tees. I also add a lightweight jacket. Next, I pack some basic toiletries and a bag of simple makeup.

The drawing on the easel catches my attention, and I gasp. Tilting my head to the side, I step closer. It looks like . . . like the start of an eye. A reptilian eye. A dragon eye. "Whoa," I breathe as goosebumps lift the fine hairs on my arms.

I glance at the baby dragon chowing down on the bacon. Why would I draw a dragon eye right before finding an actual dragon in my yard? Coincidence, right? As Twig finishes his dinner and hops into my bed, bringing the chewed-up red high heel with him, something inside of me tells me it's not a coincidence at all.

Without giving myself time to think about it, I toss a sketchbook and some charcoal pencils into my backpack and do one last look around my room to make sure I have everything. When I'm positive I do, I sneak Twig outside to the garden. While I watch him scamper among the wildflowers, I don't let myself dwell on how much my chest aches. Thinking about saying goodbye to him is too heavy of a thought. It doesn't seem fair. I just found him and got so attached, and now I have to give him away.

This is it, I think as I walk toward the outskirts of town the next morning. I don't know how long I'll be gone. Hopefully not too long. I didn't even leave a note for my dad, but that's something future me can deal with.

My nerves are a tangled mess in my belly, causing it to cramp painfully. This is probably the stupidest thing I've ever done. Meeting with my family's enemy and letting him take me to a magical world that most people think is a myth is definitely not a good idea. I could turn around and go back home. Then I won't have to deal with the Tin Man. I'll hide Twig. No one will ever know I have a dragon. And when he gets bigger, I'll find someplace else to hide him. No big deal. Right?

My shoulders slump. Of course I can't keep him. And that thought sends a bolt of pain through my chest. I rub it like that will make it all better. This stupid baby dragon just had to show up in my yard and weasel his way into my heart. But can I really trust the Tin Man to get me safely into Oz?

If I were smart, I'd turn around and go home. I'd tell my dad about the dragon and write it off as a weird occurrence before moving on with my life. But the more I think about it, the more my heart races, and not just from nerves. I've never done something like this. Sleeping around and partying are my ways of rebelling against the cage I live in. And more and more often, I find myself sinking deeper into the darkness that tries relentlessly to swallow me.

Constantly fighting my emotions and fears has worn me down. I'm tired of pasting on a fake smile for pictures. I'm sick of the act I have to put on to make people believe there isn't a care in my pretty little head. Just once, I want to have a real conversation with my dad. I want him to know how hard my mom's death was. I want to tell him how much this lifestyle has opened a pit inside of me that widens with each passing day. And eventually that pit is going to swallow me whole.

So instead of doing the smart thing, the thing I know I should do, I keep walking. Maybe I'll regret it. Then again, maybe it will be exactly what I need.

The Field takes my breath away. As far as I can see, green grass sways in the breeze. Trees dot the greenscape, white and pink flowers blooming no matter the time of year. The last bit of magic of our world keeps them vibrant and alive.

The sun seems to shine brighter here, the clouds whiter and puffier. The sky is bluer than it is just behind me. And the unsettling sensation of something alive and . . . well, magical . . . shivers over my skin.

The Tin Man stands to the side of the Field, his friends with him, all dressed in black cargo pants and Henleys. They have weapons strapped to their chests, waists, and thighs, all various kinds of blades. No guns. Bags lay at their feet, most likely holding their supplies.

The Tin Man's dark gaze is pure fury, haughty arrogance, and annoyance. He stands with his legs spread and his arms crossed over his chest. His dark hair is slicked back, and tattoos snake up his neck and twine around his exposed forearms. Piercings in his ears, eyebrows, and lip glint in the early morning light. He's dark. Deadly. And somehow, still alluring. His family is the second highest in the Camorra, and he didn't get his nickname by chance. The Tin Man's father trained him well. A hitman. An assassin. He carries out his father's orders ruthlessly with his best friends by his side. Every picture I've ever seen of him depicts the same cold detachment.

Sliding my gaze to the left, I see Matteo Rossi. The Scarecrow. He gets his nickname from the fact that he's not the brightest crayon in the box. While he carries out orders like a well-trained soldier, he's quick to laugh and always appears in pictures with his tongue down some random girl's throat. His slightly lighter gaze is intrigued, playful, and inviting. His dreads are down, and he stands leisurely next to the Tin Man with a crooked smile. A playboy with a sense of humor who never takes anything seriously. That's what I've always heard about him and that is exactly what he looks like.

And Leith Morgan. The Cowardly Lion. The most mysterious of the three. I've never seen him talk, which is why people gave him his nickname. He's timid and scared, so he keeps to himself. And like the Tin Man, he rarely smiles. His blue eyes always make him seem extra cold to me. There is nothing on the internet about him except his name and his friendship with the Tin Man and Scarecrow. But his blue eyes, wavy light brown hair, and lighter complexion don't fit in with everyone else in Girasole. Right now, his eyes are chilling as he watches me, almost as if he's dissecting me layer by layer. I can't quite get a read on his expression. Is he angry? Annoyed? Excited? Indifferent? I just can't tell.

I take a deep breath of the fresh citrus-scented air—even though there are no citrus plants around—and take the first step toward my enemies. Each step sends the butterflies in my belly swirling more fiercely. Every instinct screams at me to turn around. To not follow these three men into an unknown magical land. But instead of letting my fears crumple me to the ground, I straighten my shoulders and don my mask. The mask I've worn every day of my life.

"Well, hello boys." I shoot them my most winning smile and pop my hip, placing my hand on it.

Tin Man's gaze travels down my body, his mouth tightening as he takes in my light-pink off-the-shoulder tee, skintight ripped jeans, and purple sneakers. He shakes his head and turns on his heel, walking further into the Field.

"That's what you're wearing?" Scarecrow asks with a grin. "Not practical for what we're doing, but I approve." His light-brown eyes glitter and linger on my hips.

Lion smirks and turns to follow Tin Man. I stand uncertain for a moment with Scarecrow, trying to think of something witty to say back to him. But everything seems to have fled my mind. Instead, I stand awkwardly and nod. *Gee, great start, Daci.* I can't imagine what they're thinking about me. Actually, I can, and I push it to the far recesses of my mind. I use this mask for a reason, and I'm used to people thinking the worst of me. These three will be no different.

"Do you have everything you need?" Scarecrow eyes my backpack and the bag containing Twig with amusement. "Things aren't easy to come by in Oz."

"I'm good," I say, hoping he can't sense my uncertainty. I take off after the other two to get Scarecrow to stop looking at me. It doesn't work. He follows right beside me, and I can't stop myself from looking at him from the corner of my eye. "So, have you been to Oz before?" I ask, hoping to gain some bit of knowledge of the men I'm trusting with my life.

"Yep. I was born in Oz."

I barely refrain from tripping. "Born in Oz? But . . . the barrier . . . it's been . . ." I trail off at his smirk.

"It's a long story, but yeah. I was born in Oz. I came back with Nico fifteen years ago."

Maybe that's why I've never been able to find any information on Matteo Rossi's family whenever I fell down the social media rabbit hole. Born in Oz?

"What's it like?" I ask, unable to hide the curiosity.

He smiles coyly at me and shrugs one muscled shoulder. "You'll see."

I roll my eyes and continue walking, ignoring Scarecrow to the best of my ability. It's impossible though. His presence is like a physical weight pressing me down. We don't say anything else as we approach the other two standing amid the grasses. I gasp when I look up. A beautiful rainbow arcs through the sky. Both ends visibly land in the Field, and we're standing in the dead center. Where did it come from? I've never seen a rainbow here before, and there wasn't one just a second ago.

Tin Man glances at me, gaze flat. "Follow our lead. Don't say anything. And don't be a menace."

I rear back, hands on my hips, and open my mouth to give him a piece of my mind. But before I can say anything, he holds out one tattooed hand. He raises it chest level and swipes from left to right. That's it. I don't see any sparks or shimmering. No light or glittery particles.

But a soft wind blows my hair back from my face, smelling of the sea, which is weird because we are nowhere near a sea here. Then a vertical line appears and I blink. It spreads, slowly rotating open until an arch stands before us, a smaller version of the rainbow above. I peer inside but I can only see a blurry mix of brown and green.

Tin Man motions to Lion and he steps through the arch, disappearing. Scarecrow goes next, throwing me a wink over his shoulder as he does so. And Tin Man glares at me, waving his hand toward the arch.

"After you, princess."

Ignoring the barb, I take a breath and step inside the doorway. To Oz.

6
DACIANA

Stepping through the portal takes seconds. Warmth tingles along my skin, and the air shimmers faintly as I walk through. As soon as I reach the other side, I stop in my tracks.

An overwhelming sense of . . . completeness . . . settles over me. Something inside clicks into place, like the missing piece of a puzzle. I suck in a breath and have to blink my eyes rapidly to fight the tears building on my lashes. Girasole has always been my home. But I've never felt at peace before. Not like this.

After my mom died, it was like every good thing in the world disappeared. I know my dad loves me in his own way. But I don't think I've ever really felt like I've been *home* since my mom died. The second I stepped through the portal, I was *home.* Complete. Whole. At peace. It's a strange feeling, and I take a moment to compose myself before I look around.

And when I get a look at my surroundings, I'm further awed. I have never seen anything quite as beautiful, and it steals my breath. A little village stands before me, made entirely of stone. Brown and gray and white and red. Cracks and chips and discoloration. It's old and well-worn, but clearly loved and cared for.

Growing on every corner, on every step, on any available surface, are flowers blooming in whites, pinks, and reds. Green leafy vines climb the buildings and arch over streets and alleys. The sweet scent of flora reaches me on the breeze, mixed with the tang of salt.

The village is spread over a hill, steps winding up and down, the streets gently sloping. Balconies with wrought iron railings drip more colorful flowers from above. Vine canopies cover little cafés with round tables and chairs. Fountains burble from street corners and colorful birds splash in the basins.

And beyond the village is the brilliant blue of ocean waves with the bright sunlight glinting off the surface.

It's beautiful. And magical. And I never want to leave.

My view is blocked as Tin Man steps in front of me and walks toward the village. I hitch my bags higher and follow. Twig pops his head out of the top of his bag and his little nose twitches as he scents the air. He looks at me with large golden eyes, almost as bright as the sun. I smile at him and pat his head, hurrying my step to catch up to the others.

"What is this place?" I ask quietly, fearful of disturbing the peace.

"Oz," Tin Man says gruffly, not looking at me. His shoulders are tight and a muscle in his jaw ticks continuously.

Behind me, Scarecrow chuckles. "This is Fairyland, one of the villages of Oz, home to the fairies."

"Fairies?" I ask, glancing around. It's then that I notice the village is eerily empty. Like everyone ran and hid when we appeared.

Before Scarecrow can respond, a tiny winged creature zooms from a window and darts straight for us.

"Leith!" Its minuscule voice is like tinkling bells. "Leith, you're back!"

Pale yellow wings flutter madly, and that's all I can make out until the creature settles on Lion's upheld palm. I stare in amazement at this fairy, the size of a banana.

Leith smiles and nods, making the fairy blush a rosy hue. She ducks her head and tangles her fingers in her glittering flowy skirts, swaying her hips shyly.

As if that was the cue, the rest of the fairies come timidly from their homes. I know it's rude to stare, and I really try my best to keep my face passive, but holy shit! These are real fucking fairies, and I can't keep my jaw off the ground.

They range in height from the small one in Lion's palm to about three feet tall. I see skin tones in all colors of the rainbow, and not just skin. Scales, feathers, even bark. Some have wings, some have large ears. Some have big bulging eyes, and some have long scraggly fingers. Some fly while others walk. Some appear more humanoid than others. But all of them have an inner glow that sets them apart from me and the three guys.

Quickly, I realize the guys are more than welcome here. The fairies surround them with warm smiles and open arms. I, on the other hand, get suspicious glances and the fairies all keep their distance.

I use the moment to step back and take it all in. I'm so distracted trying to look everywhere at once, I don't notice Twig poking his head out of the bag again until he starts wagging his tail hard enough to hit me in the side.

I kneel to put the bag on the ground and I try to scoop him in my arms, but he escapes before I have the chance. He darts through the crowd of fairies, scattering them like dandelion seeds. Their tiny screams are so high pitched, they make my ears ring.

"Oh!" I say, clapping a hand over my ears. "Get back here!" I take off after him, ignoring the shocked and terrified fairies, intent on getting the dragon under control.

His little wings flap behind him and his tail wags so wildly, it shakes his entire body. He stops before a pale fairy dressed in a light-green robe with a tapered hood. Her ears are pointed and stick out from under the cloak. Blond hair trails over her shoulders in two twisted pigtails.

I skid to a stop, reaching down to grab Twig, but the fairy holds her hand out to him, a wide smile on her face. Her too-large blue eyes glow with happiness as Twig snuffles in her palm then licks it.

"I'm sorry," I say. "I didn't mean for him to get away from me."

"That's quite alright," she says, her voice high and light. She reaches the middle of my shin and is absolutely adorable. "They are just startled because we haven't seen a dragon around here in a very long time."

I glance around, and sure enough, the fairies have run off. A few poke their heads around bushes or peer through windows, but they no longer make an attempt to approach.

"Way to go, princess." Tin Man glares at me, then at Twig.

"I didn't mean to. Back off." I scoop Twig into my arms and hold him tightly. He looks around, eyes sad that the fairies are hiding.

"You need to keep him better controlled," he growls.

"Well maybe if you'd given me more warning about what we'd encounter on the other side of the portal, I may have been better prepared. This is your fault." I point a neatly manicured finger at him, the pale pink shining bright in the sunlight.

Before he can respond, a fairy approaches. At least, I think it's a fairy. She's taller than all the others, reaching to my shoulders. Her dress is simple, a plain off-white with a blue apron. And her pure white hair flows down her back.

"Leith," she says, her voice surprisingly low for her smaller stature. "It is truly wonderful to see you again." She holds her hands up to the Lion and he bends forward to take them in his own, smiling warmly. He gives them a squeeze before letting go.

"It's a pleasure to see you too, Calla," Lion signs.

I jolt. Sign language? I think back to everything I've ever seen of the Lion, but I can't remember ever seeing him sign. The others don't sign when they talk, so I assume he isn't deaf. He must not speak. Luckily, I know enough to piece together what he's saying. One of our staff members is deaf and uses sign. She's been with our family since I was a baby.

The fairy, Calla, turns to me. "You, I have never seen here before." Her gaze drops to Twig and her purple eyes light up. "And one of those hasn't been seen in a very long time."

Unsure what to say, I smile at her. "I'm Daci. This is Twig."

Her eyes narrow on me and she purses her lips like she's studying me. "Where are you from, Daci?"

"Not from here," Tin Man chimes in quickly, glancing around pointedly.

"Ah, Nico. It's been even longer since I've seen you. It must be something important to drag you back here." Calla grins at him, and I take great pleasure in watching Tin Man's jaw work as he grinds his teeth. "Come," she says, waving us forward. "Let us talk in private."

Settled at a wooden table in one of the larger buildings, I gratefully accept a cup of water. The guys look ridiculous seated at the small table, their knees almost to their chests in the little chairs.

"You can let the dragon out. You said his name is Twig?" Calla glances at the bag where I shoved Twig before coming in here.

"You sure? He's kind of a menace." I peer into the bag and meet his golden eyes. "I mean that in the most loving way possible, Twig."

He snorts like he doesn't believe me. Calla bustles around the kitchen of her home and says over her shoulder, "Absolutely. Let him explore. I'll make him something to eat."

At her words, Twig hops out of the bag and heads straight for her in the kitchen, talons clicking on the stone floor. I try to keep an eye on him to make sure he doesn't get into anything.

"So, tell me what's going on," Calla says, taking pots and ingredients from her cupboards.

"We need to talk with Nona," Tin Man says. His words are tight, like he's forcing them up his throat and through his clenched teeth.

"Mmm," Calla says. "And why is that?"

Before Tin Man can say anything else, I push forward. "I'm not from Oz. I'm from Girasole. But I found Twig in my yard the other day. A wise woman told me to come to Oz to figure out what was going on, and that Nona would be the best person to talk to."

Calla starts, but she hides it well. If I hadn't been watching her, I wouldn't have noticed her slightly widened eyes or the breath she sucks in. She turns around with a bowl of food and sets it in front of Twig. "Eat up, little dragon. Now," she says to me, "I will send for Nona. It usually takes her a few days to get here, but I'll be sure to let her know her son is here." Her gaze lands on Tin Man. "That should speed her along."

"Fucking great," he says under his breath so only those of us at the table can hear.

"You are more than welcome to stay," Calla continues, unaware of what Tin Man said. "This is the largest building in Fairyland. But I only have one extra bedroom. Daci, you can stay there." She grins, somehow turning her sweet face into something menacing. "The boys can fight over the couch."

It's been a long time since I've visited a beach. We used to go every summer when my mom was alive. After she died, my dad took me a couple of times, but then he stopped. I've always loved the ocean. The sand squishing between my toes, warm at first from the sun, then cooler the farther you dig into it. The briny scent that blows on the refreshing breeze. And of course, the sound of the waves crashing against the shore. It's always been a spot of peace for me.

The first thing I do when I step onto the beach in Oz is kick off my shoes and stuff my socks inside them. A smile spreads across my face as I step into the sand, feeling the grains shift under my feet. I leave my shoes where the sand meets the grassy plain and head straight for the ocean.

The water is the clearest blue-green I've ever seen with foamy whitecaps as the waves crest and crash gently on the beach.

Schools of small silver fish dart back and forth until I step into the water, scattering them. It's wonderfully warm against my skin, and I swear my soul gets a boost of serotonin from the contact.

Closing my eyes, I tilt my head back and bathe in the warm rays of sunshine, letting the sand under my feet shift with each wave. I breathe in the salty tang and let the waves wash away every thought I have in my head. It's the only time I'm able to clear my mind. Only the waves seem to be able to shut down every worry and the stress that constantly percolates in my brain.

It doesn't take long for the tension in my shoulders to evaporate and my breathing to deepen and even out. I don't know how long I stand there, but I'm startled out of my haze of peace by a deep voice.

"You look like you're really enjoying the beach."

I jump and turn around with my heart thundering in my chest. Scarecrow stands behind me with his arms crossed and a sly grin on his face. The breeze blows hard enough to tug a few of his locs away from his cheeks.

Brushing my hair out of my eyes, I glare at him. "It's rude to sneak up on someone like that."

He shrugs nonchalantly. "I didn't realize you were so deep in thought. Besides, I wanted to enjoy the beach too."

"Well, there is plenty of beach here to enjoy," I say with a huff and wave my hand, indicating the endless stretch of sand. "Go somewhere else and enjoy it."

Scarecrow chuckles but ignores me. Instead of walking away like I hoped he would, he steps forward to stand next to me. His shoulder brushes mine and I suddenly find the sun slightly too warm.

"Unfortunately, this is my favorite spot," he responds, sounding anything but unfortunate.

I release a breath, the tension that had just melted away already creeping back in. The thoughts that had quieted rise in volume. It's pointless to remain now. I'll never find the peace again with Scarecrow standing here taunting me. I turn around and start back toward my shoes, but Scarecrow grabs my hand and stops me.

"Where are you going?" he asks, sounding somewhat sincere.

"You ruined my peace, so anywhere else but here." I try to tug free of his grip, but he holds on too strongly. Narrowing my eyes at him, I grit my teeth. "Let go of me."

His laugh slithers over my skin and burrows into my bones. I can't help but shiver at the way it makes my stomach clench, and it's not entirely unpleasant.

"You're feisty, aren't you," he says around a grin, but he lets me go. "I'm sorry. I didn't mean to ruin your moment. You stay. I need to find Nico anyway." He's halfway to the grassy field when he stops and says over his shoulder, "Oh yeah, if you think the beach is pretty now, you should see it at night. There are fairies similar to the bioluminescent algae in Girasole that make the ocean glow when it's dark."

Then he walks away, leaving me gaping after him and rubbing my wrist where his fingers had just been wrapped around it. I swear I can still feel them there. Taking a deep breath of the salty air, I turn back to the ocean and try to find that inner peace again, even though all I can think of is the way Scarecrow's laugh made me feel completely undone.

7
MATTEO

"Well, this is the most fun I've had in a long time," I say, grinning at Nico and Leith.

Daci is talking to Calla in the kitchen. With my magic returned now that we're in Oz, I can hear every word. I know by Nico's tight expression that he's monitoring their conversation closely as well. So far, it has remained light. Purely Daci's fascination and questions about Oz.

Nico snorts. "Speak for yourself," he grumbles, shifting on the couch. The piece of furniture is tiny. Too tiny for any of us to sleep on. Nico and Leith sitting on it together barely fit, and their knees are almost to their chins. The thing groans under their weight, and I really hope it doesn't fall to pieces.

"I fucking hate this place," Leith signs, distaste plain in his movements.

I give him a small smile, letting him know I get it and I'm here if he needs anything. His experience in Oz was worse than mine, so I don't blame him for hating it here. But going so long without my magic is unbearable. It's suffocating. Like each day spent away slowly sucks more and more air from my lungs. The second I stepped through the portal, it was like my lungs expanded fully for the first time in years.

"We won't be here long," Nico promises. "I don't want to stay any longer than you do."

I refrain from speaking the obvious. This jaunt to Oz is going to be more than any of us planned for it to be. I knew it the moment Daci texted Nico. The pieces are moving around the table, slowly clicking into place, and there is nothing we can do to stop it.

I also can't stop my thoughts from returning to the beach earlier. I've seen plenty of Daci in Girasole on the news and social media, and she's always seemed like the perfectly vapid, self-centered princess everyone expects the heir to the DeRosa family to be. The last time I scrolled through her social media posts, it was nothing but selfies of her and her cousin dressed in the most expensive dresses, wearing insane amounts of jewelry that had to have cost a fortune. All she does is party and fuck—not that I'm judging the fucking part. But the moment I saw her on the beach, head tipped back, eyes closed, and a smile on her face, I knew there was more to Daciana DeRosa than I ever gave her credit for.

Talons click on the stone floor around the corner and Twig appears. His green scales reflect the candle flames lighting the room. I marvel at him. Despite having been born in Oz and spending fifteen years here before moving to Girasole, I've never seen a dragon before. They were long gone by the time I was born.

He's carrying something in his mouth, and I frown as he approaches, dropping it in front of me. It's a wooden ball. He crouches low to the ground, ass in the air and tail wagging. I raise one brow and grab the ball. His golden eyes track it.

"Do you want me to throw it?" I ask him, cocking my head to the side.

His tail wags harder so I toss the ball, wincing at the loud thud it makes hitting the floor. It rolls, and Twig takes off, talons scrabbling on the stone for purchase. He returns a second later and drops the ball in front of me again.

"Who the fuck would have thought I'd be sitting in Oz playing fetch with a dragon?" I mutter to myself.

From the corner of my eye, I catch Leith signing to Nico. "Are you prepared to see your mom?"

Nico slouches on the couch, crossing his tattooed arms over his tattooed chest. Shadows swim behind his brown eyes and he says nothing. Leith glances at me, concerned, and all I can do is shrug. Nico is going to have to deal with his shit. And sooner rather than later.

I pick up the slimy ball, grimacing at the dragon drool, and toss it again. "Things are moving forward, Nico," I say quietly, hesitantly. I've seen his anger many times and I don't want to be the focus of it. "I don't think we can stop it."

He pushes from the couch, his movements swift and feral, and stalks from the house.

"Nothing good will come from him resisting," Leith signs.

"I know. But I don't think there is anything we can do except prepare for the worst." I wait for Twig to return with the ball, but he doesn't. Worried he's gotten into something he shouldn't, I stand and go search for him.

I find him in a corner of the hallway, gnawing on something. Rushing forward, I snatch it from his mouth, ignoring the quiet rumbles in his chest that sound more like a purr than a growl.

"Well shit," I say, holding the red heel between two fingers. "Does Daci know you took one of her shoes? I don't think she'll be too pleased with this." The material is dark with slobber, and the sides have been bent and stretched at weird angles. It's definitely not wearable anymore.

I stand up, Twig jumping and trying to grab the shoe from me, but I keep it out of his reach. In the kitchen, Daci is still talking to Calla. Her green eyes are bright and filled with wonder. Her face is so expressive. She's pretty. Beautiful even. Too bad she's a snob. That won't stop me from having fun with her, though.

"Looks like Twig got ahold of one of your shoes," I say, holding up the object in question. Twig stands, staring at me with his golden eyes radiating anger. His lip curls back like he would be showing me fang, except he has no teeth. Small purr-like rumbles emanate from his chest, and it's so fucking cute I can't help but smile.

"Yeah, he got a hold of it in Girasole. I let him keep it because it was already ruined." She sighs and shakes her head. "My favorite pair, too," she mutters.

"Ah, I see." I drop my arm and let Twig snag the shoe. He glares at me before stalking away, tail swishing in indignation. Frowning, I cross my arms over my chest and watch the little dragon filled with attitude. That was not the reaction I expected from Daci. While I'm disappointed I didn't get to see her all worked up, it only makes me wonder, yet again, what kind of person she truly is. The Daciana I imagined in my head would have flown off the handle at a ruined shoe.

"I have things I need to do, and I need to send a summons to Nona," Calla says, standing from her chair and pulling me from my thoughts. "Why don't you show Daci around Fairyland? Introduce her to the fairies here."

I bow at the waist and give Daci a smirk. "It would be my pleasure." Straightening, I call over my shoulder, "Leith! We're going out. You coming?"

He appears behind me, scooching around to kneel and give Calla a hug. Calla and Nona are two of the only people I've ever seen him hug.

"Don't you dare leave without saying goodbye," she chides.

His hands flow through the movements. "Wouldn't dream of it."

"This is just . . . I don't even know what to say," Daci breathes as she wanders between Leith and me.

There's a childlike wonder in her eyes. They shine brightly, taking everything in. I watch her closely, cataloging every small twitch of her lips, every flutter of lashes. It's a glimpse under the armor she always wears—the designer clothes, perfectly styled hair, and layers of makeup. I study her and try to put together the pieces of her that I know with what I'm seeing now, and they don't match.

I could watch her marvel at Oz for hours. Her curiosity is contagious, and I put myself in her shoes. Looking around, I think about what it would be like to see it all for the first time. "It is pretty amazing, isn't it?"

"Why would you ever leave?" Her question is innocent enough, but both Leith and I stiffen.

"We have our reasons," I say quietly, hoping she drops it.

Startled, she turns to Leith. "Are you from here too?"

His face is tight, eyes hard, jaw clenched. His hands move, sharp and concise. "Yes, and I don't want to talk about it."

She glances at me, silently asking me to translate.

"He is. But he was very young when he left, so he doesn't remember it." She turns to Leith again, but before she can ask him another question, I point over her shoulder. "That's a topo fatato. Probably my favorite fairy in Fairyland."

Leith gives me a grateful look for interfering.

She whirls around, blond ponytail swinging, and a high-pitched squeal makes me cringe. "Oh my gods!" She dashes forward and drops to her knees in front of the stunned creature, holding out her hands, palm up. The mouse-like fairy with a red toadstool on its head carefully climbs into her hands. "What's your name?"

"They don't talk. One of the few who don't." I step up to her side and watch her stroke the fairy's nose with a finger. It's no bigger than a potato and almost melts at her touch. "They are really good at finding hard-to-come-by herbs, especially healing plants, and they can usually be found near streams and in tall grasses."

"You are the cutest thing I've ever seen." She smiles widely, and I catch myself staring at her high cheekbones and slightly upturned nose. A few freckles dot her cheeks and nose that I find utterly endearing. There is even a dimple in her right cheek that I'm itching to reach out and touch.

Leith smacks the back of my head to grab my attention and points to the field beyond us with wide eyes.

"Oh fuck!" I choke, taking off through the high grasses. "Twig! Put that down!"

The fucking dragon looks at me and I swear he smiles around the stick in his mouth before darting away. The problem is, that's not just a stick. It's a fucking fairy.

Leith follows me into the field. The dragon is smart, though. He evades us both, despite the fact we're faster than he is. He's too good at changing direction, using his tail like a rudder. Daci stands at the edge of the grassy expanse with her brows drawn low over her eyes. She's shouting at me and Leith, but we're too focused on Twig to notice what she's screaming.

Leith gets my attention. "I'll distract him, you catch him," he signs quickly.

I nod and stop, letting Leith get Twig's attention. Using every bit of my magic, I creep up behind Twig, barely breathing. At the last possible second, I dive for him and pin him to the ground. Leith jumps in and pries his jaws apart. Judging by the way his muscles bulge with the action, the dragon is stronger than you'd think for a baby.

The fairy jumps out of Twig's mouth, covered in slobber. Leith grabs it and holds it up.

"Are you okay?" I ask it, standing but keeping Twig in my arms. He thrashes around, trying to get back to the *stick*.

The fairy is shaking so hard I'm not sure it even heard me, but it eventually nods. "I think so," it's crackly voice whispers.

"Leith will take you to Calla just to make sure. It's a good thing Twig doesn't have any teeth yet." I bop Twig on the nose, making him go cross-eyed. "Very bad dragon, Twig. You can't eat fairies."

His head droops, tail dropping in defeat, and his chest rises and falls with a sigh. Daci sprints toward us, ponytail streaming behind her.

"What the hell? Why are you not letting him play with a

stick?" she demands, taking Twig into her arms protectively. Her breathing is fast and she's panting like she's not used to running.

"Because it's not a stick," I say, waving toward the fairy Leith is carrying away.

Daci slaps a hand over her mouth. "Oh! Oh no. I'm so sorry."

"The fairy is fine," I reassure her, taking her elbow and leading her back toward the village. "Ramo are hearty creatures. Typically, their appearance is great for camouflage. But apparently, they are defenseless against a baby dragon." I pat Twig's head, trying to cheer him up. "You didn't know any better, bud. It's all good."

Daci hoists him higher in her arms, and he rests his head on her shoulder. "Do you know anything about dragons? I feel like I'm flying blind here."

"Eh, not really. They've been gone for a long time. At least, they were supposed to be." I glance at the dragon that shouldn't exist. "Nico might know more. You could try asking him."

Daci snorts and shakes her head. "Like that will ever happen," she mutters under her breath. More loudly, she asks, "What happened to the dragons? Why did they disappear?"

"I'm not sure. From the stories I've heard, they gradually lost their power. They became weaker and weaker until they were no more. There are a bunch of myths about them and the reason why they disappeared, but that's all they are as far as I'm aware." I shrug, a slight twinge of disappointment in my chest that I can't answer her questions for her. "Even though I was born in Oz and lived here for fifteen years, I was never into learning about the history of this place. Once I was old enough to care, I was in Girasole and knowledge there is limited."

Her voice is quiet and contemplative. "It's hard to imagine such a powerful creature dying out."

I glance at her, again seeing through the armor. There is more to Daciana DeRosa than what meets the eye. There is a softness to her that I'd never expect. The way she cares for and protects Twig is intriguing. And I find myself looking forward to unraveling the layers of Daciana. To finding out who this girl really is. Once my curiosity has been piqued, there is no stopping me.

Daci, Leith, and I spend the day walking around town. I introduce her to various fairies, most of which she greets with squeals and bright eyes, and the fairies all love her. By the end of the day, we have a trail of them following us. She keeps Twig in her arms the rest of the day and only lets him go when I offer to carry him. He's small, but surprisingly heavy.

Nico is nowhere to be seen. He disappeared, but I know he hasn't gone far. We let him have his space to prepare himself for tomorrow when Nona is set to arrive. Luckily, Daci doesn't ask about him. The three of us—me, Nico, and Leith—all have our own feelings about Oz, and none of them are pleasant. My circumstances aren't as bad as theirs, and so Oz has always been a second home for me. So much so, I actually have my own place here. I haven't been back in ages, but it's here if I ever need it.

"Rock, paper, scissors to see who gets the couch?" I ask Leith as we sit in the living room of Calla's house. Daci retreated to the bedroom a while ago, taking Twig with her. Leith grins and holds out his fist. "Best two out of three. On shoot. Rock, paper, scissors, shoot." I throw paper, Leith throws scissors. "Damn! Rock, paper, scissors, shoot." I throw rock, Leith throws scissors again. "Ha! For the win. Rock, paper, scissors, shoot." I throw scissors. Leith throws rock. "Gods damn it! It's yours," I grumble. Not that any of us will fit comfortably on that thing anyway.

Leith grins and signs, "Enjoy the floor, old man. Hope you can still walk in the morning."

"I'm only three months older than you, shithead. Nico is the old man." Poor guy isn't even here to defend himself.

A soft laugh echoes down the hallway, and it draws me in like a moth to a light. It's enticing. Lighthearted and musical. I need to hear it again, closer. I need to see her face while she laughs. Do her green eyes light up? Does her dimple appear? Does she get a second dimple on the other side? As if in a trance, I head down the hall and peer into the room Daci occupies.

She sits on the edge of a bed. It's small, and she'll probably have to sleep curled up. Her blond hair has been taken down from the ponytail, and she looks as if she was in the middle of brushing it out. It gleams brightly, the golden strands catching the firelight and reflecting it back.

The bed squeaks as Twig jumps up and down, using his tail to help propel him into the air. Periodically, he stops and approaches Daci, licking the side of her face. That is what causes the giggles. Each time he does it, the gentle sound climbs up her throat, softening her features and making her look so much younger than she is.

I dig through the recesses of my memory on any information I can remember about her. She's twenty-six years old and the only daughter of Lorenzo DeRosa. She's a spoiled brat. A party girl. Her mom died when she was young, and Lorenzo remarried not too long after. I don't remember much about his new wife. The DeRosas are enemy number one to the Morellis, Nico's family.

The DeRosas and Morellis have been warring for centuries. I don't think anyone truly remembers what started the fighting, but each generation has followed along in their fathers' footsteps, continuing the madness. As the Morelli heir, Nico is expected to take over after his father steps down—or is murdered. Daci is expected to marry. The man will most likely be chosen by her father, and she'll be expected to continue the DeRosa line.

While I'm lost in thought and unable to look away from her, Daci catches me loitering in the doorway. "Um, do you need something?" she asks sharply.

I start and rub the back of my neck. "Just wanted to make sure you didn't need anything," I reply sheepishly.

"Actually, is there another blanket? Twig likes to curl up in one."

I leave and take the blanket off the back of the couch—Leith can deal—and give it to Daci. She takes it with a smile, and it sticks me to the spot. I find I can't move my feet, so I stand in the room stupidly, looking at her while trying to not look at her. Why do I have the urge to run my fingers through her hair? They tingle with the need, and I make a fist, squeezing hard. Is it as soft as it looks?

Daci raises a brow at me in question. "Was there something else?"

"No." I clear my throat but still can't make myself move. Her eyes dart around the room before returning to me. "So uh, how are you?" I wince inwardly. *How are you?* What the fuck is wrong with me.

"Fine?" Her lips twitch like she's trying to not laugh.

"I mean with everything. This has got to be a bit much for you."

She shrugs. "I don't know. Maybe it's in my head, but when I stepped through the portal, it's almost like something inside me settled. Like my body knew something was missing and it finally found it." She laughs quietly and shakes her head. "That sounds ridiculous."

Leaning against the door with my arms crossed, I study her. "Not ridiculous. I wouldn't be surprised. You're fae. A fae without its magic . . ." I'm unable to find the words to describe the travesty. "It's part of who we are. Taking it away is like taking away a limb. We've adjusted to life without magic, but there is always a gaping hole where it should be."

"When you're in Girasole, your magic disappears, doesn't it?" Her frown causes a V to form between her eyes, and I want to rub it away.

"Yeah. I've gotten used to it, just like everyone else has. But returning to Oz is . . . indescribable. To feel it return to me in a rush is powerful."

Her frown deepens, and she opens her mouth as if she would

say something but then closes it again with a sharp click of her teeth.

I tilt my head to the side. "What?"

"Do you think . . . I mean . . . Do I have . . . magic?"

"It's possible." I shrug. "If you do, I'd imagine it wouldn't be very strong unless you have a close relative who is directly descended from Oz. Most Girasolens' magic is so diluted by this point, there probably isn't much left but a spark."

"When I first came through the portal, it felt like . . . I don't know. Like something inside of me clicked into place."

I nod. "That was your magic. Even if all you possess is a spark, being in Oz will amplify that feeling. When I come back, it's always like a weight has been lifted off my chest, allowing me to breathe easier."

"What—" She stops, shaking her head. "Never mind."

I smile. "Go ahead, ask." I already know what she's going to say. And because I am who I am, I'm not going to give her the answer outright.

"What kind of Fae are you?"

I smirk and push off the doorframe. "I'll let you figure that out on your own, edainai." With a wink, I walk away, back to the living room.

Nico is still gone. He probably won't return until his mom shows up. Leith lies on the couch, legs hanging over the armrest. He looks incredibly uncomfortable, and I'm glad I lost. The floor will be much better to sleep on.

"Why are you grinning like that?" Leith asks, signs awkwardly formed from his position on the couch.

I wipe the smile from my face. "No reason."

Leith gives me a knowing look and I sigh as I settle down on the floor. I never said I wasn't going to have some fun with her. I wouldn't be me if I didn't.

8
MATTEO

Despite how much more comfortable the floor is compared to the couch, Leith is still the only one sleeping. I toss and turn on the ground, listening to his soft, even breaths. For some reason, I can't get my mind to quiet down. My thoughts constantly spin through what all of this means. A dragon showing up in Girasole is bizarre, but Nico's words from years and years ago echo in my mind. It all has to mean something.

I don't know what time it is when I hear quiet footsteps pad down the hall and into the kitchen. A moment later, the front door creaks open and shut. Giving up on sleep, I push to my feet and duck outside, looking up and down the street. Daciana's golden hair glints in the starlight as she heads toward the beach. A smile spreads across my face. Guess she's taking my advice and going to look at the ocean in the dark.

I follow, keeping my distance for now. There is something mesmerizing about just watching her, and I don't let myself think of how creepy that sounds. Seeing the way she reacts to experiencing magic for the first time is almost a taboo feeling, like I'm seeing something private that I shouldn't be. The thought is too exciting to be sane, but I don't really care at this point.

I stop in the grassy field that slowly turns to sandy beach. Daci slows her steps the closer she gets to the ocean. The waters are dark at this time of night, an inky black blob that could swallow you whole. Except for the sferalumina. The grain-of-sand-sized fairies come out at night and their light turns the ocean into a beautiful glowing deep blue-green. They move with the waves, creating a magical light show in the ocean.

Daciana sits in the sand just out of the reach of the waves and rests her chin on her knees. The soft wind blows her loose hair around her shoulders, the blond catching the light of the moon and glowing golden. I wish I could see her face. I wonder how the sferalumina's glow looks reflected in her green eyes. Is she staring at the ocean with awe? Longing? Sadness? What emotions does this sight stir inside of her? The ferocity of my curiosity takes me aback. I don't even realize I've walked halfway through the grassy field until I catch sight of something to my right.

It's only because of the glowing waters that I can make out Nico's form sitting on a hill overlooking the ocean. His elbows rest on his knees, and he's hanging his head between them, hands clasped behind his neck. I hesitate, glancing at Daci before turning back to Nico.

"Fuck," I mutter. Bros before hoes, right? As much as I want to go to her, I shouldn't leave Nico alone right now. Besides, he'll probably curse me out and send me away. Then I can at least say that I tried.

As I approach Nico, I make sure to scuff my boots in the grass so he knows I'm coming. He lifts his head to look out at the ocean but doesn't turn toward me. I sit on the ground, resting my back against the log he sits on. That way we won't have to attempt eye contact if he doesn't want to.

Neither of us speaks for a while. We just enjoy the sight of the sferalumina, something we haven't witnessed in a very long time. And I secretly keep turning my attention to Daci on the beach below us. Finally, I take a breath and break the silence.

"I'd ask if you're okay, but I can probably guess the answer to that question."

Nico huffs but says nothing.

I sigh and settle more comfortably against the log. "Look, I know you don't want to hear what I have to say, but as your friend, I feel like it's my job to at least try." When he remains silent, I take that as an invitation. "Things are moving forward whether or not you want them to. Your mom put everything into action twenty-six years ago, and there is nothing any of us can do to stop it."

"I know this," Nico growls, shifting on the log.

"I know you do," I placate. "But you're running from it. Even knowing you can't stop it, you're going to try."

"You think I should just roll over and take this bullshit lying down? I shouldn't fight for what *I* want?"

I weigh my words carefully. It's obvious by Nico's tone that he's on the verge of blowing up at me. "I think the harder you fight, the worse the situation will get. What Nona did was wrong, and I don't agree with it. I know it puts you in a position you don't want to be in. But fighting it will lead to disaster."

Instead of yelling at me, Nico seems to deflate. The energy in the air around us dissipates. "I always knew this was coming, but I was able to push it to the back of my mind. It was easy to forget about. Being the Morelli heir is something I've been able to accept. Despite the way it feels like I've been given no choice. Even though I don't want it, it's all I know. But this? This is another level entirely, and I cannot accept it."

"I get it, Nico. I really do. But I sti—"

"You don't get it, though!" he shouts. "You have no idea what it's like to be told from the moment you're born, your entire life has been planned out for you. I don't get a say in anything I do. If I push back, bad shit happens. So, yeah, if I can fight this, I sure as hell will!"

I swallow and nod slowly, carefully picking my next words. He's on edge, and one little push will send him over. "You're right. I don't know exactly what that's like. But I've been by your side long enough that I know what it does to you. I'm not blind, Nico. And I don't want you to be forced into anything. But you need to think really hard about the ramifications of this. Because you're not heartless, despite what people say about you. And if you put yourself in Daci's shoes, how does that change your opinion?"

Nico is unnervingly quiet after I say my fill. I tense, prepped for any kind of reaction. But I'm not prepared for the huge sigh he releases.

"Fuck," he breathes, then mutters something so quietly I don't catch it.

I glance down to the beach. Daci is still sitting at the edge of the water, head resting on her knees. If I go down there now, Nico will see me and I don't know what kind of reaction he'll have to that. It depends on what decision he makes. Fight it or accept it.

"What are you going to do?" I ask, unable to stop myself.

"Fuck if I know." He pushes to his feet and walks away, leaving me sitting alone and staring at Daci.

"Well hell," I mutter. Not knowing what Nico plans to do puts me in a pickle. But I am who I am, and I'm not about to act any differently around Daci until Nico makes a decision. Besides, maybe it will spur him on.

I'm just about to walk down to the beach when Daci stands. My heart sinks as she heads back to the village. Guess I missed my opportunity. Feeling worse than when I did just a few minutes ago, I wait until she's out of sight before heading back as well.

I don't know what it is, but when we first stepped into Oz, I had this strange sensation of awareness of Daci. It was like I knew of every move she made, even if I wasn't watching her. At first, I chalked it up to my fae senses being sharper with magic present. But the more I'm around her, the more I'm not sure. Watching her in the bedroom, the need to know everything about her . . . It's all too overpowering to be only fae senses.

My steps are slow as I head back to Calla's. I don't think I'm wrong about this entire situation. It's going to be more than any of us expected it to be. We won't just be dropping a dragon off on Nona's doorstep and returning to Girasole. Something bigger is at play, and we're about to find out what.

I feel bad for Leith. He despises this place. I'd suggest he return to Girasole, but I know how stubborn he is and that he needs to prove himself. Oz doesn't hold as many traumatic memories for me as it does for Leith or even Nico. For the most part, the time I lived in Oz was pleasant. The bad things that happened are overshadowed by the good. But it will be hard returning to Girasole. Losing my magic always sends me into a spiral of depression.

Not for the first time, I think about what it would be like to return to Oz. For good. But despite the prospect of my magic, the thought of leaving my brothers behind hurts worse than the knowledge of the empty pit inside of me where my magic should be. They are the only family I have left, and living without them isn't an option.

By the time I reach Calla's, my eyelids are heavy. Being in Oz always has this effect on me. Despite my concern for Nico and Leith, and the stress of what's to come, the atmosphere of Oz creates an undeniable sense of peace. Between that and my magic glowing warmly in my veins, there is a sense of ease and safety I never feel in Girasole. However, I still have a hard time finding sleep. The peace of Oz isn't enough to quiet my mind.

Leith snores softly, the only sound in the house besides the typical noises of houses settling. There are no sounds coming from Daci's room, and as I close my eyes, I can't help but imagine her sleeping peacefully with her blond hair fanned around her head. I don't know what this is with her. I don't know why I'm so desperate to get to know her. But it's with thoughts of Daci in my mind that sleep finally creeps up on me, and I tumble under with a smile on my face.

9

NICOLAI

Mattie's words echo through my mind as I stomp down the hill. *And if you put yourself in Daci's shoes, how does that change your opinion?* Fucking hell. Why does Mattie have to be so perceptive? He knows exactly what to say to make me second guess every decision I've ever made. A sharp pain in my jaw alerts me to how hard I'm grinding my teeth. It takes a conscious effort to unclench the muscles.

Fighting it will lead to disaster.

I shake my head, trying to push his words from my mind. The last thing I want to think about is Daciana DeFuckingRosa. It's bad enough I have to see Nona soon—I refuse to call her my mom —and adding anything else to my list of worries only makes the tension in my jaw worse.

Did Nona know what she was doing twenty-six years ago? Did she know who Daciana was? It honestly wouldn't surprise me if she did. Nona doesn't know how to keep to herself. Always trying to implant herself in my life. Always trying to make up for the fact that she's a shit mother. All she ends up doing is fucking me over even more.

I'm so lost in my rage, I don't realize where I'm heading until sand crunches under my boots. I freeze and look around, stomach dropping when I see where my subconscious led me. Quickly, I dart into the shadow cast by the massive hill overlooking the ocean, the hill I was just sitting on while talking to Mattie.

My gaze finds her like metal filings drawn to a magnet. She looks so small sitting on the vast beach with the waves rushing up to stop just before her feet. From my angle, I can see the side of her face lit by the glow of the sferalumina. The wind gently tugs her blond hair this way and that. And while all of that makes her look beautiful, it's the small smile tugging up the corner of her lips that I can't stop staring at.

I groan inwardly. Of course she is exactly the type of woman I'm drawn to. In Girasole, most girls have dark hair and dark complexions. I've always been attracted to the ones that dye their hair blond. It's something different in the monotony. Add her light skin to the golden hair and sharp, cutting glare of her green eyes . . .

I rub a hand down my face. Doesn't matter how attractive I find her. I remind myself of her personality. Spoiled, snobby, bitchy, and way too girly for me. I can't stand when women complain about their nails or hair, and that's something I know Daciana DeRosa is capable of.

Still. I can't bring myself to look away. And that makes the anger inside of me rise like a burning inferno. My hands clench at my sides and my breaths turn ragged enough that I wouldn't be surprised to find myself breathing fire. I try to remind myself I'm not really attracted to her. It's not real. Just some manufactured emotions that I never asked for.

It doesn't make it easier to look away. If anything, it makes it harder.

Daciana stands and turns back toward the village. I tuck myself deeper into the shadow and watch her disappear. It's not long after that I hear Mattie descend the hill and follow. I growl quietly, forcing my jaw to unclench. It's not my fucking problem.

I need to get this meeting with Nona over so we can deal with the dragon. Then I can return to Girasole and pretend none of this ever happened.

10
DACIANA

I'm sitting outside on the steps to Calla's house, bathing in the early morning sunlight. It's probably in my head, but I swear it feels different than the sun in Girasole. It's warmer. More . . . embracing? Almost like it wraps around me and gives me a gentle hug. Yeah. It's definitely in my head.

Twig darts through the little garden in front of Calla's house, chasing butterflies. I wince as he tramples flowers and plants, but Calla swore it was fine. She said the magic of Oz would replenish them. I take her word for it and watch Twig with a smile. I've never had a pet before. My dad refused to let me have a dog, saying they were filthy and flea ridden. Logically, I know Twig isn't a pet. He's a fucking dragon. A wild magical creature. But right now, as a baby, he seems so puppy-like that it's hard to not think of him as a pet.

The wooden door behind me opens and closes, and Scarecrow sits down next to me. His shoulder brushes mine, and I can't help but think of last night. The way he looked at me while he stood in the doorway, like he was seeing straight through me into my soul. It was unnerving. I'm used to guys looking at me, but never with such a penetrating gaze. Never like they could actually see the real me beneath the makeup and clothing, and I'm not quite sure what to make of it.

"I wonder how old he is," Scarecrow muses as he watches Twig with a smile. His dreads are pulled back into a ponytail today, showcasing his neck and the strong corded muscles there.

I shrug and lean back, my elbows on the step above me. "No idea."

Twig notices Scarecrow and he scampers over, butterflies scattering as he tears through their habitat. Scarecrow holds out his hand for Twig, but Twig ignores it, going straight for his face. Scarecrow falls backward, laughing as Twig pounces and attacks his face with his tongue. My belly does a weird flip at the sound of his laugh, deep and full. I clench my fists against my stomach, willing the sensation to go away.

Scarecrow manages to get Twig off him. He sits up, wiping his face and grimacing. "That's actually really disgusting."

A giggle climbs up my throat and I'm too slow to stop it. Scarecrow's face of disgust, his words, him wiping off the slobber . . . it's comical. His light-brown eyes dart to mine, pupils slightly blown, and I quickly look away. I don't like the way my stomach flutters when he looks at me.

Twig sits in front of us, watching with golden eyes that suddenly seem far older than he is. And far more knowing. His gaze bounces back and forth between us, and his ears wiggle, reminding me of when someone waggles their eyebrows suggestively. Scarecrow hasn't looked away. I can feel the weight of his gaze on the side of my face. The air around us is suffocating and it crackles with an energy that makes the hair on my arms rise.

The moment is thankfully broken when a yellow-winged butterfly flutters over and perches on Twig's nose. He goes cross-eyed trying to look at it. Then his tongue comes out, and he tries to lick the insect off, tipping his head back each time. Both Scarecrow and I laugh, the tension between us melting as we watch the dragon.

We sit there for a few minutes watching Twig until Tin Man appears on the cobbled street before us. He jerks his head to the side, silently requesting Scarecrow to follow him. Scarecrow sighs and pushes to his feet. But before he leaves, he plucks a purple and white flower from the garden.

"For you, m'lady," he says with a grin and a wink, tucking the flower behind my ear. It has to be my imagination when his fingers trail though the strands of my hair, gently brushing against my neck. Definitely my imagination, because there is no way Scarecrow would touch me like that. But telling my belly that does nothing, and it once again flips end over end in nauseating waves.

I watch the two of them disappear down the street, my fingers absentmindedly grazing the silken petals of the flower in my hair. Twig nudges my leg, getting my attention, and I snap my hand to my side.

"Want to go for a walk?" I ask him.

His eyes light up, tail swishing behind him as he jumps up and down excitedly.

"No eating fairies," I say sternly. "And don't scare them."

He bounds down the walkway toward the street, and I follow. We wind lazily through the village, waving at the fantastical fairies of every shape, size, and color. The blooming flowers scent the air, and the sun beams down on me, warming my skin. My brain still has a hard time rationalizing where I am. A magical world. A world where I strangely feel at home.

I focus on the sensation in my middle: the gentle warmth I've felt since I stepped foot inside Oz. Is it magic? Scarecrow seems to think whatever magic I might possess would be minimal, so maybe it's my imagination? Maybe I want to experience it so badly that I'm manifesting the feeling? I wonder if Nona would have an answer to that question.

Commotion in front of me draws me up short. Calla stands with a woman, a human-looking woman, surrounded by a crowd of fairies. The woman's pale-pink dress glitters brightly in the sunlight. The sleeves are long and flowing, and the hi-lo skirts are almost tutu-like. Her golden hair is curled and styled elegantly on her head. Even at this distance, her beauty shines brightly.

"That's Nona," Scarecrow says, appearing next to me suddenly.

"Shit!" I jump and place my hand on my heart as it attempts to leap from my chest. "Don't scare me like that."

He grins at me. "Sorry, edainai." His gaze flicks to the flower still tucked behind my ear and I swear his smile grows before he turns away, looking back down the street.

"Edainai?" I ask suspiciously. He called me that last night as well. "What does that mean?"

"Nona is Nico's mom. One of the Parcae," he says, ignoring my question. "She will be able to help you with your dragon problem."

Twig whirls around, a soft rumbling purr coming from his chest.

"I don't think he appreciates being called a problem." I laugh, imagining what that purr will sound like as a full-grown roar. Not that I'll ever know. The thought makes my smile drop right along with my stomach.

"I meant no offense," Scarecrow says gravely, bowing to Twig.

Twig huffs and turns around, giving his tail an extra swish for emphasis.

"You two are perfect together," Scarecrow mutters under his breath.

I raise one brow, hands on my hips. "And what does that mean?"

Once again, he ignores my question with a grin. "We should head back to Calla's. Nona will meet us there where we can talk in private."

My nerves are a tangled mess. I can't stop my leg from jiggling, and the taste of blood blooms in my mouth from how hard I'm chewing on my cheek. Something is coming. A sense of foreboding lies heavy in the air. Maybe I'm the only one who can sense it, but it's not helping me calm down.

Scarecrow sits next to me at the table, leaning back and looking relaxed like he has not a care in the world. Tin Man is a dark presence looming in the doorway to the living room, arms crossed and face a mask of indifference despite the hard set to his jaw. Lion sits across from me, tossing a wooden ball with Twig. His soft smile is charming, and I find myself momentarily distracted from my nerves.

"You're shaking the entire house," Scarecrow says, placing his hand on my thigh to stop me.

I jolt at his touch. Warmth seeps through my jeans and my nerves twist in an entirely different way. I freeze. My bouncing stops as my focus narrows on his hand. He doesn't remove it like I thought he would when I stopped. He waits until the door opens before giving my leg a gentle squeeze, and only then does he take his hand away, the heat from his skin going with it.

Calla bustles into the house with a wide smile, and behind her, Nona follows and sucks all the air out of the room. From the corner of my eye, I see Tin Man stiffen further, but I can't take my eyes off the woman standing in the doorway. Up close, her beauty is even more breathtaking. There is an otherworldly air about her, something that almost makes her seem fake. There is no way someone so beautiful could exist.

Her porcelain skin is blemish free, not a single pore visible. Every strand of shining blond hair is in its place. She's ageless. I wouldn't even be able to begin to guess how old she is. Her blue eyes travel around the room, landing on Tin Man, and her smile dims slightly. I swear, the light in the room goes with it.

"It's been a while, Nicolai. How are you?" Her voice is like ringing bells, soft, sweet, and melodious.

He doesn't answer. His eyes harden and he clenches his jaw hard enough that I can hear his teeth grinding. Tension grows in the room, and Scarecrow stands, pushing his chair back noisily.

"The lovely Nona. It has been far too long," he says with mock severity, bowing over her hand and placing a kiss on top of it.

She drags her eyes away from Tin Man and blinks. When they reopen, a glimmering mirth shines in them. Tilting her head to the side, she says, "Always the flirt. How have you been, Mattie?"

"Lost. Despondent. Drowning in sorrow. But no longer now that I lay my eyes on you." His voice ebbs and flows dramatically, and he doesn't let go of her hand.

She smiles warmly at him and tugs him in for a hug. "Have you been staying out of trouble?"

Scarecrow places a hand over his heart. "Of course. I would never dream of getting into trouble."

I snort before I can stop myself, because even I know that for the lie it is. Nona's gaze travels to me but then slides away.

"And my sweet Leith." She holds her arms open and Scarecrow steps back, making room for Lion. "How are you?" Her gaze sharpens as she looks at him closely, like she can read whatever he shows on his face. "For real."

I can't see what he signs with his back to me, but Nona doesn't look convinced. She pulls him in for a hug, and I notice she holds him a little tighter than she did Scarecrow. When they finally pull away, she looks at me.

"And you must be the reason Calla summoned me."

"Actually, I think *he* is the reason Calla summoned you." I point to Twig now snuffling around Nona's skirts.

Nona's blue eyes widen and a soft gasp escapes her parted lips. "It's happening," she breathes quietly, her gaze rising to land on Tin Man.

"What's happening?" I ask, matching her quietness, afraid to do something wrong. My gaze bounces between Nona and Tin Man, but I can't figure out what she could be talking about. Uneasiness squirms in my belly and I swallow in an attempt to work moisture back into my mouth.

Nona sits in the chair Lion pulls out for her. She studies me for a moment before holding out her hand. "I'm Nona."

I take it, not surprised to find her skin smooth and warm. "Daciana," I say hesitantly, inwardly wincing at how my palms are probably clammy.

"It's a pleasure to meet you, Daciana," Nona says with a small smile. "What do you know of Oz?"

"Not a lot," I say, shaking my head. "Just the stories that a long time ago the people of Oz closed themselves off to Girasole, taking the magic from Girasole with them. Oz has become a place of legend and myth in my world."

Nona nods with a sad smile on her face. "This is all true. You see, Oz has always been a beautifully magical place. A place of peace. And when Girasole began to grow violent, we made the decision to protect Oz from that violence to maintain our peace. Although, we didn't intend for the magic of your world to disappear. That was only one of the consequences of our actions."

"What was the other?" I ask, watching her face shift through expressions of longing, regret, and happiness.

"Dragons are connected to a dragon leader. Someone who is their guardian, protector, caretaker. That guardian was in Girasole when we created the barrier. Without her dragons, she perished. Their relationship was symbiotic. They needed each other to survive."

"That's why the dragons have disappeared," I breathe, connecting the dots. "They didn't have their guardian."

Nona nods solemnly. "They lasted longer than their guardian did. The dragons slowly faded away into nothing. And the loss of such an amazing creature sat heavy on mine and my sister's hearts. So we decided to do something about it."

Tin Man shifts, his leather jacket creaking in the silence that follows Nona's words, but I don't take my eyes from the Parcae. An unsettled feeling grows in my chest. My blood slows, while my heart pounds erratically. Whatever Nona has to say will be something that changes my life. I know it.

"What did you do?" I ask, my voice shaking as much as my hands fisted in my lap.

"My sister, Decima, is the Thread of Life, while I am the Spinner of Life. Between the two of us, we created a solution to the death of the dragons. We preserved a collection of dragon eggs, and when we were ready, I spun the threads to create a person who Decima destined to become the new guardian of dragons."

The room is silent, except for Nona's lilting voice and my harried breathing. I want to look around the room, to see the faces of Tin Man, Scarecrow, and Lion. But I can't tear my gaze away from Nona and the truth she speaks. Each word is laced with a certain finality that settles into my bones.

Nona's blue-eyed gaze is piercing as she speaks the final damning truth. "You, Daciana, are the new guardian of dragons."

11
DACIANA

Silence louder than an explosion rings through Calla's kitchen. I blink at Nona, her words not making sense in my head. They bounce around, colliding with each other, making it difficult to grasp them. And even if I could, the blood rushing through my ears makes it impossible to focus. Dragons. Guardian. Made. Fate. Destined. It's all out of order and I can't put anything together to comprehend.

Twig must sense my rapidly spiraling thoughts. He licks my fingers, my hands trembling and cold. A soft whine climbs up his throat and I absentmindedly pat the top of his head.

"I'm . . . You . . ." My voice is hoarse and raspy. I try to swallow but my tongue sticks to the roof of my mouth.

Nona smiles warmly. "I understand it's a lot to take in and there is much you will need to learn. But I'm afraid there are more pressing matters you need to attend to."

More pressing than learning I'm the guardian of the dragons? What does that even mean? What am I supposed to do with that information? All I can do is stare at Nona with wide, disbelieving eyes and try to get my heart back under control.

"My sister, Morta, the Cutter of the Thread of Life, has become angry and unstable. She is upset that Decima and I worked together to find a way around the loss of the dragons. Morta takes her job very seriously and does not believe dragons should be reintroduced into the world. They died off, and death is her job. We took that away from her and she retaliated. Her anger has warped into revenge, and she now wishes to use the dragons to release chaos upon Oz."

From the corner of my eye, I notice Scarecrow and Tin Man jerking upright, but I can't bring myself to wonder why. Nona is not done revealing things that are going to shake me to my core.

"Decima had been protecting all of the remaining dragon eggs, keeping them safe for the moment you came to Oz. Morta found them and stole them."

"Fuck," Scarecrow grunts.

"We need those eggs back," Nona continues, ignoring Scarecrow. "We need them returned to us safely so we can bring the dragons back to the magnificent power they were before."

My heart pounds so hard in my chest, I can feel it beating in my fingertips. "And I'm assuming you want me to get them back from her?" I ask, my voice an octave higher in incredulity.

Nona nods. "As the dragon guardian, it is your job to protect them."

A disbelieving laugh climbs up my throat. "You're kidding, right? You want me, an inexperienced girl, to take on a Parcae? I didn't even know magic existed until a day ago, let alone if I possess any. You say I'm the dragon guardian, but I don't even know what that means! There is no way I can take on a powerful being!" Each word gets louder and louder as they spill from my mouth. I'm spiraling. The breath in my lungs gets caught and I can't get it out. It makes my chest ache with tightness.

"I understand this," Nona says calmly, not even batting an eye at my outburst. "That is why my son and his friends will be assisting you."

Tin Man grunts. "Of course we will. And when were you going to ask us? Oh, yeah. That's right. You weren't. Because you don't ask people before making life altering decisions for them." He spits his word with disgust and hate. "You'll never change," he mutters as he storms out of the house once again.

Nona turns a pleading gaze to Scarecrow and Lion. "Please understand I had no other option. We made a mistake all those years ago by closing Oz off from the rest of the world. This is the only way to correct what I did wrong."

Scarecrow shrugs. "I have nothing else to do, and being back in Oz for a bit will be nice. You know I'll help Daci and the dragons."

Nona's shoulders slump with relief, but she turns an apprehensive look to Lion. "And you?"

Lion hesitates, shadows in his blue eyes darkening them. Finally, he takes a deep breath and nods. "Yeah, I'll help." His motions are unsure and hesitant

Nona heaves a sigh of relief. "Thank you." Her gaze travels to the door where her son disappeared.

"Don't worry about Nico. He'll come around," Scarecrow says gently.

A sad smile tugs at Nona's mouth. "I don't think he will. I can never seem to do right by him." She takes a cleansing breath and returns her gaze to me. "I know it's a lot, Daciana. But with their help, I know you can do it. You'll need to see my sister in the Emerald City first. Decima can give you all of the information you need."

I say nothing, because I don't know what to say. And I don't think it would matter. My fate has been chosen. This creature before me has created my destiny and I don't think there is a point to fighting it. Who could win against fate?

Nona snaps her fingers and a burst of glittering light spreads through the room, temporarily blinding me. The sudden sensation of something different on my feet makes me jump.

"You will need those. Never take them off. No matter what. And make sure Morta does not get her hands on them." Nona nods her head toward my feet. "They serve a dual purpose. The dragon eggs are in a state of stasis. The shoes will give you the power to imbue them with life so they can hatch. Morta will want them so she can hatch the eggs and raise the dragons to be used for evil. They also hold the power to lead you back home. As long as you wear them, Morta will not be able to kill you."

I slowly glance down and my mouth falls open. Where my purple sneakers were before, now a pair of sparkly silver flats cover my feet. A silver ribbon crisscrosses my ankles, tying the shoes on. Looking closely, I can see a faint shimmering aura surrounding them.

Nona stands from the chair and heads toward the door. "Don't tarry," she says over her shoulder, her golden hair glinting in the candlelight. "Morta is on a rampage through Oz. She's destroying towns to draw out me and Decima, most likely to send us back to our spirit state where we can't interfere with her plans. And it won't take long for her to realize you're here and wearing those slippers. She won't wait idly for you to come to her."

With those last words, Nona disappears through the door.

Silence follows. I stare at my feet and the silver shoes. Scarecrow and Lion share a silent conversation only two people who have been friends for a long time can understand. Twig sniffs the shoes then sneezes. And the silence grows. But the noise in my head is anything but quiet. Ringing in my ears drowns out every other thought that tries to rise to the surface. Right now, I'm glad for the ringing and the way it won't let me focus. I'm scared of what will happen when I have a moment to think through Nona's words.

"I should go find Nico," Scarecrow says softly. "We need to make some plans if we're going to leave soon." He stops before stepping through the door, glancing at me with none of his usual playfulness. "Are you okay, Daci?"

"I . . ." Am I okay? No. Do I have a choice but to be okay? Also, no. So I stare at my feet and say nothing, blinking and trying to sort through the raging emotions inside of me, even as I find myself shutting down.

Lion signs something to Scarecrow, but I don't pay attention to it. Scarecrow nods and leaves to find Tin Man. Lion and I sit in silence, with Twig sniffing and sneezing at my new shoes.

The next morning, I find myself standing outside Calla's house, my backpack packed and extra supplies stuffed inside. The silver shoes on my feet feel weird with the leggings and T-shirt, too fancy to go with the comfort clothes. But I didn't take them off last night, even sleeping in them. I'm not about to find out what happens if I do.

Twig bounds through the flower bed, sniffing the blooms and chasing the butterflies. The flowers he trampled yesterday have re-bloomed as if by magic. Well, it probably was magic.

Calla steps out of her house with a few last-minute provisions. "Bread and cheese," she says, handing them to Lion, who stuffs them in his bag. "You should have enough to get you to Villabosco."

"Thank you," Lion signs, then hugs Calla tightly.

A tear glimmers in her eye as she pulls away. "And don't wait so long to visit next time." She hugs Scarecrow and glances around for Tin Man. "Tell Nico I said goodbye." When she gets to me, she smiles warmly. "And you and Twig are welcome anytime."

"Thank you so much," I say, taking her hands. "Your home and village are lovely."

Scarecrow takes my elbow and leads me away, Twig dashing in front of us. The fairies of the village all gather around and wave goodbye. A few hand me flowers and by the time we reach the outskirts of the village I have a small bouquet of wildflowers. I stop to press a few between the pages of my sketchbook, not wanting to get rid of them.

"So, how do we get to the Emerald City? And where is Tin Man?" I ask.

Scarecrow glances at me with a frown, and I realize I haven't ever addressed any of them by name—given name or nickname. "Nico will pop up along the way when he's ready," Scarecrow says. "And to get to the Emerald City, all we have to do is follow the yellow brick road." He waves his hand in front of him, indicating the road that starts just outside the village.

It is indeed made up of yellow bricks. I follow the road with my eyes and find that it disappears way into the distance. "Okay. I guess we should be off then."

With the first step I take onto the yellow brick road, I swear a tingle spreads up my legs and into my soul. I scrunch my toes in the silver flats, trying to erase the sensation of ants crawling over my feet. When Twig prances onto the road, the world shudders. I brace my feet and throw my arms wide to keep my balance, and I notice Lion and Scarecrow doing the same.

"What the hell was that?" I ask as the world settles around us.

Scarecrow glances around, wide-eyed. "I have no idea," he says slowly, gaze landing on Twig and narrowing. "Come on. If we want to reach Villabosco by tomorrow evening, we need to get moving."

"What is Villabosco?" I ask, walking down the yellow brick road.

"It's the closest town to Fairyland. We'll be able to restock our supplies, rest, and prepare for the hardest part of our journey." Scarecrow winks at me and stretches his arms overhead. "We won't reach it before tomorrow evening. So I hope you like to sleep under the stars."

I groan. Lovely. I'm so far from a nature person. This entire experience is going to be terrible. We fall into silence as we walk, and my mind travels once again to Nona's words. Dragon guardian. While the thought of all that entails terrifies me, something inside of me seemed to settle when Nona spoke those words. Like my soul recognized them for what they were. It also helped me realize why I felt so strongly about protecting Twig, and why the thought of leaving him makes my heart crack open.

Still, I know nothing of dragons. I know nothing of the magical world. How am I supposed to protect a race of magical beings when I don't know what the hell I'm doing? I glance at Scarecrow. "You really don't know anything about dragons to help me?"

He shakes his head. "I know about as much as you do now.

Everything else is myth and story." He shrugs nonchalantly. "You'll figure it out, though. And I'm sure Decima will be able to help."

"What can you tell me about her?" I should probably be as prepared as possible to meet the ruler of the Emerald City.

"Not a lot. She's Nona's sister. The Parcae who measures life. She plays a part in determining fates and destinies. As far as I'm aware, she is not quite as friendly as Nona but not as vicious as Morta."

Great. That doesn't help at all. "What about the Emerald City?"

Scarecrow grimaces. "Again, not much. I've never been but I've heard stories from people who have. The road to get there is dangerous and filled with pitfalls. But once you're there, it's supposedly gorgeous."

Well, he's not a lot of help. I fall silent again. Scarecrow can't give me any information I need, so it looks like I'm going in blind. As we walk, I study him. His lithe frame with the perfect amount of muscle under his dark skin. The wind blows through his locs, tossing them to and fro. The Scarecrow. Known for his inability to be serious. Flirtatious, silly, but not the brightest. Although, I've seen him act serious already, so who knows. I should know better than others that the act one puts on in public doesn't always match who the person truly is.

"Tell me about yourself," I say suddenly, desperately wanting to distract myself from the impending spiral I'm sure to find myself in if my thoughts linger on Nona's words. "If we're stuck with each other for a while, I might as well get to know you."

He raises one dark brow at me, like he knows that's not the reason I'm asking. "Like I said, I was born in Oz. Villabosco, actually. That's where my house is. My parents died when I was young, and I was raised by my grandmother until she passed. I was on my own for a while until I met Nico and Leith when I was fifteen while they were visiting Villabosco with Nona. We bonded instantly, and I went back to Girasole with them."

"You were alone while you were that young?" I can't imagine living by myself at fifteen.

He shrugs like it's no big deal, but I can see the tension bracketing his eyes that gives him away. "It was only five years. I managed."

He was ten years old when he had to take care of himself? I can guess by the way his words are clipped that however he managed wasn't necessarily pleasant. Getting the hint, I let the conversation drop.

We walk this way for the rest of the day, stopping only for a lunch of bread and cheese. My feet and calves ache. I'm definitely not used to this much exercise. Still, even though it feels great to finally sit down, I grimace at the dirt under me. Before I take a piece of bread, I rinse my hands with water from a bottle Lion hands me, but it doesn't get all the grime out from under my nails. Gross.

I haven't seen Tin Man since we started our journey, and when I asked Scarecrow, all he said was that he'll show up when he wants to. On the road, Lion keeps a short distance behind me and Scarecrow, a silent presence that I can't ignore no matter how hard I try. Twig tires out quickly, and Scarecrow ends up carrying him for the second half of the day. We talk occasionally, conversation light and about nothing in particular. And by the time Scarecrow calls for us to stop for the evening, my legs are so worn out they feel like pieces of overcooked spaghetti. When was the last time I did this much walking?

I follow Scarecrow into the grass that borders the yellow brick road, and I sink onto the ground in front of a tree. "Oh thank gods." The fact I'm sitting in grass with who knows what kind of bugs doesn't even bother me. It feels too good to sit. I flex my feet and roll my ankles, feeling the stretch in my calves and hamstrings. The backs of my heels feel raw, and when I peek under the shoe, my skin is reddened and blistered. I groan. It's going to be a long trip wearing these shoes.

Scarecrow chuckles and sets his bag on the ground, along with Twig. "Better get used to it."

Twig scampers over to me and sinks into the grass, promptly going to sleep. I envy him. I wish I could pass out, but my stomach is rumbling. I need more than bread and cheese for dinner.

"Leith, get a fire going. I'll go see if I can hunt for something to eat." Scarecrow walks off into the sparse woods lining the yellow brick road.

I close my eyes and lean against the tree, listening to Lion gather wood and get a fire started. An owl hoots above me, and I open my eyes to look at it. It blends in, the browns, grays, and blacks of the feathers matching the bark of the tree. But its big orange eyes stare at me, unblinking. The tufts of feathers by its ears are flattened, giving it an angry appearance. I shudder and close my eyes again, blocking out the sight.

I'm dozing off when Scarecrow returns with two skinned rabbits in his hand. "Dinner!" he calls with a grin.

Bile climbs up my throat and I reflexively swallow it down. "Seriously?"

He glances at me with raised brows. "Ever had rabbit?"

"No. And I'm not about to start tonight," I mutter as I dig through Lion's bag and pull out a hunk of bread and cheese.

"Suit yourself," Scarecrow says, shrugging.

I finish my disappointing meal and curl on the ground by the tree, using my bookbag as a pillow. It takes a tremendous amount of effort to not think about what kind of bugs may be crawling in the dirt under me. Just a single thought about it and I get the itchy sensation of things skittering over my skin. A root digs into my side, and I squirm to get comfortable. It's pointless though. Sighing, I close my eyes and listen to Scarecrow talking softly with Lion. I'm surprised how swiftly sleep claims me.

12
NICOLAI

I watch her from afar, never making my presence known. Sure, it's creepy, but I need to get an idea of her character, especially when she thinks no one is looking. I haven't learned much by the time Mattie calls it quits for the evening. She's curious, which is understandable, and she seems to accept Mattie's flirting and gives it right back. But none of that is helpful or surprising. They are both known for their sexual exploits.

I perch in the tree above her and watch as she gently runs a hand over the dragon's scales before leaning her head back and closing her eyes. Leith looks around and I hoot so he knows I'm here. The girl's eyes open and land on me, wide and curious. I stare at her, like if I look hard enough I'll be able to see beneath her skin to the person she is. She shudders and looks away, closing her eyes again.

Mattie returns with rabbits. She refuses to eat them, so she eats bread and cheese before lying down. I watch her breathing, and when I'm positive she's asleep, I swoop down and shift, landing on my feet in a smooth motion.

Neither Mattie nor Leith react. They knew I was there, and they've seen me shift before. Not often, because I don't come to Oz a lot, but enough that it's nothing new to them. The dragon notices, though. His head pops up and he tracks me, studying me with too intelligent eyes.

"Twig," Mattie says quietly. "You hungry?" He holds out a chunk of rabbit meat and the dragon bounds over, tongue hanging out of his mouth.

I settle next to the fire and take some meat from Leith. Staring into the flames, I try to lose myself in thought, but the guys have other ideas.

"So," Mattie says, giving me a knowing look. "Did you figure anything out?"

I shake my head. "No. I can't tell what kind of person she is."

"Maybe if you actually spent time with her, you'd learn something." Leith's brow is raised as he signs, his mouth quirked to the side.

"She'd just put on an act," I reply.

Mattie snorts and tosses another hunk of meat to the dragon. "You don't know that. I spent all day talking with her—"

"Flirting, you mean," I interrupt.

"And she doesn't seem quite as shallow as we all thought she'd be," he continues, ignoring my interruption.

It's my turn to snort. "There is no way the daughter of DeRosa isn't a spoiled brat."

"Oh, I never said she wasn't spoiled. But she has more layers than any of us anticipated." Mattie leans back on his elbows, watching the dragon lick his paws. "I mean, look at you. The Tin Man. Heartless. Nothing but a brute. Isn't that what people say about you?"

I glare at him but don't answer because that is what they say about me. And I'm not sure it's too far off the mark.

Leith, being ever so observant as always, notices the slight shift in my expression. "You're not heartless, though," he signs. "There's more to you than people think. The same can be said of Daci."

"Honestly, it will be harder if she has a personality," I mumble, choosing to ignore my brothers.

Leith sits up and changes the subject. "Your mom left a bit out when she explained everything to Daci."

I exhale heavily and pinch the bridge of my nose. "Yeah, and I don't know whether I'm glad about that or not. On one hand it makes things easier right now, but I can't imagine how complicated it will make things later on when she finds out."

"Well, I bet talking to her and letting her get to know you will help when it's revealed." Mattie grins at me, thoroughly enjoying my discomfort.

"Fuck off, Mattie." I push to my feet and give them both a hard stare. "Don't say a word to her about it." With that, I stalk into the woods and disappear for the night.

The next day, I follow along with the others, remaining hidden in the woods. The girl and Mattie talk and laugh. There is no denying their flirting, and poor Leith is stuck with them. At one point, Mattie looks directly at me in the dark of the forest and gives me a look that says, "Grow up and grow a pair."

If I don't join them, Mattie will never let me live it down, so I leave the woods and join the group, sliding into step with Leith. The girl watches me with curiosity, and I stare straight at her, willing her to do or say something that will give me an idea of who she is. She doesn't though. Instead, she turns back to Mattie and says something that makes him laugh. My shoulders climb toward my ears. I'm not used to someone ignoring me so thoroughly.

"It's nice of you to join us," Leith signs, watching me closely and no doubt marking my reaction.

"Mattie was right," I sign back, not wanting the girl to hear what I have to say. "I'll get a better understanding of her if I try to talk to her."

Leith huffs a silent laugh. "You'll have to actually talk to her, not just grunt and curse."

"I'm not sure I can do that. What the fuck was my mother thinking?" My motions become increasingly agitated as I sign. "There is no way this will ever work out, and not just because I'm unwilling to make it work. I can't imagine a world in which the girl agrees either."

"Don't write her off before you even try to get to know her."
Leith gives me a knowing look. "You won't be any better than you
think she is."

Gods damn him. I love Leith like a brother. He basically *is* my
brother, but because he knows me so well, he knows exactly what
to say to get under my skin. He knows my hopes and dreams and
goals, and he isn't afraid to push me to help me reach them.

I spend the rest of the journey walking with Leith behind
Mattie and the girl. I listen to their conversations and watch her
closely. It's unnerving when she carries the dragon and his head
rests on her shoulder and he stares back at me like he knows
exactly what I'm doing. Or like he knows what I'm hiding. That
creature is far too knowing for my comfort.

"This is disgusting," I finally sign to Leith after even more of
their flirting.

He cracks a rare smile. "You can stop it, you know. It would
be within your rights."

"Hardly. Besides, who am I to tell Mattie he can't enjoy
himself with a woman?"

"What will you do when—"

I shake my head, stopping him. "Not a road I'm going down,
Leith."

The sun is sinking below the horizon when Villabosco comes
into view. The girl's interest is piqued and her conversation with
Mattie falls silent. Mattie shifts the dragon in his arms. That thing
has to be getting heavy. We'll have to find a better way to carry it
before we leave for the Emerald City.

We pass a few outlying buildings, most of them dark for the
night. The fae who dwell in them typically rise early with the sun
to tend to the fields and then retire early for the night. A gravel
road branches off from the yellow brick road and we follow it into
the town.

The girl takes in the two- and- three-story wooden
structures with thatched roofs. Light spills from many of the
windows, pooling in golden puddles on the gravel outside. As

we pass the tavern, raucous laughter and bawdy singing seep into the night air. A few fae are still in the streets, either heading home after work or making their way to the tavern for a drink or two.

Most of them recognize Mattie, Leith, and me. They wave and say hello. A few ask if Mattie is going to be at the tavern later. He shrugs and gives them noncommittal answers. The girl takes it all in with wide eyes. I can see the gears turning in her mind as she tries to figure out what this town is and how we fit into it.

Mattie's house is a two-story structure a couple blocks from the tavern. It's in a quiet area of the town, and without the lights the center of town has, it's quite a bit darker. The garden is slightly overgrown, like the person Mattie hired to keep it up has slacked on their job.

"Home sweet home," Mattie chimes, walking up the path. He pulls an old-fashioned-looking key from his pocket and fits it into the lock, pushing open the wooden door.

"This is your house?" the girl asks, studying the structure.

"Sure is." Mattie smiles and motions her inside. "It's been in my family for ages. Most of the furniture is ancient, but it serves its purpose." He takes a lighter from the table next to the door and begins lighting candles.

Leith goes to the fireplace and gets a fire going. The orange flames dance in the hearth and cast the room in their cozy glow.

"I'll head to town real quick and get some food," Mattie says. "Make yourself at home. Bedrooms and bathroom are upstairs. Help yourself to anything."

I sit on the creaky old couch and watch the girl closely. This house is a far cry from the opulence she's used to. She walks around slowly, looking at all the nicknacks Mattie's family has collected over the years. From what he told me, his grandma was the worst about bringing home trinkets to display.

Daci eventually sits on a chair across from me and Leith, staring into the fire. "It's weird not having electricity. It would be hard to get used to that."

I grunt, not saying anything, but Leith elbows me and signs, "Don't be a dick. Now is a good time to get to know her."

"I don't want to get to know her," I sign back, a petulant expression on my face.

The girl watches the exchange with a furrowed brow, no doubt trying to figure out what we're saying. When she notices me looking at her, she turns back toward the fire. The dragon stands in front of it, opening and closing its mouth and huffing breaths, almost like it's pretending to breathe flames.

Leith elbows me again and I pinch the bridge of my nose. "So . . ." I say, wracking my brain for something to say.

"You don't have to talk to me," she says bluntly, still staring at the dancing flames. "I know how much it would hurt your ego to stoop to my level. Conversing with the enemy's daughter. How archaic." She shudders dramatically and stands from the chair, rolling her eyes. "Come on, Twig." She waits for the dragon before climbing the stairs and disappearing.

Leith's body shakes next to me as he silently laughs. This time, it's me who elbows him. "Fuck off, asshole," I say aloud.

I don't wait for Mattie to come home with food. Instead, I head to the center of town to find my own. And to get away from the girl. This is a fucking disaster. The sooner we get her to the Emerald City, the sooner I can move on. Hopefully.

13
DACIANA

I haven't taken a bath in ages, and as soon as I saw the tub in my room at Scarecrow's house, I groaned. It's been two days since I washed up, and after traveling on the road, I feel absolutely disgusting. Thankfully, there's running water, because the first time I fill the tub, I use it to wash all the layers of filth off my skin and get the dirt out of my hair. The second time I fill it, I spend an hour relaxing in the warmth, letting my sore muscles ease.

Twig watches me with unblinking golden eyes, his tail impatiently swishing back and forth on the wooden floor. Toward the end of my soak, I pat the water, and he wastes no time hopping into the tub, sending water splashing everywhere. Giggling, I wipe my face then grimace at the puddles outside the tub.

"You are a heathen, little dude," I say with a fond smile, tickling under his chin.

I hadn't realized how dirty he was until the bathwater turns a gross shade of brown and I quickly hop out, letting Twig play. I listen to his happy trills as I dry off and put on clean clothes. Once my hair is brushed, I fight with Twig until I get him out of the tub and wrapped in a towel. He glares at me with baleful golden eyes until I tell him Scarecrow returned with food. That gets him moving.

After our meal, we claim a room and curl up in bed. Twig is out cold in seconds, his chest rumbling with quiet snores. I envy his ability to fall asleep at the drop of a hat as I stare at the ceiling. I'm exhausted from traveling, but my mind won't quiet down. There are still so many unanswered questions that keep popping into my thoughts. Each time one does, I find myself jerking back to consciousness as I mentally add it to the list of things to ask Decima. This goes on and on until Scarecrow's face pops into my mind.

He left after dinner, saying something about going to the tavern, leaving me with just Lion. Tin Man disappeared to who knows where, and honestly, who fucking cares? I sure as hell don't. But Scarecrow's flirting on the yellow brick road helped to keep my mind off the thoughts plaguing me, and I won't lie when I say I thoroughly enjoyed it.

Unable to lie here any longer, I quietly climb out of bed, making sure I don't wake Twig. I put my jeans on, struggling to get them over those stupid silver shoes. Then I fluff out my hair and sneak down the stairs. No one told me to stay inside, so I don't see the problem with leaving.

Outside, the night air is warm with just the slightest hint of chill on the wind. I have no idea what season it is, if Oz even has seasons. But the night sky above me is breathtaking. Stars and galaxies spread bright and colorful through the black expanse. I stand on the walkway and stare for a moment, marveling at the beauty we can't see in Girasole because of the lights.

When I finally pull my gaze from the sky, I make my way to the center of town. It's a straight shot from Scarecrow's house, and I have no problem finding it. All the businesses are closed for the night. I peek into the windows spotting various goods for sale. Clothing, food, candles, books, medicines. You name it, there is a store for it.

Laughter and music spill into the street from the tavern as the door opens, quieting as it closes again behind a patron. Intrigued, I make my way there, stepping across the gravel road, wincing when a few pebbles end up in my shoes. I open the door and step inside.

Immediately, warmth surrounds me from so many people crammed into a small space. A variety of scents greet me—stew, spices, beer, smoke, sweat—and it all mixes to form a disgusting combination. I crinkle my nose and scan the space, looking for an empty chair. My gaze lands on a small stage raised at the edge of the room. Sitting on a stool on the stage is Scarecrow, resting a guitar on his knee.

He strums a few notes and the crowd in the tavern instantly quiets, all attention focused on him. He doesn't seem to mind as he looks at the instrument and begins to play. I watch the crowd, all human-looking except for a few with small fairies sitting on their shoulders. Everyone stares at Scarecrow, entranced.

I've never heard someone play guitar so well. He strums the strings masterfully, bringing forth a tune that echoes through the room, sinking in my bones and settling deep within me. It's hauntingly beautiful, raising goosebumps on my arms. The sound raises emotions inside of me I wasn't even aware of feeling. Sadness, joy, fear, peace. All of it swirls together in the melody Scarecrow creates.

Then he starts to sing.

Before I know what I'm doing, I walk forward, drawn forth by the pure tenor of his voice. It steals my breath. I can't pull my gaze from him, mesmerized by the music he's making. His voice twines perfectly with the notes from the guitar, weaving to form a song that makes my soul seem to glow.

The words have no meaning to me, even though he's speaking a language I understand. It's the overall feeling of the song that brings me immense joy. Distantly, I'm aware of the word for this, for what he is, but I can't make it form in my mind. I'm too drawn to the sound, the melody, the rhythm. All of it is absolutely perfect.

Scarecrow raises his head and his gaze meets mine. He keeps singing, keeps playing guitar, but I swear it's as if the rest of the room disappears and it's just me and him. I can't pull my eyes from his. Warmth spreads through my body, starting in my chest and fanning outward. My heart beats with the same rhythm as his music.

Scarecrow sings and I fall. I fall into the darkness his music brings. It's not the dark of evil though. It's the dark you need to see the stars shining above. It's the dark of the night sky right before the sunrise. It's heavy and deep. It surrounds me in comforting arms and makes me feel . . . whole.

When the music stops, his fingers pulling away from the strings, a pregnant silence fills the room. Then the crowd bursts into applause and cheers. I stagger backward as he breaks our eye contact, like a rubber band had been holding me in place and it suddenly snapped. I suck in a sharp breath, my lungs screaming for air as if I hadn't been breathing the entire time he played.

The crowd begins chanting for more, and Scarecrow smiles and obliges. This time, the song is upbeat and catchy. The patrons stand and clap their hands or stomp their feet. A few begin to dance. Scarecrow's gaze travels to me once more, and he winks.

I now know what kind of fae Scarecrow is. Only one kind could captivate an audience like he does. Only one kind has such a beautiful and inspiring voice.

Matteo Rossi is a Faun.

Looking at him now, I can totally see it. Not just because he completely entrapped my soul while he was singing, but because of the way he moves—elegant and graceful despite his size. The way he seemed to be so at home traveling through nature, almost like it answered to him. His playful demeanor, the flirting and laughing and carefree way he moves through the world while also being sensitive and observant.

I'm not so sure he deserves the nickname Scarecrow. Matteo isn't dumb. He may play into the misconception, but I think there is a lot more to him underneath the layers of the mask he wears. Not so different from me, really.

I snag a stool as soon as someone vacates it, and I settle in to watch Matteo. He commands the small stage, and the audience is drawn to him like they are in the dark and he is the light. It's mesmerizing to watch this side of him, to see him in his element and enjoying every second of it. Matteo shines. He positively radiates joy and happiness.

Time passes in a blur, and before I know it, Matteo puts his guitar in a case then walks through the crowd straight toward me. I blink, pulling myself from the haze his performance put me in. Not once during it did I take my eyes off him. And even though I was deeply enthralled, I didn't fail to notice how his gaze traveled to me often.

Matteo stops in front of me, a faint sheen of sweat on his forehead and neck. His light-brown eyes search mine. For what, I have no clue, but I don't break his stare. A smile tugs at his lips and I drop my gaze to them on instinct, making Matteo grin wickedly. He takes my hand and leads me from the tavern, ignoring the villagers clamoring for his attention.

Outside, he doesn't release my hand, and we meander slowly back toward his house. When the lights of the center of town fade behind us, Matteo stops and turns me to face him. In the pocket of darkness, his eyes appear darker than usual. Or maybe that's not entirely due to the lack of light. He stands close to me, closer than he ever has. The heat from his body soaks into my front, and I find I want to get closer. To let his warmth swallow me whole.

"You're a Faun," I say quietly after a moment of silence.

He grins. "What gave it away?"

I glance at his hand still holding mine. Long fingers that know how to expertly pluck strings to bring forth a beautiful melody. What would those fingers feel like on my skin? Would he be able to draw music from me that I've never experienced before at a man's touch?

Matteo sucks in a breath like he knows where my thoughts have traveled. Maybe he does. Maybe his senses are stronger because he's a Faun. Maybe he can tell how that thought lights my blood on fire. He steps closer, and I can smell him. The earthy scent of a forest wraps around me and it's intoxicating.

"I wasn't expecting you to sneak out tonight," he says, voice low and quiet.

"No one told me to stay inside." I take a step closer, as if I can't stop myself from getting as near to him as possible.

"I'm glad you did."

His words are almost too quiet to hear, and I snap my gaze from his lips—which I had been staring at—to his eyes. He lifts a hand and brushes his fingers along my cheek. They're calloused from playing the guitar and they scrape surprisingly delightfully over my skin. Matteo lifts my chin with his thumb, and he gives me no chance to pull away. Not that I would have.

His lips meet mine, softly at first, barely a feather-soft caress. When he breaks the kiss, I stand on my tiptoes and chase his mouth, not ready to let him go yet. His fingers tighten on my jaw, and he presses his lips more firmly against mine. They're warm and soft and enticing. Without giving myself a chance to think twice about what I'm doing, I run my tongue along the seam of his mouth, and my stomach flutters when he opens.

Our tongues brush against each other and Matteo's other hand slides around my waist, tugging me closer to him. His body is hard against mine, and so, so warm. Wrapping my arms around his neck, I hold on and let myself get lost in the kiss. It's not hard to do. He sweeps me away with each touch, each breath, each fluttering butterfly in my stomach.

After who knows how long, Matteo pulls away. His breathing is as ragged as mine, his lips as puffy as mine feel. The silence around us is interrupted only by our breathing, until an owl flies overhead, hooting loud enough to make me jump. Matteo tracks the owl with a glare until it disappears into the darkness.

"We should head back," he says quietly, searching my face. "It's late."

I nod, my mind and body still reeling from that kiss. I've kissed a lot of guys, and none of them have ever left me this breathless and unsteady. Part of me expects Matteo to pull away, to pretend nothing happened. That's what I would do. But instead, he links our fingers together and leads me back to the house.

Inside, at the top of the stairs, he turns to me with a crooked smile. "Goodnight, edainai," he says with a wink before heading to his room.

I can't contain my smile as I enter the room I've taken for myself. Even as Twig lifts his head and stares at me like he knows exactly what I've been doing. I'm still smiling when I climb into bed and close my eyes.

14
DACIANA

One thing I don't like about Oz: no coffee. How the fuck I'm supposed to be awake and pleasant without coffee is something I have never figured out, and unfortunately, I won't be figuring it out anytime soon on this journey.

Tin Man insisted on leaving after only one day of rest at Villawhatever. And to make things even worse, he insisted on leaving before the sun had risen. The past few days, I've at least been able to have a mug of tea, but there was no time for that this morning. Now, I find myself traipsing down the yellow brick road, sans coffee, cranky and tired. Matteo tried to start a conversation with me, but I quickly shut him down. Fuck talking this early in the morning. Even Twig keeps a wide berth like he can sense my grumpy mood.

Tin Man and Lion walk ahead of me, and despite how much I dislike Tin Man—and he clearly dislikes me—I can't stop myself from admiring his ass. His and Lion's. All three of these guys are built magnificently. It must have something to do with how much magic they've been exposed to growing up.

I watch them closely, picking up bits and pieces of their conversation. Tin Man has opted to sign, most likely thinking his conversation with Lion will be private that way. I don't catch a lot since I'm walking behind them, but I can tell they are having a mini heart-to-heart, each of them asking the other how they're doing and what they can do to help the other. I find it kind of endearing, as well as baffling.

It's not so surprising to think of Matteo as being caring toward his friends. Even Lion to an extent exhibits some warmth toward others. He openly hugged Nona and Calla, and he seemed to enjoy the company of the fairies. And he's always been pleasant with Twig. But Tin Man. Tin Man is a cold, heartless bastard. Seeing him show any kind of affection toward his friends is strange to me.

"Tomorrow we'll reach the first obstacle of our journey," Matteo says cautiously, observing me from the corner of his eye and pulling me from my thoughts.

"Which is?"

"The chasm."

I huff. "And what is that?"

"It's exactly what it sounds like. A massive chasm that can only be crossed by a narrow bridge." He watches Twig trotting ahead of us. "I'll carry Twig across in my bag."

"Great. Sounds lovely," I say. A narrow bridge over a massive chasm. Sounds simple enough. Too bad my fear of heights will make it practically impossible.

Matteo snorts. "You are *so* cranky."

I shoot a glare at him, daring him to say anything else, and he chuckles, raising his hands in surrender.

The landscape slowly changes as we walk. Trees begin to pop up more frequently. They're large and topped with massive green leaves. I have no idea what kind of tree they are, but the more they appear, the more shaded the road becomes. Eventually, we're pretty much surrounded by forest.

Dappled sunlight filters through the branches, but even that disappears as night falls. The darkness seems more intense in the woods. More alive and watchful. I shudder when Tin Man calls it quits for the day, stepping off the road and into the trees to find a place for us to sleep for the night. I didn't mind sleeping out in the open the other night. The stars above and the wide-open fields were less threatening. But the closed-in forest is unsettling. Who knows what lurks in the darkness.

Lion gets a fire started right away, and I make sure to sit within the circle of light it casts. Something tells me I don't want to step away from it. Tin Man and Matteo go in search of food, and I watch Lion as he sits quietly, watching the flames dance. He glances at me and finds me staring. Before I can look away, he gives me a small smile that makes his face appear warmer than I've ever seen it.

Mouth suddenly dry, I drop my gaze to my lap. I wish I could ask him about his story. What kind of person is Lion under his mask? What's happened to him to make him this closed off from people? I jerk as one thought pops into my head, and no matter what I do to make it go away, it won't. *What would it take for him to drop his guard and let me in?*

I shake my head to dispel the thought, but it persists, floating around in my mind like a log on a river. No matter how rough the waves, it stays afloat. Luckily, the other two return and finally distract me. Unfortunately, they've caught more rabbits, and I grimace, digging through my bag for more cheese and bread. I will not eat rabbit. Nothing can make me.

When we're all finished eating, we settle down in silence. Tin Man stalks off into the darkness. Where does he keep going? Is my presence so unbearable, he can't stand to even be near me? And why does that make my chest ache? Sighing, I glance at my nails and silently pick the dirt from under them, doing my best to keep my face from showing disgust. A few nails are cracked, and I pull my nail file out of my bag to smooth them down.

"Get some sleep, Daci," Matteo says, standing up. "Maybe you won't be as cranky tomorrow."

I throw a stick at him, making him laugh, but he walks away, following the path Tin Man took minutes before. I settle down, following Lion's actions, but sleep eludes me.

After what feels like hours of tossing and turning on the hard ground, I quit trying to sleep and sit up. The noises from the forest around me make my imagination run wild. The wind blows, making rustling leaves sound like flapping wings. Branches creak and rub together, sounding like strange animal calls. And the constant chatter of nighttime insects—some familiar and others not—rise and fall in waves like the verses of an aria.

I can't help but think of the kind of creatures that stalk the night, and my imagination has no problem creating all sorts of vicious animals, conjuring thoughts of them stalking through the woods toward our camp. Twigs snap behind me and I jerk around, peering into the darkness, but I see nothing. Curling my legs to my chest, I stare at the flames.

Lion is sound asleep, and I'm so tempted to wake him to make sure there is nothing creeping up on us in the woods. But I refrain. Twig still sleeps soundly by the fire. I assume he'd wake if there was something dangerous nearby, but then again, I don't know much about dragons.

"Can't sleep?"

I jump, slapping a hand over my mouth to stifle a scream. "You fucking scared me, Matteo." My heart slams against my ribcage and my skin prickles like it's too small to wrap around my bones in the wake of the terror that shot through me.

He chuckles and sits next to me. "Sorry. Didn't mean to."

My heart slowly settles, and the fear abates with Matteo next to me. "It's so creepy out here," I whisper, looking around. "There are so many noises and things scurrying through the darkness." I shiver, squeezing my eyes shut.

Matteo hums in the back of his throat, then leans in to whisper in my ear. His voice is low and seductive as he says, "I can help you relax."

I shiver again, this time for a different reason. Swallowing, I hesitate as I think through his words. The distraction would be nice. But will he be able to tell that I'm faking? It's on the tip of my tongue to say to hell with it, but then I glance at Leith sleeping on the other side of the fire and I hesitate.

Matteo takes my decision away from me when he lowers his mouth to my neck, gently pressing his lips against the soft skin under my ear. "Edainai," he says, his breath fanning over my skin warmly. "Come here."

Unable to say no now, I slide over and sit between his legs, leaning back against his chest. His chuckle rumbles through me and I tip my head to the side to give him better access to my neck.

Matteo licks up the side of my throat before biting my earlobe and tugging gently. My eyes flutter shut, focusing on the sensation of his tongue. His hands slide over my hips and under my shirt. His skin is so warm and enticing. He traces random patterns on my belly while his mouth trails kisses down my neck. It slowly drives me wild. The touch ignites a fire inside of me that grows until I'm squirming between his legs. He stops with his finger just under the waistband of my leggings.

"Daci," he says in my ear. "Do you want me to stop?"

Do I? Yes. But also no. I want to know what his fingers feel like between my thighs. What can he do with those fingers that so skillfully play the guitar? "Don't stop," I breathe, spreading my legs wider.

Matteo releases a breath and slips one hand lower. "Fuck," he whispers harshly as his finger slides through my slickness.

I bite my lip, letting my head fall back against his shoulder. My hips lift, looking for more.

"Do you like that?" he asks, tugging my earlobe between his teeth again. "You're so fucking wet."

I whimper before I can stop myself and I glance at Lion still asleep across from us. At least, he was asleep. Now his blue eyes are open and staring at us. No. Staring at Matteo's hand between my thighs. He can't see anything, my leggings are still pulled up, but it doesn't take much to imagine what Matteo is doing.

Before I can tell Matteo to stop, he pushes a finger inside me, and I gasp at the slight stretch. His fingers work their magic inside me and against my clit. His free hand slides up my shirt and under my bra, pinching my nipple and making me groan. I roll my hips, needing more.

I'm close, but I know I'm still so far away. I'm reaching the point where I hit the wall. The wall I can't climb over or knock down.

"Fuck yeah, Daci," Matteo growls. "Take what you want."

What I want. What I want. I want to come. I want him to work those magic fingers so I can finally reach the point of someone getting me off other than myself. But it won't happen. The wall is too fucking tall. My stomach clenches at the realization that this will be no different. Tears prick my eyes, and I squeeze them shut to stop them from falling. Unable to take it anymore, I tug his hand from my leggings.

"Stop," I gasp, pulling away from him. "I . . . I . . ." My eyes burn, and I jump to my feet.

I can't look at Matteo. I can't handle seeing his expression, no doubt confused and probably disgusted with me. Why wouldn't he be? Even if he's not right now, if he ever learns I can't orgasm, he certainly will be disgusted with me then. I dart into the forest, my fear of what's hiding in the darkness temporarily forgotten in my shame.

I don't go far, because I don't want to get lost. The light of the fire is still visible, so I sink to the hard ground, leaning against a tree. Burying my face in my knees, I squeeze my eyes shut and breathe deeply, fighting the waves of anger and humiliation that try to sweep me away.

Leaves and twigs crunch under heavy footsteps, and I'm too scared to look up and see Matteo's expression. He crouches next to me, his clothing rustling softly.

"Hey," he says gently. "What's up?"

I shrug, willing him to go away and leave me alone.

"Want to talk about what just happened?" he asks. A note of concern threads through his voice.

I shake my head.

He sits next to me, settling down with a sigh. "Can you at least let me know if I hurt you?"

"It wasn't you," I say, my voice muffled.

"Well, that's good. I'd hate to think I hurt you." He falls silent for a moment before saying, "Please talk to me, Daci."

Something in his voice, in the way he said please or maybe my name, shakes something free of me. Despite not wanting to talk about this, the words are pulled from me as if by magic. "I . . ." My throat closes, making it hard to take in a breath.

"Daci," Matteo says gently, "are you a virgin?"

My head snaps up. "What? No. Not even close." I think of all the people I've slept with. All the attempts at reaching that unreachable *O* with a guy. My cheeks burn and I'm glad it's too dark for Matteo to see it. I'm a fucking slut who has never had an orgasm during sex.

"Has someone hurt you in the past?"

I clench my jaw until it hurts. I really don't want to talk about this, but I don't think he'll let it go. So I take a deep breath and bury my face in my arms again so I don't have to see him. "I'm broken." The words are jagged and cut like glass as they climb up my throat. "There is something wrong with me. I've never . . . I've never had an . . . orgasm . . . during sex," I say brokenly. "I can only come with myself," I add hurriedly.

Matteo is silent. So silent that my shoulders stiffen and I start to build a wall around myself, preparing for the worst. When I have the courage to peek at him, he's looking at me with an expression I can't read. It's like he's trying to piece together a puzzle to figure out who I am.

I make to push to my feet, to put as much distance between us as possible. "I'm a fucking idiot," I mutter. "I shouldn't have said anything."

He grabs my wrist, stopping me. "You are not broken, Daci. There is nothing wrong with you."

I huff a laugh, but there's no humor in it. "How can you possibly think that?" I blink away tears, not wanting to cry in front of him too. That is way too much vulnerability in one night.

A slow smile spreads across his face, turning more and more wicked as it grows. "While you may see something wrong with you, I only see a challenge. One I won't fail."

I open my mouth to say something but he grabs my ankles

and yanks, making me fall backward onto the forest floor. Before I have a chance to scream, he catches me, cushioning me to prevent my head from hitting the ground. Then he's hovering over me, his mouth inches from mine.

"Give me a chance, edainai. Don't write me off before you really get to experience what I can do."

Then he kisses me, and I'm lost again.

15

DACIANA

It's impossible to not get swept away by Matteo's kisses. He devours me like I'm the only thing keeping him alive. It's intoxicating. It's addicting. It's driving me fucking wild. Add to it his fingers dancing over my stomach, trailing sparks in their wake, and I'm a flame burning brightly in the dark.

Matteo moves to my neck, lavishing open-mouthed kisses there. His fingers explore every inch of my stomach, ribs, and back. He moves lower, kissing a path from just below my bra line down to the waistband of my leggings. He stops, fingers curling around the fabric. When his gaze meets mine, his eyes are darker than usual. Sexy and intense.

"Yes or no, Daci?" His voice shivers over me. His lips brush the skin of my lower stomach.

I hesitate. If I say yes and I can't come, what's the harm? He already knows my secret. So I nod. "Yes," I breathe, my voice quiet and shaky.

His answering grin is feral and makes butterflies swoop in my belly. In one smooth motion, he pulls off my leggings and panties, tossing them to the leaf-strewn forest floor. For some reason, under his predatory gaze I want to cross my legs, cover myself, keep him from seeing me. But his fingers grip my thighs like he knows what I'm thinking, and he prevents me from doing it.

His breath hitches as he spreads my legs, exposing every inch of me to him. "Fucking perfect," he mutters so quietly I almost don't hear it. Then he lowers his head and licks up my center.

My head falls back on the ground, thumping hard, but I don't feel the pain. All my focus is on Matteo and his mouth, his tongue. He completely devours me. His gaze is locked on mine, his pupils blown so wide his eyes are practically black. No one has ever eaten me out quite this good before. But I still don't know if it's enough.

Matteo throws my legs over his shoulders and lifts my hips off the ground, giving him a different angle. It sends tingles over my body, and I can't stop myself from moaning. I slap my hand over my mouth, scared to draw attention to us. The sound seems to drive Matteo harder. He adds his thumb, rubbing gentle circles over my clit while fucking me with his tongue.

Holy shit. I'm close. I'm so fucking close but I can't quite reach the finish line.

Matteo lifts his head, making me frown. "You're thinking too hard," he says, breath fanning over my sensitive flesh, his lips and chin glistening with my arousal. "Don't worry about what happens next. Just focus on each sensation."

I whimper, moving my hips as much as I can in his grasp, asking him to continue. I was so close. So close I could almost taste it.

He grins wickedly, slowly licking up my center. "I have a feeling I know what you need. A distraction to keep yourself from thinking."

He moves his hand from my stomach and wraps it around my neck, squeezing. It's not enough to completely block off my air, but it's enough to make me think I could easily pass out if he left his hand there too long.

"Tap my cheek if you need an out," he says, his voice low and gravelly. It echoes through my body like ripples in a stream.

With my air cut off, Matteo goes back to work with his tongue. I can't formulate any thought except how fucking good it feels. And how terrifying it is that with just a bit more pressure, he could take all my oxygen away. Matteo watches me closely. He watches me writhe on the ground, hips bucking as much as they can in his one-handed grasp.

The edge is right there. I can see it. Taste it. Feel it. Matteo squeezes just a tiny bit harder, and his teeth graze my clit at the same time.

And it happens. My body breaks apart with the force of my orgasm. Lightning shoots through my body. Stars explode in my vision. My legs quiver and squeeze his head. I gasp for air that I can't get into my lungs and that only seems to make me come ever harder. Matteo hums as he laps up every drop of my release and his hand loosens.

I suck air into my lungs as my body finally stills. Matteo lowers my hips and legs, closing them gently. He crawls over me, mouth still wet and gleaming, and he kisses me, stealing even more of my oxygen and letting me taste myself on his tongue.

"Good job, edainai," he says, finally wiping his mouth on his shirt.

His praise makes my body flush hot, and something like pride burns in my belly. I bite my lower lip and sit up. "Thank you," I whisper.

He hands me my clothes with a wink. "Oh, it was my pleasure." He helps me to my feet and waits for me to put on my leggings. Before we head back to the fire, he takes my hand and kisses it, bowing over it like a gentleman. "My tongue, and any other body part, is at your service. All you need to do is ask."

I slept great last night, which I'm kind of surprised at. Not only because I was sleeping on the hard ground in the creepy woods. But because I had an orgasm at the hand—er, mouth—of a guy. For the first time in my life, I came from someone other than myself. I laid on the ground with the biggest smile and thought for sure I'd be awake all night thinking about it. But my body must have been wrung out, because it didn't take long for me to fall asleep. And I slept until Matteo woke me early the next morning.

Even without coffee, my mood has been great. I feel like I'm soaring. I'm practically giddy as we continue down the yellow brick road. Twig and I play fetch as we walk with a stick he found this morning. Occasionally he takes the stick to Matteo or Lion since they throw farther. Twig seems to have caught on to my mood and he is just as bouncy this morning.

Lion signs something, a corner of his mouth pulled up, and Matteo translates. "He said you're in a good mood this morning. Did you find coffee somewhere and not share it with us?"

The glint in Lion's blue eyes tells me he knows exactly why I'm in a good mood. Feeling cheeky, I wink at him. "You can help tonight if you want."

He smiles but shakes his head, and that's the end of that conversation. I look at Matteo questioningly, but he just smiles. Okay, fine. They can keep their secrets. Twig brings me the stick and I take it, throwing it as far as I can, which isn't very far at all.

"So, when will we reach this chasm?" I ask, changing the subject. As far as I can see is forest. The yellow brick road is the only color winding through the brown and green trees. Dappled sunlight occasionally pierces the canopy above, but for the most part, it's dark and gloomy.

"Probably a couple of hours," Matteo answers. "After that we'll have an easy trek to the Emerald City."

"Are there other kinds of obstacles we will encounter?" I ask, stepping slightly closer to him.

"That will be the last one that I'm aware of. Although, there is still the risk of Morta. The fact that we haven't heard anything from her yet is slightly worrisome." He reaches out and tugs one of the braided pigtails I put in my hair this morning. "I like the hand holds." He grins at me, something seductive passing across his gaze.

My cheeks heat and I turn my head to peer into the woods to hide my blush from him. I'm not sure I'm ready to try anything more. Although, I have a feeling if anyone can make me come, it will be Matteo. He has just as much experience as I do, if the rumors are true.

The rest of the morning passes quietly in easy conversation. It's a few hours later that the forest opens up, and before us a massive chasm rends the ground.

"Wow," I breathe, stepping out into the open. "You weren't kidding."

The chasm before me is enormous. It not only spans just in front of us, but it branches off at various points, like a river used to course through it with offshoots that flowed to different locations. I approach the edge of the cliff and carefully look over at the drop below me. My head spins and I quickly step back, swallowing against the sudden dryness in my throat.

"Fuck," Tin Man growls, stepping up to the edge a little farther down from me. "The bridge is gone."

I look toward him and see two broken wooden posts sticking out of the ground. Looking to the bottom of the chasm, I see smashed bits of wood and shredded rope. The bridge. Or what used to be the bridge.

"What the hell happened to it?" Matteo asks, stepping up to Tin Man. Pebbles skitter over the edge from his boots, falling endlessly to the bottom.

Tin Man shakes his head, dark eyes scanning the chasm before us. "Morta, most likely. Trying to stop us from reaching the Emerald City."

"Is there a different way we can go? A way around the chasm?" I ask, stepping away from the dizzying edge.

"This chasm stretches all the way across the continent. There is no way around it." Matteo says, shaking his head. "We're going to have to climb down to cross it, then climb back up."

My stomach drops to my feet. "What?" I squeak, looking back toward the edge of the cliff. "I am *not* climbing down. Find another way." Crossing my arms, I glare at him.

"It's the only way," Tin Man says. He walks along the edge, looking over precariously.

Lion heads in the opposite direction, doing the same. I step back again, putting more distance between me and the endless drop. They are insane. There is no way I can climb down that and then back up. I'll never make it. I'll fall to my death before I get halfway down.

I step back again and again, until my back hits the trunk of a tree in the forest. Each breath I take gets shallower, harder to draw in. My vision blurs at the edges and my legs shake so hard, I sink to the ground. I'm going to die trying to cross this chasm. I'm going to fall, and when I fall, I'll have minutes to think about my life because that fall will last forever. At least when I hit the bottom, I'll die instantly. I shouldn't feel any pain, right?

Hands on my shoulders gently squeeze. "Daci."

My eyes won't focus. Matteo's face is blurry and wavering. The edge of my vision gets darker and darker. I hear his voice, but his words don't make sense.

"Daci, breathe," he says sharply.

I'm trying. I'm trying to pull air into my lungs, but it won't go all the way in. My chest is too tight.

His hands clasp my face, his grip gentle but still biting. The pain gives me something to focus on. Something other than my upcoming fall to death.

"Edainai, breathe. In through your nose, out through your mouth."

His voice is soothing. The timber pleasant and calming. I listen to it, still not understanding what he's saying, but just hearing his voice helps my chest ease a bit. Eventually, his words register, and I follow his lead, breathing in and out, slowly and evenly.

"Open your eyes," he says. "Look at me."

They open. I didn't even realize they were closed. He studies me, concern pulling his brows down into a V. One of his thumbs gently rubs back and forth on my cheek and I lean into the touch, letting it ground me further.

"Are you back with me?" he asks quietly.

I nod, unable to find my voice and scared it will tremble too much if I speak.

"What just happened?" he asks.

I swallow, trying to gather moisture back into my mouth. "I'm scared of heights," I whisper. Just the thought of climbing over that ledge makes my stomach churn and my head swim.

Matteo sits in front of me and takes my hands. "I won't let anything happen to you. The three of us will be there every step of the way. I promise, we'll make it as easy as we can."

I nod, but his words do nothing to comfort me. Not really. How much can they do to actually keep me safe while also keeping themselves safe? I'm so tempted to say fuck it all and go back to the portal to take me home. This isn't worth it. But one look at Twig, a stick bigger than he is clenched in his toothless jaws, and I know I can't do that. I can't leave this defenseless baby dragon to a fate of death. Because that's what will happen if I don't do what Nona said I had to do.

Take up the role of dragon guardian.

Tin Man and Lion scout the chasm and talk between them about the best option. Matteo sits with me, watching Twig play and saying nothing. But his presence eases some of my fears. That is, until Tin Man approaches.

"We found a path. Let's go." He doesn't wait for me to acknowledge his words. He strolls off toward the chasm, footsteps sure and steady.

My stomach sinks again, and I close my eyes. *I can do this. I can do this. I can do this.* With those words on repeat, I push myself up on shaky legs and follow Tin Man. Matteo snags Twig and settles him inside his book bag, uttering a few words to the dragon that I can't hear.

"We'll follow this path down to the bottom. Be careful, and don't get too close to the edge." Tin Man doesn't look at me. He doesn't give me any time of day as he steps onto the path.

A path that is barely bigger than his feet. Don't get too close to the edge? The edge is *right there!* How the hell do I not get close to it when my feet will almost hang off it? I shake my head vigorously, taking a step back.

"No," I whisper. "I can't do that."

Matteo's warmth surrounds me as he steps up to my back, his hands wrapping around my biceps. "You can do this, Daci. I'll go in front of you. Leith will be behind you. Just take your time, and don't look down."

Don't look down. Right. If I don't look down though, I'll probably step right off the edge. Matteo squeezes my arms once before stepping around me and onto the ledge. Twig's head bounces with each step where it peeks out from the bag. I take a huge gulp of air, holding it until my lungs burn, then release it. Matteo turns back and holds out his hand. I take it, fingers shaking and palm sweaty.

With a silent prayer to anyone listening, I keep my gaze locked on Twig and take that first step down onto the ledge.

16
MATTEO

Daci's hand trembles in mine. Her palm is slick with sweat, and I can hear her breathing behind me. If she doesn't calm down, she'll pass out. I squeeze her hand to get her attention.

"Keep breathing, edainai. Take one step at a time." I watch her closely, making sure she has a handle on her breathing before I let go of her hand. Her eyes go impossibly wide, and she reaches blindly for me. "I can't hold your hand and keep my balance at the same time. Keep your focus on Twig. Go as slow as you need to."

She plasters herself against the chasm wall with a whimper that goes straight to my heart. But she follows me, side stepping one inch at a time. It will take us forever to get to the bottom if she keeps up that pace, but there is no way I can rush her when her fear is so plainly painted on every inch of her body. She's trembling so hard, I'm afraid she's going to tumble right over the edge. I slide my gaze to Leith and he nods, keeping himself as close to Daci as he can get.

The path switchbacks all the way to the bottom, and I hope it doesn't get any narrower than it already is. Mine and the guys' boots barely fit on the ledge. To pass the time and help Daci relax, I start talking. I talk about nothing in particular, just random stories that pop into my head. A lot of them are childhood stories my mom told me when I was young. Fairytales and make believe.

After about an hour of traveling on the switchback path, Daci's breathing calms. I keep talking to distract her, afraid if I stop, she'll start panicking again. If I'm being honest, I'm talking to distract myself too. This chasm is ridiculously fucking high. The drop to the bottom is terrifyingly endless. My head spins whenever I look over the edge, vertigo rearing its ugly head.

I'm in the middle of a story when I hear a crack behind me, followed by rocks sliding down the chasm and Daci's scream. I whirl around to find Leith already on his stomach, reaching for Daci, who is sliding down the wall of the chasm where the ledge she was standing on broke.

He just misses her.

She plummets down, scrabbling for purchase with her fingers.

"Daci!" I scream, ripping off my bag containing Twig and shoving it at Nico.

Her scream cuts off suddenly and I find her grasping a small protrusion by one hand. She stares up at me with utter terror in her wide green eyes. The path we're on switches back and comes around, and it's at least thirty feet below her. I scan the wall, calculating distances and random protrusions along the way down.

Daci whimpers, the sound cutting through me and tearing straight into my heart. For some reason, the idea of her falling sends panic spearing through me. Not giving myself a chance to think about what I'm doing, I sit on the ledge and prepare to jump off.

"Hang on, Daci," I call, pushing myself over so I'm only holding on with one hand.

"Mattie, be careful!" Nico yells as I let go, the stress of the situation causing him to show more emotion than he usually does.

I slide down the wall on my ass, using my boots as brakes and rudder. I try to remember where the protrusions are so I can avoid them. If I hit one, I'll probably break my leg. I'm able to slow myself enough that when I hit the path below the one I just jumped from, it only slightly jars me.

As soon as my feet hit the path, I whirl around and find Daci. Her pants and cries are getting more frequent, and I can see her body shaking as she holds on with one hand. How she's managed to do so for this long, I have no idea. Adrenaline probably.

"Daci, let go! I'll catch you." I position myself below her, legs braced, and I pray we both don't tumble over the edge. Luckily this ledge is slightly wider than the one above.

A terrified squeak escapes her. "Let go?" Her voice is raised a few octaves, and so loud it echoes off the chasm walls.

"Trust me, Daci. I won't let you fall." At least not alone. If she falls, I'll be falling with her. "On the count of three. One. Two. Three."

She holds on for a second longer then lets go. No sound escapes her as she falls, and I'm guessing she's holding her breath and squeezing her eyes shut tight. I brace myself, squaring off and preparing for the impact of catching her. When she hits me, one of my feet slides backward off the edge, but I'm able to wrap my arms around her and turn my body so we fall sideways onto the path rather than into the open air behind us.

The breath is knocked from my lungs, and I lie on my back, stunned for a moment as stars swim in my vision. Daci shudders on top of me, shaking so hard. I force air into my bruised lungs and sit up, tightening my hold on her.

"It's okay," I breathe into her ear, tucking her back against my chest. "I've got you, edainai. Just breathe." I follow my own advice and work on slowing my rapidly beating heart.

Daci gasps and shakes in my arms. Panic has obviously overridden every coherent thought in her head, so I do my best to calm her down. While we wait for Nico and Leith to catch up to us, I whisper reassurances, hold her tightly, and instruct her to breathe. By the time they reach us, she's breathing normally, but she still shakes in my arms. I have no idea how we'll get her to continue to the chasm floor.

"Daci," I say quietly, "we need to keep going."

She shakes her head and shrinks into herself. I don't blame her. My heart has only just calmed from that ordeal. I can't imagine how much worse she's feeling.

"We're getting closer, edainai. I know you can do it. I'll hold your hand this time." Nico can carry Twig the rest of the way. That will make it easier for me to reach back and hold her hand while we walk. I don't even think about my actions. Instinct has taken control since I saw her fall, and it hasn't let go yet. I lean in and kiss her temple. Her skin is cold and clammy despite the heat of the sun. "Come on, edainai. We'll do it together."

I stand and step over her so I'm in front, and I reach a hand down to her. Her bright green eyes are wild and filled with fear. I wish I could take that fear away, but I don't know how. Instead, I give her an encouraging smile and wiggle my fingers. Eventually, she takes my hand, gripping it tightly.

We continue the rest of the way down the chasm in silence. I can't find it in me to tell more stories. And I don't think it would do anything to help Daci anyway. She never loosens her grip on my hand, and by the time we reach the bottom, I have lost all feeling in my fingers. I don't complain though. We made it to the chasm floor in one piece.

"The remains of the bridge shouldn't be too far ahead," Nico says, striding forward. "We need to get some wood to start a fire before it's too dark to see down here."

It's already dark. The sun can't pierce this deep into the chasm. And as it sets, it will only get even darker. We can't climb up the chasm in the darkness. And by the way the temperature has dropped, I'm guessing it will also get colder. A fire will be necessary to survive tonight.

I tug Daci along and she follows blindly. Her eyes are vacant as she turns her thoughts inward. Probably toward what just happened and how she almost died. I shudder at the thought and push it firmly away, not liking how it makes me feel. So unnerved. Angry. Desperate.

Nico and Leith use pieces of the bridge to start a fire. In the flickering light, I notice the scrapes on Daci's hands and grab her wrists to look at them more closely. There are few tears in her shirt as well, so I lift it to reveal more scrapes on her stomach. I dig through my bag until I find some first aid supplies, no doubt packed in there by Leith. He's the one who always thinks responsibly when it comes to things like this.

Daci's expression never changes as I sit her down and clean her wounds. Even when I dab the ointment on her cheek. I know that shit stings, but she doesn't even blink. Worry curls in my gut, but there is nothing I can do except make her comfortable. The scrapes aren't deep enough to require bandages, so I leave them open to the air.

There will be no hunting for food down here, so I dig dried meat, bread, and cheese from Leith's bag and hand some to Daci. "You need to eat something," I say quietly, then watch as she mechanically eats the provisions.

We're all silent as we settle around the fire, eating the food and trying to not think about what happened earlier. Twig lays his head on Daci's thigh and watches her closely. We all do. She stares at the fire with empty eyes. I don't like it. So I sit next to her and take her hand. It's cold in mine and trembles slightly. I urge my body heat into her, hoping I can warm her and help keep the worst of the shock at bay.

When Nico and Leith settle down for the night, I look toward Daci. "Do you want a distraction?" I ask, tugging one of her braids, letting my knuckles graze her neck.

She shakes her head and turns toward me. "No. I want . . . I . . ." She presses her lips together as they wobble and tears glint along her lashes in the firelight.

I understand what she's asking without her needing to use words. I lie down and open my arms for her. She curls against my side, burying her face in my chest as she cries. I rub her back and hold her tightly, whispering nonsense words into the quiet. Her body shudders against mine, and I hold her like I can prevent her from falling apart.

Each tear that dampens my shirt is like a brand that burns into my chest. And I silently vow to myself that this girl will never shed another tear again. I don't know what it is about her, but she's wormed her way inside of me already. The persistent tug of needing to be near her, wanting to know every little thing about her, has only grown the longer we spend time together. And seeing her cry makes me want to set the world on fire for ever being cruel enough to hurt her. It's wild. Completely absurd. I realize that, but it doesn't stop me from feeling all the feelings.

Eventually her tears stop and her breathing evens out, the adrenaline that kept her going no doubt draining away and leaving her exhausted. And I find, despite the situation and the reason for her lying with me, that I thoroughly enjoy her body next to mine, sharing my heat. It's a dangerous thought, and one I shouldn't let take hold.

But as I close my eyes, it creeps in. And I fall asleep with a smile on my face.

I wake, content and with the most amazing feeling of rightness. It doesn't take long to realize why that is, especially as Daci snuggles closer with an adorable, sleepy sigh. I hold her tightly for a second longer, letting myself enjoy this moment no matter how much it might hurt me later.

"Daci," I whisper, gently shaking her shoulder. "Daci, it's time to wake up. Nico will want to get moving right away."

"Yeah, wake up, princess," Nico says gruffly, stepping to where we're lying on the ground. "We need to get going."

Daci mumbles something that sounds an awful lot like "Fuck you, Tin Man" but she sits up, swiping her hair from her eyes. She looks around to get her bearings and seems to remember what happened last night. A soft exhale escapes her, and I watch in amazement as she pushes the memory aside, straightening her shoulders and raising her chin.

I sit up and take her chin in my fingers. "Are you okay?" I ask quietly, studying her closely.

She swallows but nods. "Yeah. Thank you for saving me."

I grin and wink at her, trying to lighten the mood. "Anytime, edainai."

Her brows pull down as she frowns. "What does that mean?" she asks again, annoyance clear in her voice.

I only smile at her and stand, stretching my arms over my head. "What's the plan, Nico?"

Nico grimaces and crosses his arms over his chest. "There is no way up as far as Leith and I scouted this morning. We'll have to walk and hope we find a way before it gets too dark."

"Well, that sounds promising," Daci says, tossing Twig a piece of dried meat from Leith's bag. She stands and looks around the chasm. "Are we the only ones down here?"

"I have no idea," Nico grunts, turning and walking away. "But the sooner we find a way out, the better."

We follow Nico, Twig bounding over rocks and climbing boulders. He flaps his wings as he jumps from boulder to boulder, the thin membranous tissue unable to hold him in the air. One day it will, though. I can't imagine what it will be like to see a full-grown dragon fly.

Daci watches him with a smile. It's obvious she cares a lot about this magical creature. And in my opinion, that says a lot about who she is, whether Nico wants to see it or not. She could have easily turned the dragon in to rid herself of the problem. Instead, she took it upon herself to hide him and find out how to return him to his homeland.

It's a lot cooler at the bottom of the chasm. I keep an eye on Daci to make sure she doesn't get too cold, but she doesn't seem to mind. She has apparently made it a goal to annoy Nico, and from what I can tell, she's doing a fantastic job.

Each step Nico takes, his shoulders stiffen and rise higher toward his ears. He won't last too much longer before he explodes, and it will be very entertaining when he does. Leith and I walk behind them and watch with amusement. It's not often that someone gets under Nico's skin as much as Daci does.

"You should smile more," Daci says, glancing at Nico with a frown.

Nico grunts.

"You're going to end up with wrinkles." She reaches up without breaking stride and rubs the frown lines between his eyes.

Nico stumbles a step, which is unusual for him, and he smacks her arm away. "Don't touch me."

"Oh yeah, sorry. I forgot you hate me. For no reason." With her back to me, I can't see her expression, but from her tone, I can imagine her rolling her eyes at Nico.

"No reason," he mutters and shakes his head.

"Oh, right. There is a reason." She snaps her fingers in the air. "A stupid reason. Just because we're from rival families. Even though we've never met before this journey. You made up your mind about me before ever giving me a chance." She huffs and crosses her arms. "Maybe I should do the same to you." Looking at Nico, she grins. "Perhaps the rumors about you are right. Heartless. Incapable of love. Unless it's yourself, of course. I think you're only capable of loving yourself. Although what you see in yourself is beyond me."

I snort and Leith trips over his feet as he silently laughs next to me. Nico growls and turns toward Daci, grabbing her arm and stopping her. My humor instantly fades as I take in the look of ire on his face. I tense, prepared to step in if needed, but Daci raises one perfectly plucked brow and crosses her arms.

Nico steps closer to her, staring down at her with loathing. "You know nothing about me, princess, so don't pretend to." He steps even closer, his chest brushing hers as he leans over her.

Daci's eyes widen and her lips part on a soft inhale. Her body relaxes and she seems to sway forward, as if pulled into Nico's orbit. From my position, I can see her eyes darken and her lashes flutter. Something inside of me curdles, the sight leaving a foul taste in my mouth.

Nico smiles at her, but it's not a pleasant smile. He cups her cheek in his hand, using his thumb under her chin to lift her head. "You're playing a dangerous game, princess. One you won't win."

He steps away quickly, leaving her blinking at his sudden absence. She grinds her teeth together and stomps off after him, trailing anger in her wake. Leith and I exchange a glance, a mixture of amusement and uncertainty. I hope I hide the despair slowly growing inside of me. I should never have started flirting with her. I knew nothing could come of it, but I was unable to stop myself. It's who I am, after all. But I never planned on developing feelings for her.

I rub my hand down my face and shake my head before following Nico and Daci.

17

DACIANA

This man is infuriating. But at least I can have fun being just as infuriating back to him. I spend the morning badgering Tin Man while he searches for a way out of the chasm. If I don't keep my mind occupied, I find myself thinking about yesterday and how close I came to falling to my death. Not to mention, being stuck at the bottom of the chasm with no apparent way out leaves me feeling as though the walls are going to cave in and bury us alive. Yes, distraction is much better than facing the paralyzing fear that simmers just below the surface.

"So," I say after giving Tin Man a short reprieve, "how's your dad?" I smile sweetly at him and bat my lashes.

He growls and increases his pace, making me practically run to keep up with him. Worth it though, despite the blisters on my heels. Stupid shoes. Who wears flats like this while traipsing through the wilderness?

"Is he still planning on taking out my dad? You know, a good way to get to him would be to take out my stepmom. Feel free to pass that information along. It would certainly make my life easier if that bitch was out of the picture."

Tin Man stumbles, something I find him doing a lot more when I bother him, which I find highly amusing. He swings his gaze to me, and I take great delight in the opened-mouthed shock lining his features.

"What? I may act like a party princess, but I was raised by my dad. Ruthlessness runs deep in my veins. You'd realize that if you spent any time trying to get to know me."

He grunts and turns away to keep scanning the chasm walls.

Man, getting him to talk is like pulling teeth. But I'm nothing if not determined. I study him from the corner of my eye, trying to find something else to say to him. Tattoos snake up from under his shirt, crawling over his neck and under his chin. I've never thought too much of guys whose skin is more ink than skin. But I'm not going to lie, his does something to me. The dangerous glint in his eyes combined with the lethal way he holds himself and the tats and piercings. He's the stereotypical bad guy, and for some reason, it's working for me.

I sidle closer to him until my shoulder brushes his arm. "I like your tats," I say. "They really help you play into that bad boy role. Without them, you'd look like a wimp." I grin as he clenches his jaw hard enough I can hear his teeth grinding. "Oh, that can't be good for your teeth. You should do yoga or something. It could work wonders on your tension."

He still doesn't respond. Son of a bitch. He's harder to crack than my dad's safe—which, by the way, I cracked when I was fifteen. I sigh as this game starts to bore me. Without him taking the bait, the one-sided conversation is not as entertaining. I fall back to walk with Matteo and Lion, and I grin when Tin Man's shoulders lose their tension.

Matteo slings his arm around my shoulders. "I don't know whether you're brave or stupid for poking the bear like that."

I shrug. "Bored mostly. And trying to keep myself distracted." I study my nails and grimace. They are cracked and broken from the fall. The pink polish chipped and faded. The scrapes on my fingers combined with the sorry state of my cuticles is depressing. What I wouldn't do for a manicure right about now.

It's easy to talk to Matteo. I don't feel the need to hide the darker thoughts that keep me up at night. Maybe because he held me as I fell apart the other day. Maybe because he risked his own life to save me. Whatever it is, I can't deny the connection between us, and it makes it easy for me to share with him. If I think about it too much, it raises too many questions I don't want to look too closely at.

"Well, you could have just said so." He bends down and runs his nose along the side of my neck. "I'm great at distraction." His tongue slides up my throat and he tugs my earlobe between his teeth.

I don't know how he keeps walking as he does it, but I lose my footing and trip. Only his arm around me keeps me from falling flat on my face.

He chuckles and tightens his grip on my shoulders. "Maybe we should wait until we stop for the night."

His voice is low and seductive, and it shivers over my skin like silken sheets. I can't stop the shudder that runs through my body, pure desire and need. It's quickly washed away though when I remember how dirty I am. No way I'm doing anything with him until I can clean myself, even a little bit.

Lion signs something I don't catch, rolling his eyes and quickening his steps to catch up with Tin Man. I cast a questioning gaze toward Matteo.

"He told us to get a room. But since I don't think we'll be finding one of those anytime soon, he'll just have to deal."

Lion lifts his hand and gives Matteo the bird over his shoulder.

We walk for a while longer. Matteo and I flirt and talk and it's nice. A bit of normalcy in this highly abnormal situation. We toss small rocks for Twig to chase, and Matteo cheers him on when he's able to flap his wings to keep himself aloft for longer than a second. When Tin Man stops, I look around but see nothing that looks like it could get us out of the chasm.

"I think this will be our best bet. I don't want to wander too much longer or it will start getting dark again." He studies the chasm wall in front of him with his hands on his hips.

I look at it, scanning the surface, but see nothing different about it than the rest of the chasm. "What? How are we going to climb up that?"

He points to the wall and the tiny fissures running throughout. "Using the cracks as foot and hand holds." He turns away and settles on the ground. "We'll rest for a few minutes to eat before we start to climb."

I stare at the wall with my mouth hanging open. "He can't be serious," I say to Matteo, who grimaces. "I can't climb that." My breathing hitches as my heart slams against my ribcage. I fell walking on a ledge, and now they expect me to climb up a wall using cracks as footholds? I'm going to die.

Matteo grabs my wrist and pulls me down. He hands me some food, which I mechanically eat and ignore the way it churns threateningly in my stomach. I want to turn around, walk all the way back the way we came, and use the ledge again. Then I can go home. Screw this all.

But just like the last time I debated it, Twig catches my attention. He bats a small pebble around on the chasm floor, chasing it and pouncing on it before batting it away again. He's a baby still. He'll die if I don't continue this journey. Is that something I can live with burning a hole in my conscience? I already know the answer. No, I can't. So when Tin Man stands and brushes off his pants, I sigh and follow his lead.

"Don't fall this time, princess." Tin Man doesn't even look at me as he says this, shouldering his bag and turning to face the chasm wall.

I open my mouth, a sharp retort on the tip of my tongue, but Matteo grabs my face in his hands and forces me to look at him. "Leith will climb above you. Follow his path. Put your hands and feet where he does. I'll be behind you, helping if you need it."

I squeeze my eyes shut and suck in a ragged breath. With my eyes closed, I don't see Matteo lower his face. But he tilts my head back and presses his lips against mine, softly at first, then more firmly. When he pulls away, I open my eyes. "What was that for?" I whisper, my lips still tingling where he touched them.

"Why not?" He shrugs with a smile. "Think of it as a promise. You'll get more of that when you reach the top."

As far as incentives go, that's a pretty good one. I'm not sure it's good enough to risk my life for, but I nod and turn toward the chasm wall. Tin Man is already on his way up, sending small pebbles skittering down. Matteo hands me my bag, which is quickly turning more brown than white, and I shoulder it with a frown. Poor thing probably can't be salvaged. He then gets Twig into his bag and stands behind me. I watch Lion closely as he reaches, digging his fingers into a crack and hauling himself up.

"Remember, rock climbing is mostly using your legs to push yourself up. You shouldn't be using your arms to pull." Matteo gives me a gentle pat on the ass, which I ignore for the time being.

When Lion is far enough up, I stick the toe of my fancy silver slipper in the crack and push, reaching for another crack higher up. My fingers scrape the rock and I hiss at the pain, a remnant from my fall yesterday, but I shove it deep inside. This is only the beginning. It's going to get worse as I go.

The first few feet aren't too bad. I'm too focused on sticking my toes and fingers where they need to go to pay attention to anything else. But the longer I climb, the harder it gets. My fingers ache. No, not just ache—they fucking hurt from gripping the rock wall so tightly. When I let go to reach for the next crack, my hands and arms shake.

My feet aren't doing any better. The thin material of the shoes does nothing to pad my feet from the rough terrain. My toes feel bruised and scraped raw. Some fucking magical slippers. Shouldn't they protect my feet? My thighs burn and shake as well, threatening to give out at any moment. Each inch I gain takes all the effort I have.

Glancing up, I groan. I'm only halfway there.

"You got this, edainai. You're doing great." Matteo has been talking the entire time. I don't know how he manages to do that and not fall, but he does. He gives me encouragement and praise, and honestly, it's the only thing keeping me going.

I want to prove to him that I can do this. I want to show Tin Man I'm more than a pampered princess. I want him to choke on his words when I climb over the top of that wall. I want them all to look at me with pride and respect. Why I want that, I'm not sure. But I do. It burns deep within me, bolstering me and fanning the flames that keep me going, foot after foot after foot.

When Lion climbs over the top of the wall, I almost cry. Then he reaches down a hand and I grasp it. He pulls me up, and I collapse on my belly on the hard ground. My lungs are on fire, along with the rest of my body. I can't feel my fingers or toes, although my heartbeat throbs in them. I'm too exhausted to even cry with relief. All I want to do is curl up and go to sleep.

"You did it," Matteo says, rubbing my back as he sets his bag down. Twig jumps out and scurries over to Lion. Matteo lies down next to me and exhales. "I told you you could."

All I can do is grunt, and I barely manage that.

"Let's go," Tin Man says brusquely.

"What?" I croak, lifting my head to glare at him.

"We're wasting time." He sets off without a second glance.

Lion gives me an encouraging smile before following Tin Man, and Twig prances after him. Neither of them looks the least bit fazed by the rock climbing.

I groan and my head falls back to the ground, smacking my forehead painfully. But it's minimal compared to the rest of my body.

"Sit up," Matteo says gently, helping me to a sitting position. "I'm pretty sure there is a hot spring not far from here. My guess is Nico is heading that way." He takes my hands and grimaces.

They are bloody and bruised. My nails cracked and ragged. My fingers are so stiff, I can't even bend them. A faint white light wreathes Matteo's hands, and it spreads to mine. I gasp as the sensation of cool water flows over them. The ache disappears. The cuts heal. Bruises still darken my fingertips, but the rest is gone. I flex my fingers and stare at Matteo in wonder.

He smiles sheepishly, rubbing the back of his neck. "I don't have a lot of healing magic, but most Fauns possess a little bit. It comes from nature. I can heal minor scrapes but nothing major."

"That's amazing," I breathe, staring at my mostly healed

hands. When I return my gaze to Matteo, he's looking at me with something shining in his eyes I can't quite read.

That tug in my middle, the string that pulls me to Matteo, makes itself known, and I find myself closing the distance between us. He meets me halfway, wrapping one hand behind my neck. His eyes darken, his pupils expanding to practically turn his gaze black.

"As promised," he breathes roughly, then presses his lips to mine.

This kiss feels different. It's intense and overpowering. It steals my breath and makes my heart flutter strangely. As if possessed, I climb into Matteo's lap, needing to be closer to him. A soft groan rumbles in his chest and does something funny to me. I brush my tongue along his, suddenly wishing there was less clothing between us.

When Matteo pulls away, he doesn't go far. He buries his face in my neck and breathes deeply. "I think"—he stops to swallow—"I think that about covers your reward." His lips press gentle kisses along the sensitive skin of my throat, under my chin. "We should probably catch up to them."

I nod, but I don't move and neither does he, until an owl flies overhead and hoots loudly. I frown, looking into the clear blue sky. It's early for an owl to be awake, but maybe it's different in Oz. Matteo stiffens and slowly stands, taking me with him. Before he turns away, he tucks a stray strand of hair behind my ear, brushing his knuckles over my cheek.

"Let's get to the hot spring," he mutters, his eyes still glazed with lust. "We can continue this there."

18
DACIANA

By the time we reach the hot spring, it takes all my willpower to not whimper with each step. My feet are absolutely killing me. These stupid shoes don't have the best support to begin with. Then the climb up the chasm wall did a number on my toes. Somehow though, they still look brand new, despite the battering they've taken during this journey. I have a feeling my feet won't look so good when I take them off. If I ever can take them off. I know I could ask Matteo to heal them like he did with my hands, but I'm too stubborn to do that. The need to prove I'm not just a pampered princess has taken hold.

I limp down the slight grassy incline to the rocky terrain surrounding the spring, treading carefully to avoid any loose stones. The water is a deep crystal blue, and I can see all the way to the smooth pebbles lining the bottom. Steam wafts from the surface, billowing gently in the breeze. The heat reaches me even on the shore, and I groan at the prospect of stepping into that warmth.

Movement beside me catches my attention. I turn my head to find Tin Man and Lion stripping out of their clothes. Tin Man's body is covered in black ink, swirling lines and geometric shapes, beautifully detailed designs and rough sketches. His body is a canvas of artwork, and I have to force my gaze away from him.

Lion has a few tattoos on his chest and back, but nowhere near the amount as Tin Man. His body is no less beautiful though. They are both cut with muscles that flex with their movements. When I realize they are stripping down completely, I whip my head forward, face burning from more than the steam. I want to look. I want to see what they look like completely naked, but I also don't want to go there. Because once again, those questions I want to avoid asking myself rise to the surface.

Splashing lets me know it's safe to turn back to them, and I watch Tin Man submerge into the water, spraying droplets as he comes back up and whips his head side to side, slicking back his dark hair.

"What are you waiting for?" Matteo asks, stopping next to me and pulling his shirt over his head.

I let myself look at him, at the grooves of his muscles cutting through his dark skin. I don't see any tattoos. He watches me with a glimmer in his eye and a smirk on his lips.

"Like what you see?" he growls, his voice low.

I shrug, turning back to the spring. "It's passable."

He laughs darkly and I have a feeling he'll make me pay for that remark. "What are you waiting for?" he asks again.

I hesitate, glancing at my shoes. The idea of walking around in soaking wet shoes makes me cringe. It won't do any good for my already battered feet. Matteo notices me looking at them, and he purses his lips.

"I think you can take them off long enough to bathe. We'll put them back on as soon as you get out." He kneels and unhooks the straps wrapping around my ankles. His fingers burn where they touch my skin, and I'm surprised they don't leave a visible mark. He gently removes one shoe and sucks in a breath. "What the hell, Daci?" he growls, looking at me. "Why didn't you say anything?"

I look at my foot and grimace as he removes the second slipper. It's gross. My feet have never looked so awful. Blood and dirt cake my skin. Blisters bubble on my toes, a few having popped, leaking pus and more blood. My toenails are broken and the pink paint chips off in most places.

"Daci," Matteo says sternly. "You should have said something." White light wreaths his hands again, and this time the sensation of cool flowing water covers my feet, healing the blisters and cuts. The dirt and blood remain, but that will wash away in the spring.

I can already tell his magic healed the soreness as well, and I flex my toes, sighing quietly. "Thank you."

Matteo stands and helps me to my feet. "Next time tell me." He studies me, making sure I understand, then he turns toward the spring, stepping out of his boxer briefs.

I don't look away from him. His muscled back and perfect ass are mouthwatering. As if he can sense me looking at him, he looks over his shoulder and winks.

"Meet me out there. We have to continue what we started earlier." With that, he steps into the water and dives under.

I take a breath and slowly strip out of my clothes. The prospect of continuing what we started is only overpowered by the prospect of the hot water soaking into my sore muscles. I quickly unbraid my hair and let it fall over my shoulder as I step into the spring, hissing at the heat. I take my time slowly sinking deeper, letting myself adjust to the temperature.

I look around for Lion and Tin Man, suddenly nervous about them seeing me naked, but Tin Man is nowhere to be found, and Lion is relaxing against the far side with his eyes closed. But Matteo is watching me with a hungry, predatory look in his eyes that makes my stomach do somersaults.

I swallow and continue submerging into the warmth. When the water is up to my shoulders, I exhale. The heat is amazing. It's like I can feel the layers of grime and dirt washing away, and my muscles loosen and relax for the first time in a while. My hair is frizzy from the humidity and I duck my head backward, letting the water soak in and remove any dirt and grease. I sigh heavily at the pure bliss this hot spring is giving me.

Matteo stalks toward me, water rippling in his wake. His chest is visible above the surface, shiny and glistening with water. But it's his eyes that hold my attention. Dark and hungry. He reaches out and takes my hand, tugging me through the water until I'm right in front of him. His fingers gently land on my sides before he tightens his grip and tugs me even closer until I'm pressed against him.

Skin to skin with the heat of the spring around us, I gasp. His dark gaze falls to my lips and something crosses his expression. "You look beautiful," he says, his voice low and rough. "With your skin flushed from the heat."

My stomach clenches at the rawness of his words. Then again as his fingers trail down my cheek to my throat. He lifts my head with his fingers and then he kisses me.

It's deep and devouring. There is something urgent and primal in the way he kisses me this time, like he's trying to claim me. I get lost in it, letting myself fall into the depths of the kiss until my lungs burn with the need to breathe. Only then do I pull away to suck in a breath, but Matteo chases my mouth, claiming me again and again until my head spins.

His fingers are unyielding on my hips and neck, holding me to him so I couldn't get away if I wanted to. And I don't want to. I press myself closer, his body so hot and hard against mine. His skin is warm and smooth under my fingers, wet from the spring, and so inviting.

I slide my hand under the water, tracing his abs lower until I grasp his hard cock in my hand. He hisses against my mouth, his hips thrusting forward almost as if he can't control them. I want to get my mouth around him, but I can't, so my hand will have to do. He's thick and so big. My stomach flutters at the thought of him inside me and I whimper just thinking about it.

The sound does something to Matteo. He wraps my legs around his waist, and I gasp when my core slides against his cock. I move my hips, searching for more friction, trying to find the right angle to rub my clit against his hardness.

"Fuck, edainai," he groans, squeezing my ass almost painfully.

Matteo walks us toward the bank, kissing my neck and throat, nipping at my sensitive skin and making me writhe even more against him. I don't know how he does it—I'm too focused on the heat building in my core and spreading through my veins—

but he lifts himself to sit on a rock, keeping me straddling his lap. The rock scrapes against my knees but I don't care in the slightest.

"Edainai," he murmurs against my neck, gripping my hips tightly. "Do you want this?"

I hesitate, my hips faltering. Yes, I really do. But at the same time, what if I can't come? I close my eyes, trying to hide myself from Matteo. If he can't look into my eyes, he can't see into my soul, right?

His fingers gently trace my jaw. "Daci, it won't make me think of you any differently. Whether you come or not, I want to try. I want to feel you wrapped tight and warm around me." His thumb rubs my lower lip. "But only if you want that."

I open my eyes and stare at him, trying to determine how sincere his words are. I find nothing but honesty in his gaze, and desire burning in the depths. I swallow and nod. Anxiety, lust, hope . . . it all swirls in my gut, making me feel nauseous. But Matteo kisses my jaw, then my throat, then my collarbone.

"I'll take care of you, edainai," he whispers, his breath warm on my skin.

The heat from the spring warms the air, but it's chilly outside of it. My nipples pebble, and Matteo bends his head down, sucking one into his mouth, swirling his tongue around the peak. My back arches and soft sigh escapes me. He pinches my other nipple in his fingers, rolling it into a tight peak, tugging it gently, and heat spreads through my body to my core, making my clit pulse with need.

"Matteo," I breathe, clinging to him and digging my nails into the skin at the back of his neck.

He growls, releasing my nipple. "Hearing you say my name like that does something to me, edainai."

He releases my other nipple and slides his hand south, finding my clit easily and circling it with his thumb. I cry out, the pleasure sharp but not enough still.

"How wet are you? Are you ready for my cock?" His thumb

slides lower to my entrance, and he groans. "Fucking hell, Daci. Already so wet for me."

"Please, Matteo," I beg. "I want to feel you inside of me."

He makes a pained sound in his chest, dropping his head to my shoulder and biting the spot where it meets my neck. "Fuck," he breathes.

He lifts me in his strong grasp, his muscles flexing with the movement, and I reach between us with one hand to grasp his cock. My fingers don't even meet, he's so thick. I've never been with someone so big, and anticipation shoots through me, hot and needy. I'm instantly grateful for my IUD as I angle him at my entrance and he slowly lowers me down. The head of his cock slips inside, and I bite my lip at the sensation. It's fucking perfect.

But then he lowers me even more. He stretches me, filling me so slowly it's almost unbearable. Each inch makes me think I can't take any more, but he doesn't stop. And soon, he's all the way inside. I breathe heavily, cataloging the sensations of his cock inside me. Matteo's fingers grip my thighs hard enough to leave bruises.

"Fucking hell. So fucking perfect," he breathes, his chest rising and falling rapidly. "You feel so fucking perfect, edainai."

I lift myself with my legs, sliding off his cock before sitting back down slowly. We both moan. He feels . . . amazing inside me. His cock hits every spot I need it to. It doesn't take long for me to start moving earnestly. He helps me, lifting me up and pulling me back down.

"Take what you want, edainai. Take everything you need." He watches me intently, his eyes burning darkly.

His thumb finds my clit again and I cry out at the pure fire he creates inside me. My pleasure rises higher and higher. It's a tidal wave that wants to crash to shore. But it stops. I hit that wall. That fucking wall I always do. The wall that I can't seem to tear down. I whimper in frustration and heat burns my cheeks in shame.

"Stop thinking, edainai," he breathes in my ear, his thumb

never stopping those maddening circles. "Clear your mind of everything but my cock inside you."

I bite my lip and try to do as he says, but I can't. I can't get out of my own head. I knew this would happen. I should never have agreed to even try. Tears burn the backs of my eyes, and I squeeze them shut so he can't see them. So he can't see my shame and embarrassment.

His fingers grip my chin, but instead of keeping my face toward him, he turns my head to the side. "Open your eyes, edainai."

I do as he says and find Lion standing a short distance from us, leaning against the edge of the spring. One elbow rests on the ground outside, his other hand below the surface, but the water around him moves in turbulent waves. His blue gaze is glued on us, and I suck in a breath when I realize what he's doing. He's pleasuring himself while watching me and Matteo fuck.

Matteo leans in and whispers in my ear. "How does that make you feel? Knowing Leith is getting off while watching us?" His thumb presses a little harder on my clit and my hips buck. "Leith doesn't sleep with women. He doesn't sleep with anyone," Matteo continues, his voice low and seductive in my ear. "But he loves to watch. Should we put on a show for him?"

Heat spreads through me at his words and I rock my hips, watching Lion as he watches me. I've never had someone watch me while I have sex. It feels . . . dirty and shameful. But something deep inside of me curls in delight, sending pleasure burning through my blood.

"Fuck," Matteo groans. "That's it. Show him how fucking beautiful you are as you fall apart on my cock. Make him wonder what it feels like to be encased in your warmth as it pulses and squeezes." His words falter as my pussy does just that.

His words drive me higher. No one has ever talked this dirty to me before and I think I like it. My hips move faster and Matteo matches my speed with his circling thumb. I notice Lion's hand beneath the surface of the water moves in time with my hips, like he's imagining his hand is my pussy, and that thought makes me gasp.

"That's it, edainai," Matteo breathes, his voice harsher and more on edge. "You're so close, aren't you? You're squeezing my cock like a vise. Let go. Let yourself fall, edainai. I'll catch you."

So, I do. Something inside me opens and my pleasure sweeps through me, pushing me over the edge. Matteo curses as I come, my body shuddering as I cry out. It seems like it never ends, just wave after wave of unending bliss. Matteo grips my thighs and thrusts his hips up harder and harder until he groans, his cock twitching inside of me as he comes. I look over at Lion, and he's hunched over, breathing heavily, his hand slowing then stopping.

My gaze travels back to Matteo and I find his light-brown eyes staring at me, shining with something that almost looks like pride.

"Edainai," he breathes, tucking a wet strand of hair behind my ear. "You are amazing."

I did it. I fucking did it. I had an orgasm during sex. My eyes burn and I blink them hard, not wanting to fall apart after having sex. Matteo pulls me against him and holds me while my heart slows. I don't even know what to think right now. My body is limp and pliant in his arms, and I float lazily in a post-orgasmic bliss I'm not used to experiencing.

Instead of trying to process what happened, I close my eyes and enjoy it.

19
DACIANA

Back on the road after the hot spring break, I definitely pick up on tension between Matteo and Tin Man. When we emerged from the spring, Tin Man was sitting on the bank, dressed and watching Lion play with Twig. His gaze immediately snapped to Matteo's and something passed between them that was charged and full of tense energy.

That charged energy has followed us the entire day. Neither of them has spoken to each other, but they pass glances back and forth that probably mean more than any words they could speak. I hang back from both of them. The unsettling tension that radiates from them makes my stomach clench, like I've done something wrong but I don't know what it is.

Lion keeps pace with me while we travel, and I glance at him from the corner of my eye often, only to find him already studying me, and he doesn't hide the fact that he's watching me. My mind travels back to the hot spring and the way Lion watched me and Matteo. The way his arm moved under the water and the hungry look in his gaze as he chased his own pleasure. It made something inside of me flutter warmly, having his attention on me while I rode Matteo's cock.

Matteo mentioned something about Lion not sleeping with anyone but enjoying watching. Questions burn my tongue and I want to voice them, but I swallow them back. I can't ask without giving away that I know sign language. Also, that seems incredibly personal, and I don't think I want to open that can of worms.

So we walk in silence, occasionally glancing at each other while lost in our own thoughts. Twig picks up on the tension hanging heavy over the group, and his usual antics have been toned down. He watches all of us, studying us like he can figure out what's going on in that little dragon brain of his. Fuck, for all I know, he can. I have no idea how smart dragons are. Twig has always seemed abnormally intelligent for an animal.

When we finally stop for the night, I huff a sigh of relief. The soak in the hot spring soothed my muscles, and Matteo's magic healed my wounds from climbing the chasm wall, but I'm still sore and tired. What I really need is a soft bed and a long night of rest. But I know that won't be happening any time soon.

Lion gets a fire started and I sit on the ground, waiting for the warmth to surround me. This uncomfortable silence has wormed under my skin and chilled me. Matteo has always been cheerful and flirty. But he hasn't said a single word to me once we hit the road. And the only thing that changed was the fact that we had sex.

I groan and drop my head into my hands. It was great sex. The best I've ever had. I mean, I had a freaking orgasm. But if it makes the rest of the journey this uncomfortable, I wish we hadn't done it.

When I look up, Lion is staring at me with a raised brow and crooked smile. I shake my head and frown at him. "What's so funny?" I demand.

Of course, he doesn't answer me. But he glances at Tin Man, who stalks off, disappearing in the distance. Matteo sighs heavily and follows, leaving me and Lion alone.

The fire catches, and I scoot closer, warming my hands. It's not really cold outside, but I can't get rid of the chilled feeling I've had since we left the hot springs. Twig curls next to me, his chest rumbling like a purr as I run my fingers over his green scales. The firelight reflects off them, making them look darker than they are. I take comfort in his presence and use it as a reminder as to why I'm doing this in the first place. It's not to flirt with Matteo or have sex with him. It's to figure out who I am and how I can save this dragon next to me.

I dig through my bag and pull out my sketchbook. I've seen so many beautiful things since entering Oz, and I want to make sure to capture as many of them as I can. The sound of my charcoal pencil scratching across the paper gets lost in the hissing and popping of the fire. Even as I draw, my mind stays firmly stuck on Matteo, and I don't realize what I'm drawing until it's complete.

Matteo's eyes. Dark with long lashes. I somehow managed to capture the carefree and flirtatiousness of him in just this sketch of his eyes.

I study the drawing until Tin Man returns alone with a few rabbits. He kneels by the fire to prepare them without a word or glance. Lion takes one look at his stormy expression and leaves. He fucking leaves me with Tin Man to deal with his anger.

"What a fucking dick," I mutter under my breath.

Apparently I wasn't quiet enough, because Tin Man's shoulders tense and he looks up at me. I glance away, my cheeks burning. I hope the fire hides the rosy tint.

I'm drawn back to watching Tin Man. All these men are like magnets to me. I find myself watching them, wanting to get closer to them. I understand it and it makes me squirm uncomfortably. Tin Man's movements are sure and swift as he skins and cleans the rabbits. He makes it look like something he's done thousands of times, and for all I know, he has. Because honestly, I don't know anything about this man. He's the son of Father's enemy. That's all I know. The rest is rumor. And if he is basing everything he knows about me off rumor, then he doesn't know me well at all either.

The firelight plays along his skin, the muscles of his tattooed forearm flexing with movement. Between his moving and the firelight, his tattoos seem to writhe on his skin like living things. A lock of dark hair has fallen across his forehead into his eyes, and my fingers itch to brush it back. I squeeze my hand into a fist, trying to erase that weird and sudden urge.

I mean, there is no denying Nicolai Morelli is a sexy motherfucker. The tattoos and piercings, his dark stare and broad shoulders, all play into the dark and depraved man that he is. I think there is probably some part of every woman who finds that bad boy personality intriguing.

Too bad he's an ass with a horrible attitude.

I must have lost myself in thought, because I start when a stick with sizzling meat is shoved in my face. I blink and lean back, finding Tin Man kneeling in front of me with a skewer of roasted rabbit.

"Eat this," he says, his voice full of gravel. "You can't survive on bread and cheese."

My stomach roils at the scent of the meat, and the thought of it touching my tongue and squishing between my teeth makes bile climb my throat.

He must see something in my expression because he frowns. It's not one of his usual agitated frowns though. This one seems more curious and thoughtful. "Are you a vegetarian?"

"Gods no," I say, shaking my head. "I love a good steak. But I've never eaten rabbit before. Just the thought of it . . ." I swallow hard.

His lips twitch, almost like he wants to laugh, but he stops himself. "Take it," he says, gruffly. "It tastes like chicken."

I do as he instructs, only because I know he's right. I can't survive on cheese and bread, not to mention we're running low on it. He tosses a few chunks to Twig, who wakes up to devour them in one bite before lying back down.

I hesitate, turning the stick over in my fingers. Tin Man watches me, unblinking, and that dark gaze makes me shiver. I think it's the most he's looked at me, ever, and I'm not sure I like being on the receiving end of that intense stare.

Sucking in a deep breath, I take a bite of the meat, wincing as some juice squirts out of it. I don't give myself time to taste it. Just chew and swallow, washing it down with water. Tin Man snorts and sits back to eat his own dinner.

I eat the rest of the rabbit the same. Taking bites, chewing quickly, swallowing forcefully, and chasing each bite with water.

I'm sure it's not bad tasting, I just can't get it out of my head that I'm eating a rabbit. I take the last bite, shuddering as I do, and toss the stick into the fire, watching it catch and burn.

After a few moments of silence except for the cracking of the fire, Tin Man shifts, drawing my attention. When I look toward him, I find him already staring at me.

"What?" I ask, not bothering to make my voice friendly.

"The other day, you said something," he says quietly.

I wait for him to continue, but he doesn't. I raise one brow and tilt my head. "I've said a lot of things. You'll have to be more specific."

He huffs and crosses his arms in agitation. "You mentioned your stepmom."

"Ahh," I say, leaning back on my hands. "What about her?"

"You don't like her?"

My gaze narrows on him and I take a moment to study his face, searching for a reason why he'd want to ask me this. I see nothing that gives me any clue, but I can probably safely assume it's to gather information to use when he returns to Girasole, to give to his dad.

I hesitate only for a second, thinking through my options. Telling Tin Man why I don't like Melanie doesn't really give him anything to use against my family. I already told him the best way to get to my dad was to take her out. Not that my dad would care if she died, but because not being able to protect his own wife would make him look weak.

I should be ashamed I told my enemy that. But I can't find it in me to care. It wouldn't phase me one bit if Melanie was removed from my life. Not to mention, all the violence and bloodshed I grew up with has hardened me. But that doesn't mean I like it. I don't enjoy living such a regimented life. It's too similar to living in a prison. Yes, a plush, rich prison. But a prison all the same. This is the first time I've been away from home. Ever.

Taking a breath, I look into the flames. "She's a bitch," I say simply. "She's jealous that my dad loves me more than her. It pisses her off that she was his second choice, and he'll always love my mom more. She hates that he buys me things just because, and he doesn't do the same for her. She's spiteful and never misses an opportunity to say something degrading or bitchy to me." I shrug, closing my mouth at the tirade that escaped when I first started talking. I'm not sure why I said all of that, but once I started, I couldn't stop. "She made my life a living hell," I finally say, words barely audible over the crackling fire.

Tin Man says nothing, but he continues to study me for a moment longer before turning away.

"What about you?" I ask, risking a glance at him. "Why don't you like your mom?"

His jaw clenches and he shakes his head, like he's not going to answer me.

"I answered your question. The least you could do is answer mine." I hesitate, chewing my bottom lip before saying, "I won't use it against you."

He gets my meaning. I won't tell my dad and use the information to help us get ahead in the game. Tin Man studies me to make sure I'm telling the truth, and I leave my gaze open and honest.

Finally, he sighs, rubbing a hand down his face. "For starters? She left me when I was a baby. I didn't see her again until I was five. She has a habit of popping in whenever she feels like it and disappearing just as quickly." He shakes his head and grinds his teeth. "She's a master manipulator and a pro at playing the innocence game. Or the victim game would be a better term for it. Whenever she pops in, it's usually to drop something in my life that causes more harm than good. It's a game she's played for so long, I don't think she realizes she does it."

More questions burn inside me. Like what things she's done to him to make him hate her so much. There is more to his feelings for her than what he told me. It's easy to see in the way he acts around her and whenever her name gets brought up. But we're definitely not in the position for me to ask that personal of a question.

"So," Tim Man says after a few beats of silence. "You like to party?"

I whip my head in his direction. Is he making small talk? A look of discomfort crosses his features, and he rubs the back of his neck. I pull my bottom lip between my teeth and give his question serious thought before I answer.

"I wouldn't say I like it," I say, my words slow and thoughtful. "It's a way to pass the time. An entertaining distraction." I shrug one shoulder and frown. Partying has always been about getting drunk enough to not feel anymore. It's a means to an end. The end being finding the next guy to sleep with in the hopes I can prove to myself that I'm not broken. Not that I'd ever tell him that. "Sometimes, it's more work than it's worth," I say honestly. The process of getting ready and then forcing a smile on my face for so long a period of time. Not to mention finding a guy to sleep with, then doing it. Then the resulting crash of emotions when I realize I really am broken.

He studies me, parsing through my words like he can find the deeper meaning between them. "That's what tattoos are for me," he says, causing my breath to hitch. Tin Man is talking to me like an actual person and not dirt on the bottom of his shoe. "It's a distraction. A way to prove to myself that—" He shakes his head and clamps his lips shut.

My ears perk up but I keep my face neutral. A way to prove to himself that . . . what? I'm dying to know, because that's what partying is to me too, or at least sleeping with every guy I can. A way to prove I'm not broken. What does Nicolai Morelli have to prove to himself?

"When did you get your first one?" The question spills from my lips before I can even think about it. My curiosity is piqued at the openness Tin Man is showing me.

He scrunches his face almost comically. "Fuck, I don't know.

Fifteen, maybe? It's been so long." He lifts his shirt to expose his muscled, tattooed torso.

My eyes greedily soak it in, taking in all the ink and dips and grooves of him. He points to a tattoo on his side, just above his hip. Two eagle talons crossed to form an X. I recognize it as the Morelli family symbol. It's faded, the lines blown out a bit from age. But it doesn't keep my gaze for long.

A beautifully detailed snake winds around it, the ink a darker and crisper look of a new tattoo. The tail snakes down his hip under the waistband of his pants. The body winds up and over his ribs with the head disappearing under Tin Man's raised shirt. The details are mesmerizing. Breathtaking. I wouldn't be surprised to find the thing writhing and slithering, it's so realistic. And before I know what I'm doing, I'm leaning over to trace the body of the snake with my fingertip. Tin Man's skin is warm and smooth, not cold and lifeless like I always imagined it would be. He sucks in a sharp breath, and when my finger reaches the waistband of his pants, awareness slams into me.

I yank my hand back, clutching it to my chest. I stare at him with wide eyes, searching for something to say. Do I apologize? Do I compliment the tattoo? It doesn't matter what I want to say, I don't think I could peel my tongue from the roof of my mouth anyway.

His dark eyes burn into me, the fire reflecting in their depths. He slowly lowers his shirt, and it takes all my effort to keep my gaze on his face and not his body. What the fuck did I just do? What possessed me to touch him like that?

Tin Man opens his mouth to say something but then closes it. He stares at me for a moment longer, and I can't tear my gaze away from his. Something crackles in the air between us. Something that lifts the hair on my arms and steals my breath. When Tin Man finally looks away, I sag as I'm released from his penetrating gaze. He says nothing further, just stares into the fire, watching the flames dance. But the muscles of his jaw tense.

I flop backward, tucking my bag under my head for a pillow.

My heart is racing. My breath stutters in my lungs. I stare at the sky above me and the thousands of pinpricks of light from the stars. My fingertip burns as the phantom memory of Tin Man's skin against mine keeps popping into my head. No matter what I do to push it away, it keeps coming back.

So I stare at the stars and press my fist to my chest until my eyes slide closed and I fall asleep.

20
DACIANA

There is smoke in the distance. Twig is the first to notice it. He stops, head lifted and nostrils flaring. When he turns toward the left, we all see it. On the horizon, gray smoke billows, backlit by an eerie orange-colored sky.

"What is that?" I ask, turning to Matteo.

He frowns, and I can see him mentally calculating distances to figure out what could be burning. "That isn't . . . That couldn't be . . ." He turns to Lion and Tin Man with wide eyes.

Lion swallows thickly and nods. "It is," he signs, his movements jerkier than usual like he's stressed or uncomfortable. "That's a fae village."

"Motherfucker," Tin Man curses. He doesn't hesitate as he sprints into action, running off the yellow brick road and into the grassy field.

We all follow him, and as we get closer to the burning village, the acrid scent of smoke gets worse. It burns my nose and throat, making me cough. Matteo stops and pulls a shirt from his bag. With a knife, he cuts it into four long pieces and wets them before handing each of us one. He helps me tie mine around my nose and mouth. It helps a little, but as the heat of the burning fire increases, it quickly dries the fabric.

When we get close enough to see the extent of the fire, we all stop. The destruction is unbelievable. The town must have been mostly wooden structures, and all that's left are burning piles of timber. Not a single building remains standing.

"How . . ." I trail off in a coughing fit. There is no way every single building has already burned to the ground.

Matteo shakes his head, his eyes reflecting the flickering orange flames. "The buildings had to have been knocked to the ground before the fire even started." He bends to pick up Twig and keep him from running into the burning village.

"And each building was lit individually. There is no way it spread so evenly," Tin Man adds.

I look closer and realize he has to be right. I'm no fire expert, but every single building is burning at the same general speed. Rather than what I would expect from a typical fire that spreads outward as it goes.

"Who . . ." I trail off again as Lion steps forward. There is no question *who* caused this fire.

Lion walks into the village, heedless of the fire or the ash raining from the sky. He stops beside a dark bundle on the dusty street. A bundle I refuse to look at too closely. He slowly kneels to the ground and stares straight ahead at the dancing flames on either side of him.

"Leith, we need to keep moving," Tin Man says. "There is nothing we can do here."

Lion ignores him and continues to kneel on the ground. While I know Tin Man is right, it seems heartless to move on so soon. These people deserve some kind of remembrance.

There's a tug inside of me. A gentle pulling sensation that draws me forward like a hook embedded in my middle. I've felt it before, with all three of these guys, and it's so unsettling it makes me shiver despite the heat of the flames. I plant my feet and take a cleansing breath, ignoring the acrid scent in the air, but it doesn't help. Before I realize what's happening, I'm shaking off Matteo's grip and walking toward Lion. I have no idea why I'm drawn to him, but it's like I can't ignore it. When I reach him, I kneel, keeping my gaze on his profile. I can't look at the object in front of me. I know what I'll see, and I can't deal with that.

His light-brown curls blow in the scorching wind, and his blue eyes glimmer with tears that spill over and track down his cheeks, only to dry instantly. I don't hesitate to reach out and wipe them away. His eyes close and he leans into my hand.

"L-Leith," I say, stumbling over his real name and not the nickname society gave him.

"There were children here," he signs, his movements slow and despondent. "Innocent children who didn't deserve this."

I purse my lips and hesitate. If I say something, he'll know I understand sign language. But it doesn't seem like the time to ignore him. "Yeah," I say quietly, pulling my makeshift mask down. "I know."

He doesn't even blink when I respond to him. "She can't get away with this," he signs more fiercely.

"No. And she won't. We won't let her. We'll make her pay for taking all these innocent lives."

He nods and reaches behind his head to tug off his shirt. Carefully, he lays it over the small body. I keep my gaze trained on Leith, not wanting to see the small shroud-covered bundle. We sit for a few more minutes in silent mourning for this village and the people who lived here. It's the least we can do.

When the heat gets to be too much for me, I touch his cheek gently. "We should go," I whisper. With his fae hearing, I know he can hear me over the hiss and pop of flames. "There's nothing else we can do here. But Morta is out there. And we *will* deal with her."

He nods and stands swiftly before reaching to take my hand and help me to my feet. We're silent as we walk back to the others, and I ignore their scrutiny when their gazes bounce back and forth between me and Leith. Tin Man digs through his bag and pulls out a spare shirt, tossing it to Leith, who quickly puts it on.

No one speaks as we continue our journey. We walk long into the night, wanting to put as much distance between us and the village as possible. Matteo carries Twig the entire time, the baby dragon looking just as forlorn as the rest of us feel. When we do finally stop for the night, Leith walks off into the darkness without a word.

Again, that pull tugs me toward him, and before I know it, I'm following him, using the moon's light to guide me. I find Leith kneeling by the edge of the stream, washing the ash from his skin. I join him without saying a word and do the same. The silence is comfortable between us, despite the heaviness from earlier.

"Do you know how I ended up in Girasole?" Leith signs, sitting back and making himself comfortable.

My breath catches. Is he going to tell me his story? "No, you're a mystery to me."

He gives me a small smile and it lights up his entire face, but it falls as he begins his explanation. "I was born in a small village in Oz. It was so small, it didn't even have a name. I wouldn't be surprised to find out it doesn't exist anymore. Everyone was poor and barely surviving, but no one had the resources to up and leave to start over in a new place."

He takes a moment, his gaze turning inward. I give him all the time he needs. A small rock catches my attention, and I dig it from the dirt, tossing it into the stream. Leith watches the ripples as he continues.

"The first seven years of my life were happy. Or as happy as we could be. My twin and I would finish our chores early so we had time to play. My mom always took it easy on us."

Twin? I had no idea Leith had any siblings. His hands tremble the more he shares, and it makes my chest ache.

"You don't have to share this, Leith," I whisper.

He shakes his head. "No. I do. I don't know why, but I need you to understand me." His blue eyes are so earnest when he looks at me, so I nod and wait for him to continue. "My dad got sick. It started slowly. He would have episodes where he would become someone entirely different. Someone hateful and violent. We didn't have money for a doctor, so we just did the best we could.

"But it kept getting worse. Within a year, the dad I knew was gone. He locked my brother and me in the cellar. My mom couldn't do anything because he would hurt her if she tried. We lived in that cellar for two years. It was freezing down there, and we had no blankets or anything to sleep on. We'd get food whenever he remembered to feed us."

I blink, realizing tears are blocking my vision. Leith is hunched over, making himself smaller, almost like he's back in that cellar. I place my hand on his thigh without thinking, and he swallows thickly.

"My mom would sneak down there with us occasionally. She'd bring us what she could, but she was too scared of getting caught. She promised us she was going to get us out. Every time she left, I kept that hope. My brother, though, gave up quickly. One time when my mom visited, he yelled at her. He told her to stop lying to us. My dad heard and found her in the cellar, bringing us food."

A tear falls down his cheek and I wipe it away. I want to hug him. I want him to stop. He's reliving the pain, and I realize with a jolt that I don't like to see him hurting.

"He dragged my mom out of the cellar by her hair. I ran after them, but my brother stopped me. I stood on the steps and watched him beat my mom until I thought she'd died. When he was done, he turned to me and my brother. My brother pushed me behind him, and my dad grabbed him by the throat. He squeezed until my brother's lips turned blue. Seeing the life leave my twin's eyes was like having a piece of my soul ripped out. When my dad dropped his body, I snapped. I screamed and screamed. I told him I wanted to kill him. I wanted to see his body bleed and break and die."

I'm barely breathing as Leith relays his story. And Leith is looking at the creek with empty eyes that make me hurt. Tears stream silently down my cheeks as I think about that scared little boy watching his twin brother be murdered by their father.

"Until that moment, I never had any indication I had magic. But as soon as the words left my lips, they floated in the air before us, golden and shimmering. Beautiful despite the hate that created them. And then they wrapped around my dad. I watched as his body bled, broke, and died. Just like I said."

I'm unable to hold in the gasp. He turns to me, eyes wary and waiting for judgment or fear. He won't find it from me, though. When I say nothing, he continues.

"My mom screamed. She looked at me like I was a monster. She tried to get up, to run from me, but she was too beaten to do it. She screamed. She yelled for help. So I ran. I ran and ran until I couldn't run anymore. I lived as an orphan in random villages, stealing for food and clothing. I was angry. Always so angry. And every time I'd talk to someone, I'd end up hurting them. So I just kept running.

"I ended up in Fairyland and Nona found me. She knew right away what I was, and she took me in. She brought me to Girasole for Nico's dad to raise. And the rest is history."

"You haven't spoken since then, have you."

He shakes his head. "Not since Nona found me. I was always too scared to try to learn how to control my magic. After three attempts and hurting the people who were trying to help me, I gave up. It's not worth the risk."

"You're a crocotta," I whisper. A creature that kills with its voice. It can mimic any language, any person, and wield it as a weapon.

He nods. And when he looks at me, he looks broken and alone. He's waiting for me to run. To show my fear and disgust just like everyone else probably has. But I'm not afraid. And I'm not disgusted. I know he doesn't like physical relationships with others, but I can't stop myself from climbing onto his lap and wrapping my arms around him. He's stiff at first, then he wraps his arms around me and shudders with relief. He buries his head in my neck and his tears are warm as they land on my skin.

"You are not a monster, Leith," I say gently, running my fingers through his hair. "You're not a bad person."

It all makes sense now. How people think he's cowardly because he doesn't talk. But they have no idea. This man is incredibly brave. And incredibly strong. He lived through a horrendous past, and he didn't let it ruin him. He could have turned into the monster he says he is, but he didn't.

We sit like that for a few minutes, and when he pulls away, I frown at the distance between us, even though it's just inches. It's the closest I've been to him, and I want to savor every second in his arms.

Thank you, he mouths then leans in to press a kiss to my forehead.

My stomach erupts into butterflies at the sensation of his lips on my skin. I smile and wipe the lingering tears from his face. "No need to thank me."

He stands, easily lifting me with him, and sets me on my feet. We walk back to the others, shoulders brushing. A fire is blazing merrily, and I swallow back the image of the village wreathed in flames. Leith stares at the fire with shoulders hunched around his ears. An empty look still lingers in his blue eyes.

I sit and tug on Leith's hand, silently asking him to sit next to me. He's still lost in his own grief and trauma. I don't want him to be alone. So when he sits, I scoot closer. I don't touch him, because I don't want to make him uncomfortable, but I let him know I'm here if he needs me. After a moment, he adjusts and lets his thigh rest against mine.

Matteo stares at us with curiosity and a bit of awe. I don't think they are used to seeing Leith get close to someone. Matteo meets my gaze and raises his brows in question, but I don't respond. This is between me and Leith.

"Does anyone want me to go hunt for food?" Tin Man asks quietly. Even he seems affected by what we saw. Shadows hide his dark eyes, and his posture is slumped, like what we saw has drained him of his energy. Not so heartless after all.

We all shake our heads. Our appetites fled in the sight of that horrendous act of violence. Even Twig doesn't seem to care about food right now. He watches me and Leith, and stays close to Matteo's side, almost like he's giving us privacy.

"What was that town?" I finally ask after a long silence.

Matteo purses his lips, and Leith looks at his lap, leaving Tin Man to answer. "It was one of the few villages comprised of only fae." He looks toward Leith before cautiously saying, "It was the last one of its kind."

Leith closes his eyes and swallows. If I were to guess, the little village he came from must have been one of those fae-only villages. If the one that burned was the last of its kind, then that means Leith's village is gone. I have no clue if that's a relief to him. I put my hand on my leg palm up and let him make the decision. He takes it, threading our fingers together and squeezing tightly. His skin is clammy and cold, and I urge my warmth into him.

"Was it Morta?" I ask, even though I already know the answer.

Tin Man nods. "If not her hand directly, then her bisso galeto on her orders."

"Bisso what?"

Tin Man looks at me impatiently. "Bisso galeto. A creature the size of a pony, with the head and body of a rooster, wings of thorns, and tail of a snake. Morta controls them somehow. She makes them do her bidding. My guess is it was them that caused the destruction."

Matteo shudders. "The thorns on their wings are coated in poison. One scratch is all it takes to paralyze and shut down all body functions."

Tin Man continues, "Since it didn't appear anyone fought back or tried to stop the fire, I'm guessing an entire host of them were sent to take out the villagers first. Then they destroyed the buildings and set them on fire."

"That's awful," I breathe, placing my hand on my throat. "All of those people."

We lapse into silence again. Leith doesn't look at the fire. He lies back and stares at the stars. The others also lie down and close their eyes, Twig laying his head on Matteo's chest. I tap Leith's shoulder to get his attention. He slides his blue eyes to me.

"Are you okay?" I sign, wanting to keep our conversation silent.

He shakes his head, eyes going unfocused. "No. Seeing that child, it reminded me of my brother. I was thrown back to that moment my dad dropped his limp body to the floor. I can still hear the thud."

I clench my teeth. It's so hard to not reach out to him. He needs comfort, but I don't know how to provide that without touching him. His eyes focus on me, and he holds out an arm.

"You want me to lie with you?" I ask, my signs small and hesitant. I try my hardest to not show my surprise or excitement.

When he nods, I curl next to him with my head on his shoulder. He wraps his arm around me and holds me tightly. I exhale, trying to memorize what it feels like to be in his arms. When the sun rises, I know things will go back to normal. So I'll take this moment and tuck it away for when I need it most.

I fall asleep to the sound of his heartbeat and the feel of his kiss on the top of my head.

21
LEITH

I wake sometime in the middle of the night. I'm not sure what woke me, but I immediately feel Daci sprawled on top of me. Her head rests on my chest. Her arm is wrapped around my waist. And one of her legs is thrown over mine. I wait for the paralyzing sense of dread that I always feel when someone touches me against my will. But it doesn't come. Instead, the warmth of her body, her weight on top of me, sends a different sensation through me.

It starts as tingles over my skin, not unpleasant, then spreads to a gentle burning fire. The sensation travels through me until it settles in my dick, and I find myself getting hard. *Fuuuck.* Why does this girl have that kind of effect on me? I have never gotten hard from someone touching me. Ever. The only times I do is when I watch someone else.

I lie still for a few minutes, willing my dick to deflate but it doesn't. Sighing, I gently untangle myself from Daci. She whimpers quietly and her brow furrows. I freeze and wait for her to settle back down before heading to the creek.

It's dark and quiet. The only sounds are the nighttime insects singing their song and the gentle rush of water over the rocks in the creek bed. I settle against a large boulder facing the direction of camp and free my dick from my pants. Masturbation is the only way I ever get off. And even then, it's usually just to take the edge off. I've never found the act particularly sexy.

I've only been at it for a few seconds when footsteps crunch through the dead leaves on the ground. I freeze, but when I see Daci emerge from the darkness, the fire in my middle spreads to my limbs. Her steps falter when she sees me, and her mouth drops open in a silent gasp. And in the light from the moon, I catch her cheeks turn an adorable shade of pink.

Her body tenses in preparation to turn and flee, and before I know what I'm doing, I crook my finger at her, never once stopping the up and down motion of my other hand. She hesitates, biting her lip in a way that makes me squeeze myself harder. I'm afraid she'll walk away, but instead, she takes an uncertain step toward me, then another.

I nod toward the tree across from me, and Daci slowly sits. Her eyes are wide as she watches me, the pink in her cheeks now there for an entirely different reason. When she starts squirming, I grin and nod again, this time my gaze falling between her thighs.

Daci swallows and I can hear it in the quiet that surrounds us, but she slowly lifts her hips enough to tug down her leggings and panties. When she hesitantly spreads her legs, I almost curse aloud. I rub my thumb over the tip of my cock, gathering the moisture beading there and spreading it down my length.

Her breathing hitches and I find mine doing the same when she slides her fingers through her folds. I can hear her slickness, and it makes my dick even harder. Just knowing that her watching me pleasure myself got her that wet is fucking hot.

Daci circles her finger around her clit, mouth parting on a soft inhale, before she slides them lower and pushes two inside of her. I groan and my hips jerk just imagining her fingers as my dick. Warmth pulses in my middle, a pool of molten fire that slowly takes over my body. As my hand moves faster and faster, so does Daci's. Her breathless pants echo my own, overtaking the gentle rush of the water behind me.

I can tell she's getting close. Her movements turn more harried and less refined. Her legs spread wider, giving me the perfect view as she fucks herself. In the moonlight, I can see the shine of arousal on her fingers and my mouth waters at the sudden desire to taste her. Why does she have this effect on me? I've never had these kinds of urges before, and now they pulse through my body strong enough to make me tremble.

Daci whimpers and closes her eyes, but she opens them again almost immediately, as if she doesn't want to take her gaze from me. I nod, and Daci moans as her body begins to shudder. It's so fucking erotic to watch her fall apart on her own fingers. All it takes is one more pump and I find myself erupting all over my own hand.

Silence falls around us again as our breathing slows. Once again, I act without thinking. Pushing onto my hands and knees, I crawl the short distance to Daci and take her hand, bringing her fingers to my mouth. She tastes like nothing I've ever tasted before. Her eyes widen and her lips part. Those fucking lips. I suck every last drop from her fingers.

Once I'm satisfied, I sit back on my heels and give her a smirk. She blushes from the tips of her ears to her chest, then she hurriedly tugs up her leggings. When she stands, her legs tremble and she fists her hands against her stomach.

"Thank you," she whispers. "Goodnight."

I watch her walk away with the goofiest grin on my face.

That certainly wasn't in the cards. I never planned on jerking off while Daci touched herself. And I certainly never planned on sharing my story with her. Very few people know the truth. In fact, I can count on one hand the number of people who do. But that child's body lying motionless on the ground dragged up all the trauma I worked so hard on repressing. I couldn't shake the image from my mind of the life leaving Landon's eyes and his body hitting the ground.

I've spent twenty-three years with that memory haunting my every step. Most days I can shove it so deep inside of me that I don't think about it. But every now and then, it creeps up on me like a tiger stalking its prey. And every time it rears its ugly head, it leads to the memory of the absolute terror and disgust in my mother's eyes. The way she looked at me like I was a monster instead of her child.

I'd never admit to anyone—although I'm sure Nico and Mattie know—that the moment my mother chose to fear me instead of love me haunts me worse than my twin's death. A child wants nothing more than for his parents to love him unconditionally. And I was born to two who wanted nothing to do with me.

As I was sitting by the stream washing the ash from my skin, the little boy inside of me was too close to the surface to repress. I felt so tired. So alone. And in that moment, with Daci sitting next to me, I wanted someone to comfort me for once in my life. I wanted someone to look at me with understanding and caring.

Maybe that's why the words spilled from me before I could stop them. Or maybe it has something to do with the way Daci is like a magnet, drawing me to her no matter how much I try to stay away. In her presence, the trauma I constantly fight with quiets. She brings me peace that I've never felt before. I don't know why or how, but I know that I like it.

I was terrified to tell her what I was. If she had shown the same fear and hate as my mother, I probably would have broken beyond repair. But she didn't. I saw surprise in her beautiful green eyes, but it was quickly swallowed by understanding and compassion. And when she climbed onto my lap and wrapped her arms around me, a piece of my broken soul smoothed over. It was like she healed me, just a tiny bit, in a way no one else has ever been able to.

When I look at all the things Daci does for me, I can't help but wonder what makes her so special to me. The magnetism, the quiet in my mind, the way my skin doesn't crawl at her touch like it does for anyone else—in fact, I find myself craving it. It's the only reason I can explain what happened last night.

I can't help but think we shared something special. Not a word was uttered between us, but I feel like more was said by our actions and the way our gazes met over the distance. Even though she didn't touch me and I didn't touch her—until I licked her essence off her fingers—I've never been more aroused in my life. I don't know what it means, except that I know nothing can come of whatever it is. That thought alone makes the healed piece of my soul shrivel a little.

Sighing, I click my tongue at Twig. I walked him to the stream so he could get a drink before we continue our journey. Daci was still asleep, and I had to carefully extract myself from her when I woke. Waking up with her wrapped around me was . . . strange. But definitely not unwanted.

Twig ignores me and instead jumps into the stream, sending a wave of cold water rushing over my boots. I frown at him, and I swear the bastard smirks back at me. Kneeling on the bank, I splash him, making him shake his head to get rid of the droplets sliding down his face. His golden eyes narrow before he uses his wings to send more water my direction. Little fucker. I jump back, narrowly avoiding the splash, and cross my arms over my chest.

I click my tongue again and point to the ground at my feet. Twig shakes his head and stares at me, unblinking. I stare back.

"You won't win a staring contest with him. Believe me, I've tried."

I whirl around to find Daci picking her way toward us as she lazily throws her hair into a messy bun on top of her head. She gives me a shy smile before turning her attention to the dragon.

"Out. Now," she says sharply, stopping by my side.

Twig huffs, a puff of smoke curling from his nostrils.

"Don't make me come in there and get you. I promise you'll regret it." She crosses her arms over her chest and glares right back at the dragon.

My lips quirk as I watch the showdown between Daci and Twig. She looks absolutely adorable. Twig stares at her for a moment longer before dropping his head and wading out of the stream.

Daci points toward the camp. "If you look pathetic enough, maybe Matteo will dry you off with a spare shirt."

She watches Twig before turning back toward me with a grimace. "The older he gets, the worse his attitude gets." She sighs and shakes her head. "I swear this is like raising a child while being a single parent."

"Well, at least you have me, Mattie, and Nico to help you now," I sign, grinning.

Her smile falls as she looks at me, and I know what's coming. Normally, I would cringe away from the questions I already see brewing in her eyes. But with Daci, I find myself waiting expectantly for them.

"Are you okay?" she asks quietly.

I give her a small smile and nod. "Yes. Thank you for last night. *All* of last night."

She blushes and casts her gaze to the ground. "Can I . . . Can I hug you?" she asks timidly.

Instead of answering, I step up to her and wrap her in my arms. She sucks in a sharp breath before winding her arms around my back and squeezing. The touch quiets my mind immediately, and I rest my chin on the top of her head, exhaling. Who would have thought I'd search out comfort from another person?

Daci pulls away, but only far enough to tip her head back to look at me. There are so many questions swimming in her eyes, and as much as I want to answer them, I don't think I'll be able to. At least not right now. This is all too new for me. I'm still trying to come to terms with this strangeness. It doesn't help that I have a sudden desire to lean down and kiss her. And by the way she's looking at me, that's not something she'd be opposed to.

Mattie's laugh echoes through the trees from the camp, shaking me out of . . . whatever this is. *Fuck.* This is the last thing I should be doing. I step away from Daci, ignoring the way some of the light leaves her eyes as I do.

"We should get back," I sign. "Nico will want to leave soon."

Daci nods and walks away. I follow her, my steps heavier than they were just a few minutes ago.

22
NICOLAI

Taking Mattie's advice is harder than I thought it would be. I don't like to admit I'm wrong, and by getting to know Daciana, I have a feeling I'll learn she's not the person I thought she was. Just that talk we had the other night proved there is more to this girl than I thought. Not to mention whatever passed between her and Leith. I've never seen him open to anyone besides me and Mattie.

Then there is the bigger issue at hand. The one where my mother is involved, and that is what is making this so fucking hard for me. If I get to know Daciana and learn what kind of person she is, what if I end up liking her? Not only is that going to end in disaster because she's the daughter of my father's rival, but it would mean I'm not in control of my life. And I refuse to let my mother win.

And to top all of it off, Mattie is sulking now because I was a jerk to him. He can't keep telling me to talk to Daciana, to get to know her, if he keeps sticking his dick in her. It doesn't work both ways. Either I pursue her, or he does.

I don't even want to fucking pursue her. This is just a mess. I'm a mess. I can't make up my fucking mind and I feel like I'm being torn in half.

I growl, kicking a rock out of the way and sending it skittering over the ground. Twig bounds after it, batting it between his paws like a kitten with a ball of yarn. My frustration draws all their attention, and they look at me with various expressions. Daciana with curiosity. Mattie with echoing frustration. And Leith with knowing. I fucking hate them all at the moment. But I choose to step up next to Daciana. For better or worse.

The question I ask comes out of nowhere. I hadn't even realized it was on my mind until I voice it. "How come you haven't asked me about your uncle?"

Daciana exhales slowly and purses her lips. I remind myself that now is not the time to notice how kissable they look. "What's there to ask?" She shrugs and forces a laugh up her throat. "It was years ago, and I know who gave the order."

I grimace. "Yeah, but I was the one who acted on that order."

"My family knows the risks that come from being part of the Camorra. My dad could have stepped away anytime. My grandfather could have made the choice to raise his son differently. Death is inevitable in the Camorra, and I can't find it in myself to feel sorry for someone who knew what they were getting into." She pauses, and her next words are so quiet I barely hear them. "Maybe that makes me heartless after all."

Her heartless? Hardly. It's me with that nickname for a reason. I don't know how she can stand next to me and talk casually after everything I've done. I have more blood on my hands than a surgeon. Her uncle's included. She should hate me for what I've done to her family.

"I know there will be more death in the future," she says, looking straight ahead. "I know you'll be the one holding the knife. And I know my family will bleed more than it already has. You're wondering how I can stand to talk to you, aren't you?" She looks at me with a raised brow, and I can't find the words to answer. She doesn't need me to anyway. "My family is just as guilty. And if I'd been born a boy, my hands would be stained just as red as yours. No one is innocent in the Camorra."

I open my mouth to respond but stop. She's right. And gods, the bleak outlook she has on life is so depressing. It's unfortunate that it's true, though. I study her, processing what she said and trying to fit this image of her into the spoiled princess I know from Girasole. Why the fuck did Mattie have to be right? Why can't she be the snobby bitch she pretends to be? Seeing this side of her makes everything so much harder.

I don't want to see the depths of her. I don't want to know how smart she is. Or how capable and caring she can be. I want her to be the vapid blond that spreads her legs for anyone and everyone. It's the only way I can keep my resolve. Desperate for something to grab to to keep my dislike of her, I jump on the first thing that pops into my head.

"You know sign language," I say, accusingly.

She stiffens next to me and ducks her head, letting her blond hair fall forward to hide her face. "Um, yeah, I do."

"So you just decided to not tell us? All the personal conversations we had thinking you couldn't understand us, and the entire time you were eavesdropping?" I think back to everything we've discussed, mainly about her, and cringe.

She shrugs. "You never asked. You just assumed I didn't know. I'm guessing there are a lot of things you assume about me, and I'm willing to bet most of them are wrong." Her voice holds a challenge, like she's daring me to say something just so she can prove me wrong.

I'm learning, though, that she would be correct. So, instead of saying something, I drop it. That way I can keep my preconceived notions about her. Ignorance is bliss. We walk quietly for a few minutes until the silence becomes too heavy for me, and I once again search for something to say. "So, you don't have any siblings, right?" I ask, attempting to make some small talk that won't backfire on me.

She trips over her own feet, whipping her green-eyed gaze to me. "Yeah," she says slowly, nodding. "Just me. My mom got sick with cancer when I was young, and she was unable to have any more kids." Her voice is soft, and her eyes take on a distant look full of sadness and anger.

"I'm sorry," I say, my voice rough and uncertain. Am I trying to apologize? Why do I feel the need to let her know that I actually *am* sorry that she lost her mom so young? Is it because I essentially did too? Fuck. How did this already turn into a conversation I regret?

She shrugs, trying to pull off nonchalance but failing. "I'm pretty close to my cousin. At least, as close as we can be with her always sharing things with her dad." Her tone is bitter, and her smile doesn't fool me for a second.

I nod. "Yeah, I understand that. Family loyalty and everything."

She studies me from the corner of her eye. "I have a feeling we probably have more in common than we realize," she says quietly.

Her words almost make me stop in my tracks. I never really thought about how similar our lives must be. We're both children of the Camorra. We've grown up living with violence and bloodshed. We've been taught from the very beginning, family first and only. I've never thought about how lonely it gets. I got incredibly lucky with Mattie and Leith. Not to mention my little sister. But Daciana? She's on her own.

She faces forward again, and I take the opportunity to study her. I've never denied she's beautiful. She's always looked like she doesn't belong in our world. Rather than the tan skin and dark hair and eyes most of us Girasolens have, Daciana is fair. Her hair looks like gold flowing over her shoulders. Her green eyes are absolutely stunning. She's too thin for my liking, but I get why she keeps her figure trim. Being in the spotlight all the time does things to one's mind. I would know.

"You have a little sister, right?" she asks suddenly.

I tense, immediately going on alert. She must notice how quickly my guard goes up, because she shakes her head.

"I'm just . . . trying to get to know you," she says quietly, almost shyly. "I didn't mean . . . I wasn't trying to . . . fuck." She grimaces and glances at the sky, growling. I hate to admit how adorable she looks doing it. "This is so fucked up. We can't even talk to each other without the other thinking we're trying to gain information to use for our advantage. I don't know why I'm even bothering." She hangs her head and watches her feet as she walks.

The defeated look on her face makes me scowl. I don't like it. And I don't like that I don't like it. Everything with this girl is a vicious cycle, but I can't stop myself from trying to make her smile again.

"Yeah, I have a little sister. Well, half-sister, technically," I say, looking straight ahead and praying I'm not making a mistake. "Her name is Giorgia. She's ten years old and an absolute menace." I can't stop the smile from spreading on my face when I think about her. "She swears she's going to marry Mattie, and whenever she sees him, she plasters herself to his side. She has a big heart and an even bigger attitude. I'm scared to think what she'll be like as a teenager."

When I look at Daci, she's staring at me open-mouthed, and I realize it's because she's never seen me smile. I clear my throat and rub the back of my neck as heat creeps up my throat.

I lift the sleeve of my shirt, revealing the only colored tattoo I have. A unicorn holding a knife, surrounded by pink and purple flowers. "I asked her to design a tattoo for me, and this is what she came up with."

Daci laughs, and her face completely lights up. I notice a dimple in her right cheek, and I can't stop staring at it. "It suits you perfectly," she says, still giggling.

I'm actually enjoying my time walking with her. We talk about nothing in particular, but as soon as Mattie calls for us to stop for the night, a cold sinking sensation settles in my gut. I can't get attached to her. Talking to her was a bad idea. The more I get to know her, the harder it will be to walk away at the end of this.

Needing to get away for a minute, I tell them I'm going to look for food. I don't really try though. I wander aimlessly and try to shut down the nagging in my brain that this is what I'm supposed to be doing. Just because fate says it is, doesn't mean it's what I want.

I keep telling myself this as I walk back to camp with two rabbits dangling from my hand. Leith is still out hunting, but Mattie and Daci are sitting by the fire. I slow my steps when I hear their conversation.

"What's up, Matteo?" Daci asks, keeping her gaze on Twig.

"Nothing," he shrugs.

I watch Daci's face fall, and something in me rears its ugly head. If she prefers Mattie over me, isn't it for the best?

Mattie sighs and sets his water down. "Look, it's not my place to tell you what's going on," he says, practically whispering. Probably afraid of me overhearing him. "This involves Nico, and it needs to be him who tells you. I've been trying to convince him, but he won't listen to me. And I think I may have pushed him too far." He looks at Daci, clearly begging her to drop it, but she doesn't.

"So, we're just going to act like nothing happened between us?" she asks incredulously.

Mattie closes his eyes and shakes his head. "No," he says quietly. "Because I don't want to pretend nothing happened." He looks at her, begging her to understand. "I like you, Daci. You're not at all what I expected, and you speak to my Faun in a way no one else ever has."

I suck in a breath. For him to admit that is huge. Fauns fall hard and fast when they want to, and what he just said . . . There's something more happening here than any of us realize. First Leith, now Mattie?

"But . . ." Daci prompts, because there is a definite *but* in his statement.

His smile is brittle and his eyes look incredibly sad. "But, again, Nico—"

"What about me?" I ask, finally stepping out of the shadows and making myself known.

Daci jumps and startles Twig. He glares at her and rolls off her lap, waddling over to Mattie, who gives the dragon a boop on his nose before standing. "Come on, Twig. Let's go help Leith find some dinner. Nico and Daci need to talk."

Fucking Matteo. I'm tempted to beat his ass to a bloody pulp, but that's not something friends do. However, one could argue that leaving me in this position isn't something a friend would do either. I get it. He thinks Daciana needs to know, but I disagree. Unless I decide to act upon things, there is no need for her to know. And do I want things to move forward?

Daciana looks at me expectantly, and I heave a breath as I sit next to her. Her green eyes have a silver tint to them in the moonlight, and I find myself staring at her. She quirks one brow, and her lips pull into a teasing smile.

"So," she prompts. "What do you have to tell me?"

And that breaks the spell I was under. I turn away and grimace. "You need to be more careful in Oz," I mutter, grasping the first thing I think of that will start an argument. It's easier to fight with her than be real.

Daciana's back straightens and she tips her head up in that infuriating way she does when she looks down her nose at people. "Excuse me?" There is no denying the sass in that tone.

"You almost fell off that cliff. And in the process, Mattie risked his life and could've died. Be. More. Careful."

She gapes at me before spluttering. "Are you serious? You think it was my fault I almost fell?" She spreads her arms wide and laughs without humor. "Do you really think I threw myself off that cliff to put Matteo's life in danger? You're fucking nuts, Tin Man."

I glare at her. The anger that always flows just under my skin rises to the surface. And hearing her call me that only pisses me off even more. "That's right. After all, I'm heartless. Why wouldn't I think you'd do something like that?"

"This is insane. There's no point in arguing with you. You're too stubborn and arrogant to ever think about anything except yourself."

Fuck. I'm doing this all wrong. I'm only proving to her I'm the heartless bastard everyone says I am. And for some reason, that makes my chest ache. I don't want her to think that of me. "You're right," I say through my gritted teeth.

Her head whips in my direction and she stares at me open-mouthed. "Wh-what?"

"I'm only thinking of myself. And I started this argument to avoid a conversation I didn't want to have."

"Well," she says quietly. The fight visibly leaves her. She leans back on her hands and studies me. "Then what conversation were you trying to avoid? It's what Matteo was talking about, right?"

I shake my head and grimace. "Nothing. Mattie needs to keep his nose in his own business."

"Something tells me this 'business' involves me too." She crosses her arms, and I swear if she'd been standing, her stance would have widened in preparation for a fight. Again. It's annoyingly attractive, and the way it excites me to see the fire in her eyes is alarming.

Just then, the wind blows, sending her scent to me. The fae in me reacts immediately. My blood heats so suddenly, it steals my breath. The pull I've been fighting against grows so strong, my vision narrows until all I can see is Daciana. I take a deep breath to clear my head, but her scent floods my nose again and makes every inch of me come to life. There is no fighting it this time. No matter how hard I try, I can't fight the hook that's embedded inside of me.

My hand wraps around her throat and I pull her toward me. I get one quick look at her surprised face before I press my lips to hers. She freezes for a moment, her body stiff and frozen. My other hand slides into her hair and I tug the strands roughly in my fingers. She sways into me then, her mouth parting on a soft inhale, and I take the opportunity to slip my tongue inside. A low moan climbs up her throat, and the sound does something to me. I'd already lost all control of my actions, but right now, it's as if I'm possessed.

Before I know what I'm doing, I'm pushing her to the ground and pressing my body against hers. She's so small under me. She feels so frail, like my bodyweight alone could snap her in half. But I can't lie to myself. She feels so fucking good.

Her hands twine around my neck and she pulls me closer. I growl low in my chest as her legs spread and my hips fall into the cradle of hers. Oh, fuck. I'm in trouble. I know I should pull away, but I can't stop. And by the way she's gripping me, she doesn't want me to stop either.

There are millions of tiny sparks in my chest spreading outward and taking over my entire body. Everywhere she's touching me burns. And deep inside, a fire grows, something primal and urgent sparking to life that is overwhelming. That sensation alone gives me the power to pull away.

I stare at her for a second, with her face flushed and her eyes still closed, her lips kiss-swollen, and her pulse thundering under my thumb. In the silver moonlight she looks like a goddess. Deep inside of me, I know if she opens her eyes and I see them dark and glazed with lust, I'll dive back in and never resurface.

I push to my feet and shift faster than I ever have. My wings flap hard and carry me high into the sky and away from the temptation that is Daciana DeRosa. But it doesn't matter how far I fly, she's there. Her taste is in my mouth. Her touch branded onto my skin. She's in the blood rushing through my veins.

I'm already in too deep.

And I was in too deep before I kissed her. She caught my interest the second I got her text asking for help. Just the fact that she reached out to me, her enemy, told me she was either incredibly brave or insanely stupid. Then with every obstacle we've come across here in Oz, she's proven just how determined she is.

She didn't fall apart when she found out who she was. She didn't quit when she fell in the chasm. As much as I hate to admit it, Mattie was right. There is more to her than the party princess act she puts on in Girasole. She's probably more similar to me than I'd like to admit as well.

Fuck. Me.

Now I need to decide. Do I tell her about what my mom did? Do *I* accept what my mom did? I'm not sure I have any other options. It's either accept it and tell Daciana, or walk away.

I'm not sure I can walk away now.

When I finally fly back to camp, Mattie and Leith have a fire started. Daciana is nowhere in sight, and panic briefly flares through me before I spot Twig lying next to Mattie. She wouldn't go far without that dragon.

When I shift and land, I glare at Mattie. "No more. Stay out of my business."

He doesn't say anything, but he shakes his head in disappointment, his dreads swaying with the movement. Leith keeps his gaze on the fire, refusing to get in the middle of whatever this thing is between me and Mattie.

"Where is she?" I ask.

"Cleaning up at the creek over there," Leith signs and tips his head in the direction of the creek I heard when I shifted.

I debate going to find her, but if I did, what would I say? I'm sorry I kissed you, it won't happen again? Or I'm not sorry I kissed you and now you're stuck with me? Neither of them sound like something Daciana will want to hear.

So instead, I walk around the fire to sit as far from Mattie as I can get. There's a sketchbook on the ground where Daci was sitting earlier. I glance at the page and almost trip. Sitting next to the charcoal pencil on the creamy white paper is a brown and white feather. An owl feather. One of my feathers. And drawn on the page is a rough sketch of a pair of lips. My lips.

I sigh and flop onto the ground. I can still feel her mouth against mine. I could walk to that creek and kiss her again. I could strip her out of her clothes and see what the rest of her tastes like. I could claim her completely. A small voice in the back of my mind brings me up short. Matteo already has. He knows what she tastes like. He's seen her coming undone. Fucking bastard.

Instead of dwelling on the volatile emotions inside of me, I lie in the grass and close my eyes. I don't want to look at her when she comes back. I don't want to know if she'd look at me, or what her expression would be. It's best if I stop things now before they go any further.

When her footsteps crunch the grass, I even out my breathing.

She hesitates briefly when she walks past me, but then I hear her settle next to the fire. The sound of her charcoal scratching across the page piques my interest. Is she finishing the drawing of me? Or is she scratching it out and starting one of Matteo?

Nope. Not going there. I can already tell I won't be getting any sleep tonight, so I push to my feet and shift back into my owl. This way I can keep watch while remaining as far from her as I can.

23
DACIANA

The landscape slowly changes to wide-open rolling hills covered in wildflowers. The yellow brick road winds through them like a brightly colored ribbon. It's peaceful, with the gentle breeze and the clear blue sky above us. The weather in Oz is always perfect, according to Leith. The magic of the land keeps everything alive and happy. The days are comfortably warm, and the nights hold the slightest hint of a chill that makes sitting by a fire relaxing. At least, it's relaxing unless you're dealing with Nicolai Morelli.

I don't think I've ever burned so hot before as when he kissed me. Even when Matteo and I had sex. There is something about Nicolai. He does everything so intensely, and that includes kissing. It was brutal, consuming, and mind blowing. His hand on my throat sparked a burning desire deep inside of me. And his tongue tangling with mine . . . there are no words for what he made me feel.

Then the next day he was freezing cold with me. Hot then cold. That's Nicolai's MO. I sigh heavily as I make my way between the grassy hills. Leith looks at me with a raised brow and I shake my head. No point in complaining about Nicolai to his best friend.

"Keep your eyes on the horizon," Matteo says. "The Emerald City should be coming into view soon."

Sure enough, we round a large hill and I stop dead in my tracks. The Emerald City looms before us, a vibrant green city built into a hill. A blue-green lake stretches between us and the city, and the sun reflects off the gentle waves.

"How do we get there?" I ask, stepping up to the lake. Twig

hops forward and sticks his nose in the water, creating ripples that spread far and wide. He sneezes, causing the water to spray over my feet and shins.

Matteo steps up next to me, his shoulder brushing mine. It's the most we've touched in a while, and if I'm being honest, I miss it. He points to the middle of the lake. "See that boat out there? It'll take us to the other side."

I watch the boat drift closer to us, faster than it should be able to considering it doesn't have a motor. There is no one steering it, and I'm once again reminded of the magic of Oz.

When it reaches the shore, Leith hops in first and the craft doesn't even shift in the water, holding steady as Nicolai follows. Twig jumps in and settles on Leith's lap, looking over the edge of the boat. Matteo takes my hand and helps me climb in. His fingers linger with mine a moment too long, and Nicolai coughs pointedly. I shoot him a glare. If he's going to get possessive, he needs to figure out what the hell he wants. Come to think of it, I guess I should too. I can't keep playing three games. I probably shouldn't be playing any game.

There are three rows of seats in the small boat. Leith claimed the one near the end and Nicolai claimed the one in the middle. Before I can sit on the seat at the other end from Leith, Nicolai scoots over and gives me a dark look. I sigh and sit next to him, letting Matteo take the last seat.

As soon as Matteo is seated, the boat takes off. It rocks gently on the smooth water. I try to watch the glassy surface as we float over it, but Nicolai's thigh presses against mine, and the heat from him steals all my focus. I can't keep my gaze on the green city growing larger the closer we get to it. My eyes travel to Nicolai, only to find him already looking at me.

The air surrounding us crackles, and I suck in a sharp breath. It's as if nothing else exists except Nicolai and me. His dark gaze is both freezing and burning. It penetrates all the way to my soul, and I find it hard to breathe with that intense focus on me. Then his eyes drop to my mouth, and my stomach clenches in a way that makes me squirm. When he lifts his gaze back to mine, a small smirk curls the corner of his mouth and the bubble of lust I found myself in pops. Insufferable, arrogant, moody bastard.

I scowl at him and turn toward the Emerald City just as the boat docks. When I stand to hop out, Nicolai takes my hand and helps me. I don't fail to notice the subtle look of contention he gives Matteo. Once we're all on the shore, the boat takes off toward the center of the lake again.

I thought the Emerald City was beautiful from far away. But up close it's breathtaking. The city gets its green color from the myriad of plants and vines that crawl over every building. And each structure is built into the grassy hillside, with a cream cobblestone street winding back and forth from the ground to the very top of the hill. At the top, a large building sits looking out over the city, the white walls shining in the late afternoon sun.

"Decima lives in the palace at the very top," Matteo says, following my line of sight.

Decima, the measurer of the Thread of Life. The one in charge of each person's fate. Is she the reason I'm the guardian of the dragons? Hopefully she can give me some answers and help me figure out what exactly I'm supposed to do.

The people of the Emerald City are just as enchanting as the building at the top of the hill. They vary in every way possible. Size, shape, color, personality. There are human-looking fae walking among tiny fairies like the ones I met in Fairyland. There are fairies flying through the air while others crawl on all fours. Larger fairies ride horse-like creatures, and smaller fairies hitch rides on tiny carts pulled by more fairies.

It's chaotic and loud, cheerful and mesmerizing. There are too many things for me to look at, and I quickly get dizzy trying to take it all in. Twig stands at my feet, stunned into immobility at the bustling creatures before us. None of them spare us a glance, at least until they notice Twig. Then they stop and stare. Soon, the rumblings of hundreds of fae and fairies carry through the street as the news of Twig spreads like wildfire.

Before we know it, an army of fae marches toward us. Their green uniforms blend into the landscape. Only the golden trim and thread makes them stand out. A fae woman approaches. She has the look of a commander of some sort, with golden ropes looped around her shoulders. Her eyes are glued to Twig, and I slowly bend to pick him up.

I grasp Twig tightly in my arms, my palms slick against his green scales. My gaze travels over the guards, taking in their serious expressions and the hands gripping sword hilts. I attempt to swallow, but my throat has gone dry and my tongue sticks to the roof of my mouth. Nicolai and Matteo shift to stand in front of me, and I duck slightly to hide behind them. Leith's presence at my back helps calm some of the nerves that boil and bubble inside of me.

"That is not something that has been seen in Oz in quite some time," the woman says in a deep melodic voice. When she raises her gaze to mine, weariness lines her face. "Who are you?"

I hesitate, unsure of what I should give away. Nicolai didn't prep me at all, once again. So I do what I do best and don my mask of haughty princess. "We're here to see Decima," I say, lifting my chin and hoping she doesn't notice how my voice trembles with fear.

The woman laughs darkly. "Even having a dragon isn't enough to warrant a meeting with one of the Parcae."

Seriously? If a dragon isn't a good enough reason, what the hell would be? But before I can open my mouth to say something that would probably get us into trouble, Nicolai clears his throat to get the woman's attention.

"I'm Nicolai Morelli. Nona's son." His last two words are practically growled through gritted teeth. "We're here to meet with my aunt."

The woman's skin, as dark at Matteo's, turns ashen and she quickly straightens. "Of course. Apologies. Please follow me."

Nicolai looks at me with a smirk and winks before he follows the guard. I'm so shocked, it takes me a moment to catch up to them. But by the time we reach the top of the hill, I'm huffing and puffing. Twig is heavier than a ton of bricks in my arms, but he gave up walking long ago.

"I'm too out of shape for this shit," I mutter, trying to catch my breath as I tip my head back to stare at the building.

The white stone of the structure peeks from under the vines that climb over the entire thing. There are no doors or glass in the windows or doorways. The entire building is open to the elements and the fresh breeze scented with flowers.

The guard woman leads us inside, where we find ourselves in a massive foyer made of white marble. Golden candelabras line the walls with flames that glow silver-white, providing enough light to illuminate the dark space.

We follow the guard through the palace until we get to a large arched doorway covered in hanging vines. She parts the vines and ushers us inside. My jaw hits the floor, and Matteo has to poke me in the back to get me moving again. The large circular chamber is all white marble. A massive golden chandelier hangs from the domed ceiling with more silver-white flames. Golden pillars line the walls with green vines climbing up to the ceiling.

But what caught my attention first was the beautiful woman sitting on a golden throne with leafy green vines snaking around it. Her tan skin practically glows, and her long dark hair curls in gently cascading waves. Her eyes are mirrors to Nicolai's.

"Nephew," she says in a smooth, high voice. "I haven't seen you in many years."

Nicolai nods and stops a few feet from the raised dais. He doesn't smile at her or say anything. Just waits expectantly with a slightly hostile expression.

She sighs. "You still haven't forgiven me or your mother yet, have you." It's not a question, and even I can see the genuine sadness that gleams in her eyes. Still, Nicolai says nothing, so Decima turns her attention toward me. "And you must be Daciana and Twig. It is a pleasure to meet you both."

I startle. "How did you know our names?" I ask, holding Twig tighter to my chest. The dragon narrows his eyes at her, his small body vibrating with tiny growls.

Her knowing smile chills me to my bones. "We have a lot we need to discuss. But first, I'm sure you would like to rest and get cleaned up. Rooms have been prepared. Please, make yourselves at home and we'll talk later."

We don't have any choice but to let the guard lead us to a separate part of the palace, similarly styled in white, gold, and green vines. We get to our rooms, and I take one look at the golden clawfoot tub in the bathroom. I know exactly where I'll be spending the next hour of my life.

My hair is half dry when there is a knock on my door. Twig's head pops up from where he's napping at the foot of the bed. His nostrils flare and he jumps down, rushing to the door. By the time I get there, his tail is wagging so hard his entire body wiggles back and forth.

"Seriously? You don't get this excited to see me?" I say, wondering who could be at the door. When I pull it open and find Matteo's grinning face, my humor fades. "Really?" I give Twig a look, and he returns it with one of his own that I interpret as "Deal with it."

Matteo bends to scratch under Twig's chin, then the dragon takes off down the hall. I pop my head out to see where he's going to find him stopped in front of another door, clawing at it pitifully. Leith pokes his head out and smiles as Twig bounds into his room. He sees Matteo standing in front of my door and gives us a knowing smirk before he heads back to his room and Twig.

"Traitor," I mutter about the dragon. "What do you want?" I ask, hands on my hips.

"Ouch," Matteo says, placing his hand on his chest in mock hurt. "Is that anger really necessary?"

I narrow my eyes at him and tip my head to the side. "Oh, I don't know. You and Nicolai are both so hot and cold with me. One minute you guys are all over me, the next you won't even look at me. Maybe I'm sick of the bullshit."

Matteo's expression falls into something serious. "You're right. I'm sorry. You don't deserve that."

"No, I don't. So why are you here?"

He slides his hand under his dreads to rub the back of his neck. "Can I come in?"

"Depends on why you want to come in. Again, why are you here?" I'm more than fed up with the bullshit he and Nicolai have put me through. And I don't know why I care so much in the first place.

Matteo sighs. "Can we talk?"

"About what?" I ask, not budging from the doorway.

"Daci, please."

It's the slight pleading in his voice that makes me take a step back, letting him enter my room. I head for the big round bed decked out in creams and greens, then I think twice about that and head toward the bench in front of the open window. I brush the gauzy white curtain aside and stare out at the landscape.

The blue-green lake at the bottom of the hill twinkles in the light of the setting sun. Everything is cast in an orange glow that makes the entire Emerald City look like it's caught on fire. From this high up, I can just make out the citizens scurrying about in the streets, heading home for dinner.

Matteo sits next to me on the bench. It's too small for both of us. His leg and arm brush against mine, and I have a feeling he sat here for that very purpose. He knew his presence would scramble my brains.

"So," he says quietly, looking out the window with me. "What do you think of the Emerald City?"

I shrug. "At first glance, it's beautiful. But I've learned that first impressions aren't always what they seem."

"That's fair. I guess the lives we live in Girasole tend to make us think the worst of things."

I snort, very unladylike, and shake my head. "Matteo, what do you want?" I pin him with my stare, letting him see how much I'm done with this bullshit.

He leans his back against the side of the window, kicking one leg out into the open so he's straddling the windowsill. I could give him one push and he'd fall. It's entirely too tempting.

He sees me calculating the distance and he smirks at me. "If you want to push me, I'd let you. It's the least I deserve."

I cross my arms and keep my gaze on the lake. Despite how much training my dad put me through, I've never been good at mastering my expressions. I've gotten good at the uncaring bitch, but since being in Oz, that mask is cracking, and I'm not sure I can keep it in place for whatever Matteo has to say.

"Things are complicated, Daci," Matteo begins. "I can't tell you all of it, because it's not my place. And no matter how much I try to convince Nico to fill you in, he refuses. But . . ." His hand brushes my jaw, fingers tugging my chin so I'm forced to look at him. "I really like you, Daci. I enjoy the time we spend together. I really enjoy kissing you . . . and other things."

I tug my chin from his fingers and turn back toward the lake. The orange glow has faded into the dark blue that makes everything look flat. Tall lampposts cast silver-white puddles of light on the winding street, and the last citizens make their way home.

"Daci," Matteo whispers, drawing my gaze from outside to him. "What do *you* want? You've shown interest in all of us, if I'm being honest. We've had sex. You've kissed Nico. You managed to get close to Leith. You're not exactly innocent in all of this either."

I swallow thickly because he's right, and because I don't know what I want. This time when I try to look back outside, he doesn't let me. When I look into his eyes, I feel something inside of me bloom, like a flower opening its petals to catch every ray of sunshine. Matteo is the sunshine, and my soul wants it. It makes my breath catch.

"You can't ask me to talk and not return the favor, Daci."

I pull from his grasp and stand, walking across the room. The way he says my name . . . Damn it! "I . . . I don't know." My words are so quiet, I'm not sure if he heard them.

"That's not an answer."

"What do you want me to say, Matteo?" I ask, turning around with my arms spread wide. "That I like both of you? All three of you?" I shake my head with a wry smile. "Not only does that make me the slut everyone says I am, but it also makes me the biggest idiot in Girasole. What happens when all of this is over? We return home and go back to being enemies? Because don't forget, I'm a DeRosa and Nicolai is a Morelli."

"I haven't forgotten that," he says quietly. "But who knows what happens when this is over. And you're not a slut."

I shake my head again because that doesn't answer anything. He admits to liking me. Nicolai . . . well, I don't know what the fuck is going on there. And I *do* like them both. I like all *three* of them. How the fuck does that not make me a slut?

"So what?" I whisper, voice breaking slightly. "I'm supposed to choose?"

Matteo smiles and pushes to his feet. "No. You don't have to choose, edainai."

My heart pounds faster with each step he takes toward me. When he's standing in front of me, my breath freezes in my lungs. The way he's looking at me. It's like . . . like . . .

His lips brush against mine and all coherent thought flees. We haven't kissed in so long. I missed it. His kisses are gentle yet insistent. And when he threads his fingers through my hair, tugging my head back, I'm lost.

24
MATTEO

Gods. I've fucking missed this girl. Even though we've been traveling together, I've kept my distance to respect Nico. But he's clearly got his head so far up his ass, he can't see what's right before him. I'm not going to putter around with my thumbs up my ass and miss my shot. His loss. My gain.

It's wild how fast this girl has climbed into my heart. With every obstacle we've faced, she hit it head on, despite her fears and hesitations. She's stronger than anyone thinks. She is more caring than anyone gives her credit for. The mask she wears in Girasole hides the amazing person she is, and each crack that has formed in Oz has given me glimpses of the real her. And I want that mask to come off entirely.

As soon as my fingers thread through her silken hair, she melts for me. Her body goes pliant in my hands, and I step closer to feel her softness against me. When I run my hand to the small of her back, she rolls her hips against mine with a soft moan. It's my undoing.

I pick her up and carry her to the bed, gently laying her in the middle of it. She's flushed and hazy eyed when I step back, and that primal part of me almost purrs in satisfaction. *I* made her look like that. It's because of *me* she's squirming on the mattress, wanting even more.

"Daci," I whisper onto her neck between kisses. "Do you want me to stop?" When she doesn't say anything, I pull away, studying her face closely. "Daci. Do you want me?"

She already admitted it in her own way. But I want to hear her say it. I *need* to hear her say it. When she still says nothing, something inside of me shrivels and dies. I take a step back from the bed, preparing to leave.

A panicked expression crosses her face, and she sits up. "Don't go," she says quietly. "You want me to choose between you guys, and I don't think I can."

"What if you didn't have to choose?" I ask.

Her brow furrows and she stares at me. "That doesn't . . . How would I . . ."

"Don't worry about the details. Just answer the question. What if you didn't have to choose?"

I see the moment she realizes what I'm saying. Her lips part on a soft inhale and the flush in her cheeks deepens. Oh yeah. She's into that idea.

"Give me five minutes," I say, smirking at her.

I've never run so fast in my life. The marble floor is slippery, and I slide right past Nico's door. My shoulder twinges painfully when I grab the doorknob to stop myself.

"Nico!" I shout, pounding on his door. "Nico!"

He wrenches his door open, shirt off and pants unbuttoned. His dark eyes are wide as he scans the hallway behind me. "What is it?"

"Do you want Daci?" I say breathlessly.

He startles, staring at me incredulously. "What? Why the hell are you banging on my door like we're being attacked to ask me if I want the girl?"

"Just answer the fucking question," I growl. "Do you want her? Forget about *everything*. Forget about who she is. Forget about what she is. Do you want her?"

A muscle in his jaw ticks and he runs his hand through his hair.

"Don't lie to yourself, Nico. For once in your life, do what *you* want."

When he meets my gaze, I know I've won. He swallows thickly, then nods. "Yeah. Yes, I want her," he says hoarsely.

I grin and grab his arm. "Then come on. And don't bother buttoning your pants." I rush past Leith's door. He'll be down for this, I already know. But I need to ease Nico into it. Too many balls—literally—in one game will throw him.

My grin stays in place when we burst into Daci's room and find her sitting on her bed, knees drawn to her chest. Her gaze falls on Nico behind me and her mouth drops open. I step out of the way so she can peruse his body. More tats than skin, chiseled abs, large chest. The dude is good looking. Even I can't deny that. I reach behind my head to grab the neck of my shirt and yank it over my head.

"What the fuck, Mattie?" Nico growls. Either he still hasn't caught on to my idea or he's about to shut it down.

I pray to every god I've ever heard of that he doesn't walk out of this room. Or throw me out. Daci watches me as I crawl on the bed toward her. She doesn't move and lets me push her gently to her back.

"You said you wanted both of us," I say, making sure I speak loud enough for Nico to hear me. "So, here we are."

Her breath hitches and she glances over my shoulder at Nico. It's so fucking hard for me to not look as well. Especially as silence falls in the room. I find myself holding my breath until Nico walks to the head of the bed and tugs down his pants. He sits on the edge in his underwear and his gaze burns hotly as he looks at Daci.

I give her a cocky grin, hiding the relief that rushes through me like a tidal wave. I have no idea how this will go, but I'm sure as hell going to figure it out. Nico is demanding and controlling in everything he does. I suspect it will be the same in the bedroom.

I lower my lips to Daci's neck and kiss along the column of her throat. My fingers skim under her shirt, teasing and playful. When I sit back on my heels, she pouts, and those perfectly pink lips tempt me to dive in for a kiss. But I refrain and look toward Nico.

"What do you want me to do?" I ask, surprised at how breathless I sound already.

He looks caught off guard for a moment, then he relaxes with a small smile. "Take her clothes off."

Daci shivers at his words and I watch her skin pebble. She reacts to everything so perfectly. I don't hesitate to tug her shirt over her head. Her creamy skin is mouthwatering and so, so smooth under my fingertips. I lick up her abdomen as my hands snake behind her to unhook her bra. Neither Nico nor I can take our gazes from her breasts when I toss her bra to the floor.

Nico is the first to move, bending low to lick around her nipple before sucking it into his mouth. Daci makes a sound that snaps me into action. With no finesse whatsoever, I pull off her jeans and panties, tossing them to join the pile of clothing on the floor. The silver slippers glitter in the lamplight, and I hesitate briefly before leaving them on.

I already know what she tastes like, and while I'm dying to taste her again, it's only fair to offer it to Nico. I step back and give him a knowing smirk. "All yours, brother."

The speed at which Nico dives between her legs almost makes me laugh. Almost. But the moment he grips her thighs and spreads her wide, her mouth parts and her tongue darts out to lick her bottom lip. When Nico finally licks up her core, Daci moans and lifts her hips. I watch them for a moment. I watch Nico make her squirm. I watch Daci grab his hair and squeeze his head between her thighs. But I also watch her gaze cool as she begins to get inside of her own head. And that just won't do.

I kneel on the bed and bend down to kiss her. "Stop thinking, edainai," I mutter against her lips. "Let us give you what you want."

I cup her breast before pinching her nipple and rolling it between my fingers. Based on the past two experiences I had with her, I know she likes pain. And I know she needs something extreme to distract her from her anxiety. So as I deepen the kiss, I'm already planning how to do just that.

It doesn't take long for her to reach that wall I know she hates.

I can sense her frustration, so I catch Nico's attention. Because we've been through so much together, and we've been friends for years, all I have to do is look pointedly at his hips and he catches my meaning.

We both pull away from Daci to strip out of the rest of our clothes. She eagerly drinks in Nico as he stands at the foot of the bed. He cuts a powerful image with his piercings and tattoos. His hair is mussed from Daci's fingers and his eyes are darker than I've ever seen them.

I let Nico take the lead and he crawls over Daci, kissing her deeply. He kisses rougher than I do, but that's just who he is. Dominant and demanding in everything he does. Daci whimpers and lifts her hips, and I curse. They look good together on that bed. Naked and writhing. Both straining for the other.

"Nicolai, please." Her voice is rough and breathy, and I find myself grabbing my dick and squeezing the head.

"What do you want, Daci?" Nico asks darkly. He teases her by running the tip of his cock through her wetness, and all three of us moan.

"I want . . . I want you. And I want . . ." She turns to me, her green eyes big and bright. "I want Mattie."

Fuck. She called me Mattie. Only Nico and Leith call me that. Hearing it on her tongue almost makes me fall to my knees. I squeeze my dick harder, imagining my hand is her warm, wet pussy.

"Shit, Nico. Just fuck her already," I growl, kneeling on the bed by her head.

Nico's laugh is dark, and it makes Daci shudder. But the way her pupils blow out, I know it's not from fear. I watch her expression carefully as Nico slowly slides his cock inside of her. The little gasp of pleasure she makes. Her mouth falling open and her eyes dropping closed. The way her face goes slack with each inch he pushes in. She's fucking gorgeous.

Nico makes a sound low in his throat, and I know exactly

what he's going through. There is nothing like sliding into Daciana DeRosa. It's heaven. It's euphoric. It's . . . home.

I impatiently wait a couple of minutes, giving Nico his moment. But my dick is aching and I want her mouth wrapped around me. I take her chin in my fingers and turn her head toward me.

"Open up, edainai," I command, and she obeys. Perfectly. I rub my thumb along her bottom lip before sliding it inside her mouth and pressing down on her tongue. "Do you want to take us both at the same time? Do you want to come around Nico's cock while I come down your throat?"

She stares at me with such desperation that I grin at her.

"So dirty, edainai," I mutter, taking my dick in my hand. With my other hand, I lift her head, supporting her neck and giving her a better angle to take me.

When I slide past her lips, my eyes fall shut. This is the second-best place my dick could be. Nico is currently in the best place. I would never call Daci a whore, but she definitely knows how to give a blow job. Both of my hands are behind her head now, and I try my best to keep my thrusts shallow. But it's fucking hard.

Nico's hips slowed while he watched us, but now he picks up his pace, fucking her thoroughly. Each thrust makes a noise climb up Daci's throat, and I can feel each vibration. It fans the flames even more until I'm burning from the inside out.

This is the hottest thing I've ever done. Sharing a woman with my brother is something I've never considered, mainly because I didn't think Nico would ever go for it. But Daci isn't just a woman. Not for either of us. Nico meets my gaze. It's something I would've thought would be weird, but in the moment, the connection is mind blowing.

I can tell by the set of his jaw and the speed of his hips that he's reaching his point. And I'm right there with him. Daci's brows are slowly lowering as her frustration rises. So I grasp the back of her head and slam my cock down her throat, holding her there and blocking her air flow. She swallows reflexively, and it takes all my willpower to not come.

"Edainai," I grit between my teeth. "Let go for us."

Her orgasm takes her. And as her throat constricts around a scream, I find my own release. It burns through my veins and sets my body on fire. Daci swallows around my cock, milking every last drop from me. Nico grunts, and the mattress stutters as he finds his own release. I pull out of Daci's mouth, wiping her lips with my thumb. She gasps for air, her green eyes watering.

"You did so good, edainai," I breathe, bending down to press a soft kiss to her mouth. "So fucking good."

Her cheeks are already flushed, but they turn an even darker red at my praise. She looks stunning with her hair tousled, eyes heavy, and a rosy blush covering her body. Something in my chest constricts. I look at Nico and see him staring at Daci with a look that I'm sure mirrors my own. He rubs his chest absently, and I look down to find myself doing the same.

Daci glances between us, and I can see the embarrassment creeping into her expression and overtaking the post-orgasmic haze. That won't do. I climb into bed with her and tug her into my arms. Her head fits perfectly on my shoulder. And when she tangles her legs with mine, my stomach does a weird little flip.

"You gonna join us?" I ask Nico with a smile and pat the bed on the other side of Daci. "There's plenty of room."

He stares at us for a moment, but I get the feeling he's not really seeing us. Then he grabs his clothing from the floor, his movements jerky and rushed, and he heads out the door.

Daci stiffens in my arms. "Did I do something wrong?"

It's not like her to sound so small and uncertain. I don't like it, and I want to rush after Nico and beat him to a pulp for making her feel like she did something wrong. I squeeze her tighter and kiss the top of her head.

"No, edainai. You did nothing wrong. Nico's just . . . he has a lot to work through." I kiss the top of her head again, lingering to inhale her scent of rose mixed with whatever soap she used in her hair during her bath. Apple maybe. "You were perfect, edainai." More than perfect. There aren't words to use to describe what she just did for me.

She sighs like she's not content with my answer, but she cuddles closer to me, and it doesn't take long for her breathing to even out.

25
DACIANA

It takes me a moment to climb from the darkness of sleep. I lie still, thinking of how rested I feel. It's been awhile since I slept so well and when I think about what happened last night, and whose arms I slept in . . .

I sit up so quickly my head spins. Blinking through the stars dancing in my vision, I look around. The bed is empty. And so is the rest of the room. My heart sinks, even though I try to tell myself it's no big deal. It was just sex. Nothing else. But the nagging in my head won't stop. I admitted my feelings for both of them last night. And they both walked out on me.

I flop back down on the bed and my movements cause something to flutter in my peripheral vision. There's a slip of paper on the pillow next to mine, and my fingers shake when I pick it up.

Good morning, edainai. I'm taking a shower. Meet me for breakfast?

A giddy smile spreads across my face, and I quickly hop out of bed and into my own shower. I wash faster than I ever have, and it's only when I'm stepping out that I realize I have no idea where or what time he wants to meet.

I knock on his door, but he doesn't answer. I knock on Leith's door, and he also doesn't answer. I hesitate in front of Nico's and chicken out. I said what I needed to last night. The ball is in his court now.

I aimlessly wander down the hall, peeking into alcoves and sitting rooms. But it's like the palace is deserted and I'm the only one left. Just as I decide to head for the stairs and check on the main level, a maid comes around a corner carrying a broom and dustpan.

"Oh, good morning," she says, curtsying as best she can with her hands full. "Are you looking for your friends? They are in the small dining room at the other end of the hall."

"Thank you so much."

When I step into the small dining room, I find Leith and Mattie sitting at a small table with empty plates in front of them. Twig is under the table, munching on what looks like a pile of bacon.

"You ate without me? What happened to eating together?" I ask, coming up short.

"You weren't here. I thought you didn't want to eat with me." Mattie shrugs and sits back in his chair.

"You didn't tell me when or where. I spent the past ten minutes wandering the halls looking for you."

"Oh. Oops." He gives me a lopsided grin and pats the chair next to him. "I guess I didn't think of that. Come here. We can get you something to eat."

Leith rings a small bell on the table while I sit next to Mattie. As soon as my butt is in the chair, he hooks his foot around the leg and drags me closer to him. I give him a look and he taps me on the tip of my nose.

"Good morning," Mattie says, voice low and quiet. "How'd you sleep last night?" A knowing smirk tugs up his lips, and I quickly glance toward Leith to gauge his reaction.

Based on the smile he's directing toward his empty plate, he knows exactly what happened last night.

"I actually slept great, thank you." I mean the thank you to be in response to his asking the question, but of course Mattie takes it differently.

"It was my pleasure. Literally."

I roll my eyes and see Leith silently laughing as he plays with his fork in the leftover syrup on his plate. "Oh hush," I say to him.

"You're just jealous."

Leith's head snaps up, his blue eyes burning like the hottest fire, and he gives me a look that makes my insides squirm. "Next time invite me and I won't have to be jealous," he signs.

My jaw hits the floor, but before I can say anything, a server appears and places a plate in front of me. The smell of buttery pancakes and syrup, crispy bacon, and fresh tea distracts me from Leith's comment. I dig in, not realizing how hungry I am until the food is under my nose. While I eat, Mattie and Leith discuss our next move.

"Sometime today, we should be getting a summons from Decima," Mattie says, watching me shovel food in my mouth. "We need to make sure we ask the right questions."

Leith nods in agreement. "Daci needs to make sure she asks about her magic. Not just being a dragon guardian."

"I think we'll ask about the entire history of Oz and Girasole." Mattie gives Leith a knowing look. I can't be sure, but I swear I see Leith hesitate for a second before agreeing. "Are you finished, edainai?" When I nod, he takes my hand and pulls me to my feet. "Then let's go explore the palace."

Leith nudges Twig with his boot, and they both follow us to the door.

"Thanks for dragonsitting Twig last night. I hope he was good for you," I say, looking over my shoulder.

Twig huffs, a puff of smoke curling from his nostrils, and he glares at me with an adorable growl.

Leith smiles and signs, "He's always good. Don't forget he's just a baby. And dragons are more curious than other creatures."

We're halfway down the hall when Nicolai's door opens and he steps out. His gaze lingers on me for a second longer than it does Mattie or Leith, but it's empty and cold. Something inside of me shrivels and dies at that look.

"Decima is waiting for us. Come on." He turns and leads us toward the stairs.

My shoulders drop with my heart. It's like nothing happened

between us last night. Or maybe last night was just an easy fuck for him. Getting his turn with the DeRosa princess. It obviously didn't mean to him what it meant to me.

Mattie squeezes my hand, but I take a breath and put my mask back on. Now isn't the time to deal with this anyway. Decima is waiting for us. And hopefully I learn something about who I am.

The room Nico leads us to isn't the grand room we met Decima in yesterday. This is a smaller, more intimate setting. A pair of dark-green couches face each other across a low table with a small green fire burning through the middle of it. A white wingback chair is placed at the head of the table, and Decima sits grandly in it, wearing a dark-green velvet dress.

Mattie leads me to one of the couches and pulls me down next to him. Nicolai and Leith take the couch across from us. Servants appear with trays of tea with little containers of honey, sugar, and milk, placing them on the table. The fire parts around the trays like . . . magic.

Twig stands on his back legs, front paws landing on the table with soft clicks of his talons. He stares into the fire with big golden eyes, opening and closing his mouth like he can use the fire to create his own.

"Good morning," Decima says, receiving a porcelain cup from a servant. She takes a sip and closes her eyes in happiness. "I hope you found your accommodations acceptable?"

We all nod and give her various hums and grunts of agreement. Mattie pours a cup of tea and adds sugar and honey before handing it to me. I take it, even though I'm not a huge fan of tea. If I can't have coffee, tea is better than nothing.

"Do we want to start with pleasantries or skip right to the reason you're here?" Decima looks at me with dark eyes, and it takes a monumental amount of effort not to shrink before her gaze.

I glance at Twig and smile at the creature. "Let's skip the pleasantries and start at the beginning," I say, remembering Mattie and Leith's earlier conversation.

Decima nods and sits back in her chair. Her voice takes on a wistful tone, her eyes going distant. "Thousands of years ago, Oz and Girasole lived peacefully side by side. Travel between our countries was plentiful, trade was good, and all were happy. Then the Camorra was started by your distant relative." She looks to Nicolai, who doesn't seem surprised to hear his family was the start of the Camorra. "At first, things continued as they had been. But year after year, more violence began to spread from Girasole to Oz.

"The damning moment, the final straw for Oz, was an attack on a small village on the outskirts of Oz. Some members of the Camorra razed the town to the ground over a petty grudge. There were no survivors."

I hadn't heard this story. I knew Oz closed their borders because of violence in Girasole, but I didn't know the violence had spread to this peaceful place. By the look on Decima's face, it was devastating.

"My sisters and I knew we couldn't let things continue as they were. There was no hope in talking sense into Girasole. Already the Camorra was too deep. Grudges and enemies abounded. There was no chance of peace being created between the Camorra families. So my sisters and I decided to take Oz out of the picture. With our magics combined, we created the shield that essentially made Oz forgettable.

"What we didn't expect was the impact it would have on Girasole. It took so much power for us to create the shield that we accidentally took the magic from Girasole. We took all of it."

And as a result, all the fae of Girasole lost their powers. We essentially became human, as over time the little bit of magic left was used up. The weather became unpredictable with seasons that fluctuate. For the fae currently living in Girasole, it's just life. We don't know any different. But after spending time in Oz, I've realized what we're missing. And it's heartbreaking.

Decima continues, "But the worst consequence of our actions was the loss of the dragon guardian. She was in Girasole when the shield was created. Without her magic, without the connection to their guardian, the dragons began to die. Once, our world was filled with the magnificent creatures." She looks at Twig with amazement and sadness. "But slowly, their numbers dwindled. Their health declined. Then they were no more."

I rub my chest, the thought of these beautiful creatures slowly disappearing making my heart ache. All three of the guys' expressions are similarly sad.

"When a nest of eggs was found, Nona and I knew we had to do something. We didn't tell our sister, Morta, as death is her realm. When the time was right, the two of us used our magic to hatch one of the eggs. The baby wouldn't survive long without a guardian, so I decided to bestow the gift of dragon guardian to the one Nona had chosen as her son's mate."

Silence falls in the room, and I repeat the sentence in my head, sure I'd misheard her. The dragon guardian. Nona's son. Mate. As the words repeat over and over, my breath begins to rattle in my lungs, and my heart races so hard it's painful. That can't be right, can it?

Nicolai Morelli is my mate?

It takes a moment for Decima's words to register in my mind. They bounce around inside my skull like gibberish. As each one settles into place, my skin prickles, feeling too tight over my bones. I look to Nicolai for clarification. He holds himself incredibly still, his usually tan skin pale. But when he turns to his aunt and glares, I know this wasn't a surprise to him. He knew this entire time, and he never told me.

"What?" I choke out, my voice strangled like something is lodged in my throat.

Mattie squeezes my hand, and I turn my attention to him. He

gives me a small encouraging smile, but he's not surprised by this news either. And neither is Leith, by the look of sympathy on his face. They knew. All of them knew. I pull my hand from Mattie's and lean away from him.

"Hey, edainai—"

I stop him with a sharp shake of my head and an accusing stare. Of all of them, I think his betrayal hurts worse. But then again, Nicolai fucking slept with me. He slept with me knowing he was my mate, and I had no idea. My chest caves in, and I'm not sure how I keep my chin high. Twig senses the rapid change in my emotions and he comes over to hop onto my lap, resting his chin on my shoulder. I take comfort in his warmth and the weight of his head.

"You didn't know," Decima says slowly, studying the group. She gives her nephew a reproachable look. "That disappoints me," she says so quietly I almost don't hear it. "All of you leave us. I would talk to Daciana alone."

Nicolai is the first to stand, pushing up swiftly from the couch without giving me any further acknowledgment. Leith stands slower, but he refuses to meet my gaze, and the slight flush of his cheeks tells me how bad he feels about all of this. Mattie is the last to stand, his stare on the side of my face like the warmth of the sun, but I refuse to look at him.

"Daci . . ." he whispers. I close my eyes and turn away. Luckily, he gets the hint, and he follows the others out the door.

Decima sighs heavily, rubbing her brow. "I'm sorry. You shouldn't have found out like that, but I never assumed my nephew would be so—"

"Cruel? Uncaring? Heartless?" I snort without humor.

She tips her head side to side. "I was going for stubborn, but those work too."

"Can you explain it to me? The mate thing?" Since Nicolai clearly wasn't going to.

"I'm not sure how much Nona told you," Decima begins. "She fell in love with Nico's father, but she couldn't stay with him. He was part of the problem. He continued the violence we worked so hard to protect Oz from. When Nicolai was just a baby, she had to leave. But she thought she'd gift him one final time, something to show him how much she loves him."

"A mate," I say lifelessly.

"Yes. She had me give him a mate. It backfired on her, though. When Nicolai found out, he was furious. He never had a good relationship with his mother. She was always in and out of his life, mostly out. And to him, it looked like she didn't care. Then he took her gift as a way to meddle in his life. To take his choice away. It was just another way for her to embed herself in his life when he wanted nothing to do with her."

I rest my elbows on my knees and rub my eyes hard enough to see stars. I get where he's coming from. I understand why he feels the way he does. But that doesn't make up for him not telling me. It's my life too. I'm just as involved in this as he is. To not tell me . . .

"I'm truly sorry you found out this way," Decima says again.

I shake my head. "No. I should be thanking you. I probably never would have known had you not said something." My voice trembles, and I swallow thickly to keep the tears from building. I focus instead on my breathing. Even as shallow and uneven as it is, it's better than thinking of Nicolai.

"There is more to the story, if you would like to hear it now. Or we can wait."

I shake my head again and pat Twig's neck. "I need to know everything. Tell me." There isn't time for me to dwell on this.

Decima nods. "As I'm sure you know, Morta stole the eggs in her anger. With her thirst for revenge, she will do what she can to hatch them and raise the dragons to be used for evil. Those eggs are the last hope we have at saving the dragon race."

Twig looks at me, his golden eyes so unfathomably sad. I can't imagine him being the last of his kind. To never see another dragon again after this. It's not right.

"Morta can't be killed," she explains. "As a Parcae, if our

bodies are killed, our magic returns to our temple, where it will wait until it's given a new body. If you can deal with Morta while you're saving the eggs, do it. But don't risk yourself or the eggs. It is your duty as the dragon guardian to bring this magnificent race back to life. You must go to Morta's palace and save the dragons."

26
DACIANA

The next day comes too soon. I spent the afternoon following Decima's revelation moping in my room. Letting the guys' betrayal get to me will only make the rest of this task even harder. So I let myself wallow in my feelings for a day, but now I need to put the mask back on. I need to become the DeRosa princess version 2.0. Ruthless, heartless, and bitch queen.

The guys are already waiting for me outside the palace. Seeing Nicolai standing there, uncaring of the fact that he hurt me, makes me see red. My chest grows tight with anger and I can't breathe until I dispel this energy. I don't give Matteo or Leith the slightest glance. But I step right up to Nicolai and swing. My open palm connects with his cheek with a satisfying *crack*. I don't wait to see his reaction, just step past him and head toward the gates where Decima is waiting.

I clench my fist and grimace. Holy shit, that hurt. My hand stings, but damn was it worth it. I hope he has a handprint for days.

"This will help you find Morta's palace," Decima says, handing me a rolled paper map. "Good luck, Daciana. The fate of the dragons rests on your shoulders."

"Should I have magic?" I ask her. After the bomb she dropped yesterday, I completely forgot to ask this question.

She looks surprised for a moment before schooling her features. "You should be able to talk to the dragons." Her gaze drops to Twig, and she furrows her brow.

"So I'm supposed to protect the dragons but I have no extra

special powers to help me do that?" I bend and lift Twig into my arms. Why haven't I been able to talk with him?

"That's why I fated you to be the dragon guardian. With your mate's powers, you would have had some protection." Her dark eyes flick over my shoulder to Nicolai. She steps closer to me and lowers her voice so only I can hear. "He'll still protect you, even if he is too stubborn to admit he was wrong and refuses to see what's in front of him. And the other two will as well."

For some reason, I already knew that. I never once doubted their protection. From the first moment I met with them and they saw Twig, I knew they'd watch out for me.

"And . . ." Decima purses her lips as she thinks through what to say. "I think there might be more at work than just the fates I put into play." Her eyes scan all three guys behind me with a puzzled expression.

"What does that mean?" I ask, hefting Twig higher in my arms. He's almost too heavy for me to carry now.

The smile Decima gives me is nothing short of mysterious. "You'll see." With that, she steps back and the guards open the gates.

I only wait long enough to toss Matteo the map without looking at him. Then I walk away with my head held high. I carry Twig halfway down the hill, then I set him on the ground. "Don't eat anyone. Don't pee on anything. And stay where I can see you."

He gives me a baleful look before taking off down the street. To his credit, he remains in my eyesight. To his discredit, he scares a tiny fairy selling mushrooms. The fairy knocks the crate over and the fungi fall to the ground, rolling down the hill.

"Oh!" I clap a hand over my mouth and rush over to the fairy. "I am so sorry." I hurry to grab as many mushrooms as I can and place them back in the little crate. "I'll pay you for them. How much?" I stand up and pat my pockets, belatedly realizing I have no money. Nor do I know how money works in Oz.

A hand slides into my vision over my shoulder, holding a bag that jingles with coins. "This should cover it," Matteo says, dropping the bag by the crate.

Damn. So much for my dignified exit. I give the fairy a smile and continue on my way. Matteo tries to catch my hand, but I yank it away and continue after Twig.

"Daci, wait," he calls.

I turn around long enough to give him a look that would burn him alive if I could breathe dragon fire.

He stops with a grimace and lets me continue without him. By the time I reach the bottom of the hill, Twig is already there batting a rock around on the ground. I'm more out of breath than I should be, except I spent the time practically stomping in frustration whenever I thought about the mate thing.

I have a mate. Someone I was destined to be with. Someone I should love unconditionally, and who should love me unconditionally. It's hard to even wrap my mind around it, because mates disappeared when magic did. But it explains so much. This entire time my soul knew Nicolai was safe, despite the fact that he's my enemy. I never once questioned whether he'd keep me safe. He always felt . . . right.

I have a mate. But he wants nothing to do with me. And he kept it from me. Despite me admitting I wanted him, and us having sex—great sex—he still kept it from me. That's what hurts the most. Realizing that the person who is supposed to be my mate could hurt me so badly is like reliving my mom leaving me. The abandonment I ignore daily rears its ugly head.

It hurts. It hurts so fucking badly.

Twig and I walk to the lake and wait for the boat to float ashore. Unfortunately, it's not fast enough to beat the guys, and they join me shortly after, so I'll be stuck with them on the tiny craft. But I'll be damned if I have to sit next to one of them.

As soon as the boat touches the shore, I hop in. Twig follows me and perches on the first bench facing the lake. The guys are silent as they climb in, but I feel the presence like an added weight on my shoulders. When the craft takes off, Twig hops from my lap and climbs onto the edge of the boat. I watch him carefully because I have no idea if he can swim. It would be just my luck if he were to fall in and drown right now.

He sticks his tail in the water and turns to look at me. I swear he's grinning when he whips it into the air, spraying me with droplets. I screech and duck, but it's no use. Cold water slides down my face and makes me shiver. Matteo chuckles behind me, and my shoulders tense. Twig is a smart dragon. He can read the tension between all of us, and he's been sticking close to my side. When Matteo laughs, Twig turns toward him and narrows his golden eyes. That shuts Matteo up. I give Twig a grateful smile and a scratch under his chin. At least I have him, and I know he'll remain loyal to me.

Twig spends the rest of the ride swishing his tail back and forth, and I do my best to ignore the looming presence of the Tin Man, Scarecrow, and Lion behind me. When the boat finally docks, Twig and I climb out, and I impatiently wait for the guys. I don't know the direction I'm supposed to go. And I hate that I still have to rely on them for something.

Matteo pulls out the map and spreads it on the ground. While Nicolai and Leith crouch next to him to study it, I wander a short distance away, enjoying the beautiful rolling green hills. I avert my gaze from the yellow brick road. While it wasn't an easy journey here, there are memories I made on that road that I'd rather not think about right now.

"We need to go southwest," Matteo says, and I turn around enough to see which direction he's pointing.

As soon as I get the information I need, I take off without them. They won't be far behind me, but at least I get a semblance of being on my own. Away from the guys who hurt me. Unfortunately, the farther we go, the more my mind keeps traveling back to them. I find myself simmering in a stew of anger, shame, and abandonment. So, I turn my focus to my supposed magic.

Twig waddles ahead of me, occasionally flapping his wings

and jumping. The most he's able to lift himself is a couple feet before he crashes back to the ground. He's determined though, and that's better than what he was able to do a few days ago.

Hey, Twig, I say in my mind. Nothing. I purse my lips and try again. *Twiiiiig. Can you hear me?* His butt wiggles as he walks, but he doesn't acknowledge that he heard me. If talking to the dragons involves magic, shouldn't I feel something inside of me? Some kind of spark or ember or something that indicates magic? Wouldn't I have to use that to talk to him?

I take a deep breath and roll my shoulders back. I've never been good at meditating, but this walk is pretty mindless. Maybe I can focus inward while walking. Emptying my mind is impossible. Even if I were to close my eyes, that only increases the presence of the guys behind me. I look at the sky, hoping the even terrain doesn't trip me.

Blue. Blue as far as I can see. Only blue. Blue. Blue. Blue. Twig is green. But other dragons will probably be different colo—nope. Quit wandering, stupid mind. Empty. Like the sky. Empty. Breathe in. Breathe out. Feel each breath. Feel my heart thumping. Thump. Thump. Empty. Breathe. Thump.

I stumble when a burst of warmth pulses inside me. It was only there for a second, but I swear I felt it. *Do it again, Daci. Empty. Breathe. Thump.* Nothing. *Again. Empty. Breathe. Thump.* Nothing.

I growl in frustration, kicking at the grass as I walk. Twig turns around to look at me and quickly hops to my feet. I scoop him into my arms, grunting at his weight. "I'm going to figure this out," I whisper so only he can hear me. "I'm going to figure out how to use my magic, and I'm going to save the dragons."

His golden eyes, so wise beyond his years, shine brightly. He bumps his head against my forehead, almost like his way of telling me he believes in me. I kiss his nose and set him back down.

And I spend the rest of the day trying to find that warmth again.

I never do.

That night by the fire, I pull out my sketchbook and lie on my stomach. It amazes me I don't even think twice about the possible bugs crawling in the dirt beneath me. I've come a long way on this journey. The flickering of the flames isn't the best light source, but my fingers have been itching to draw all day. The landscape is so beautiful, and I want to capture it.

However, as soon as my pencil starts to scratch across the page, I know I'm not drawing a landscape. Eyes take form. Human eyes. I fill the page with eye, after eye, after eye. When I'm done, I hate to admit to myself that I can identify each one. They belong to Nicolai, Matteo, and Leith. Some are squinted like they're smiling or laughing. Some are closed. Others are open wide, windows to the soul. But each one is easily identifiable.

Frustrated with myself, I turn the page and try again. This next sketch starts to take form, and I grunt when I realize it looks a lot like Matteo. I flip the page again, almost ripping it in my agitation. When the next sketch starts to look like Leith, I stop. I flip back through the pages and progressively get more and more pissed. Each page is filled with something related to the guys.

I growl and in a burst of hurt and anger I stand and toss my sketchbook onto the flames. I don't stay to watch it burn. Instead, I walk away and let the fire burning inside of me keep me warm as I settle further away from the guys. I'm close enough to still feel safe, but far enough away to feel alone.

It's a feeling I'm used to. So why does it hurt so badly all of a sudden?

"We're coming up on the Living Wood," Matteo says a few days later.

I refrain from stating the obvious that I could tell by the forest getting closer and closer each mile we walked. I've said a total of ten words to them since we left the Emerald City. And I've slept apart from them as well. Twig has kept close to my side, sensing the emotions brewing inside of me.

I feel like I'm on a rollercoaster. One moment, my anger is so hot it could burn the world to the ground. The next, my heart aches like it's been cut open and bled dry. And in between, I strengthen my resolve and determination to not let them get the best of me. I'm not sure I'm succeeding, but I sure as hell won't give up.

"Let's try this again," I mutter to myself as I keep walking toward the woods. I take a deep breath and look at the sky, clearing my mind of everything. It's still hard to do, but the more I've practiced, the quicker the quiet settles in my mind.

I turn my focus inward, to the spot where I felt that burst of warmth. In my mind, I imagine my hands scooping deep inside of my belly. I imagine a pool of liquid that faintly glows reddish-orange puddling in my hands. It's warm, like the heat from a fire, but it doesn't burn me.

When the liquid begins to undulate, I force myself to not startle and keep my mind focused on the magic in my hands. It slowly coalesces into a small ball of light, burning a bright reddish-orange. It dances like a flame, waving back and forth. The warmth grows, spreading outward from my middle until I feel as if I'm standing in front of a bonfire. It's comforting. Welcoming.

Keeping my focus on the ball of fire, I send a thought into the ether. *Twig.*

The dragon bounding in front of me stops so suddenly, his ass flips over his head and he tumbles to the ground. He lies on his back and tips his head so he can look at me upside down. *Mama?*

I freeze in my tracks, one foot lifted mid-step. Mama? Is that what I am to him? Emotion swells in my chest, and I swallow the lump that forms in my throat. There is no stopping the tears that build along my lashes as I rush to him. He flips over and meets me halfway, hopping up and down. A laugh bubbles up, mixed with the tears that spill down my cheeks as I plop on the ground and scoop him into my arms.

I found my magic, I say to him.

His rough tongue scrapes lightly as he licks the tears off my cheeks. *Mama.* He buries his head in my neck, his breath warm against my skin. The wings on his back flutter happily, and I hold him tighter.

Yes. I am. Nothing has ever felt so right as this little dragon calling me his mom. Except maybe . . . I look up to find all three guys staring at me and Twig with confusion. No. I won't go there. I won't think about how right they all feel as well. Or how the connection I've always seemed to have with Nicolai is the same I have with Matteo and Leith. I *can't* go there.

They're staring at us, Twig.

The dragon lifts his head and turns a baleful glare on the guys. *I'll eat them for you. Just say the word.* His voice is a strange mixture of childlike growling, and combined with those words, I can't help but laugh.

Maybe later. I might need their help saving the dragon eggs. I set Twig down and push to my feet. *Come on. The sooner we get there, the sooner we can be done with them.* Even if I'm not sure I want to be done with them.

As we approach the Living Wood, uncertainty floods my veins. The trees loom ominously in front of us, a swath of darkness breaking up the green of Oz. Twisted trees with gnarled branches reach for the crooked and broken yellow brick road that disappears into the gloom. There are no leaves on the trees. Instead, all the leaves are littered on the ground, brown and dying. There is no sound except a faint wailing wind that rattles the branches and makes them knock into each other with hollow-sounding thuds.

I stop a distance away from the edge of the forest, but the shadows still fall across me. A chill shivers down my spine and I rub my arms to ward off the eerie sensation of being watched. Behind me, the guys are talking between themselves, most likely planning the best path to get past this obstacle.

I peer into the darkness. It's so complete, I can barely see anything. But I swear I see yellow eyes watching from behind a few of the trees. I take a step closer, and they wink out. Maybe I was imagining things. I look at the tree closest to me and frown. Is that a face on the trunk? Drawn to the vision, I take one more step toward the Living Wood.

Before I know what's happening, something whips out from the forest and wraps around my middle. Then the ground disappears from under me and my stomach dips as I'm lifted high into the air. My strangled scream is cut off as the pressure around my middle tightens.

I frantically look around and find myself being held by a branch. My nails crack and break when I try to dig them into the wood around my waist, but it's no use. All that seems to do is piss the tree off even more. It squeezes harder and I gasp.

Mama! Twig shouts in my head at the same time Matteo screams, "Daci!" He reaches up with one hand like he could grab me and pull me down. Twig takes a step closer to the woods, and Leith jumps forward, grabbing him and holding him tightly so he doesn't get snatched as well.

I glance to the ground, at the three guys standing with mixed expressions of anger and fear, and I swallow thickly. My vision swims when I realize how high I am and my skin prickles with a cold sweat. I squeeze my eyes shut and bite back a whimper. So high. So fucking high. If the tree drops me, it's going to hurt.

"Stop moving, Daci!" Nicolai yells. "It's only going to make it squeeze harder."

Easy for you to say with both your feet firmly on the ground. I grit my teeth and take a deep breath, hoping to calm my racing heart and keep myself still.

"We're going to get you down, Daci. Don't worry." Matteo's face is pale, and he fists his hands against his stomach. He looks at Nicolai and says something, but I'm too high up to hear it.

Nicolai nods and takes a step back before shifting.

27

NICOLAI

Gods, there is nothing better than this. The only thing I miss about Oz is my magic and being able to shift. The wind blowing through my feathers as I climb high into the sky is better than any drug. But I don't have the time to revel in the euphoria of flying. Daciana's sounds of pain are clearly audible in my owl form and they focus me immediately.

Before flying into the woods, I study the branch around Daciana's waist. It's holding her tightly. I can see just how hard from this position, and the grimace on her face tells me it's starting to hurt. With one last look at the ground to make sure Mattie is ready, I fly straight for the tree holding Daciana.

I keep my head on a constant swivel, waiting for a branch to try to whack me out of the air. I've seen a bird hit by one of these things before, and it wasn't pretty. Feathers and guts went everywhere. I'd rather that not be my fate. I duck when a branch comes swinging my way, and swoop back up toward Daciana.

Her screams have stopped, and she's gone still as she watches me. I risk a look in her direction, and I swear I see worry gleaming in her eyes, but that can't be right. She fucking hates me, and I don't blame her. I deserve all of her hate. I don't let myself look long. These trees are fast, and I need to keep my focus.

While I dive-bomb the tree and dodge its branches, it slowly loosens its hold on Daciana. I check again to make sure Mattie is in position. With me distracting it, he's able to get closer to the trunk where Daciana will be dropped. But checking on Mattie almost costs me.

"Nicolai! Look out!"

Daciana's shout gives me the warning I need to tuck in my wings and drop fast, narrowly avoiding a branch. It was close though. Too close. I felt the bark skim across my tail feathers. I don't have time to reflect on it, or on how Daciana called my name, on how she saved me. She whimpers, and I watch as the branch holding her loosens enough for her to slip through. She falls, a scream ripping from her throat. I keep flying, keep distracting the tree long enough for Mattie to catch her and step away into safety.

Once they are out of reach of the trees, I fly out of the woods and swoop down, shifting before I land. With two feet on the ground, I take one step toward Daciana, arm outstretched and her name on my tongue, but I freeze.

She's already pulling away from Mattie, despite how she's shaking. It's impressive, really, to watch her don the mask. She closes her eyes and takes a breath, shoving everything down into the darkest parts of herself. When she opens her eyes, the DeRosa princess is back.

I don't like how much I hate the sight of it. Watching the mask slowly come off during our journey to the Emerald City was one of the things that endeared me to her. I watched as piece by piece the real Daciana was revealed. And there was no denying how much her soul spoke to mine. I don't know how I kept my distance for so long. And now I've fucked it all up.

Daci approaches Leith and takes Twig from him. She looks at the dragon and whispers to him before kissing the top of his head. Something has happened between them, and if I were to guess, I'd say she finally learned how to use her magic to communicate with him. And she did it without help from anyone. My chest fills with pride, and that pisses me off. And getting mad that I'm pissed only sends me into a further spiral. Why can't I make up my mind? Do I want her or not? Is it too late to change my mind?

"Let's go," I say gruffly, unable to keep my anger at myself from creeping into my voice.

Mattie watches Daci with as much desperation as I feel. But

he shakes his head and takes a drink of water. "I'll go first. Leith and Daci follow behind me. Nico, you bring up the rear. We're the only ones with night vision, so we need to make sure they stay on the path."

Leith waits until Daci glances at him, and he signs, "We have to stay quiet in there. Let Mattie get us through."

Daci nods but turns away from him. He looks just as crestfallen as the rest of us. I'm surprised the guys don't hate me for this. It's all my fault for not telling her the truth and not letting them tell her either. They kept it a secret for me, and now it's backfiring on all of us.

Mattie takes a breath before he begins to sing. The language is fae, but I don't bother trying to translate it in my head. Of course, as a Faun, he has a beautiful voice. It's the only thing that can get us through the Living Wood without being attacked. His song will tame the wildness of the trees.

The first step into the Living Wood is like taking a step into a dark cave. It's cooler without the sun. Even though there are no leaves on the branches, the sun doesn't reach the ground here. As Mattie's voice pierces the darkness, the trees still. Their branches quit swaying in the wind, and the clacking falls silent. Soon, Mattie's song is the only thing we can hear.

I split my attention between our surroundings and Daci's back. She's stiff and doing her best to avoid touching Leith. Her gaze remains on the ground in front of her, and she's probably trying to make sure she doesn't trip on anything. Twig's head swivels back and forth as he watches our surroundings from the safety of her arms.

Leith doesn't break his stride as he reaches over and gently tries to take Twig from Daci. She holds on tightly for a moment, but eventually she gives in. Carrying him for so long would be hard for her. Since I first saw the dragon in Girasole, he's doubled in size. He has to weigh close to twenty pounds by now. Daci's eyes are frozen emeralds as she looks at Leith. There is nothing in her gaze even remotely like the way she used to look at us. And the crestfallen expression on Leith's face is mirrored on my own.

I have a lot of time to think about things as we walk, and I wish I didn't. I have no idea how to repair what I broke between us. There wasn't much there to begin with, but I have a feeling her admitting to wanting both me and Mattie the other night was her way of telling us she has feelings for us. Or *had* feelings for us. I don't think it was purely because she wanted to have sex. Then I went and screwed that up.

But that night with her and Mattie was mind blowing. I'd been fighting the bond I felt in my chest this entire time in Oz, and I finally caved that night. The way it glowed inside of me, the pure happiness I felt with her, it terrified me. Because not only did I know I was keeping this secret from her, but I also knew I was one move away from giving in to the bond. And I wasn't ready for that.

Now, my chest aches. Thinking of how I hurt her, thinking of the distance she's put between all of us. It's like a chasm I don't think I can get across. I don't know how to repair that bridge. And it's that realization that tells me I've already lost. It doesn't matter how much I hate my mom for forcing the bond on me. It's there, and I want it. I want Daciana DeRosa.

I glance at Daci just in time to see her foot catch on a root. Without thinking, I reach out and grab her arm, yanking her back up. I don't let go though. Not until she turns around and meets my gaze in the darkness. My eyes are probably glowing eerily, but she stares straight into them, and she lets me see everything she's feeling.

Hurt. Betrayal. Heartbreak. Anger.

Hate.

I recoil at the ferocity of her stare. If we didn't have to be quiet, I'd try to say something. I don't know what I'd say, but I desperately want to smooth the turmoil I see in her gaze. It's probably a good thing I can't speak. I'd probably mess it all up even more.

When we finally get free of the Living Wood, Mattie's voice is hoarse. The trees are beginning to get restless, so when the light pierces the darkness, indicating we're safe, I heave a sigh of relief.

We make camp a few miles from the forest, and Mattie collapses, chugging water and wincing. "Holy shit, that hurts," he rasps.

"Don't talk," Leith signs. "We'll get a fire going, and I'll search for a topo fatato to find some healing tea leaves or something."

Daci wanders a ways off like she's done every night since the Emerald City. It makes me nervous, especially the closer we get to Morta's territory. In a couple nights, I'll have to tell her she can't do that anymore. I'm sure it will piss her off more.

As I get the fire going and Leith searches for a topo fatato, Mattie digs in his bag and pulls out Daci's sketchbook. After she tossed it in the flames, he jumped up to fish it out. It's only slightly scorched on the edges, and the inside pages are all intact. When we saw all the drawings of us, it only made my chest ache more. I refuse to look at any of them anymore. But Mattie looks through the stupid thing every night.

When Leith returns with a handful of leaves and gets water boiling, I break the silence. "Something isn't adding up," I say quietly, making sure my voice doesn't travel to Daci where she's settling down next to Twig.

"What do you mean?" Mattie whispers, probably the most he can manage at this point.

"Well, I know Daci is my mate. Even if my lovely mother hadn't told me, I feel it." I rub my chest absentmindedly. The glow isn't as bright as it was that night in Emerald City. But it's still there, and I take comfort in that. "But, you guys seem just as affected by her as I am."

Mattie stares unblinking at the fire, but he also rubs his chest. I've seen him do that a few times around her, and it's made me suspicious. Leith looks at me, and his expression is nothing short of shocked.

"You can't be saying what I think you're saying." His motions are rushed, making his signs more difficult to read.

I lean back and think through everything. "She immediately connected with you, Mattie. And while that's not entirely surprising, you act differently around her than you do anyone else you've ever been with."

Mattie nods slowly, still staring into the flames.

"And I don't think I even need to mention you, Leith. You've let her in where no one else has ever gotten. She's like a star all three of us have found ourselves orbiting around. You can't deny it."

Mattie finally looks up, his eyes shining. "I've felt . . . something. I don't know how to describe it other than a warmth in my chest."

At his words, Leith's head perks up. He looks back and forth between me and Mattie multiple times before finally signing, "No way."

My gaze drifts to Daci's sleeping form outside of the firelight. "I think all three of us are her mates."

The next day, I notice Mattie and Leith looking at Daci through a different lens. It's like they can finally put a name to what they've been feeling. Now, instead of the intense emotions they've had toward Daci without understanding why, they are seeing her as their mate. They now know why they would protect her above all else. They understand why they would destroy the world for her.

And she's not even acknowledging them.

"I'm sorry, guys," I say, swallowing my pride. "This is all my fault. You tried to talk sense into me but I was too stubborn to see it."

Mattie shakes his head. "There was no way you could have

known it would impact me and Leith too. Besides, you have your reasons. We can't fault you for that."

I nod, but it still sits uneasy with me. If I hadn't fucked up so badly, things might be very different right now. I don't have time to think about my mistakes though. In the distance, I notice a splash of red in the green fields of Oz.

"What is that?" I ask, looking at Mattie.

He squints, then frowns. "It looks like a flower field?" He pulls out the map and studies it. "There is nothing listed on the map about flowers. And seeing how big it is, there is no way it wouldn't be on the map."

I keep a close eye on it as we get closer. It doesn't take long for me to make out the type of flower. "Papaveri," I say, and immediately tense. "Papaveri are Morta's flowers. She leaves them on people's graves after she accepts their souls."

"Do you think it's a trap?" Leith signs.

"It's absolut—Daci, stop!" I take off after Daci, who is running as fast as she can toward the flowers.

Her laugh drifts back to me, and Twig bounds after her, tongue lolling from the side of his mouth. She's too far ahead though, and either can't hear me or is ignoring me. I push myself harder, but I already know I'm going to be too late.

She takes the first step into the papervero field, then the second. It's with pure joy on her face that she spins around and dances further into the flowers. I follow her, not even stopping to think about my actions. I need to get Daci out of there.

"Don't follow us!" I yell over my shoulder to Leith and Mattie. "Keep an eye out for danger!"

When I turn back around, I can't see Daci anywhere. I suck in a breath, and a cough tickles my throat. The air smells strange. Not like the usual sweet, sort of spicy scent of a papavero. I frown but keep scanning the flowers for any sign of Daci.

It doesn't take long for my limbs to grow heavy. My movements turn sluggish, and so do my thoughts. It's like wading through a pool of honey. I open my mouth to yell, either for Daci or the guys, but all I do is cough. My legs can no longer hold me up. They shake and tremble, and I fall to the ground.

I catch a glimmer of gold just a few feet in front of me. Daci's hair. I crawl on all fours, and each inch takes all of my effort. Twig stands next to her, golden eyes wide with worry, and he flaps his little wings uselessly. When he sees me, he jumps over her body and rushes to me.

He takes my hand in his mouth and tries to pull me to Daci, but he's too small and I'm too heavy. I can't go any farther. My body won't obey me. With my last bit of energy, I push myself forward and reach for Daci's hand. My fingertips graze hers, and my eyes close.

28
DACIANA

The world is fuzzy, and I feel like I'm floating. The last thing I remember is fog and the heaviness of exhaustion. I couldn't walk any farther and I sat down in the field of beautiful red papaveri. Now, when I look around, it's like the world is disappearing. I rub my eyes, but it doesn't help. I don't see Twig anywhere, but there is a path through the flowers that I hadn't noticed before.

Pushing to my feet, I walk along the path, and a strange sensation in my middle makes me pause. It's like during and after the fire, when Leith needed me. It's the same feeling I get around Nicolai and Mattie. Are the guys here with me? Do I want to find them? Another sharp tug and I decide to follow my instincts.

It appears to be a maze. A papavero field maze. I trail my fingertips over the soft red petals, making the flowers sway on the stems. It's gorgeous. A never-ending field of papaveri. I think I got my love for flowers from my mom. She'd spend hours upon hours in the garden outside our house. Tending to the roses and the beehive were her favorite things, until she became too weak to do so.

The path twists and turns, and I often have to double back when I come to a dead end. At first, I wander aimlessly and just enjoy the peaceful moment. I don't let myself think about the strangeness of the situation. But eventually, the quiet becomes too heavy. And the tugging in my middle becomes too incessant.

I let the pull lead me where it wants to go. I don't know which of the guys will be at the end, but I know one of them will. Why is it that I have this connection with all three of them? I get why I'd feel this way for Nicolai. But I feel the same way for Matteo and Leith.

The tugging is getting stronger, and I slow my steps as I round a corner. Nicolai is on the other side looking harried. He's breathing heavily as if he's been running, and his eyes are wild. Strands of his dark hair fall in every direction from running his hands through it.

"Daci," he breathes, taking a step closer and reaching for me. "Are you okay?"

I step back automatically and his face falls. "I'm fine," I say primly, lifting my chin.

He looks around then back at me. "We're in a dream-like state," he explains. "The papaveri are a trap set by Morta. She cast a sleeping spell on them."

Ah. That explains the weird wispy look and the way my body feels like it could float away. It also explains why I can't seem to dredge up the fear I know I should feel. "Then how do we get out of here?" I have no doubt he'll yell at me when we wake up for rushing headlong into the flowers without second thought.

"To break a sleeping spell, we have to admit a truth," he says, looking me in the eyes. "It will take us back to Mattie, Leith, and Twig."

"Twig was with me." I frown. "How come he isn't here?"

"I don't think the magic of the papaveri can affect a dragon."

I nod like that makes all the sense in the world, but magic is still a mystery to me. Crossing my arms, I stare at Nicolai. "So, what's your truth, Tin Man?"

He frowns when I call him that, but he steps closer and scans my face. "I'm sorry," he says simply. "I was scared. My mom has controlled my life from the very beginning. And my dad isn't any better, as I'm sure you understand. It's why I get tattoos and piercings. It's one thing I have control over." He shakes his head and lifts a hand like he's going to reach out to me, but he changes his mind and lets it drop. "I didn't tell you because I never intended on acting on it. I didn't want to give in to my mom's designs. But I couldn't keep fighting the attraction I felt toward you. I hurt you and I regret that more than anything. I *want* to be your mate, Daci."

I stare at him. His words flow over me and I listen to each one, cataloging how it makes my heart beat faster and faster, and not in a good way. My chest grows tight, and I find myself squeezing my hands into fists until my nails cut painfully into my palms. The anger rises like a tide that sweeps everything else away. I understand why he didn't tell me, and I can appreciate that. I know what it's like to not have control over your life and want to hang on to every bit of control that you can.

But the part I can't forgive is that he slept with me. He listened to my truth. He heard me say I wanted him. And he slept with me without saying a single word. If I hadn't found out from Decima that he was my mate, I'm not sure he ever would have told me.

"Do you want my truth?" I ask, without giving him any reaction to what he told me.

He nods and swallows, looking slightly scared. Good.

I cross my arms over my chest and stare him straight in the eyes. "Ever since my mom died, I've never felt truly at home. My dad does his best, but his main priority is the Camorra. I may have lived in the mansion my entire life, but it was never a home after my mom's death." I swallow back the tears that burn up my throat as I think about my mom. "Then I came here. I discovered Oz. And most importantly, I found you. I found you and instinctively, I think I knew what you were. After years of aimless wandering, I felt home again." My voice cracks on the word *home*, and I close my eyes, feeling the tears building on my lashes. "Then you betrayed me," I whisper, opening my eyes and letting him see all the anger and hurt. "And now, I'm back to wandering. Searching for a place to call mine." I harden my tone and straighten my spine, practically spitting my next words. "You say you want to be my mate, but I want *nothing* to do with you."

I have one second to see the devastation on Nicolai's face and marvel that someone so expressionless could look so heartbroken. Then the world explodes.

When I wake up, I immediately know something is off. I'm . . . empty. I roll over and bring my knees to my chest, groaning. Everything hurts. My body, my head, my chest. It's as if I've been beaten half to death. After taking a few deep breaths, I open my eyes. I'm in a sparse forest, but I can already tell the forest isn't in Oz, and not just because it's lacking the otherworldly aspect.

I know I'm not in Oz anymore because my magic is gone. My body is cold without it, like that spark kept me warm. And inside, I'm hollow. My heartbeat echoes in an empty cavern.

I look around, gasping for breath that doesn't fill my lungs enough. Why am I here? What happened? I push to my feet, ignoring the way my body screams in pain, and I stumble through the woods in a frenzy, gaze constantly searching. The longer I go without any sign of Twig or the guys, the harsher my breathing becomes until I stagger to the nearest tree. The bark is rough under my fingers, and I curl them, digging my nails in, uncaring of the dirt that lodges under them.

"Twig?" I rasp. Frantically, I turn my head this way and that, looking for any sign of the baby dragon. The forest is still. Not even a breeze blows by to rustle the leaves above my head. My throat burns as I swallow, and I suck in a ragged breath. "Mattie! Leith! Nico!" The only answer is my hoarse call echoing back to me.

My knees tremble and I fall to the forest floor. I don't know what happened. One moment I was in Oz, the next I'm back in Girasole. Something went terribly wrong. I choke on a sob. Where's Twig? Is he still back in Oz? Will he be okay without me? I clutch at my chest and curl into a ball. Why does it hurt so bad?

Why does it feel like something vital has been ripped from my body, leaving the wound open and bleeding?

After what feels like an eternity, I'm able to draw in a somewhat steady breath. I look up and see my house in the distance, the garden sitting quietly between us. I hope for a second that it's a dream, like the papavero field, but everything is too crisp in my vision. There is no fog or wavering images. It's real. I'm not sure what else to do, so I push myself to my feet, groaning in pain. The silver slippers are still on my feet. Still shining as brightly as the day Nona put them on.

I'm in a daze as I stagger past the garden and toward the servants' door in the back of the house. I have no clue how long I was gone, but I'm hoping I can sneak up to my room and figure something out. Of course, I have no such luck.

As soon as I step into the kitchen, every single gaze turns to me. Their reactions are all the same. Shock, surprise, joy.

"Miss Daciana!" Mara shouts, breaking the silence. "Oh! What's happened ta ye? Where ha' ye bin? Are ye okay?"

She bombards me with questions, and I can only stare blankly and blink at her concern. Panic crawls up my spine, slowly climbing higher and higher. Each inch makes it harder to breathe. I'm going to explode in a messy pile of anxiety and fear if I don't get it under control.

Stella, the head of our housekeeping staff, shoos Mara away. "That's enough, girl. Give the miss some space." Stella looks me over with concern, then wipes my cheeks with her thumbs. It's only then that I realize steady silent tears flow down my face. Stella takes my arm and gently leads me from the kitchen. "Let's get you upstairs to the bath. I'll let your father know you've returned. He's been worried sick."

The next few hours pass in a blur. I'm aware of Mara returning and helping me bathe and wash my hair. Her endless chatter is nothing more than sounds in my head. All my attention is on keeping my heart from beating out of my chest and taking steady, even breaths. Each time my thoughts travel to Twig or the guys, I lose all the progress I made at keeping calm, and I have to start all over again.

The warm water of the bath does nothing to banish the chill that seems to have permanently settled inside of me. I can't stop my body from shivering, a few of the tremors so violent they make me slide further into the tub. How easy would it be to let myself slip all the way under the water?

I don't even realize Mara has gotten me out of the tub and into a comfy pair of pajamas. Somehow, she gets me to my room and situated in my bed, while Stella brings me dinner. I'm not hungry, though. Just cold. I can't stop shivering, so I lie down and drag the covers to my chin, swallowing against the bile that climbs up my throat at the scent of the food on the bedside table.

As soon as they leave, my dad barges in despite Stella telling him I need rest. I quickly close my eyes and even out my breathing, praying he falls for the act. The edge of the bed dips as he sits, and he rests his palm on my shoulder.

"Daci, mi rosa," he says roughly.

He hasn't called me his rose since my mom died. Tears threaten to give me away, but I somehow manage to hold them back. He sighs heavily and tucks my wet hair behind my ear before leaving.

The door closes behind him, and I curl in on myself and let the tears fall.

29

DACIANA

The next three days last for months. Time crawls as I mope in my room. I refuse to talk to anyone, even my dad. I'm pretty sure everyone thinks something horrible happened to me. And I'm not positive my dad isn't trying to place the blame on the Morellis just as a reason to fight them. I don't have the energy to tell him otherwise, not that he'd listen to me anyway.

If it weren't for the silver slippers and the ragged appearance of my nails, I'd almost think everything that had happened was a dream. I spend all my time trying to figure out what went wrong. Why was I sent back to Girasole? Nicolai said I needed to give him a truth, so I did. I just don't understand. And I have no idea how to get back to Oz without him.

It's not just the lack of magic that's making me feel empty inside. I miss Twig. I miss him so much, I feel sick to my stomach. It's hard to drag myself out of bed knowing he won't be greeting me. Eating food is impossible because I know he won't be there begging for some. Missing him is like missing a limb.

If I'm being honest with myself, I miss the guys, too.

I got used to their presence. Their solid comfort and safety that was always with me. Even after the Emerald City, when I refused to acknowledge them, they were there. Always behind me. Always waiting to step in if I needed help. And it's not just Nicolai I miss. I know he's my mate, and his absence hurts like something was torn from my chest. But Matteo and Leith hurt just as bad. Again, I wonder why. Why do I feel this way toward all three of them? Especially after how much they hurt me.

I can't go on like this. Empty. Alone. Missing pieces of myself that make me whole. I need to go back. I need to save the dragons. I need . . . I need *them.* And what will happen to Twig without me? If there is no dragon guardian, there is nothing to keep him alive. I could never live with myself knowing I let him die.

As soon as it's dark, I put on an old pair of gym shoes and a black hoodie. When the house is quiet, I sneak out. The walk to the Field is long, but I walked so much in Oz, this feels like a breeze. The Field is dark and eerie, but as soon as I step foot in the tall grasses, a sense of peace overcomes me. It's not complete, but it's like a small portion of my broken insides have been smoothed over.

I walk through the grass, heading for where I thought we went through the portal. But even if I find the spot, I don't have magic to open it. Still, I try. I walk around aimlessly, silently begging Nona or Decima to hear me, to let me through. Nothing happens. Each step I take makes my heart sink lower and lower until I have nothing left in me. I fall to the ground and let more tears fall. My heart hurts so bad, it physically feels like my chest will crack open and I'll bleed out.

If I can't return to Oz, what will happen?

I sit in the Field, letting the bits of magic this space possesses ease my soul. It makes me feel close to them, like I could just close my eyes and when I open them, they'll all be there, waiting for me. I let my tears run their course before I stand and trudge back to my house just as the sun is peeking over the horizon. Before I can make it to my room, I run into my dad on the stairs.

"Daci," he says, surprised to see me. "Where were you?"

"I went for a walk." My voice is lifeless even to my own ears. I can't fake it, no matter how much I want to.

He frowns. "Get cleaned up and meet me in the council room. We need to talk."

I don't even have it in me to find an excuse. I failed. I wasn't enough to save the dragons.

After I listlessly clean up, I head to the study. The persistent layer of fog that has settled over me is almost comforting at this point. It helps keep me numb. And numb is better than feeling . . . everything.

I'm not surprised to find my dad's most trusted friends seated around the long table. A sinking feeling settles in my gut, but I gather the fog around me tighter and ignore it. Once I'm seated next to my dad, he begins.

"As you all know, Daciana was kidnapped by the Morellis," he says sternly.

A heavy weight presses down on my shoulders. I figured this is what he would claim. I could stop this here. Tell him the Morellis had nothing to do with this, but it wouldn't do any good. Once my dad has made up his mind, it's impossible to change it.

"We have video evidence of the Morelli heir accosting Daci at Gormond Park with his two thug friends," my dad continues.

What? They have footage of me meeting with Nicolai? That shakes some of the fog from me. I glance at my dad, and he pats my hand soothingly. With each word my dad utters, I climb from the depths of my despair.

My dad pulls a picture out of a folder in front of him and holds it up for everyone to see. It is indeed from the night I met with Nicolai, but the angle worked to my advantage. There's a tree in the way, so you can only see me standing in front of Nico when I attempted to stop him from leaving. There is no sign of Twig.

I gape at my dad. How the hell did he get this? How did he even know to look at the cameras from the park?

"Of course, we can't let this stand. They attacked first, and we will retaliate." He looks at me, and there is nothing fatherly in his expression. Only the businessman, the Camorra leader, he has become. "Daci, tell us what you can of your captivity."

I stare at him blankly. He wants me to share with all these men what happened to me? What if I had truly been kidnapped? What if I had been beaten and raped? My dad thinks I would share this private information with all these men?

What happened to him caring about me being back? Where

did that man go? All he's happy about is that he thinks he can get information from me on how to take the Morellis down. I swallow, because I do indeed have information that would crumple them. Giorgia Morelli. Nico's half-sister. But I would never share that.

The knife cuts deep as I realize the role I truly play in my dad's life. While I always knew, there's something about this situation that brings everything to light. One would think a father would be more concerned about his daughter's safety after she disappeared. But, instead, he's going to exploit it. I'm a tool. Not even a weapon. Just a tool to be used so he can get what he wants.

It has been this way for as long as I can remember. He used me first as a cute little girl to play the innocent child who accidentally stumbled into meetings to overhear information. Then as the young woman to spread her legs for our family's advantage. The thought is sickening. And I've been complacent in it this entire time. Never trying to stand up for myself. Only going along with everything because I didn't know what else to do. Because I thought it was what I was supposed to do.

The fog evaporates into smoke as a spark ignites in my chest. My anger slowly fans the flames until a raging inferno billows inside of me. My hands shake when I place them on the table and push to my feet. "You have no idea what you're talking about," I say quietly, the venom in my tone clearly audible, and I walk from the room. Normally, I'd be worried about what my insubordination would do, but I don't care anymore. I'm not going to play into my father's hands.

In my room I fall to my knees, grabbing a pillow from my bed and screaming into it. I scream out all my hurt—from my dad, from the guys—I scream out all of my anger, betrayal, and desperation. I meant it when I told Nico I never really felt at home here. The lack of nurturing from my father, and the life of a Camorra princess, created an environment that was cold and lonely. My mom took all the love and warmth with her when she died.

On shaking feet, I walk to the desk along my wall. The piece of furniture is a massive wooden thing, old and fancy. It was a gift from my dad when I started drawing. I stand in front of it and close my eyes, breathing deeply in an attempt to ease my trembling, before I grab the edges and pull. The thing barely moves, but I don't give up. As soon as there is enough room to get my fingers between it and the wall, I wedge them in and use every ounce of strength I possess.

Inch by inch, the desk moves. When it's far enough from the wall for me to fit behind, I drop to my knees and scan the ground. It's there. Where I always knew it would be if I only cared to look. The necklace my mom gave me the night before she died. The golden bee pendant on a delicate golden chain.

My fingers shake as I pick it up. The chain is broken where I yanked it from my neck. I sit back and stare at it. Time hasn't affected it at all. It still shines like it's brand new. I've held on to my anger for so long now. When I was younger, it was hard for me to understand why my mom lied to me. Why she didn't just tell me the truth. I understand now that it was her way of protecting me, of trying to preserve my innocence.

But she could have told me she wasn't doing well. Instead of promising me she'd see me in the morning, she could have told me. I could have spent that last night with her saying goodbye. I would have grown up without that feeling of abandonment that always lingers like a weight on my shoulders. Instead, I wrapped myself in anger like a cloak to protect myself from the hurt. But living with that anger took a toll on me. Now, when I think about my mom's death, all I feel is exhausted. Is it fair of me to continue to be angry at my mom for leaving me? I know she didn't choose to get sick.

How different would my life have been if my mom hadn't died? Maybe this place would have felt more like a home. Maybe I wouldn't have been used like a tool and instead loved like a daughter.

Or maybe I never would have felt at home anywhere. Because maybe home isn't a place.

Even Oz wasn't home, despite the comfort I felt there. If I truly think about it, I don't think it would matter where I go. It wasn't until the safety and care I received from Nico, Mattie, and Leith while in Oz that I felt a semblance of belonging. Maybe it's just the mate bond between me and Nico. But that doesn't explain what I have with Mattie and Leith. Or why, deep inside, I don't think I'll ever be home unless I'm with all three of them. And, of course, Twig.

Twig. Images of the guys taking care of him along the journey pop into my head. Mattie carrying Twig on his back. Leith throwing sticks for Twig to fetch. Even Nico always making sure Twig was fed. Even though I'm sure I was a handful and needed lots of looking out for, they always made sure to keep an extra eye on Twig. Fuck. Why does that do funny things to my insides? Why do I picture the four of us raising a bunch of dragons together? The realization slams into me so hard, I gasp for breath.

Home *isn't* a place. Home is wherever *they* are.

What was it Nona said when she gave me the silver slippers? Besides giving me the power to hatch the dragon eggs, they would always lead me home. At the time, I thought that meant they were a way to get back to Girasole. But they aren't. Those silver slippers are a way to get back to my guys. My home.

I push to my feet and throw the closet door open, praying Mara didn't toss the shoes. I find them pushed to the back of the bottom shoe shelf and my hand shakes as I grab them. Wasting no time, I put them on and run.

I run for the Field. For Oz. For my guys. For my home.

30
LEITH

I stand with Mattie and watch Nico follow Daci into the papavero field. What kind of trap could Morta have set? It's killing me to wait here and do nothing when Daci could be in trouble. Ever since Nico suggested Daci could be our mate, a missing puzzle piece clicked into place.

There is zero doubt in my mind that Daciana DeRosa is my mate.

I have never been big on physical touch. But after my father locked Landon and me in the cellar, I went five years without it. The most I ever got was sitting shoulder to shoulder with Luca. When my father beat my mother and killed my twin, when my mother turned her back on me, I think something inside of me broke.

All I knew for so many years of my life, the most important years of a child's life, was pain and suffering. It took me a long time to learn that touch does not equal pain, but I've never been able to shake the discomfort I get when someone touches me.

Mattie and Nico are different. I've never trusted anyone as much as I trust them, and still I prefer them to not touch me. But with Daci, I find myself craving her touch. When I saw the burned body of that child in the village, Daci's hand on my cheek brought me back from my dark thoughts. When she hugged me in the woods, the ghosts of my past disappeared. And when I let her lie with me that night, my mind quieted enough for me to actually sleep.

There has always been something about Daci that has given me comfort and calmed the storm that always seems to rage inside of me. I wondered what it was, and now I know. But now I'm standing here, doing nothing, and my instincts are screaming at me to run into the field and find her.

Mattie is just as jittery next to me. He's bouncing on his toes, eyes scanning one end of the flower field to the other. "How long do we wait?" he asks.

I don't answer because I don't know. Nico would want us to wait here until he gets back, no matter how long that takes. But Mattie and I won't last that long. With each minute that passes, my anxiety grows until it's lodged in my chest, constricting like boa and suffocating me.

Twig returns and Mattie and I take a step forward, but it's only him. He keeps looking back at the flowers with droopy ears. He starts to pace back and forth in front of us, his tail swishing angrily behind him. Every once in a while he'll huff, and a small puff of smoke curls from his nose.

"I can't wait much longer," Mattie says as he rolls his neck like he's trying to shake off an unsettling feeling.

I still don't bother to answer, because he knows I'm in the same boat. Besides, my fists are clenched so tightly, I don't think I can relax them enough to sign.

After another few minutes, motion bursts from the papavero field. A brown owl climbs high into the sky. Mattie and I both tense as Nico flies over the flowers. We hold our breath, watching him make one loop, two loops, three. Then he turns toward us and my heart sinks.

Nico shifts and lands in front of us. His eyes are wild as he looks around. "Did you see her?"

"Not since she walked in the field. What's going on, Nico?" Mattie asks, his voice trembling slightly.

"It was a sleeping spell," Nico explains hurriedly, continuously spinning in a slow circle, searching. "I met her in the dreamscape, and like you have to do to break a sleeping spell, we admitted a truth," he says. Mattie and I nod impatiently. We know what sleeping spells are and how to break them. "I . . . I think she lied. I think she wanted to hurt me as badly as I hurt her."

I close my eyes, feeling my body sway as his words sink in. If she lied, who knows where she was transported to. There is no way to know, no way to track her. She would have just disappeared.

"What the fuck!" Mattie screams, pulling at his locs. He looks around helplessly. "What do we do now?"

"I'm going to keep searching, but I don't think it will be of much use." Nico takes off without another word, shifting and flapping rapidly to gain height.

I don't bother to watch him. I already know she's gone. We hurt her, so it doesn't surprise me that she would want to hurt us back. Even if she didn't understand the severity of lying under a sleeping spell, any harsh words she could have spoken to Nico were well deserved.

Twig hangs his head and his wings flutter pathetically. I scoop him into my arms and he buries his head in my neck, breathing his hot breath against my skin. He's gotten heavier, but I don't put him down as I turn around and head back the way we came.

Twig has grown despondent. It's been two days since Daci disappeared, and he hasn't left my room in the Emerald City. He barely moves from his spot on the foot of the bed, watching the door, waiting. I have to force him to eat and carry him outside to do his business. When I bring him back in, he returns to his watchful position.

I'm almost as bad as he is. We spent the first day trying to think of ways to find Daci, but we came up empty handed. Decima was our only hope, and she's off in another part of the realm dealing with something. After that first day of failure, I've kept myself to my room with Twig.

Mattie joins me every morning and we sit in silence, lost in our own thoughts. When the sun sets, he returns to his room. Nico spends all his time flying over the city and surrounding lands to the point where he's almost collapsed from exhaustion. And his attitude has been shit. Not that I can blame him. We're all running on a short fuse. It's like without Daci, we've forgotten how to exist.

"I feel empty," Mattie says quietly, staring out the window.

"Like you're missing something important," I sign in agreement.

"Yeah." He rubs his chest, and I know exactly what he's describing.

That spot where a golden warmth pulsed has gone cold. A gaping wound that won't stop bleeding. And unless we get Daci back, I don't think it will ever stop. I have run through a thousand scenarios on how and where to look for her, but I keep coming to three conclusions.

One, she'll make her way back to the Emerald City if she can. Two, she has made the decision to not come back to us at all. And three, she's unable to return. And if it's the third option, I don't know what to do about it without knowing where she is.

"There really isn't any tracking spell we can use?" I sign for the hundredth time.

Mattie rubs a hand down his face, as exhausted as I feel. "Decima is the only one who can help us, and who knows when she'll be back."

I close my eyes and let my head thump against the wall. Staring out the window all day has yielded nothing. Even though we don't stop. Either we'll see Daci returning, or we'll see Decima. But I'm losing hope.

"Fuck!" I sign, standing in a burst of angry energy. "How can we ever call ourselves her mates if we just stand around like this and do *nothing*?"

"What the hell are we supposed to do without knowing where she is?"

"I don't know." My movements are agitated and sharp, just like my emotions. "We should check Girasole, Villabosco, the places she's been to in Oz."

"How the hell do we get there? It will take us forever, not to mention the bridge across the damn canyon is broken." Mattie sighs in frustration, tugging his locs back jerkily. "If we wait for Decima, she should be able to give us an idea."

Fuck, he's right. And I hate that he's right because it means sitting and waiting and feeling useless. A low whine draws my attention to Twig. "Is it just me, or are his scales looking duller than usual?" I ask Mattie.

"Yeah," he says, quietly. "I don't think he's acting like this purely from missing Daci. His health is declining already. I don't think she's in Oz anymore."

My heart clenches and I have to take a deep breath to keep from falling on the ground. Without her, Twig will die. There will be no more dragons. And I'm not so sure Mattie, Nico, and I will survive either.

On the third day without Daci, I'm carrying Twig through the palace gardens, trying to get him some fresh air. He hasn't eaten anything today, and I haven't been able to make him. He's barely opened his eyes long enough to look at me. The dark emerald color of his scales has turned more sickly looking, almost as if there is a brownish tint to them. Like they are dying as he does.

Hang in there, buddy, I think. *Don't give up yet.* It's hard to sound sincere when I'm losing hope.

A flutter of wings draws my attention to Nico as he shifts and lands in the garden, grasping the back of a bench to keep from falling over. His face is pale, and his hair hangs limply on his head. He's barely able to stand straight.

"You should rest," I sign numbly around Twig in my arms. Everything is numb lately.

He shakes his head. "I can't. I'm going to eat then go back out there."

"I know you blame yourself for this, but killing yourself won't solve anything."

"You don't know anything," he mutters.

I lay Twig in the grass in a patch of sunshine, hoping to warm him up. His inner fire has gone out, and he's cold to the touch instead of warm like he usually is. "I know you're blaming yourself for not telling her. I know you blame yourself that Mattie and I are going through this. I know—"

"You don't know anything, Leith!" he shouts. "Just because you're so observant, doesn't mean you've pegged me. So keep your mouth shut about me."

I take a step forward, my own anger rising at his words, but before I can reply, a soft voice floats to us from the doorway.

"Please don't fight."

I whip my head in that direction, my heart stuttering to a stop. And there she is. My mate. Beautiful, healthy, and very real. I fall to my knees, heedless of the pain, and blink tears from my eyes.

"Daci," Nico breathes roughly. He takes a step toward her and stops.

She looks at him with a hard expression that makes his knees buckle. She definitely hasn't forgiven him. Which means she probably hasn't forgiven me.

But when she turns her gaze on me, her face softens. "Why are you crying, Leith?" she asks with a voice as soft as her expression.

My hands tremble as I sign, "Because I thought I lost you before I ever really had you."

Her eyes widen at my confession. I've never really indicated how I feel about her, and my heart pounds with nervous energy. I've kept my distance out of respect for Nico, but now I regret that. Will she accept me or not? Will she forgive me for how badly I've hurt her?

She studies me for a moment, then she's walking toward me and kneeling. "Leith," she whispers.

I pull her into my arms, and she climbs onto my lap easily. Her touch soothes the emptiness I've felt these past few days. Her warmth, her weight, her arms wrapped around me. I don't deserve it.

"I'm sorry," I say against her neck. My words are hoarse and more air than anything, but she hears me. "I shouldn't have kept it from you."

Daci's breath catches in her chest, and she pulls away to look at me with wonder. A faint smile plays about her lips, even as her eyes redden with tears. "You did it for your friend, because he asked you to. I can respect that, even if I don't like it."

"Daci," I say. My hands cup her face, and she leans into the touch. "Nico isn't your only mate."

Her body goes incredibly still, pupils contracting. "What?"

"I'm your mate, too. I realized it right before you disappeared." My voice is less hoarse, but still breathy. I'm too scared of projecting it.

Rather than disbelief or anger like I expected, she looks relieved. "That makes so much sense," she whispers almost to herself. Before I can say anything, she sits up tall. "Twig!" She jumps to her feet and looks around, spotting him in the patch of sun where I laid him. She gasps and runs to him, falling to her knees.

I kneel next to her. "He's not been doing good since you were gone," I sign. "If you needed proof you're the dragon guardian, I think this is it."

"Twig," she breathes, hands hovering over him. She runs her fingers over his scales, and I watch in awe as the color shimmers under her palm, the green intensifying before fading back to the lackluster brown. Daci stifles a sob and scoops Twig into her arms. "I'm so sorry, Twig," she cries. "I'm so sorry. But I'm here now. I promise, I won't leave you again."

It's amazing to watch Twig transform from the sickly baby dragon he'd become back to his normal, healthy self. Inch by inch, his scales shimmer then turn emerald. His ears perk up, and his tail swishes lazily. Even his wings look sturdier than they did before.

He opens his eyes and he stares at Daci with so much love, it breaks my heart. Then he licks up the side of her face, and her laughter carries away the rest of the cold that had settled inside me.

31
DACIANA

I hold Twig tightly in my arms. When I picked him up, he was almost lifeless. His body was cold, and his scales were brownish. I was scared he was dead. But when I touched him, he transformed. The emerald green of his scales came back. His body warmed. And the best part . . . he licked me.

Mama.

I choke on the lump in my throat. *Yes. I'm here. I'm so sorry.*

He rests his head on my shoulder and relief sweeps through me so fast, I fall backward. Leith reaches out lightning fast to catch me. Leith. My mate. My *other* mate. I look at him, and my heart stutters. He's watching me with his blue eyes, taking everything in like he's memorizing my features in case I disappear again.

He tucks a strand of my hair behind my ear, grazing his fingers along my neck, and I shiver. "I'm glad you're back," he signs.

"We should probably talk," I say. Turning around, I look at Nico, who has been standing in silence, watching my reunion with Leith and Twig. "All of us."

Nico's eyes are endlessly dark as he stares at me. He opens his mouth but changes his mind. Shaking his head, he turns around and walks out. I follow with heavy footsteps, and not just because I swear Twig has gained even more weight since I last saw him.

It was easy to forgive Leith and Mattie. I understand why they didn't tell me about Nico being my mate. Their priority was to their friend first and I can appreciate that. But Nico is another matter. I'm not sure how to forgive him yet. When I think about what he did, it still hurts.

Before we get to Mattie's room, Leith takes Twig from me. I don't want to give him up, but he really has gotten heavy. And I know as soon as Mattie sees me, he's going to try and hug me. So I reluctantly hand him over. His big golden eyes never leave me though.

In front of Mattie's door, Nico steps aside. He watches with what I can only assume is envy. I feel a pang of regret for hurting him, but then I remember what he did to me. I knock twice then push open the door. Mattie sits on the windowsill, gazing outside. He doesn't even turn around.

"Go away," he says quietly, sounding nothing like the Mattie I've come to know.

"But I just got back," I say lightly.

He tenses, every muscle in his body going stiff. In the reflection of the window, I see him close his eyes and swallow, but he doesn't turn toward me. "Daci?" he breathes, almost like he's afraid if he says it too loud, I'll disappear again.

I walk to him and grip his chin to make him look at me. "Mattie."

He shudders and throws his arms around me, pulling me onto his lap. He curves his body around mine and buries his face in my neck. "I am so, so sorry," he whispers brokenly. "You deserve so much better. I should have told you, and I'll regret that for the rest of my life."

"Stop." I tug on his locs to pull his head up so I can look at him. "I already told Leith. You were being a good friend, and I would never expect you to choose me over him."

He shakes his head. "No. No, I will always choose you over him. Daci . . ."

"I know. You're my mate."

His expression almost makes me laugh. A mix of wonder, surprise, and bewilderment. He closes his eyes. "Say it again."

"Matteo Rossi, you're my mate."

"Daci, you will always come first. I should have told you."

I shake my head. "You didn't know I was your mate. There is

nothing you need to apologize for. You told me over and over that you wanted to tell me but it wasn't your business. And I get that."

He's gearing up for an argument, so I stop him the only way I know how. I lean forward and kiss him. His hands thread through my hair and pull me closer. And damn. I really missed this man. Just being in his arms again settles me in a way nothing else can. When he deepens the kiss, I completely lose myself. At least until Nico clears his throat.

Oh. Right. I pull away and shake myself, trying to clear the haze of Mattie's kiss from my head. He smirks at me like he knows exactly what kind of effect he has on me. I put some distance between us, because otherwise I'm tempted to dive back in for more.

"I think we should talk about this," I say, tossing my hair over my shoulder and trying to calm my racing heart.

"About you and Mattie kissing?" Leith signs with a grin that steals my breath. He sits on the edge of the bed and lays Twig next to him. The dragon sets his head in Leith's lap but still keeps his gaze on me.

Mattie snorts. "It's understandable to be jealous watching me kiss Daci, but you should hide it better. It's not very flattering."

I duck just in time to avoid a pillow thrown for Mattie. He chuckles and I find myself smiling at their antics. I haven't seen either of them this free or happy ever.

"If this is going to turn into a fuckfest, I'm out of here," Nico says, voice dripping with venom. He leans against the closed door with crossed arms and a clenched jaw.

Mattie's humor fades quickly. "Of all the people in this room who should be pleasant, it's you."

"I'm trying," he grits through his teeth. "But watching my mate kiss and flirt with my two best friends while completely ignoring me isn't exactly easy."

I sober quickly at his words. Because he's right. Even though it's his fault he's in the position he's in, I don't need to rub it in his face, no matter how good it feels. I'm better than that.

"And whose fault is that?" Mattie bites out.

"Guys, seriously. Stop fighting. I don't like it. If we can't talk like adults, then we might as well give up now."

"What do you want to talk about?" Leith signs.

"For starters? How about the mate thing?"

"You seem surprisingly calm about it. And how did you figure it out anyway?" Mattie laces our fingers together, and I get momentarily distracted.

"Um, well, Leith told me he was my mate, and I just assumed you were too. It felt . . . right. A lot of things made sense when I found out. Like, how I never once feared for my life when I was with you guys, when in reality I should have been terrified Nico would use me to his advantage." I shrug. "I think finding out was more comforting than surprising. It answered the questions I was asking myself."

"It's not exactly common to have more than one mate," Mattie says carefully. "I'm curious why you have three. Is that something common for dragon guardians?"

I shake my head. "I don't think so. Decima said something to me before we left. She said she had a suspicion there was more at work than what she put into play, or something like that. She seemed kind of surprised."

"Well, whatever the reason," Leith signs, "I'm not going to complain about it."

"So you guys are okay with this?" I wave my hands, indicating all three of them. "You don't mind sharing?"

Mattie shrugs. "For you, yeah I'd share. But honestly, it's really only like sharing with Nico. You know, because Leith is a freak." Another pillow sails for Mattie's head. He ducks, but he isn't fast enough. It smacks him in the face, and he laughs. "I'm kidding, Leith. You know I love you."

"Well, the feeling is not mutual," Leith signs, but his lips quiver with suppressed laughter.

"Did we get this settled?" Nico asks with impatience. "I'd like to talk to Daci alone."

My laughter dies and I straighten my spine. "Yeah. I think that about settles things."

"Can we talk?" Even with his clipped words, his anxiety is evident in the way he won't meet my gaze and rubs the back of his neck.

"Yeah. We can talk."

Nico takes me back to the garden. An awkward silence falls between us, and we both stop and stand in front of a fountain, trying our hardest to not look at one another. The fountain is a depiction of the three Parcae carved into white marble: Nona, Decima, and Morta.

Nona looks ethereal with her curled hair piled on top of her head and a flowing dress swirling around her legs. Decima looks stern, yet the artist managed to capture the kindness in her eyes. The kindness I saw when I met her. And Morta, the Parcae I haven't met yet. She also looks stern, but there is no kindness in her eyes. Only a cold, empty expression.

I shiver looking at Morta. Eventually, I'm going to have to face her, and I have no skills to use to my advantage. I can't fight, and my magic doesn't seem to be useful in combat. I'm going to have to rely on the guys, my mates. Some of the tension leaves me when I think about them.

The questions and uncertainty I felt about all of them disappeared when I found out what they were to me. It was a relief being able to put a name to the feelings. And it only solidified my confidence that they will protect me no matter what. Even Nico, despite our strained relationship.

I sit on the edge of the fountain basin, enjoying the cool mist that showers me from the water's spray. When I look up, it creates a glittering rainbow in the sunlight. Nico paces in front of me and I give him the time he needs to gather his thoughts. While I wait, I trail my fingers through the water and let the koi fish nibble on my fingers.

"The first thing I want to say," Nico begins suddenly, "is that I'm sorry. I was wrong and it wasn't right for me to hide something so important from you. And I never should have slept with you without you knowing what we are."

"I think that's what hurts the most," I say quietly, keeping my gaze on the fish. "That should have been a positive memory for me, being with my mate for the first time, but instead now I just think about how I felt when I realized I'd been lied to." I wrap my arms around my middle. "And then you just walked out, like it was nothing. Like I was just another number to add to your tally." My voice trembles slightly as tears burn the back of my throat.

"And you don't deserve that." His voice is softer than usual, lacking its typical blunt edges. "I wish I could go back and do it over. Differently. Seeing the pain in your eyes will haunt me forever. I never want to see you hurt again, especially by my hand."

"Why did you do it?" I whisper, running my finger over a large orange koi and keeping my gaze safely away from Nico. "I mean, I know it was because you didn't want to feel like your mom was controlling you. But was any of it because you don't want *me*? Am I the reason you fought so hard against it?"

Strong fingers grip my chin and force me to turn around. He's kneeling in front of me, staring at me with such intensity it makes me shiver. "No. Never." His dark-brown eyes swim with so many emotions, and I find myself falling into them. "I was torn because of our family differences. I knew I shouldn't want you the way that I did. And when I realized I *did* want you, I hated it because I didn't want to give in to my mom's meddling. I told myself I didn't want you. I fought against the feelings I had and denied them with every breath. But it was never that I didn't want you. Wanting you was the problem."

This softer side of Nico makes my insides squirm. I grew so used to the distant, sharp-tongued asshole. This Nico is something I don't know how to deal with. I don't know what to feel about what he just said.

I take a breath and pull my chin free. Looking him in the eyes is too hard. "I understand why you didn't tell me. And I can't say

I wouldn't have done the same in your position. But it really hurt, Nico. A lot. I don't know how to forget that."

Nico presses his forehead against my thighs and wraps his arms around my calves. "I will do everything I can to show you how much I regret what I did. I will live the rest of my life fighting for your forgiveness, even though I don't deserve it. If you give me one more chance, I swear I won't let you down, Daci."

I can't help but run my fingers through his hair, and his body shudders at the touch. The strands are silky and smooth and the dark brown glimmers in the sunlight. I weigh his words, and I want to forgive him. I really do. But my heart is still too tender to completely give in. But I can definitely give him another chance.

"Okay," I say quietly.

Nico releases a breath and squeezes my legs tighter. "Thank you, Daci. I promise I won't let you down again. I'll be everything you need me to be."

I left Nico in the garden, and as I stepped inside I heard the telltale swish of wings flapping. As I walk back to my room, I mull over his words. I don't doubt his sincerity. I think he really is sorry for how he hurt me. But like I told him, it's still too raw for me to completely jump back in with him. It's going to take some time.

When I get back to our rooms, I pause outside of mine. I missed my mates, and the thought of going to my room by myself makes me feel lonely all over again. So I knock on Mattie's door. He doesn't answer. I try Leith's next, and he also doesn't answer. Frowning, I head back to my room, deciding to take a bath and relax instead.

But when I open my door, Mattie and Leith are there. Mattie is sprawled on the bed, tossing a dagger up and down, catching it by the blade and making me cringe. Leith is sitting on the floor in front of Twig, feeding him bacon so Twig doesn't have to lift his head from the bed. Spoiled dragon. All three of them look at me when I enter. Twig's tail twitches happily as he munches on his food. Mattie and Leith scan me for any signs of me being upset or hurt.

"How'd it go?" Mattie asks.

I shrug and plop onto the bed next to him. "It's hard. I know he's sorry and regrets what he did, but it still hurts, you know? I just don't know what to do."

"Take your time figuring it out. Don't rush into anything just because he's your mate and you feel like you need to. You need to heal your relationship first or else it will fester." Mattie toys with the end of my ponytail as he talks.

"When did you get so wise?" I ask with a smile.

Leith looks up with a wry grin and signs, "He's not wise. He's just pulling words from his ass and hoping to sound smart."

This time, it's Mattie who throws a pillow at Leith, who isn't fast enough to dodge it. I chuckle, already feeling lighter just from being with the two of them.

Mattie taps the top of my head. "Hey, come here." He holds out his arms and I roll over to snuggle against him. "What happened? Where did you go?"

I release a breath, shivering at the memory of pain bursting through my body when I woke up. "I lied," I whisper. "I thought I was telling the truth, but deep down, it was a lie. The world just . . . poof," I say, using my hands to help describe what happened. "When I woke up, I was back in Girasole. It wasn't until I realized what you guys mean to me and remembered what the silver slippers do that I was able to get back here. As soon as I stepped foot in the Field, I was transported back to the Emerald City."

Mattie shakes his head and tugs me closer. "I missed you," he whispers.

"I missed you too," I say. "I missed you both." Looking at Leith, I give him a smile that he returns.

"How much?" Mattie asks. There is no denying that seductive and playful tone.

I push up so I'm leaning over him. "Do you want me to show you?"

A slow grin spreads across Mattie's face, making my stomach flutter. "Yes please."

Leith clears his throat and we both look at him. "Hold up," he signs as he stands. He scoops Twig into his arms and drops him in the bathroom before shutting the door. "He's too young to see this."

Small growls echo into the room, fiercer than I've ever heard, and the thump of his body hitting the door follows.

I shake my head, but I grin. "What's he going to see that he shouldn't?"

Mattie slides his hand to my waist and slowly slips it under my shirt. "Leith and I worshipping you," he breathes against my neck, making me shiver.

I cut my gaze to Leith, who I know doesn't like physical touch, but his eyes are glued to the bit of exposed skin on my belly. Mattie pushes me to my back, and I lift my arms so he can tug off my shirt. Each inch of skin he exposes, he traces with his mouth. Heat pools in my core, spreading through my veins, making me crave more.

My gaze follows Leith as he prowls toward the head of the bed. He watches Mattie toy with my nipples with a hungry expression, his cock pushing hard against his pants. I suddenly want to see him. All of him.

"Take off your clothes," I say breathlessly. "I want to see you."

Leith grins and follows my orders, slowly stripping out of his clothes. My fingers itch to touch him. His body is cut perfectly. Lean and muscled. I want to trace every inch of his skin with my own, but I refrain, fisting the sheets in my grasp instead.

"Your turn," Leith signs, sitting on the edge of the bed. He slowly strokes his cock, working a bead of pre-cum from the tip.

I don't get a chance to even try to take off my pants. Mattie chuckles and yanks them down, tossing them to the floor with my shirt. "I'm so fucking glad I don't have to share you right now," he growls. His fingers bite into my thighs as he spreads me wide for him.

Anticipation curls in my gut, and he makes me wait while he slowly strips out of his own clothes. By the time he kneels between my legs again, I'm whimpering and squirming, trying to get him to touch me.

He grins. "I am going to feast on you, Daci."

And that's the only warning I get. He dives between my legs and does exactly what he said he was going to do. He feasts on me. The noises that fall from my lips don't even sound like me as he draws me closer and closer to the edge. Leith watches it all with a heated gaze that only makes me burn even hotter. When I reach that impenetrable wall, I whine, yanking on Mattie's locs to try and pull him even closer to me.

He looks up with a grin, his lips and chin glistening with my arousal. "Leith doesn't know what he's missing out on."

"Mattie, please," I beg, lifting my hips in a plea for more.

Mattie grasps my hips and effortlessly flips me over onto my stomach. I keep my gaze on Leith and the way he lazily strokes himself, watching everything Mattie does to me. My back arches when Mattie lightly runs his fingers down my spine, followed by his lips.

"Get on your hands and knees, edainai. Between Leith's legs," Mattie breathes against my skin.

My limbs are already shaky, but I do as he asks. With Leith's cock in my face, I lick my lips. I want so badly to taste him, but I won't do anything unless he wants me to. But being able to see him watching me, and seeing how turned on he is just by watching, makes my core clench.

"She's blushing," Leith signs with one hand.

Looking at his intense gaze only makes me blush harder. He grins wickedly and squeezes his cock, making my core clench. Mattie chuckles darkly and grabs my hips, tugging me back against him. His body is so hot against mine and I writhe my hips, searching for what I want. He groans and my stomach flutters at the deep guttural sound.

"Fuck, edainai. Don't do that or I'll lose all control." Mattie runs his hands over my skin, touching every inch of my body. A combination of tingles and lightning ripple outward from his touch.

"Maybe that's what I want," I say, my voice breathless and slightly needy.

He chuckles. "You're going to have to be patient, edainai. I'm taking my time."

Despite his words, he runs the tip of his cock through my wetness, making us both groan. My hands hurt from how hard I'm fisting the sheets on either side of Leith's hips. *Don't touch him. Don't touch him. Don't fucking lick his abs like you want to, Daci.* I have to keep chanting to myself to make sure I don't do something stupid and freak out Leith. It's always on his terms.

"Please, Mattie," I beg, pushing my hips back again.

"I love hearing you beg." It's all the warning he gives me before he grabs my hips and slides inside.

I gasp and let my head fall forward, causing my ponytail to slide over my shoulder. It brushes against Leith's thigh, and he sucks in a breath. When I look at him, I can see the indecision on his face. He's fighting his instincts, like he wants to touch me but can't quite bring himself to do it.

I try to reassure him with my expression that it's okay, he doesn't have to, but Mattie grabs my ponytail and wraps it around his fist, tugging me up until my back is against his chest. The sharp sting of my hair pulling in my scalp drags a groan from me. Each thrust of Mattie's hips drives me higher and higher, and Leith's hungry gaze on my body sends licks of fire over my skin wherever it touches.

"Do you like Leith watching?" Mattie asks in my ear, his voice strained. "Look at how much he enjoys seeing you come undone."

Mattie loosens his grip enough for me to look down at Leith.

His blue eyes are so dark, they are almost black. And the rhythm of his hand has become jerky and more rushed.

"Yes," I breathe. "I like when he watches."

Leith grins wickedly at me before reaching up with his free hand to pinch my nipple. I gasp and arch my back as much as I can. He rewards me with the same treatment on the other side.

Mattie lets go of my hair and slides his hand around my neck. The anticipation in my gut increases, knowing exactly what Mattie intends to do. I keep my eyes on Leith, watching as he pleasures himself. Watching as he plays with my nipples. Watching as he watches me. Something goes taut between us, and I whimper as my desire climbs even more.

"Do you want to come, edainai?"

Words are too hard right now. Only a strangled noise comes from me, but I grasp his wrist in both of my hands, digging my nails into his skin.

He chuckles, hips never faltering, and he finally squeezes my throat. At the same time, he slides his hand around my hip and rubs my clit in maddening strokes. As my body begs for oxygen, the peak is right there. I can almost reach it . . .

"Be a good girl and show Leith how pretty you are as you come, edainai. Let go for him."

My orgasm slams into me, making my body shudder. Strangled noises escape past the hold Mattie has on my throat. Leith's breath catches and he squeezes his cock hard, hand moving faster and faster until his body jerks as he finds his release.

Mattie doesn't let go, and he doesn't stop thrusting his hips or rubbing my clit until my body is completely drained. Only then does he loosen his hold, but he doesn't let go. He slides his other hand back to my hip and he grips it tightly as he slams into me again and again until he grunts and shakes as his orgasm barrels through him.

As soon as Mattie releases me, I fall forward, not even thinking about landing on top of Leith until I'm already lying on him, skin to skin.

"Shit," I mutter through numb lips. "I'm sorry." I try to push myself up, but my arms are still too shaky.

Leith shakes his head and wraps his arms around me. I melt against him, not caring one bit that I'm lying in cum. Mattie collapses behind me and wraps his arm around my middle. Together, the three of us lie skin to skin as our heartbeats slow and we come down from our euphoria.

"You did so good, edainai," Mattie finally says, kissing my shoulder. "I'm proud of you."

Warmth curls in my gut and I smile sleepily, snuggling closer to both of them.

32
NICOLAI

Even though Daci hasn't completely forgiven me, she's at least talking to me. We're on the road again, still intent on stopping Morta. With Decima's aid, we used a portal to skip over all the obstacles we faced the last time. Now, we're all on our guard, and I think Daci finally realizes the importance of listening to us and being careful. And I don't think it's because of how she was transported back to Girasole, but rather her seeing how affected Twig was by her absence. It's like she finally realized and accepted her fate as dragon guardian.

Despite being on high alert, this has been the most pleasant part of our journey. There are no secrets between us anymore, and the tension has almost completely dissipated. At least between Daci and the other two. Between me and her it still crackles like electricity whenever one of our gazes lingers longer than it should. But she won't act on it, and I'm okay with that. For now. It's the least I deserve. But eventually, I hope she can let me in.

Twig is the first to notice it. The sudden scurrying of topo fatatos all around us. It starts with just one, then two, then ten. Seconds later, hundreds of topo fatatos are crawling over our shoes, running for their lives.

Mattie quickly snags Twig from the ground, stopping his playful snapping at the creatures. "What the hell?" he asks, watching the flood of fairies.

"What's going on?" Daciana asks, careful to not move her feet.

Leith turns to me. "Something is chasing them," he signs hurriedly.

I nod in agreement and shift, flapping my wings to lift me off the ground. With my vision enhanced, I can clearly see the rushing fairies as they run from . . . holy shit. I land carefully, parting the stream of topo fatatos before shifting. "Lu gattu puzzu." A catlike fairy, massive in size and reeking of sulfur.

"Fuck," Mattie curses, handing Twig to Daciana. "Hold him. And stay back." He grabs her face in both of his hands, forcing her to look at him. "Please, don't move from this spot." He kisses her quickly and turns to wade through the rising tide of topo fatatos.

I give her a stern look, telling her with that alone to listen to Mattie and not get involved in this. Then, Leith and I join Mattie and march toward the creature chasing the fairies. They part for us, making our way easier.

"What's the plan?" Leith signs, blue eyes scanning ahead for the gattu puzzu.

"I'll distract it," Mattie says. "You two take it out."

Leith and I nod, right as the creature crests a hill. It's larger than a direwolf. Its black fur is matted and sticking up in all directions. Orange eyes take in the scurrying topo fatatos and it licks its teeth, pointed and sharp, perfect for tearing fairies into bite-sized pieces. The wind carries its scent to us, and I gag. That sulfurous stench curdles my stomach and makes my eyes water. Fucking horrendous creatures.

Mattie darts forward. With his Faun abilities he's light on his feet, and fast. He reaches the gattu puzzu in a second. I can hear him taunting it, not that the creature can understand a word Mattie says. But the bigger prey gets the gattu puzzu's attention. It forgets about the topo fatatos and focuses instead on the more satisfying meal in front of it.

Mattie draws the creature back down the other side of the hill and out of my and Leith's sight. We hurry forward, drawing our knives as we go. When we crest the hill, neither of us wait to make our move. I throw my first dagger. It sinks into the spot between the gattu puzzu's shoulder blades. The creature growls and whips its head back and forth. Leith throws his dagger a second after me. His embeds into the creature's back thigh. It stumbles, giving us time to get closer.

It's been a while since we've fought a magical creature in Oz, yet we fall into the rhythm of the battle seamlessly. The combination of our training back in Girasole and our fae instincts makes this fight a breeze. Mattie keeps the gattu puzzu distracted while Leith and I slow it down with thrown daggers.

I wince when the cat manages to get past Mattie's guard. A jagged claw rips through his thigh, causing him to stumble and curse. If we don't take it down now, the scent of Mattie's blood will rile it up even more. Not to mention draw the attention of other monsters.

Leith spots an opening when the creature rears up to bat away one of my knives. He darts forward, ducking to avoid its claws, and slides past in the grass. His knife slices through the gattu puzzu's stomach as he does, and the rotten stench of its intestines fills the air as they spill from its body.

The gattu puzzu collapses into a pile of matted black fur and gooey insides. The three of us stand around, breathing heavily, making sure the creature doesn't get back up. When I'm positive it won't, I scan Leith for injuries and find Mattie is the only one bleeding.

"Good work," I say, pulling my knives from the creature's body. "Let's get back to Daciana and we'll take care of your leg."

Leith and I loop Mattie's arms around our necks and help him limp back to our mate. She's standing where we left her, bottom lip pulled between her teeth as she bounces on her toes in concern. Twig is still in her arms, and he's staring at the topo fatato sitting on Daci's shoulder. As we get closer, I realize it's not just any topo fatato. It's the queen of the topo fatato. A small golden crown of flowers sits perched on her tiny head.

I bow respectfully. "Lu gattu puzzu is dead. You are safe."

Her shoulders slump in relief and she places a hand on her heart, nodding her head in thanks. When she hops off Daci's shoulder, the swarm of fairies follows her back the way they had run from.

"What . . ." Daci slowly sets Twig back on the ground once the last topo fatato has disappeared.

"Lu gattu puzzu," Mattie explains with a grimace, "is a horrid creature. It could eat hundreds of topo fatatos in minutes. They usually live in the mountains, but I'm guessing Morta lured this one down to come after us. But because we saved the topo fatato, the queen will spread the word. If at any time we need help, all we have to do is ask. If there is a topo fatato near us, they'll give their life for us." He winces as he explains, shifting weight off his injured leg.

Daci drops her gaze to Mattie's leg and presses her lips together. "You're hurt." She sets Twig on the ground and helps Mattie sit in the grass. "What the hell happened?" Her face pales as she takes a good look at the wound.

Mattie's pants are shredded, as is his skin, and blood flows freely from the claw swipe. "It's just a scratch," he says with a forced grin.

Leith kneels next to Daci and digs through his bag. He pulls out healing creams and bandages, along with a suture kit. "This needs stitches," he signs, settling in the grass.

Daci pales even more, and she swallows loudly enough for all of us to hear. "Um, do you need me?" she asks shakily.

"Don't like the sight of blood, princess?" I tease, hoping she doesn't take it as an insult. "I thought you were more bloodthirsty than that."

"Not when it's coming from one of my mates," she replies faintly.

I quickly grab her arm as she wavers, and I drag her a short distance away. "Sit down," I instruct. "Don't look at them."

Her breathing is coming in sharp pants, and I realize she's on the verge of either fainting or having a panic attack. I gather her hair in my hand and lift it off her neck, blowing gently to cool her down. She shivers but ducks her head to give me better access. I try not to stare at the graceful curve of her neck, but damn I want to sink my teeth into it.

"Before all of this happened, before Oz and Twig, what did you want with your life?" I ask. "I know what was expected of you, but did you want that?"

She's quiet for a moment before saying, "No, I didn't want what my dad had planned for me. An arranged marriage to someone I probably would have hated. A life of violence. Constant worry about my safety and the kids I no doubt would have been forced to have. Who wants that kind of life?"

I nod, even though she can't see me. "What did you want then?"

"I wanted to be an artist." Her words are so small and quiet, the wind almost carries them away. She says it like she's ashamed to want something like that.

"I think you would have been a wonderful artist," I say truthfully. I've seen the sketches in her notebook, and I've been curious to see them come to life on a canvas. "What medium do you paint with?"

"Acrylics mostly, but sometimes watercolors."

We're quiet for a moment, and I let myself picture one of her sketches of me done in watercolor, sitting on an easel. Her breathing has calmed, so I drop her hair and sit next to her, not quite ready to leave this peaceful bubble we've found ourselves in.

"What about you?" she asks. "Do you want to take over after your dad?"

"No. But honestly, I don't know what else I'd do. Blood and violence are all I've known for so long. It's really the only thing I'm good at."

She looks at me then, and I swear it's like being bathed in warm rays of sunshine. "I doubt that's true."

"You think?" I stare into her green eyes and watch her smile. When she smiles at me, it makes me think I can take on the whole world and win.

"Who knows. Maybe you have a hidden talent for gardening?"

I snort and shake my head. "Just because my grandma is good at gardening, doesn't mean I am. That gene passed me over."

Her smile fades, but the warmth in her expression remains. "You're a protector. That's what you're good at."

She says it so earnestly, I can't help but think about it. And maybe she's right. I take my job of protecting Giorgia seriously. The same goes for Daci. I'd give my life to keep both of them safe. So maybe that is what I'm good at.

Before I can say anything, a topo fatato scurries past us with something clenched in its teeth. I turn around to find it giving Leith a leaf of some kind. Leith bows his head in thanks and places the leaf over Mattie's stitches. When I see him start to wrap the wound, I help Daci to her feet.

"The coast is clear now," I say.

She bites her bottom lip maddeningly. "Thank you for distracting me."

I'm not prepared for her to stand on her tiptoes and press a kiss to my cheek.

33

DACIANA

We take it easy for a day to give Mattie's leg time to heal. Whatever kind of ointment Leith used did wonders though. He said it's something that can only be found in Oz, but Nico's dad has a stash of it back in Girasole in case of emergencies. It's why they have very few scars

The second day after the attack, Mattie's limp is almost gone, and he insists we pick up our pace. "The sooner we get there, the sooner this ends and we can move on with our lives."

I frown at his words. What exactly does "move on with our lives" mean? I hadn't put much thought into what happens after we deal with Morta. When I first came to Oz, I assumed I'd be returning to Girasole. But I don't think that will be the case now. Being the dragon guardian means I have to remain here, with the dragons.

I can't imagine Nico staying. He has to return to his duties in Girasole. And Leith hates it here. Mattie could go either way. So when this is over, will it *all* come to an end? Can I live without my mates? Do they even want to live with me?

Nico bumps my shoulder with his own. "What's that face for?"

"What face?" I ask innocently, hoping to avoid this conversation. That ever-present fear of abandonment makes itself known, and to keep myself from getting hurt, I try to change the subject. "Is there a specific place where the dragons lived? Or did they just live all over Oz?" Twig perks his head up at my question.

Nico narrows his eyes, but he answers, "They lived everywhere. Dragons lived in packs called flights. It was similar to wolves in terms of having an alpha for protection of the flight, but at the same time, females tended to be the dominant ones that control flight dynamics."

"What exactly does a dragon guardian *do*? I don't have any special powers to protect them, so how am I supposed to guard them? And what do they need guarding from? Aren't they, like, the top of the food chain?"

Nico's lips twitch at my rapid-fire questioning. "They are the top of the food chain. I don't think it's necessarily guarding the dragons, but more like keeping an eye on them."

"Like a dragon babysitter?" I ask incredulously.

This time he smiles. "Basically. Dragons tend to be very hot headed. They need someone to occasionally keep them in check. The dragon guardian is alpha over all dragons, so they'd listen to you."

My heart sinks. The idea that I will be in charge of *all* dragons is overwhelming. That is a responsibility I don't think I'm ready for. Back in Girasole, I was barely functioning as an adult. Partying, drinking, fucking. That's what I'm good at. Keeping a bunch of magical creatures in check? That seems impossible.

"You won't be alone, Daci," Nico says, uncharacteristically quiet. "And you'll be starting with baby dragons. That should be easier."

I glance at Twig prancing between Mattie and Leith and snort. "That might actually be more difficult. I can't imagine trying to raise multiple little menaces."

"I have no doubt you can do it."

I'm startled by his sincerity, and I slow my steps to look at him. Why does this man make my emotions fluctuate so much? I know I'm going to forgive him. Honestly, I already have. It's harder to let him back in though. But if he keeps this up, I'll melt before I'm ready.

"You don't believe me?" he asks with a crooked smile. "I had my doubts about you when we started this journey. A pampered princess in the wilds of Oz?" He snorts and shakes his head. "But you surprised me from the very beginning. You never complained, even though I could tell you didn't enjoy sleeping outdoors and every time you broke or chipped a nail you'd scowl for hours. You did things I didn't think you could do, like climbing the chasm wall. And every time something happened to you, you got back up without a fuss." He shrugs and when he steps closer, I don't back away. "You're stronger than you give yourself credit for. You're stronger than *anyone* gives you credit for. I've never seen someone more determined to prove others wrong. So, yeah. I know you'll be able to do this."

He's only a few inches from me when he stops talking. Even though I hear his words and they resonate inside of me with happiness and pride, I can't focus on them. He's so close I can feel his body heat, and it makes my stomach do funny backflips. I hate how much I miss him. I can still feel his kiss, demanding and devouring.

Nico takes one more step, and his chest brushes against mine. I look up at him, and when I do, his dark eyes are bottomless pools. He cups my cheek, rubbing his thumb back and forth, and my eyes fall closed. Butterflies erupt in my stomach when his breath fans across my lips, and I know he's leaned in. His nose brushes against mine and I stop breathing.

"We should catch up to them," he whispers, then he pulls back.

I blink when he walks away without a backward glance. What the hell was that? My heart pounds, and I watch him with a glare. That bastard. I hurry my steps to catch up, and when I step next to him, he doesn't even look at me.

"I know the questions about the dragons were a distraction," he says calmly, as if nothing just happened between us.

"What?" I ask, still not able to completely focus.

"Something else is bothering you," he clarifies. "Something that Mattie said earlier, about going on with our lives."

My heart drops and the dazed feeling evaporates. "Oh," is all I manage to say.

"Spill it, Daci."

I sigh and look at the ground, too scared to show him this vulnerability. "What happens when this is all over? Not with the dragons. I get that part. I think. But what about . . ." I'm unable to voice the words.

"What about us? All of us?"

I nod. "Yeah."

He shrugs. "I'll stay here with you. At least, I will if you want me to. I know Mattie will as well. And while Leith hates Oz, I think he likes you more. So I wouldn't be surprised if he stays too."

I stop in my tracks again. "You mean you'd give up everything in Girasole to stay with me? Your family. The Camorra. All of it?"

He takes my hands in his. "I know I haven't been the best at showing you how I feel. And I know I've made some big mistakes. But I'd do anything for you, Daci. I'd follow you to the ends of the earth if you asked me to. Hell, I'd do it even if you asked me not to. I'm not going anywhere. And I'm going to prove that to you."

I'm opening my mouth to reply, but Mattie cuts in. "Um, guys? We have a big problem."

Normally, I wouldn't take Mattie too seriously. His big problem could very well have been he lost a bet to Leith. But a tremor in his voice gives me pause. Nico must sense this as well because he turns to see what's going on.

In the distance, a dark cloud approaches. I'm taken aback because I haven't seen any clouds except big puffy white ones that drift by on a lazy breeze. This cloud is ominous. It churns almost like it's a living thing. And as it draws closer, I realize it *is* a living thing.

"That's not a cloud," Mattie says.

"No, it's not. Bisso galeto." Nico's face is set in grim determination. "Morta's puppets."

I swallow as fear floods my system. "How do we fight them?" My voice is shrill, and I take a step back like that will keep me safe.

"We don't." Nico kneels on the ground and opens his bag. He swiftly shoves Twig inside with a few words to convince him to stay before slinging it onto his back.

"What do you mean 'we don't'?" I look at Mattie and Leith, and they share the same grim expression as Nico. "Mattie?"

He steps up to me and hands me two daggers. "Fight. That's all you can do. But against that many, it won't be enough."

"What? So we're just going to die right here?" Are they out of their minds? We have to do something!

Mattie takes my face in his hands and leans down to kiss me. "She'll want you alive. You need to stay strong and remember what your goal is. Find the eggs. Get them out. Kill Morta if you can, but don't risk it if you can't."

"Mattie!" I reach for his shirt, but he steps away too quickly.

Leith replaces him. "Remember how strong you are. Remember what you're fighting for." His signs are slower than usual, like he wants to make sure I catch every word. Then he too kisses me before stepping away, leaving me reeling for many reasons. First being that that was our first kiss. And possibly last.

By the time Nico is in front of me, my eyes burn. They can't be saying what I think they're saying. Right? "Don't make me do this alone," I whisper shakily to Nico. "Don't leave me."

A muscle in his jaw ticks as he looks at me. "I won't let you fight this alone, princess. I promise."

Behind him, Mattie and Leith take up fighting stances, and in front of them, the dark swarm of bisso galeto draws closer. The flapping of wings becomes deafening and the light dims as the mass covers the sun. I get my first good look at the creatures, and my blood runs cold.

They are just as Nico described. They're the size of a small pony, with the head and body of a rooster and the tail of a snake. Their wings are tipped in thorns, and I remember those thorns are poisonous. There's no way we can fight them off.

Nico steps in front of me, and Leith steps behind me. Before I know it, the beasts descend on us. All three guys jump into action, stabbing and slicing. Mattie is fast, darting here and there with animal grace. Leith isn't as fast, but he's just as deadly. His movements are more calculated, and he takes the time to analyze each shot. And Nico is breathtaking to watch. He's powerful and fierce. Each move he makes is filled with rage and violence.

I have no idea how to kill one of these things. I'm more likely to stab myself, honestly. My training in self-defense can only take me so far. So I do my best to duck out of the grasp of their chicken-like claws. One gets the shoulder of my shirt and the seams tear with a rip, but it misses skin. I swipe out blindly, feeling my blade connect with something. The unholy screech of a dying rooster makes my vision blur, and I cover my ears with my hands.

My heart thumps so fast in my chest, and it's hard to draw in breath. I'm trembling so hard in my panic, I almost fall over. I can't fight them off. All I do is crouch and duck. Crouch and duck. With an occasional blind swipe that usually misses. I'm useless. Just a distraction the guys don't need.

Even with the dead bodies lying around us, the bisso galeto just keep coming. The guys are breathing heavily, their strength fading. Blood oozes from various injuries on all of them, and each one is like a knife to my heart. Every injury inflicted on them resonates so deeply inside of me, I'm surprised I don't see the same injuries mirrored on my skin.

Time seems to slow as I watch a bisso galeto swoop down behind Nico and wrap its massive claws around his middle, trapping his arms. The creature flaps its wings and lifts Nico off the ground.

"Nico!" My shout is lost in the fray, but his gaze finds mine.

He thrashes in the creature's grip, but it doesn't loosen. No matter how hard he fights, he can't get free. Even if he were to shift, the creature would squash Nico's owl in an instant. I see the moment Nico knows it's the end for him. His eyes turn soft, and he gives me a small smile. My stomach drops to my feet. The world seems to narrow so just he and I exist. I shake my head and scream, running after him like I could do something to stop him. But I only take three steps before I'm wrapped in claws as well.

My scream is cut short as the vise-like grip around my middle tightens, but I never take my eyes off Nico. I watch in horror as the bisso galeto flies over the woods and drops him. Nico flails, grabbing the bag from his back and shifting it to his front. He wraps his arms around Twig, even as he careens toward his death. I still can't scream, even though I'm screaming inside, but my mouth is open in silent despair. His body falls, falls, falls. Then he crashes through the trees, and I can't see him anymore.

No. No. No! My heart thunders in my chest so hard, I can hear the echo of it in my ears. I swear it sounds like Nico's name.

A pained shout draws my attention from the spot where Nico disappeared, and I turn my head to find Mattie being carried with claws pierced through his middle. Blood runs freely from the wound and drips like raindrops to the ground. This creature takes Mattie over the woods and drops his body as well. I'm living in a nightmare. Watching my mates injured and falling to their deaths, and there is nothing I can do to save them.

Silent tears stream down my face as I try to gasp for breath. The harder I struggle, though, the tighter the grip around my waist becomes. As the creature carrying me flies further and further away, I frantically scan the sky for my last mate. Leith is also in the grasp of a bisso galeto, but instead of being dropped, the creature carrying him follows the one carrying me.

After a few minutes of struggling against the claws around my middle, my vision darkens at the edges. No matter how hard I try to draw in a full breath, I can't. The panic and tears only make everything worse. The tearing in my heart, the images of Mattie and Nico falling, the bag with Twig wrapped in Nico's arms, is a weight upon me that suffocates more than the squeezing of the claws. I glance behind me toward Leith. His gaze is glued on me, and his pained expression is the last thing I see before everything goes black.

34

DACIANA

I fight as I rise to consciousness. If I can stay asleep for a bit longer, that's more time I don't have to think about what happened. The dark void of nothingness is welcome compared to the sinking fear and agonizing despair. Just one thought about Mattie and Nico, one mental image of their bodies falling, drives me to insanity. I lost two of my mates before I ever really had them. I lost Twig.

I roll over and curl into a ball, ignoring the discomfort that tells me I'm lying on a hard stone floor. It doesn't matter anymore. I'll never be truly comfortable again. There will always be this aching emptiness inside of me where they should be. It's like a missing rib. I know it's gone, I can sense it's absence, and the pain it causes is debilitating.

The only thing that gets me to open my eyes is knowing Leith is still alive. At least he was when the bisso galeto carried us away. And Nico attempted to save Twig. I have to keep telling myself he's still alive. There is no other reality I'll accept. I force myself to sit up and push down the tears that well in my eyes. I don't have the luxury of mourning right now.

Looking around, I find that I'm in an empty room. The red stone floor is cold underneath me, and the dark brown walls seem as if they are closing in. Standing, I stumble to the door and attempt to open it. I'm not surprised to find it locked. I go to the window next. I appear to be on the second floor. It looks out over a small fenced-in barnyard. The window won't open, of course, and there is nothing in this room I can use to break the glass. Instead, I take in the surroundings outside.

People work in the fields, or I suppose they must be fairies. They are short in stature and willowy. Their skin ranges from a blue so pale it's almost white, to a dark, royal blue. They go about their business in a determined fashion, yet there is something about them that makes them look defeated. Maybe it's the way they never look up from the ground or the way their steps seem heavy and tiring. Or maybe it's the set of their shoulders, slumped and rounded, that makes them look as if their will to live has been beaten out of them

As I look out the window, I remember Mattie's last words to me. *"You need to stay strong and remember what your goal is. Find the eggs. Get them out. Kill Morta if you can, but don't risk it if you can't."* Even though thinking about him makes me wrap my arms around my middle and fold in on myself, I know I can't give up. They wouldn't want me to. There will be time to cry for them, and now is not that time. I have a task to complete. But first, I have to figure out how to get out of this room.

I don't have to wait long. A soft knock on the door is followed by the sound of a key scraping in the lock and the bolt turning over. I spread my legs and ball my hands into fists. I may not be good at fighting, but that won't stop me from trying. But the moment I spot the pale blue woman poking her head inside my room, I deflate.

She looks terrified. Her brown eyes are wide in her face, and her fingers grip the door handle hard enough to turn her knuckles white. She's wearing a dark-gray dress with a white apron, and a white kerchief covers her dark-blond hair. She's clearly a servant of some kind, and obviously being forced to do this.

I make myself relax, curving my shoulders inward to appear timid and frightened. Taking a step back from the door, I clasp my hands in front of me. "Who are you? Where am I?" I ask shakily. "Where's Leith?"

"My name is Hota. I'm to bring you to Morta," she curtsies low, her voice high and quiet. "I also need to warn you not to attempt to escape. The bisso galeto are everywhere. And they are watching."

My heart trips over itself, but this is my goal. I need to figure out where Morta is hiding the eggs. I motion her to lead the way, and I follow. I make sure to study my surroundings as we go. We appear to be in a sort of medieval-style manor. The floors are roughhewn stone and the walls are dark wood. Torches line the hallway, giving off acrid black smoke that burns my eyes. The doors we pass are black wood with rusted iron handles and locks. I see no other people besides the blue-skinned fairies and the rooster-like monsters that make my blood run cold.

Hota takes me to the stairs, which curve down in a half spiral to the first floor. It's not much different on the lower level. It's more open with windows that let in the light, but it's still dark and foreboding. I follow Hota to a door carved with three stars. Two of the stars have been scratched out, like someone angrily took a knife to them.

"Just do as she asks," Hota whispers, "and you'll be fine."

She knocks and opens the door, gently pushing me inside. My eyes immediately travel to Morta. There is no other possibility for who the woman sitting in the large wooden chair could be. She looks like her sisters, only older and more vicious. Her hair is long and straight, gray streaking through the black. Her narrow chin and sharp cheekbones give her a witch-like appearance. But it's the cold look in her green eyes that stops me in my tracks. There is nothing remotely warm in that gaze.

"Daciana DeRosa," she coos in a low melodious voice. "I've been waiting for you."

I say nothing. And not only because I don't know what to say. My body seems to have frozen in her presence. Fear leaks through my bloodstream like ichor, poisoning me and keeping me from doing anything.

"My sisters have been very naughty." She shakes her head as she stands and rounds the desk. Her black dress billows behind her, the long sleeves trailing over her fingers. A simple golden brooch in the shape of a snake adorns the breast of her garment. "It's unfortunate they got you mixed up in all of this. If they had left well enough alone, you could have continued living your peaceful life." She tsks and stops in front of me, looking down her sharp nose. "Now, you'll have to pay the price for their arrogance."

I try to swallow, but my throat is too dry. What do I do? I need to find out where the eggs are. I need to get her out of the picture. How do I do all this alone and without powers?

A sharp black-painted nail scrapes down my cheek, making me flinch. "Help me hatch the eggs and I'll treat you fairly."

I clench my jaw and shake my head. "No."

Her green eyes flash dangerously, and she backhands me hard enough to knock me to the ground. Pain flares in my cheek and I taste the coppery flavor of blood on my tongue. I blink back tears and press my hand to the burning skin.

Morta squats down, grabs one of my silver slippers, and pulls. "Then give me the slippers."

"No," I growl again through the blood pooling in my mouth.

I try to yank my foot away but I'm not fast enough. Still, even though she pulls with all her might, the slipper stays firmly on my foot. Morta screeches and tries harder, pulling on my foot until my leg hurts. I kick out with my free leg and connect with her stomach. When she falls backward, I scramble to my feet.

Morta is too quick though. She shoves me against the wall and bares her teeth. "Take. Off. The. Shoes."

"No," I grit out with a glare.

Her face turns an alarming shade of red before she takes a deep breath and steps back. Smoothing down her black skirts, she composes herself amazingly quick. And when she gives me a smile, my stomach clenches.

"That's fine. I always have a backup plan. Either you'll give me those shoes or you'll become my puppet. The choice is yours.

Let's see what we can do to help you decide." She grabs my wrist and drags me from the office.

I try to pull free, but her grip is inhumanly strong. I fight the entire way back up the stairs and down the hall. Unease pumps through my bloodstream. I tremble in her grasp as every possible horrible scenario rushes through my mind. She stops in front of the door next to the room I was in. With a wave of her hand, the lock clicks and Morta shoves me inside.

I wince, falling to my hands and knees painfully, but my gaze immediately goes to Leith. He's chained to the corner of the wall, and the black metal shimmers faintly with a hint of reddish-orange. Cuts and bruises cover his body, and his left eye is purple and swollen shut. Even looking beaten to death, he watches me with deadly focus.

"Leith!" I cry. I try to crawl to him, but Morta grabs my hair and pulls me to my feet. Tears spring to my eyes at the prickle of pain in my scalp, and Leith growls, tugging at his chains until they rattle.

"Let me lay down a few ground rules," Morta says calmly, stepping to the side, her fist still clenched in my hair. A bisso galeto struts into the room. This one looks more human-like, but I'm unable to pinpoint exactly what about it makes me think that. "If you act out"—she shakes her hand holding my hair, causing me to jerk back and forth—"you're silent friend here will pay the price." She turns to Leith and smiles coldly. "And the same goes for you. So it will behoove you to behave and do as I ask."

Leith stops fighting against the chains. He's breathing heavily and blood oozes from the iron cuffs around his wrists. The sight makes my stomach churn. He doesn't take his eyes off me though.

"Now," Morta says, letting me go. "Give me the shoes."

Dread curls in my gut, but I stand firm. "No."

Morta's smile could chill even the most frozen river. I don't see what she does, but the bisso galeto moves. It reaches out a clawed foot and slices through Leith's stomach. It's not a deep cut, but it's enough to well with blood and make him hiss through his teeth.

I lurch toward him, a scream lodged in my throat, but Morta forces me to the ground with an invisible force. It pins me on my hands and knees, squeezes my chin, and forces my head up to watch Leith bleed.

"Let's try again." Morta's voice is entirely too cheery, and I want nothing more than to rip her fucking heart out. "Give me the shoes."

Leith shakes his head, silently telling me not to give in. I want to though. I want to give her the shoes so she won't hurt him. But I trust Leith. So I swallow and take a deep breath.

"No." The word isn't as sure as it has been the past few times I told her no. But I still mean it.

Again, the bisso galeto moves to Leith. This time, a gash opens on his thigh. This one is deeper, and he grunts at the pain. I scream and fight against the forces holding me down, but it's no use. Tears stream down my cheeks and fall to the ground. Still, Leith doesn't take his eyes off me.

Morta sighs. "I'm not going to lie, I'm impressed you haven't caved yet. Let's try it again. Give me the shoes."

My chest aches with how hard I'm crying. The sobs shake my body even in Morta's constraints. Leith shakes his head again, his blue eyes endlessly sad. I can't do it. I can't watch him be tortured.

Seeing this on my face, Leith's eyes harden. *Don't do it,* he mouths. *Don't give her the shoes.*

I close my eyes and suck in a ragged breath through the tears. "No," I whisper.

This time, Leith screams when the bisso galeto pierces his arm all the way through. My vision wavers and only Morta's magic keeps me from collapsing.

"Stop," I breathe. "Please, stop hurting him."

"Then give me the shoes."

I sob. It's on the tip of my tongue to say yes. But then I remember Nico and Mattie. I remember Twig. I remember their bodies falling from the sky as Morta's wicked creatures let them drop. If I give her the shoes, their deaths will be in vain. But can I watch Leith be tortured more? The certainty in his eyes, even through the haze of pain, tells me I can. I have to.

"I will never give them to you," I spit.

Morta clicks her tongue in disappointment. "Let's try something else, shall we?"

At her words, Leith's eyes widen in fear. His face pales even more and he shakes his head. I take a breath, because I know what's going to come this time.

Morta turns to the bisso galeto and dismisses it from the room before turning her attention to Leith. "Order her to take off the shoes." She points a finger at him, black manicured nails glinting dully in the low light. "But don't even think twice about doing something stupid. You won't live long enough to finish your sentence. And Daci will follow you soon after."

My stomach drops. She knows what Leith is. That's why she kept him alive. Because with his magic, he can make me do anything. The reddish-orange shine in the black chains shimmers then disappears. But Leith doesn't open his mouth. Instead, he clamps his jaw shut tight and gives me an apologetic look.

I don't have time to prepare myself, and even if I had, there is nothing I could have done. Fire sears through my veins. I scream and thrash, but I can't move. My body is burning from the inside out. My blood boils and sizzles. My bones melt. And through it all, I scream and scream and scream until I can't scream anymore.

Leith roars, pulling at his chains, ignoring the way his injuries open even further. But there is nothing he can do. When the fire subsides, I hang limply in Morta's bonds. My heart races so fast, I'm worried it will stop completely. My lungs ache with how hard I'm breathing.

Morta doesn't give me a chance to recover. "Order her to give me the shoes."

A tear slides down Leith's cheek, but he shakes his head.

Again, fire burns through me. I open my mouth to scream,

but nothing comes out. If I had been free, my body would be writhing on the floor, but I'm frozen in place while my insides burn. Leith struggles so hard, his tendons pop. The chains groan where they are embedded in the wall. I keep my eyes on him. I steal all the strength I can from his gaze. But it's not enough.

Morta's fire rages longer than the last time, and soon my vision darkens. The last thing I see is Leith fighting to get to me but failing.

35
DACIANA

Everything hurts. My body feels like it's been run through an incinerator then hit by a Mack Truck. I groan as I roll over on the hard floor. Peeling my eyes open, I look at my hands and arms, surprised to find my skin unblemished. I thought I'd find it charred and peeling from my bones.

But the pain won't keep me down. The only thing I can think about is Leith. There was so much blood pooling around him before I passed out. I crawl to the wall, knowing he's right on the other side, chained and unable to move. With my hands on the rough wood, I lean my face against it.

"Leith," I say, my voice more of a croak than anything. "Leith," I say louder. There's no response. I clear my throat and attempt to gather moisture in my mouth to swallow. "Leith!" Still nothing.

I choke back a sob and flip around to lean against the wall. Just that bit of movement drains me. A fine sweat coats my entire body, and my limbs tremble from fatigue. I don't think Morta would kill him. He's too valuable to her. If she can break him, he'd be a powerful weapon in her hands. But at the same time, he's stubborn and strong. He won't break easily, and if Morta gets tired of his games . . .

I cut off that line of thinking. I can't afford to let myself fall into that trap. I need to be strong. I need to find the eggs.

A knock on the door makes me groan, but when Hota enters, I relax. She sets a bucket of water in front of me and hands me a cloth. "Here. You can wash up. Her Eminence has ordered you to do chores today."

I move slowly, giving myself time to think of what to say. "Leith. Is he . . ."

"He's okay," Hota says quietly, looking at the closed door. "Her Eminence had someone heal his wounds."

My stomach sours because I know she only had him healed so she can do it all again. "Hota, how did you come to work for Morta?"

She glances at the door again before saying so quietly, I barely hear, "It wasn't a choice. My people were living peacefully when Morta came and took over. We're at her mercy now."

So I could have a potential ally in . . . "What are your people called? I'm not from Oz."

"Ariatan. We're air fae."

Their blue skin makes sense now. I nod and choose my words carefully. "I understand you have to be careful, but would your people be willing to help me? I promise I will do what I can to save you."

Hota's pale-blue face drains of even more color. "What you're asking is incredibly dangerous," she whispers.

"I know. And I wouldn't ask if it wasn't important. It's not for me. I'm the dragon guardian, and Morta has the last remaining dragon eggs. I need to get them to save the dragons."

Hota's eyes go impossibly wide. "Dragons?"

I nod, and my heart squeezes when I think about Twig. He's alive. He has to be. I know Nico managed to save him. I'll accept nothing less. "This is the last chance to bring them back. Please help me."

Hota studies me for a moment before nodding. "I'll talk to my people. We'll do what we can."

I almost sag with relief, but I keep my chin high as I finish washing. With the ariatans' help, I may just be able to do this. I just hope I don't get them all killed in the process.

Hota wasn't lying. Morta is working me to death. I have been moving non-stop since I stepped out of my room. Sweeping. Mopping. Dusting. Laundry. Even cleaning out the ash in the fireplaces. I haven't had a single bite to eat since I got here, and the longer I go, the weaker I become.

My stomach is an empty hole, rivaling the one in my chest where Nico and Mattie should be. Waves of nausea mix with hunger like a rollercoaster that leaves my head spinning. Morta is going to get her wish. I'm going to die of hunger, and she'll be able to take the shoes.

Whenever I feel myself giving up, I remember the dragons. I imagine Twig and his puppy-like antics. I feel Mattie's touch on my face and see Nico's eyes as they pierce my soul. I hear Leith's screams as he's tortured to keep me safe. If I give up, I'll be letting all of them down. So I push myself further. I force myself to keep going for one minute longer.

My back twinges as I push myself into a kneeling position. I'm covered in soot head to toe, and my fingers ache from holding the scrubbing brush. When I stand, my head swims. Stars burst in my vision, and I sway on my feet. A passing ariatan notices and rushes off. When I reach for the mantel, I miss.

My knees hit the floor hard enough to bring tears to my eyes, but I barely notice. Darkness creeps into my vision, and I know I'm seconds from passing out. Small worn brown shoes appear in front of me, then a small blue face. The ariatan that saw me wavering on my feet. He slips me some bread and cheese before rushing away.

I shove the food in my mouth, heedless of the soot staining my fingers. It's not enough to sate my hunger, but it does stop my shaking and clear my vision. I sit for a few moments, letting the carbs boost my energy, and when I stand again, the room doesn't spin quite as bad.

I slowly make my way to the second floor, being extra careful on the steps because killing myself by falling down them would just be embarrassing. At the top, I take a moment to catch my breath and look around. There's a guard in front of Leith's room and my heart sinks. I was hoping to sneak in there.

Still, I walk that direction and keep my chin high. I have no idea if the bisso galeto can understand spoken language, or reply, but I figure it can't hurt to try. "Can I see him?" I ask quietly, ignoring the slight tremor in my voice. These things are terrifying.

It shakes its head, and my heart drops. I figured as much, but it was worth a try. Still, the tears come unbidden. If I could see him once, maybe touch him, it would give me the strength I need to keep going.

I don't know what the bisso galeto sees in my expression, or why he changes his mind, but he opens his beak and hisses quietly, "One minute."

I hold my breath as he steps aside, and I don't waste any time slipping into the room. Leith is still chained to the wall. He's sitting in the corner with his legs pulled up to his chest and his forehead resting on his knees. At the creaking of the door, he lifts his head and gasps.

I rush to him and throw myself in his arms. The chains barely let him wrap me in a hug. I bury my face in his neck, and I have to fight the urge to break down in tears. He holds me tightly for a moment before pushing me away so he can look at me. His blue eyes scan my soot-covered face with concern.

"I'm fine," I whisper. "But I only have a minute. The ariatan are going to help us. At least, as much as they can. We just need to stay strong." Even as I say this, my voice wavers. Because even if we succeed in getting the eggs, Mattie and Nico . . .

Leith closes his eyes and pulls me back in for a hug. Of course he knows exactly what I'm thinking. I lost my mates, but he lost his best friends, his brothers. I have to remember I'm not the only one suffering.

When I pull away, he cups my cheeks in his hands, the chains clanking with his movements. From the corner of my eye, I notice the reddish-orange hue in the metal again. He swallows roughly. "Be careful," he whispers hoarsely. "Please. I can't lose you too."

When he presses a kiss to my forehead, I almost lose it. How will I stand up and walk out of this room without him? But the door squeaks open, and I make myself get up. I give him one last lingering look before leaving. Tucking away the feeling of his touch, his arms around me, his lips on my skin, I strengthen my resolve.

I *will* find the eggs. And I *will* take Morta down in the process.

The next day, Hota gets me early in the morning and brings me to the pig yard. It reeks of manure, and mud and pig shit squishes under my shoes. Despite this, they glitter in the sunlight. It's as if nothing can tarnish them.

"Her Eminence wants you to clean the sty today." She looks around before lowering her voice. "I'll make sure someone brings you food and water. It gets hot under the sun here."

And she wasn't lying. As the sun rises higher in the sky, so does the temperature. There is no breeze to cool the sweat sliding down my face and back. My skin steadily turns a rosy shade, then straight up red as the sun burns me. I've never tanned well. I get my porcelain coloring from my mom, and we both burn under the sun.

The stench at least isn't so bad anymore, probably because I'm used to it. But shoveling shit is hard work. Each scoop and lift makes my back ache something fierce. Blisters have bubbled up and broken on my hands, leaving bloody streaks on the shovel handle. Even though it hurts, I'm too exhausted to really notice.

I think my body is going into shock, or I'm burying everything so deep inside of me, I can't find it. I'm on autopilot as I work, my mind blank and full of cotton. I don't even hear someone approach until slow clapping draws me from my numb haze.

"Well, well, well," Morta drawls. "The pampered princess can do hard labor. Who would've thought."

I straighten, cringing at the fire lancing through my lower back. Somewhere along the way, I've lost my fear of this woman. Maybe I'm just so exhausted and over it all, I can't bring myself to find any feeling. I glare at her and imagine my hands wrapped around her throat, squeezing and squeezing until all the life leaves her worthless body.

Morta chuckles as if she knows exactly what I'm thinking. "Oh yes. There is still some fight in you. Guess I'll have to work you even harder. But don't worry. I'll get there. And when I do, you'll gladly hand those shoes over to me."

She turns on her heel and walks away. A sudden burst of anger works through my hazy numbness, burning away the fog shrouding my mind. Without thinking, I grab a bucket of water and toss it as hard as I can at Morta. She's far enough away, it barely reaches her, but the water sloshes to the ground and splashes up, droplets flinging everywhere. Some of them land on her heels.

Morta shrieks. It's an unholy sound that causes my vision to blur. She jumps and spins around, looking at the puddle on the ground in front of her. I think I see fear in her eyes, but she blinks and it's gone, leaving nothing but pure hatred behind. Even with that deadly look, I can't find it in me to be afraid.

"You'll pay for that, girl," she snarls.

When she turns back around and walks away, I swear I see smoke curling from her feet.

I spend the rest of the day in the pig pen, but my mind is elsewhere. Morta's reaction to the water was a little extreme. Sure, no one likes to get splashed with water. But the way she completely freaked out seems strange to me. And I swear I saw smoke where the water touched her. Am I so fatigued and hungry that I'm imagining things?

I'm walking slowly back to my room, nibbling on a piece of bread an ariatan snuck me, when Hota rounds a corner. She heads for me and slows her steps, but she doesn't stop walking. Instead, she says quietly as she passes me, "I know where the eggs are."

I almost trip over my feet, but I force myself to keep walking. Holy shit. If she knows where they are, this can all be over! I school my face into a mask of exhaustion. It's not hard because I am utterly spent, but I need to make sure I don't give anything away. The bisso galeto guarding Leith's door always watches me closely. He hasn't let me back in to see Leith, but Morta also hasn't tried to use us against each other again.

In my room, I collapse to the floor, and I'm so tired the hard stone doesn't even bother me. I'm about to drift off when my door opens. Hota brings me a plate of bread and cheese. It's the only *legal* meal I receive. The rest of the bread is snuck to me throughout the day.

She sets the plate down. "You can't get to them without dealing with Her Eminence first," she whispers.

My stomach drops. I was hoping to take the eggs and run, but apparently that won't be an option. "Do you know how to do that?"

She shakes her head. "We've been watching for a long time, but no one has spotted any weaknesses." She smiles sadly before leaving.

I eat my bread and cheese and mull over her words. No one has found a weakness yet. But everyone has a weakness. Did she show me hers when I splashed her with water? I don't have any answers when I lie down and close my eyes.

36
LEITH

Four days.

Four days have passed since we were ambushed by the bisso galeto. Four days since my brothers . . .

I bite hard on my lower lip, using the pain to wipe away the tears that build behind my eyes. That is one thought I will never be able to finish. And right now, I can't afford to fall into the pain losing them causes. Daci is my priority, and I need to find a way to get us out of here.

Unfortunately, I have no good options. The chains holding me to the wall were made with arum, a rare flower found in Oz that nullifies magical powers. Even if I were to try to use my magic, I wouldn't be able to. And I know my magic doesn't work on the Parcae. I found that out when Nona saved me all those years ago. So no matter how hard I try to come up with a plan, I get nowhere.

Groaning, I shift against the wall. Every part of me aches. Morta had me healed after the first torture session, but only enough to stop the bleeding of the worst injuries. My wrists have been rubbed raw by the chains, and every movement sends fire through them. I'm sore from sitting in the same position and not being able to get up and move around. It's maddening.

But the worst is knowing my mate is out there and I can't get to her. I have no idea if she's hurt or hungry. There's nothing I can do to keep her safe or help her through her pain at losing two of her . . .

I shake my head roughly, attempting to shake that thought

right out of my mind. If I fall into it, I'll spiral until I'm useless to Daci. Not that I'm not useless chained to the wall like I am. With a substantial amount of effort, I unclench my jaw and take a deep breath, re-focusing myself to find a plan to get us out of here.

I've just settled into some semblance of calm when the lock to my room clicks and the door groans open. My breath catches as hope flutters inside of me. I haven't seen Daci since she snuck in here, and if I can lay eyes on her it will calm the rolling fear that won't go away.

Unfortunately, it's not just Daci. When Morta pushes my mate into the room, my stomach clenches and fear floods my system. A cold sweat breaks out over my skin because I know what's going to happen next. If I thought losing my brothers was hard, being used as a weapon against my mate is one hundred times worse.

Daci falls to her knees with a muffled shout of pain, and I clench my fists. She looks up at me through a curtain of tangled blond hair, and I can see the fear shimmering in her green eyes. She knows what's coming next as well. Somehow, we both have to stay strong enough to survive this.

"It's a lovely day today, isn't it?" Morta coos, gently brushing Daci's hair from her face. The dark bruise-like circles under my mate's eyes spark a fire inside of me. She looks utterly exhausted. "Your little princess here has been worked so hard and she's so tired, I have no doubt she'll cave today."

Despite the fear and exhaustion, Daci's gaze hardens as she looks at me. She gives me a subtle shake of her head, and I know she's still able to fight this. My girl is stronger than anyone gives her credit for. Now the question is, will I be able to stay strong?

Morta tests my resolve when she grabs Daci's hair and yanks her head back, eliciting a whimper from my mate. "Shall we begin?" Morta waves a hand and the reddish-orange of the arum in the chains holding me back disappears. Somehow, she's able to nullify the effect in the hopes I'll use my magic. "Make her give me the shoes."

Bile climbs up my throat, acidic and burning. I swallow it down and clench my jaw shut. *I will not cave. Daci is strong. She can handle this.* My gaze meets Daci's, and her green eyes remain hard, even as her breathing increases. She won't want me to give in. So I say nothing.

Morta sighs dramatically and snaps her fingers. The scream that comes from Daci pierces straight to my soul. It flays me alive and peels the skin from my bones. My heart splinters into thousands of pieces, and there is nothing I can do but watch as my mate writhes on the ground in agony.

Even knowing it won't do any good, I pull on my chains. I pull until they creak and groan against the pressure. But no matter how hard I try, they remain firmly embedded in the wall. I can't tear my gaze away from Daci. The tendons in her neck pop as she strains and screams. It seems like it lasts for hours. In reality, it probably lasts only seconds. When Morta pulls her magic back into herself, Daci slumps on the ground, shoulders heaving as she pulls air into her lungs.

"Daci," I croak, my voice unused to being used. When I open my mouth to say more, I feel a shimmer inside my veins. Golden light flickering as my magic comes to life. I clamp my mouth shut and shove my magic so far inside myself, I'll hopefully never find it again.

Daci lifts her head. Tears stream down her cheeks, but she shakes her head at me again. "Don't," she whispers.

Morta clicks her tongue. "This is so tiring." A blade appears in her hand, and she grabs Daci's hair again, yanking her head back to expose her neck. "I'd hoped I could convince you to make a decision. You have two choices, how hard can it be?." She gazes down at Daci in irritation. "Either give me the shoes or do what I ask of you. I don't want to hurt you even more, but you're giving me no other option."

A ball of ice forms in my gut and Daci's eyes go impossibly wide. I strain even harder against my restraints until my muscles shake and burn. I'll do it. I'll cave if she threatens Daci's life. I know without a shred of doubt I'll give in.

Faster than an asp, Morta swings her arm and blood blooms from Daci's right shoulder. The pain doesn't register at first, then Daci screams again, clapping a hand over the wound. I watch with horror as her blood seeps through her shirt and between her fingers. Then Morta strikes again. This time her left thigh. Daci collapses to the ground with a pained shout.

A growl climbs up my throat, and I thrash against the chains. Watching Daci's blood pool on the floor sends me into a frenzy. The mate bond between us flares, so hot it almost burns inside my chest. Every instinct as a mated fae male is firing, and I can't act on a single one.

Daci screams again. She writhes on the ground as Morta uses her magic to torture her even more. The movement causes her wounds to bleed faster, but Morta doesn't stop. She watches me with a smile and a raised brow, waiting for me to cave. And I'm so fucking close. I can put an end to Daci's pain. I can make Morta stop. All I have to do is say the words. *Take off the shoes.* My chest aches and my eyes burn. I can make this all stop.

As if she can sense what I'm about to do, Daci lifts her head. Sweat plasters her hair to her forehead. And even though her face is pale and contorted in pain, her green eyes focus on me. "Don't. You. Fucking. Dare," she grits out between clenched teeth and sharp breaths.

Morta sighs and she must pull her magic back in, because Daci stops writhing on the ground. Her body shudders and twitches at the lingering pain, and her chest heaves, but she looks at me with such strength and determination it cracks me open. My beautiful, strong, stubborn mate.

"Now you're just mocking me," Morta says, walking in a slow circle around Daci. She cocks her head to the side, studying her limp body on the floor. "I suppose I can wait a bit longer. Breaking you will be so satisfying."

Morta grabs Daci by the hair again and pulls her to her feet. Daci struggles but has no choice except to get her feet under her. I watch The Parcae drags my mate from the room, blood dripping onto the tile floor in her wake. As the door shuts behind them, the tears break free and I let myself cry for my mate.

37
DACIANA

The next day, I'm in the kitchen filling a bucket of water to mop the kitchen floor. My hands have never been so pruny before in my life. And my nails are absolutely atrocious. They're cracked and chipped and broken in jagged pieces. For the first time, I don't care. Looking good doesn't mean anything to me anymore. Right now, all I want is to save the dragons and for me and Leith to get out of here.

When Morta returned me to my room, she healed my wounds, but the lingering pain from her magic hasn't abated. Every inch of my body throbs and burns. I can still feel her magic flowing through me, searing every nerve, cell, and tendon. Exhaustion weighs heavily upon me, and each move I make takes tremendous effort. I want to curl into a ball and give up. But I can't. And I won't.

The bucket is half full when I hear footsteps behind me. Glancing over my shoulder, I freeze. Morta stands in the kitchen, looking as out of place as I would have just a few weeks ago. She sneers at me and places her hands on her hips.

"Come with me, girl."

"Where?" I cross my arms and give her my best haughty look. It's hard when I look and feel like a street urchin though, dirty and ragged and broken down.

"It doesn't matter where," she snaps. "You're coming with me." She tries to grab my arm, but I jerk to the side out of her grasp.

"Tell me where we're going first."

"Fine. It will only make you dread it more." She studies her perfect nails, not chipped and broken like mine. "We're going to visit your friend. This time it will be him that bleeds."

My blood runs cold. Not again. Not so soon. I can handle being tortured by her. I would gladly accept the pain, but I'm not sure I can watch my mate bleed again. Leith almost gave in yesterday. I felt it along the bond. His resolve slowly shriveled and dried up until only desperation remained. Will that be me today? Will I be the one to give in and hand Morta the shoes that give her the power to hatch the dragon eggs? I have to end this now. I can't let her take me to Leith's room.

I brace myself, spreading my legs wider, and take a deep breath. "No."

Morta smiles. "What did you say?"

It's hard to ignore that rapid pounding of my heart as I face off against the Parcae, but I can't let her hurt Leith. "I said no. You're not going to use us against each other anymore. I won't go with you."

Her smile spreads. "I'd like to see you try to stop me."

She reaches out a hand and the burning begins. I fall to my knees, screaming in agony as I burn from the inside out. I dig at my skin, trying to peel it from my bones, hoping to ease the searing heat inside of me. It wouldn't surprise me to find my skin bubbling and popping with smoke curling from it.

Smoke.

The bucket of water is still in the sink. If I can get to it, I can pour it on Morta and pray I'm right about my suspicions. It's the only possible weakness I can think of, and it's worth a shot. I have nothing to lose. She's going to torture me and Leith no matter what happens. So I think about Mattie and Nico and Twig. I use their memories to strengthen me and push the pain away. The image of Leith bleeding and straining against his restraints is the armor I need to fight against this wave of magic.

Gritting my teeth, I climb to my hands and knees. I only have one shot at this, and I can't let her see what I'm doing. So I close my eyes and swallow the pain. Screaming, I leap to my feet and reach for the bucket. My fingers curl around the wooden rim and I grasp it, pulling it from the sink. It takes all my strength to hold on to it. My fingers are numb and twitching from Morta's magic.

Morta realizes what I'm doing. She ducks to the side as I toss it, distracted enough that the fire burning inside me disappears. In the process, the bucket slips from my hands and I accidentally throw it across the room. The water hits Morta's hand and she shrieks, the sound once again piercing my ears and making my vision swim. She clutches her hand to her chest, hiding it in the fabric of her dress, but not before I see the skin bubbling and smoking.

So water *is* her weakness. I quickly look around, but the bucket is too far away and will take too long to refill. I need another way to get her wet and quickly before she recovers too much. The silver pipe connecting the sink to the wall catches my attention and I leap for it, hitting the ground hard enough to make me grunt.

I wrap my hands around the pipe and pull. It doesn't budge. Behind me, I hear Morta moving and I glance over my shoulder to see her standing straighter, reaching her other hand out toward me. I brace my feet against the wall as leverage and pull with everything I have. The pipe groans, but it doesn't break.

Come on, Daci. You can do this. For Mattie and Nico. For Twig and the dragons. For Leith.

I close my eyes, clenching my jaw. I pull so hard, my muscles shake. But Morta gets to me first. Her magic slams into me again, harder than it ever has. Fire ignites inside of me, and pain sweeps from my head to my toes so fiercely, I almost black out. But it causes my body to jerk violently, and I refuse to let go of the pipe. As I jerk, the pipe breaks away from the wall.

Freezing cold water sprays into the kitchen, drenching me. Morta screams in agony and the fire inside me disappears. I spin around to find her scuttling backward on her ass, trying to get away from the steadily growing puddle. Where the water touches her skin, it bubbles and smokes. Her green eyes are wide in fear and anger, and when she pins me with a stare, I suck in a breath.

This is it. This is my opportunity. I lurch forward and grab her ankles, tugging with all my remaining strength. She flails, but the closer I pull her to the water, the weaker she becomes. I'm able to grab her shoulders and I hold her under the spray of water, feeling her body tremble under my hands. The black dress she's wearing becomes baggier on her frame, as her body slowly gets smaller and smaller.

Smoke fills the room, billowing from her in great gray waves that make me cough, but I don't let go. Her body melts into mist. Her scream echoes in the kitchen before fading away into nothing. I'm too stunned to move, so I sit in the freezing water next to the empty clothing and shiver and gasp until Hota finds me minutes later.

She sucks in a sharp breath and drops down beside me. "You killed her?"

I shake my head. "She can't be killed since she's one of the parcae, but she's been reduced to a spirit form until her sisters give her another body to inhabit." My words are numb, like my body. I still can't believe I did it. Any minute now, I'm sure to wake up and realize it was all a dream.

Hota digs through the clothes in the puddle and hands me the golden snake brooch Morta always wore. "Take this and show it to the guard outside Leith's door."

I don't ask why, I just do as she says. Shivering and leaving a trail of water in my wake, I head to Leith's room and show the guard the hairpin. His eyes widen and he bows his rooster neck low.

"My lady," he hisses. He opens the door and unlocks Leith's chains before leaving.

Leith looks at me in confusion then lurches to his feet and wraps me in his arms, picking me up off the ground. I bury my face in his neck and let all my emotions spill out. Exhaustion. Fear. Despair. It pours from me in heaving sobs that shake my body. Leith holds me through all of it, rocking back and forth to comfort me.

When I no longer have the energy to cry, I step back. "She's gone," I say hoarsely. "I got rid of Morta. We can get the eggs and leave."

"What about the bisso galeto?" he signs.

I look at the hairpin in my hand and frown. "I don't think they'll be a problem anymore."

And I'm right. No one stops me from following Hota into Morta's chambers. The eggs are hidden under a floorboard in her closet. I almost laugh at how human-like it is, to hide something under the floorboards like that. Like a teenager hiding something from their parents.

But I handle the chest carefully, setting it down so gently. There is no lock on the chest, which surprises me. I flip open the lid and gasp. Six eggs are nestled snugly inside. They're about the size of half a watermelon, and their scale-like shells range in colors from gold to red, and black to purple. I run my finger over the purple one. It's warm, like an ember of fire exists within it.

I look at Leith in amazement. "We did it," I whisper.

His eyes are lined with tears as he looks at the eggs and signs, "I can't believe I'm looking at a real dragon egg."

"We need to find Twig," I say quietly. "Ni-Nico stuffed him in his bag before the attack." I swallow the pain that rises at the thought of Nico.

Leith loses the awestruck smile on his face. He nods. "We'll find him. And we'll bring them all home."

I clutch my chest at the sharp burst of pain that radiates outward. Bring them home. Find my mates' bodies and make sure they are burned upon a pyre like the fae do. I stare blankly at Leith, unable to process what he said. Or maybe just unwilling to process my loss. I lost my mates and my baby dragon just as I found them. How cruel can fate be?

Leith takes my face between his palms and studies me. Whatever he sees makes him sigh. Instead of trying to comfort me, which would be pointless, he kisses my forehead and leads me from the estate.

"Keep it. You earned it." Hota curtsies to me before tucking the golden brooch into my hand. "With it, you can control the bisso galeto." She sees me shiver and she chuckles. "They don't have to be used for evil. Also, you don't have to use them at all."

I nod but cast a sideways glance at the large rooster-snake standing off to the side. He's apparently the captain of the bisso galeto, and he's patiently waiting for my orders.

"Thank you," Hota continues. "Without you, we'd still be stuck under Morta's thumb. We're free now because of you, and we'll be eternally grateful. If you ever need anything, please don't hesitate to ask. And you're always welcome here."

I give Hota a quick hug before turning to Leith. "I don't know what to do with this," I say quietly, holding up the brooch.

"They can help us search for Twig," he signs. "From the air, the search will go much quicker."

"That's a good point. Okay. Do I just . . . ask them?"

He quirks a smile, tucks a stray lock of hair behind my ear, and signs, "Yes, you just have to ask them."

I take a deep breath before I face the commander. The image of claws piercing Mattie's stomach haunts me. I can still smell the acrid smoke of the burned village. Although I know it was at Morta's orders, these creatures still carried out horrendous acts of violence.

"We would like your help searching for my baby dragon," I say as calmly as I can, ignoring the way my skin crawls just talking to one of these creatures.

The commander steps toward me, and it takes everything I have to not back away. "It would be our pleasure," it hisses, bowing its rooster-like head. "And we would also like to thank you for rescuing us from Morta's clutches. The things she made us do . . ." The creature's eyes go distant. Then he shakes his head, feathers rustling, and lowers himself to his belly. "Climb on."

What? Climb on? He expects me to ride on him? Leith is strapping the chest of dragon eggs on the back of one of the beasts, and he gives me an encouraging smile. Hesitating, I weigh my options. If I don't accept the ride from this thing, it will take me forever to find Nico, Mattie, and Twig. Do I have any other choice? With one last glance at Leith, already settled on the back of his rooster, I give in.

I grimace as I grab feathers and pull myself up, but it doesn't seem to hurt the creature. When I'm sitting on its back, it shakes back and forth to settle me more firmly. I mimic Leith's posture and lean forward over its neck, wrapping my arms around it. There is no warning. An undignified squeak crawls up my throat as the bisso galeto flaps its wings and takes off into the air.

I spend the first five minutes with my eyes squeezed tightly shut. But eventually I remember the reason for being up here on the back of this creature. I pry my eyes open and swallow as I look at the ground. It swims alarmingly under me, and I wrap my arms tighter around the bisso galeto.

"I can't do this!" I shout to Leith.

If he answers, I have no idea, because I can't open my eyes no matter how hard I try. My body will not respond to my command. The feathers under my hands turn slick with sweat from my palms. We're so high up. And no matter how hard I try not to think about the height, it's the only thing my mind will focus on.

The creature under me rumbles, and I realize it's laughing. "Keep your eyes closed," he hisses. "I'll look for you."

I don't know how much time passes. All I'm aware of is the sensation of the bisso galeto's wings flapping under me, and the wind pulling my hair from its braid. My grip never loosens, and I'm honestly surprised I haven't choked the creature to death. I only open my eyes when Leith's sharp whistle pierces through the wind. He's pointing to his right and when I look, I almost fall from the bisso galeto's back at the ground swimming below me. That was a bad idea. *Don't look down, Daci.*

It makes a quick descent, sending my stomach into my throat, but I swallow it back down. As soon as it lands, I jump off and I don't know where to look first. At Nico lying motionless on the ground, or at Twig, sitting by his side with his head on Nico's chest.

Twig's head snaps up when we land, and his golden eyes go impossibly wide. I bite back tears as he runs toward me and I dash forward to scoop him into my arms, holding him tightly to my chest. Small rumbling noises vibrate against me, and I have to fight back the tears that want to spill over.

"Are you okay?" I whisper, running my hand down his smooth neck.

He nods and something that's been wound tight inside of me loosens. Twig is okay. That's one less thing I have to worry about. But when I turn my attention to Leith, the tears I was trying to hold back spill over.

He kneels next to Nico's body. There is something unreadable in his expression, and I slowly make my way over, my entire body shaking.

"He's still alive," Leith signs slowly.

"What?" I drop to my knees and run my gaze over Nico, stopping on his chest. It rises slowly, barely noticeable. When I place my fingers on his neck, a slow but steady beat pulses against my fingertips. "He's alive?" I choke out around the lump in my throat. "Nico," I breathe.

Twig hops from my arms and takes up his position next to Nico with his head on his chest. Just then, movement in the brush to our right draws our attention. A small topo fatato scurries out and places a berry in Nico's mouth.

"Have you been keeping him alive?" I ask through my tears. The tiny fairy nods before scurrying away again.

"We need to get him to the Emerald City," Leith signs.

"What about . . . what about Mattie?" My voice cracks on Mattie's name. "Maybe . . ." I'm unable to finish my thought, because if it's not true, I'll be heartbroken all over again.

Leith nods and picks up Nico. He settles him on the back of a bisso galeto before climbing up after him. I help Twig settle into Nico's backpack before climbing onto my bisso galeto. Once again, I close my eyes. Watching the ground swoop past makes my stomach feel as if it's going to crawl up my throat.

This search takes longer, and I'm scared Leith is about to call it when he whistles and points again. I try not to hold my breath as we descend, but I'm so scared I'll find Mattie's dead body.

When we land, I hop off, and my legs almost give out. Mattie lies on the forest floor with a host of topo fatatos scurrying around him. Leaves have been placed on his stomach, and some sort of brown paste has been slathered under the leaves.

I fall at his side, hands hovering over his body. His chest also rises, but much slower and shallower than Nico's. I bite back a sob and address the closest topo fatato. "Thank you for keeping him alive," I breathe, nodding my head in a bow. "We'll take it from here."

The creatures bow back and scurry away, leaving me and Leith alone with Mattie. He's so pale. Dried blood crusts the ground under him, and I have to fight back a wave of panic. He's still alive. And if we get him to the Emerald City, everything will be okay. It has to be.

I climb back onto the bisso galeto, and Leith lifts Mattie up in front of me. I'm careful of his injuries, but I hold him tight enough to make sure he doesn't fall. When Leith climbs onto his rooster-snake, we take off for the Emerald City where hopefully we can save my two mates.

38

DACIANA

After Mattie and Nico are settled into their rooms for healing, a servant escorts us to Decima's lounge. She's sitting in the green velvet chair in front of the table lit with golden flames. Once again, Twig rushes for the table, eyeing the fire with something that almost looks like envy.

Decima's gaze goes straight to the chest in Leith's arms. "You got them," she breathes. "And are they all whole?"

I nod and open the chest. "All six look unharmed. But don't they need to be incubated or something?"

"No, thankfully. Now that they are in your possession with the silver slippers, they'll begin to hatch. Once that happens, they'll need to be placed near a fire. But until then, they are fine."

"And when will they hatch?" I ask.

"Nona and I intervened with Twig. But the rest will hatch naturally within a couple of months now that you are here."

I bite my bottom lip and look at the ground, suddenly nervous. "Will you . . . will you help me? I still don't know what I'm doing, and I really don't want to mess this up."

Decima gives me the kindest smile she has yet. "Of course I will. But I have a feeling you won't need much help from me." Her gaze flicks to Leith briefly before returning to me.

"Thank you again, for helping Nico and Mattie. I really can't tell you how grateful I am for that."

Her smile turns slightly wicked. "Oh, I can imagine. Interesting, isn't it? Even though I am in charge of fate, it still sometimes makes its own rules. Lucky for you."

Heat rushes to my cheeks and I duck my head. "Yes, well . . ."

"You can put the dragon eggs in the garden," Decima says, ignoring the way she just embarrassed me. "They'll enjoy the sunlight, even though they don't need it. I'll place a guard on the eggs so they'll be safe, and I'll let no one into the garden except you."

"Thank you." I bow my head. "And what about Morta?"

Decima sighs and looks like she wants to slouch in her chair and hang her head. She does neither though. "Her spirit has returned to its resting place—a temple where our magic originates from. She'll remain there until Nona and I decide what to do with her. But you needn't worry. It will take us quite a long time to decide what to do."

I nod and hesitate. Slowly, I pull the golden snake brooch from my pocket and hold it out to her. "I don't want this," I say quietly. "I know the bisso galeto aren't evil, but I can't forget the things they did under Morta's control." And I don't want another responsibility. Raising the dragons is going to be hard enough.

Decima takes the brooch with a nod. "I'll keep this somewhere safe. We don't want someone like Morta to get their hands on it."

She dismisses us and we head to the garden, where Leith sets the chest on the ground in a patch of sunlight. The scales on the eggs shimmer and shine, throwing rainbows all around.

"They're really beautiful, aren't they? Do you think the dragons will be the color of their egg?" I ask.

He shrugs. "I have no idea. Guess we'll find out in a couple of months," he signs.

I turn to face him, suddenly overwhelmed by so many emotions. I'm relieved we got the eggs. I'm nervous about being a dragon guardian. I'm anxious for Mattie and Nico to wake up. I'm scared to confront Nico again, to forgive him and move on. I take a shaky breath, on the verge of losing it entirely.

Leith, as always, is more observant than I give him credit for. Even though he doesn't like to be touched, he pulls me into his arms as soon as he sees how much I need his hug. I melt against him, letting him hold my weight. When I think I have my emotions under control, I pull away, not wanting to put him in a situation that makes him uncomfortable.

Leith doesn't let me go far though. He looks at me with an expression that makes me almost lose it again. "I love you, Daci," he whispers.

And with those four words, I crumble. Leith catches me and pulls me into his arms again. This time, I don't try to hold back my tears. I let them fall and purge my past fears and insecurities. I let the tears make way for my future, clearing a path for my three mates and the dragons we're going to have to raise together.

Leith wipes my tears with his thumbs and searches my eyes. "I hope those were good tears," he signs.

I laugh and nod. "Yes, they were. And I love you, too."

I'm rewarded with the brightest smile. And then Leith wrecks my world completely. He frames my face in his hands and bends down to kiss me. I gasp, and he slips his tongue past my lips, brushing it against mine. I hesitate, not sure what to do with my hands, but Leith takes control and solves my dilemma. He grasps my wrists and raises them, lifting them to the back of his neck. My fingers tangle in the soft curls of his hair and Leith grabs my waist, tugging me close against him.

I lose myself in his kiss and the way his tongue caresses mine. Little sparks sizzle every place where our bodies touch, even through our clothing. I catalogue and memorize the way the hard planes of his body feel against mine. Strong, sure, and safe. It's not very often I get to be wrapped in his embrace, and each time he gives me this opportunity, I cherish it.

When Leith pulls away, it takes a tremendous amount of self-control to not chase his mouth. But I take a breath and step back, smiling at the dazed look on his face.

"I think I could get used to that," he signs slowly, making me smile even wider.

"Me too."

I haven't left Mattie's side in two days. Before Nico woke up, I would split my time between their rooms. But now that Nico is awake and back to his usual asshole self, I've taken up residence in Mattie's room.

Twig, Leith, and Nico are usually with me, but I find myself alone for a rare moment, and I take advantage of it. I don't feel comfortable talking to Mattie while they are here. Not because I'm worried about them judging me or anything like that. But because it seems too personal.

"Hey," I whisper, sitting next to him on the bed. "I miss you, Mattie. I think you'd be proud of me and how I handled Morta. And I can't wait to show you the dragon eggs. Twig has taken to lying with them a lot. I think he feels like a big brother." I sigh and run my finger over his bottom lip. "But it's not the same without you. So, please wake up. I need you." I toy with one of his locs and smile. "You need to get your hair done. It's looking kind of rough." I know that would drive him insane. His hair is always perfect, and knowing I said something bad about it . . .

"My hair looks fine," he rasps.

I jolt and pull my hand away as a slow grin spreads across his face. "Mattie!" I have to refrain from throwing myself on top of him and squeezing until he pops. "Are you . . . Do you need . . . What can I . . ." A million questions run through my head, and they all tumble together, making it impossible to get out what I want to say.

"Just lie with me?" he asks, finally cracking his eyes open. "My head is stuffed with cotton balls, I think."

"No cotton balls," I whisper, snuggling down to rest my head on his shoulder.

"What happened? Tell me everything."

I launch into the tale, starting from watching him get gutted, to returning to the Emerald City with the eggs and two bodies.

When I'm done talking, he takes a deep breath and shakes his head.

"You defeated her on your own?" he breathes. "I always knew you could do it. You're a tough cookie when you need to be."

"It was . . ." I swallow, ignoring the way my eyes burn. "It was so hard," I choke out. "I thought you and Nico were . . . and I . . . it was just . . ."

"Shhh," Mattie mutters, holding me tighter. "Everything worked out. It will take more than some flying rooster-snakes to take me and Nico away from you."

I huff a snotty laugh and bury my head in his chest. "Don't ever leave me," I whisper. "Please."

Mattie tangles his fingers in my hair and tugs to lift my head. His eyes shine so brightly as he says, "I promise, edainai. I will never leave you."

"What does that *mean*?" I ask again, blinking back tears.

As usual, Mattie only smiles and kisses my forehead before changing the subject. "Where are the others? They don't care about me enough to sit by my bed while I'm injured?"

"Psh, we've been here almost the entire time," Nico says, stepping into the room, followed by Leith. "We went out to check on Twig and the dragon eggs."

"Glad you're awake," Leith signs, sitting on the other side of the bed. "Your hair looks like shit, by the way."

I stifle a laugh, and Mattie glares. "My hair looks fine. I was just half dead a day ago. You could give a guy a break."

I ignore the words that make my insides shake with fear. Mattie being half dead. Nico unconscious. It was not an experience I ever want to go through again. Leith and Nico both smile, but Nico's smile fades when he sees my haunted expression.

"So," Nico says, sliding his hands into his pockets. "What now?"

My heart slams against my ribcage at his words. "What do you mean?" I try to hide the tremor in my voice, but I don't think I succeed very well.

"We rescued the eggs. We got you to the Emerald City. Isn't that what we were supposed to do?"

I stop breathing. Nico and I had this conversation before we were attacked. He said he was going to stay with me, even if I didn't want him to. And I do want him to. So, now he's saying he won't? He's watching me like he's looking for my reaction, and I don't know what kind of reaction he's looking for. So I do my best to keep my face blank.

Mattie takes my hand, drawing my attention to him. "I think the question should be, do the eggs have to stay in the Emerald City? Ultimately, wherever the eggs end up is where Daci ends up. And wherever Daci ends up is where I end up."

"Agreed," Leith signs, giving me an encouraging smile.

Two-thirds of the tension inside me melt away. But there is still one-third making my insides twist uncomfortably. I look at Nico and find him already watching me. Still not knowing what he's looking for, I glance away. It will be better if he can't see my expression when he says he'll be leaving.

"Daci," he says quietly. "Can we take a walk?"

I nod but look back at Mattie before I stand. "Don't do anything stupid while I'm gone. You better still be in one piece when I come back."

"I can't promise that." He grins at me then gives me a soft kiss.

I follow Nico down the hallway. The silence stretches between us like a rubber band about to snap. Each step I take increases my anxiety until my palms sweat and my heart races. Communication between us has been difficult from the start. Being from rival families started us off on the wrong foot, and Nico keeping the secret of me being his mate derailed us completely. Before the attack, I thought we were working on improving things between us, but maybe I was wrong.

I can never tell with him. He's always so cold and distant, and it's impossible to read him. Wouldn't it be better to come out and say what I feel? No mincing words, no sugarcoating? Just simple, honest truth? I'm too exhausted to keep going on this way. My steps slow, then I stop. Nico turns around with a frown. He opens his mouth to say something, but I don't give him the chance.

"I don't want you to leave," I say simply. "I want you to stay with me, wherever I end up. I want to be with you, Mattie, and Leith." I close my eyes, afraid of seeing his reaction, but when I do, I see him falling from the grip of the bisso galeto. My voice trembles as I continue. "I almost lost you, and I realized being mad at you isn't worth it. Thinking I lost you forever hurt more than your betrayal." I shake my head and swallow, opening my eyes to see his desperate expression. "I don't want to be angry anymore. I don't want to hurt anymore. I just want . . . you."

Nico sucks in a ragged breath then takes three large steps to close the distance between us. He cups my cheeks gently, lifting my chin and molding his mouth to mine. While he may hold me gently, his kiss is anything but. It's rough, demanding, obliterating. He invades my senses completely, and I lose myself willingly.

I've gone so long without his kiss, without his touch, it's like I'm starved for it. I can't get enough of his hands on my skin, his lips against mine, his tongue . . . I break away with a moan and slide my hands around his neck. Nico grips my ass and lifts me, helping me wrap my legs around his waist. With sure and steady strides, he walks us to his room, kicking the door shut behind him.

Within seconds, I'm on his bed and we're both stripping out of our clothes like they're on fire. Then he's leaning over me, kissing along my collarbone, over my shoulder, biting my nipple. His fingers find every sensitive part of my body and he drives me wild with his touches. When he claims my mouth again, it's frenzied, like we're scared we won't get this moment again and he wants to imprint himself on my very soul.

I can't tell him he already has because he steals all the breath from my lungs with each kiss, each touch, each soft exhale.

Nico pulls back, eyes wild, but he swallows and tucks a strand of hair behind my ear. "Are you sure, princess? I don't want you to regret this."

I pull his head down to kiss him, spreading my legs so his hips settle in the cradle of my thighs. "I won't regret it, Nico. You're my mate, and I'm not going to fight it anymore."

His eyes fall closed and he shudders over top of me, but I catch a glimpse of a rare smile before he kisses me again. This one is slow and deep. It consumes me from the inside out, and I lose all sense of myself until he rocks his hips and his cock rubs against me. The sound I make is borderline embarrassing, except he makes one almost the exact same.

"Please, Nico," I beg, scratching my nails down his back and lifting my hips. "Please don't make me beg for you."

His dark eyes devour me, and they spark with something feral and heated. "But what if I want you to beg?"

I whimper and lift my hips again, searching for his touch. "Then make me do it later," I almost growl. "Right now, I want you to make me come so hard I see stars."

"Fuck," he hisses, taking himself in hand and lining up with my entrance. "As the princess commands."

He slides in with one smooth thrust of his hips, and I gasp. The stretch is exactly what I need, and I close my eyes and let the pleasure build. Nico's breathing steadily turns more ragged, his movements less refined. But I'm not there yet. And as that wall creeps up, so does my panic.

Nico must sense something, because he pauses and searches my face. I try to turn away, but he stops me with a strong grip on my chin. "Daci?"

The tears are already threatening, so I close my eyes to hide them. It's no use though. Nico sees through it. I don't want him to think he did anything wrong, because it's not him who's the problem. It's me. It's always me. So I take a shaky breath and swallow my shame.

"It's . . . I can't . . ." Or at least I try to. It's so much harder to admit out loud, especially when you're already so vulnerable in the middle of having sex.

Understanding flashes across Nico's face, followed closely by a wicked sort of delight. "I get it now. Why Mattie always chokes you." He gives me no warning before rolling us so I'm on top. His eyes are darker than the deepest pits of hell as he slides his hand up my body and wraps his fingers around my throat. "Take what you need, princess. Use me."

The way my body reacts instantly to that. I ride Nico while he slowly increases the pressure around my throat. Each gasp of air I squeeze past gets smaller and smaller, and the fire inside me burns hotter and hotter. Nico's free hand slides between us, and he rubs circles around my clit until my entire body is shuddering. I'm so fucking close, and it's not until he squeezes hard enough to cut off all oxygen that I'm finally able to let go.

The stars that burst in my vision could either be from lack of oxygen or the orgasm, but I feel so good breaking apart I don't even care. The fire that rushes through my body seems like it never ends. And it isn't until Nico releases my throat and I suck in lungfuls of air that he grabs my hips and flips us. He pounds into me until his rhythm stutters and he groans my name against my neck.

I'm unable to move. All I can do is lie there with Nico on top of me while I catch my breath. I feel thoroughly wrecked and I don't regret it at all. Accepting what's between us was exactly what I needed. All three of these guys are as essential to me as the air I breathe. Almost losing them was an eye-opener that I'm ashamed to say I needed.

But all that matters now is that I'm whole. I'm complete. I'm home.

39
DACIANA

"I'm sorry," Nico says sometime later.

I don't know how long we've laid in his bed, but I have no desire to get out. Nico is so warm and comfortable. With his arms around me, I know I don't have to worry about anything hurting me. If I could stay here with him forever, I would.

"Sorry about what?" I ask sleepily.

Nico continues to trail his fingertips up and down my arm. "I didn't keep my promise to you."

He sounds so broken as he says this, and I can't help but push up on my elbow to look at him. "What are you talking about? What promise?"

"I promised you I wouldn't let you down again. And I did. I broke my promise and I'm so, so sorry."

I frown, studying the heartbreaking dullness in his eyes. "You haven't let me down, Nico."

"I wasn't there to help you. I let myself get carried off by a bisso galeto. You had to face Morta on your own, thinking Mattie and I were dead. I should have been there but I wasn't, and I let you down."

"Nico," I breathe, cupping his cheek. "You didn't let me down. Even if you had been with me, you wouldn't have been able to do anything. Leith was used against me. The only time I got to see him was when one of us was being tortured. If you had been there, I would have had to withstand watching two of my mates being tortured. I don't think I could have survived that. I would have given in."

He doesn't look convinced, shaking his head and clenching

his jaw, but he lets it go. I lean down and kiss him, slowly and leisurely, before laying my head on his chest again.

"I lied, you know," I say after a beat of silence. "In the papavero field. I told you I wanted nothing to do with you. And I told you I thought I'd found my home but then you betrayed me, and I felt like I was wandering again. It was all a lie."

"Yeah, after you disappeared, that was a pretty good sign that you lied." His words are laced with an angry growl. "I told you you had to tell the truth."

"Yeah, well, I was angry and you didn't tell me *why* I had to tell you the truth. So it was kind of your fault."

He huffs and grabs my chin, forcing my head up so I'm looking at him. His dark eyes are hard and accusing. Nico definitely has a temper, and before it can get any worse and ruin the moment, I kiss him.

"That won't distract me," he says after I pull away.

"I wasn't trying to distract you. I just wanted to tell you that I found my home."

Before he can say anything, his bedroom door opens and Leith enters with Mattie's arm slung over his shoulder, supporting the other man's weight.

I sit up, clutching the sheet to my chest. "What the hell? Mattie, you should be in bed."

"I was in bed," he says breathlessly. "But you weren't there so I had to come find you."

Leith helps him settle next to me, and Mattie takes a moment to catch his breath. His skin is still pale and a sheen of sweat glistens on his forehead, but his eyes are bright as he looks at me and Nico.

"If I didn't help him, he would have crawled over here," Leith signs, trying to clear his name. "It was tempting, but I figured you'd be pissed if I let him do that." He hops onto the dresser and perches there, watching the three of us in bed with an amused smile.

"I gave you two plenty of time," Mattie says, reaching for me. "And I was lonely. Leith isn't as cuddly as you."

"Leith isn't cuddly at all," Nico mutters. He crosses his arms over his chest and leans against the headboard. My pissy, heartless Tin Man is back.

I smack his chest then sit next to him, helping Mattie lay his head in my lap. Despite Mattie being injured, a smile spreads across my face. I'm finally with all three of my mates without anything between us. No anger, hurt, or lies. And it's amazing.

"I see you smiling," Leith signs with his own grin.

"Hush," I sign back.

"So, what's the plan?" Mattie asks around a yawn.

I tug the covers up to his chest. "You need to get some rest, that's the plan."

"Rest is boring. I want to know what we're doing next."

Nico takes my hand and threads our fingers together. "I think that's up to Daci. Where do you want to raise the dragons?"

I shrug, suddenly feeling all the pressure. Whatever choice I make is where we'll ultimately end up living. "Shouldn't it be a group decision? I mean, it involves all of us. And I know nothing of Oz."

Mattie hums in the back of his throat. "We already told you, edainai. Where you go, we go. Just say the word."

Before I can think of the possibilities, I sigh. "Mattie. What does that mean? Please tell me." I grab his locs and tug.

He chuckles and turns his head to look at me better. "It's fae for 'baby girl.'"

My stomach flutters. The butterflies inside me swirl to life at his look, the softness of his gaze, and the meaning of his words. Baby girl. I bite my lip to keep from smiling, and force my thoughts to the possibilities of where we can live. While I enjoy the Emerald City, it's too busy and chaotic. Not to mention dragons probably need a lot of space. So somewhere in the country would be best. But not too far in the country, because I'm still a city girl at heart.

"What about somewhere outside of Villabosco? There would be plenty of room for dragons, but still close to a town for supplies and all that." I hold my breath and try to gauge all their reactions at once. Mattie and Leith smile, but Nico just shrugs.

"I think that's perfect," Leith signs.

"Agreed." Mattie beams up at me and it makes my heart flutter.

I turn to Nico, waiting for him to shoot it down, but he leans over and kisses me. "I already told you. I'll follow you anywhere."

I close my eyes and swallow back the tears that burn up my throat. "If there's one thing I learned in all of this, it's that home isn't a place. Home is where your heart is happiest. And mine is happiest with you guys. You are my home."

A week later, I find myself standing outside of my dad's house in Girasole. Decima was able to send us here with her magic so we could at least inform our families that we were alive but not returning home. I left Twig with the guys in the forest next to the house, seeing as showing up with any of them—Twig included— would only cause more problems.

I take a breath and shake out my arms, mentally preparing myself to face my dad. Slowly, I open the front door and make my way to his office. He's sitting behind his desk, piles of paper stacked everywhere. I'd hoped he would appear somewhat distraught at my disappearance again, but he looks like he always does when he's dealing with Camorra business. Serious, composed, and calm.

I knock on the doorframe before stepping into the office and closing the door behind me. He looks up and his eyes widen. He pushes to his feet then rounds the desk and stops in front of me, looking me up and down. A frown slowly creeps onto his features when he notices how well put-together I look. Nothing like I did the last time I returned home.

"Daci," he breathes. "Are you okay? Where have you been?"

"We need to talk," I say, brushing past him and sitting in front of his desk. I wait for him to take his seat before I launch into my planned speech. "I'm not doing this anymore. I understand how important the Camorra is to you, but I've come to the realization that it's more important to you than I am. I'm ashamed at how much I played into your plans and willingly accepted them as normal. I'm not a tool to be used to further your place in the Camorra. I'm not a slut you can whore out to get information from your enemies." My fingers grip the armrest so tightly, they turn white. Just recalling what I've done in the past for my dad makes shame heat the back of my neck. "For too long I let you buy me with jewelry and clothes, and I foolishly believed you actually cared about me. My eyes have been opened, and I won't be returning to that way of life again.

"I'm not coming back home," I continue, my voice cracking at the emotion I'm trying to keep hidden. Despite everything, this is still hard to do. Lorenzo DeRosa is still my dad, and I love him despite everything. "I just want you to know that I'm safe, and I've found a place to call my home. You won't be able to reach me there, but I can tell you that I'm happy. Finally. I've finally found my place and my happiness. And as much as I want you to understand that and be happy for me, I know all you're thinking about right now is how this will impact you in the Camorra." I sigh and push to my feet, ignoring the shock on my dad's features. Reaching into my bag, I pull out a letter and place it on his desk. "If you could give this to Sophia, I'd really appreciate it."

Without a backward glance, I walk away. I leave the only place I ever thought was my home, the person I thought cared for me over everything else. My steps are surprisingly light as I head to the forest and the three guys and the baby dragon who have shown me how wrong I was. I was never at home here. My dad wasn't the only family I had. When I see them waiting for me on the edge of the woods, I smile.

40
NICOLAI

I wasn't really surprised at how well Daci handled telling her dad she wouldn't be returning to Girasole. That girl has done nothing but prove over and over again how strong she is. What does surprise me is the nerves I feel facing down my own father. This seems like a chapter of my life I'm closing the door on. The chapter that has been the only thing I've known, the only thing I've ever seen for my future.

That is, until I met Daci. She stormed into my life and destroyed everything I thought I knew about myself and my life.

I stand in his office and let his words wash over me. Of course, the first thing he did was yell at me for disappearing and shirking my duties. I ignore all of it and let him get it out of his system. I won't be able to get a word in until he's done. While he yells, I study his features because this very well may be the last time I see him. Our relationship isn't terrible. He cares about me more than I think Daci's dad cares for her. But like with all children of the Camorra, he sees me as something to be used. That never bothered me, and it still doesn't. But it does make this easier to do.

I look a lot like my dad, thankfully. There isn't much of my so-called mother in me. His hair is graying at the temples, but it's the same dark brown as mine. A few wrinkles crease the corner of his eyes, the same brown as mine. And I know the lines by his mouth from frowning so much will match the ones I get when I'm older.

When he finally runs out of steam, I ask, "Can I talk now?"

He narrows his eyes at me but nods.

"I'm leaving. I'm stepping down from my position in the Camorra, and I will no longer be carrying out your orders. Something has come up, and I'm moving to Oz, so you won't be able to reach me."

With each word I speak, red slowly creeps up my dad's neck into his face. His jaw clenches and he fists his hands on his desk. I ignore it and keep talking.

"Mattie and Leith are going with me. I know this will impact your position in the Camorra, and I'd like to say I'm sorry, but really, I'm not. I'd also like to hope you would listen to me when I ask you to stop the violence, but I also know that's pointless." I hesitate before saying, "Thank you. For everything. Even though I didn't necessarily have the childhood a kid should, you still brought Mattie and Leith into my life, and I'll be forever grateful for that."

"Nicolai!"

I ignore his strangled shout and walk out of his office, a weight I wasn't even aware existed lifting from my shoulders. As I round the corner, I bump into Giorgia. She stares up at me with large, watering eyes.

"You heard everything, didn't you?" I sigh and take her shoulder, leading her into the library.

She sits on the couch next to me and I almost crumple at seeing her stricken expression. "You're leaving?" Her voice wobbles, and her lips tremble.

I was planning on telling her I was leaving, but I didn't think through how horrible it would be to actually leave her. "GiGi," I say quietly, tucking a black curl behind her ear. "Something has come up, and I have to return to Oz."

A tear slips past her lashes, and she looks up at me with her big brown eyes. "You're not coming back?"

I swallow the lump in my throat. "I met someone. My mate, actually. She has to remain in Oz. There is no way I can leave her."

"Your mate?"

I nod. She knows enough about me and Oz to know what

that means. I watch a range of emotions flicker over her face. Happiness, despair, fear. "GiGi." I reach for her hands and find them clammy and shaking.

"Take me with you," she whispers, tears sliding down her face. "Don't leave me behind."

My heart cracks and splinters into thousands of pieces. "GiGi, I can't. Dad would—"

"He'll use me," she says, her voice gaining strength. "Without you here, he'll use me to continue climbing the ladder." She shakes her head violently, her black curls bouncing. "Please, Nico. Please."

My blood freezes at her words. Giorgia is too wise, too old, for her ten years. As is the way with all children of the Camorra. But what she said is the absolute truth. Without me, my dad will turn his attention to her. Daci flashes in my mind. She was around Giorgia's age when her mom died, leaving her to be raised by her dad. And look what he made her do.

Fire erupts in my belly at the thought of Giorgia going through what Daci did. There is no way I can walk away from her and leave her to that fate. I pinch the bridge of my nose and curse.

"Okay, listen to me closely," I say. "Oz is nothing like Girasole. My mate, Daci, has two other mates—Mattie and Leith. She is also the dragon guardian, so we'll be raising baby dragons."

When I mention Mattie, her brown eyes narrow, but as soon as I say dragons, she gasps. "Baby dragons?" She bounces on the couch. "Nico, please, please, please take me with you!"

I look into her brown eyes and see the excitement shining in them, hiding the fear at being left behind. "I've never been able to say no to you," I mumble.

She squeals and throws herself at me, wrapping her arms around my neck. "Thank you, Nico!"

I push her away gently and give her my most serious expression. Of course, it has no effect on her. "Here's the deal, though. You have to tell Dad. And you can only pack one bag."

When we meet the others in the forest, I can't help but smile at their reactions to seeing Giorgia. Leith smiles and opens his arms for a hug. Mattie rolls his eyes and pats the top of her head. Daci raises a brow and stares at me questioningly.

"Giorgia, this is Daci, my mate." I take Daci's hand and squeeze it gently. "Daci, this is my sister, GiGi."

GiGi plants her hands on her hips and stares up at Daci with a glare. "I heard Mattie is your mate," she says through clenched teeth. "I just want you to know, I already claimed him as my future husband."

Mattie chokes and covers his grin with his hand. Daci's mouth opens, but nothing comes out. She looks at me, eyes begging for help, so I take pity on her and kneel on the ground.

"GiGi, this is Twig."

That gets her attention, and I smile as she squeals and falls to the ground to pet him. With GiGi distracted, I look at the others.

"I can't leave her behind. Without me home, my dad will use her. The same way—" I cut off, looking at Daci.

Daci sucks in a breath and glances down at GiGi, who's rubbing Twig's belly like a puppy. "No. You can't leave her to that kind of life," she whispers. "Of course she can come with us."

I lean over and give her a soft kiss. "Thank you."

"As long as she knows Mattie is mine," she growls.

I laugh and step back to take in the people and the dragon before me. Daci was right. Home isn't a place. It's the people you surround yourself with.

Daci looks at me, then the others. Her green eyes shine as she takes my hand. "Can we go home now?"

EPILOGUE
1 YEAR LATER
DACIANA

"No! No! Megan, drop it!"

I shake my head and continue working on my painting, tuning out Mattie's shouting. With six baby dragons and one toddler dragon, sometimes that's all we do.

"Leith, stop her! She has a squirrel in her mouth!"

Of course she does. Megan loves all animals, even if they're terrified of her. One time we found her in a tree trying to sit on a bird's nest. Nico got her down before she could crush any of the eggs.

I tune back in to my painting and frown. The color isn't quite right. I add a smidge of blue to the mixture of paint on my palette and nod. Perfect. Just as I touch the brush to the canvas, a thump on the roof makes me jump. "Fucking dragons," I curse, looking at the smear of paint where it isn't supposed to be.

"Fucking dragons!" Nico yells, echoing me from outside. "Get off the damn roof!"

Two more thuds follow, along with the drag of tails swishing back and forth. Then, an even louder thump that causes the roof to groan.

"Damn it, Twig!" Nico shouts. "You know better. Get off the roof. Now!"

Twig growls low in his throat and the glass in the windows rattle. Apparently a two-year-old dragon is the equivalent to a fifteen-year-old girl. Moody, sassy, and argumentative.

I sigh and place my paintbrush in the cup of water next to my easel. Looks like I won't be getting any painting done today.

When I step outside, I stop in my tracks. I figured I'd be stepping into pure chaos, but what greets me is pale in comparison to chaos. In fact, there isn't a word to describe what I see.

Mattie is chasing Megan, her white scales shimmering beautifully in the sunlight. And she does indeed have a fluffy squirrel tail hanging from her mouth. At first, I think Leith is playing tug-of-war with Chomp, but upon closer inspection I realize he's trying to pry the ladder from the jaws of the burgundy-colored dragon. That also doesn't surprise me. Chomp got his name for a reason. A small fire burns behind Nico, and when I look closer, I can just make out the charred remains of a bookcase Nico was building for me.

"Fuck!" Nico shouts, falling to the ground and covering his head as Twig sails down from the roof, just barely missing him. "You are the worst sort of menace."

I chuckle and turn around, looking up at the roof. Ophelia, Lilly, and Bruiser are tussling on the tile shingles Leith and Mattie painstakingly installed. "You guys, get down from there," I call to them. "You know better. And if any shingle is broken, I'll use one of your scales to replace it."

They immediately cease their fighting and flap down to land in front of me. I give each of them a scratch under their chin and pat on the head before they wander away to get into more trouble.

"Where's Magnus?" I ask, turning to Nico.

He shrugs, too concerned with pouring buckets of water on the flames.

"How'd the fire start?"

"How the fuck do you think?" he growls. "Twig sneezed. Of course it had to be right on the bookshelf. I was almost done!"

That's an unfortunate occurrence around here, and one I'm not looking forward to when the six babies start breathing fire. Twig has gotten better at controlling it, but he still sets accidental fires when he sneezes—which is a lot because he likes to sniff the wildflowers. We're going to have to find a way to keep them from burning the house down.

I pat Nico's back and leave him to his task while I glance around. Sure enough, I spot a glint of gold next to the massive oak tree by our house. Mattie, Leith, and Nico single-handedly built our house in the year since I rescued the eggs. There are still a few things that need doing, but the house is livable. And I love it. They made sure to add lots of bedrooms and bathrooms, a library, a massive kitchen, and an art studio. Mattie even has a music room.

I approach the golden dragon and sit next to him. Magnus frequently lies in the tall grasses by the tree, watching the rest of the dragons get into trouble. His eyes are the color of a stormy sky, a blue-gray mixture that churns when you stare at them. Those eyes seem far too wise for a dragon so young—even more so than Twig's were. I have a feeling Magnus will end up the alpha of this dragon flight.

He sets his head in my lap, and I stroke the warm scales on his neck. "Why aren't you out there causing trouble for the guys?"

He huffs and small puffs of smoke curl from his nostrils. *They have enough to deal with. If I made any trouble, they wouldn't be able to handle it.*

Oh yeah. Alpha material for sure. "Well, I'm sure they appreciate that."

We sit quietly and watch the chaos unfold, occasionally commenting on one dragon's skills or places where another could use some work. Twig was a huge help for me when the dragons first hatched. He took his role as big brother very seriously. But as soon as Magnus began showing signs of his dominance, Twig stepped back. Since then, Magnus has shown me what it is to be a dragon guardian. Twig will always be my baby though.

When Nico finally gets Twig's fire put out, he joins us in the shade under the tree. "If I would have known how much work raising baby dragons was, I would have returned to Girasole in a heartbeat."

Magnus growls deep in his chest. *I still don't like this one.*

"You're not winning any points with Magnus," I tell my mate.

Nico glares at the dragon. "Yeah, well, he hasn't won any points in my book either."

These two definitely haven't hit it off. I'm guessing it has to do with both of their alpha-like personalities. Any time Nico tries to get close to me, Magnus inserts himself between us. He doesn't have any problems with Mattie or Leith. Just Nico. I find it endlessly entertaining. Two strong-willed males butting heads. One of these days, one of them will win, and I'm betting on Magnus.

"Why don't you go round up the babies and head in for dinner," I suggest to Magnus. "They should go to bed early tonight. They've been outside playing for a long time today."

Magnus and Nico stare at each other for a moment and I almost roll my eyes. But eventually Magnus dips his head in my direction and waddles off to gather the babies. Nico spent a lot of time with a couple of villagers from Villabosco building a barn for the dragons, although barn sounds too primitive.

The dragons basically live in a mansion next to our house. We even hired a cook to make them food, and someone to clean their house. It's ridiculous really. But honestly, it takes a lot off our plates, which are already full. Raising dragons is a full-time job.

As soon as Magnus is gone, Nico tackles me to the ground. "Finally," he says, burying his face in my neck.

I laugh and thread my fingers through his dark hair. "Tell me how you really feel, Nico."

"I think you can feel that for yourself," he says, voice low and gravelly.

And indeed, I can. Nico rubs his hips against my thigh, and I have to stifle a groan. "I'm so gross right now," I say, gasping as he bites the spot where my neck and shoulder meet. "I need to shower."

"Or," he says, licking up the column of my throat. "We could head to the hot spring. GiGi won't be back until tomorrow. It's the perfect opportunity."

Giorgia has been attending school in Villabosco and is thriving here. She loves taking care of the dragons. And even though she's grumpily accepted my mating to Mattie, we get along really well. She also has a great relationship with Decima, which is where she is right now. Giorgia spends one weekend a month with Decima in Oz, where she gets ridiculously spoiled.

"Did someone say hot spring?" Mattie asks, looking down at us.

"I did, but I wasn't inviting you," Nico growls.

Laughing, I push Nico off and sit up. "Let's *all* go to the hot spring. Nico can share."

LEITH FOUND this hot spring while hunting one day. It's not as big as the one we visited when we first came to Oz, but it's private and cozy. Perfect for the four of us. Large pine trees completely block it from the outside world. Stepping between the branches is like stepping into another world. The sounds from the forest outside dim, leaving the gentle lapping of the water against the edges of the rocks the only thing you can hear.

The boys waste no time stripping out of their clothes and wading into the pool. I watch them eagerly, taking in their muscles that shift under their skin that already glistens in the heat. They are too beautiful for words. And they're mine.

I slowly remove my clothes, enjoying the sensation of their gazes on me. When I turn around, my heart flutters in my chest. All three of them stare with hunger as they take in my naked body. I throw my hair into a bun on top of my head as I step into the water, hissing at the heat.

Nico wastes no time. He rushes forward and wraps his hands around my waist before pulling me against him. He kisses me like he's trying to devour me, and I melt against him, wrapping my legs and arms around him. The heat from the hot spring is no match to the heat that builds inside of me from Nico's kisses.

Without breaking the kiss, Nico carries me across the pool to a natural stone bench inside the hot spring that lifts us out of the water and gives us enough room to move. He sits down and I straddle him, my hips moving instinctively against his. Mattie hovers behind us, and he trails his fingers down my back, starting at my nape and ending just above my ass. I shiver at the touch and Mattie chuckles.

"You are so responsive," he says, his voice low and full of gravel. "I fucking love it."

Mattie's mouth replaces his fingers, nipping and kissing at my shoulders and neck. He wraps his hands around me and pinches my nipples, making my back arch. I gasp as the movement makes me grind on Nico's cock, and he greedily swallows the sound. Mattie keeps tugging and pulling, the pleasure turning to pain, but he doesn't stop until I whimper pathetically.

"Are you ready for us, edainai," Mattie whispers against the shell of my ear, making me shiver again.

I break away from Nico and nod. "Yes, please."

Leith lifts himself onto the bench and stokes his hand up and down his cock. I watch him and bite my lower lip. He smirks at me and squeezes the tip, milking a drop of pre-cum from the slit.

"Come on, guys," I whine.

Nico laughs darkly, but he lifts me and I grab his length to angle at my entrance. When he lowers me down, I moan. He stretches me perfectly, and I rise on my knees once before sitting back down. Slowly. Torturously. It draws a groan from him, and his fingers tighten on my hips until I know they'll leave bruises.

I hear foil tearing behind me, then Mattie drops an empty lube packet on the edge of the hot spring. Where the hell he got that from, I have no idea. But I stop moving on Nico and wait impatiently for Mattie. It took me a while, but after lots of patience from them, I can now take both Mattie and Nico at the same time. And it's my favorite thing.

The first press of his cock against my ass makes me tense up instinctively, but Nico knows exactly what to do. He gently rubs his thumb over my clit and turns my head so I'm watching Leith.

"Relax, princess," he whispers in my ear. "Leith is dying to watch you take both of us. You know how much that turns him on."

I whimper as Mattie pushes the tip inside, but I keep my gaze on Leith and watch as his blue eyes darken and his hand moves faster. Laying my head on Nico's shoulder, but keeping my eyes locked on Leith, I relax my body. Mattie slowly pushes inside, and it doesn't take long for the burn to disappear.

I'm impossibly full with both their cocks inside of me. My legs are already shaking when Mattie pulls back, and I have to use Nico's shoulders as leverage to lift myself up. He helps me with his hands on my waist, and he holds me steady as Mattie thrusts into my ass again. They alternate like this, and it doesn't take long for me to become completely useless.

I can't do anything except grip Nico's shoulders, digging my nails into his skin hard enough to draw blood. Leith watches with hunger as my pleasure builds higher and higher. The noises that fall from my lips would be embarrassing if I wasn't with my mates. I'm coming completely undone. There isn't a coherent thought in my head as the fire in my middle spreads.

But the best part of all of this is that I no longer have to worry about that fucking wall that always got in the way. All three of them know exactly what to do and somehow, they always know exactly when to do it. Right as I reach that first point of frustration, Mattie wraps his hand around my throat and squeezes. When I try to breathe air into my lungs and I can't, my body explodes.

Lightning sizzles through my veins and I break into millions of tiny pieces. My body shudders and shakes as my orgasm crashes through me with wave after wave. Mattie and Nico don't stop, drawing every last drop of pleasure from me.

I collapse onto Nico's shoulder, limp and completely spent.

Through my half-lidded eyes, I watch Leith as he hunches over, his body trembling as he finishes. Mattie and Nico come together, both of them emptying inside me with a chorus of groans.

Silence falls around us once again, only our harsh breaths echoing in the quiet of this hot spring oasis. Leith gives me a sweet smile and brushes sweaty strands of hair away from my face.

Mattie drops gentle kisses along my shoulders and down my spine. "You did so good, edainai," he says quietly.

"Absolutely perfect," Nico rumbles, hands rubbing up and down my thighs.

I hum contentedly in my throat and bask in their loving attention. My heart swells to the point that I'm afraid it will burst, but at least that means I'll have died happy. We let the silence surround us as we all come down from our high. This feeling of pure relaxation is something I enjoy the most about living with my mates. Within the safety of their arms, I can enjoy myself and not worry about anything.

Unfortunately, the peace doesn't last long. Leaves rustle outside the circle of pine trees, and branches snap and break. The guys stiffen, hands going to weapons they don't have on them.

"What the fuck is that?" Nico growls, stepping in front of me protectively.

Before any of us can answer him, a puff of smoke curls from the trees, followed by an emerald-green snout and glaring golden eyes.

"Son of a bitch, Twig," Mattie says, hand over his heart that is no doubt thumping as hard as mine is.

Twig steps from the trees and narrows his gaze on the four of us before shaking his head.

"Judgmental little shit," Nico mutters. "I'll fuc—"

I slap the back of Nico's head, cutting off whatever crude thing he was going to say. "Watch it. He's still just a toddler."

Leith grins while he signs, "He's going to have trauma to deal with when he's older. Seeing his parents have sex? Poor dude."

Twig huffs again, sending another curl of smoke into the sky.

Then he flaps his wings once and launches himself into the hot spring. Water splashes everywhere, and again when he surfaces, shaking himself like a dog.

The guys curse and groan, and I smile. This is my family. This is my home. And there is nowhere else I'd rather be.

Acknowledgments

And once again, I find myself having to write acknowledgments. It never gets easier. But first, I'd like to thank my readers. If you weren't reading these books, I wouldn't be able to keep writing them.

I need to give a huge shout out to my betas! This book was a hard one for me to write, and it was a mess for quite a while. Without their input, The Last Dragon of Oz never would have seen the light of day.

As always, I have to thank Lou. A lot of things went down while writing this book, and she helped to keep me sane while also helping me brainstorm and problem solve.

And of course, my family. My hubby is always so supportive of me and gives me the time and space I need to write and edit. And my son, who gives me inspiration when I see how excited he gets while reading his own books.

About the Author

Whitney L. Spradling is a neurospicy, full-time Occupational Therapist and autism mama, who has had a dream to write and publish a novel since she was a little girl. She lives outside of Cincinnati with her husband, son, and two cats.

She is a strange mixture of Disney adult, elder emo, and board game nerd with a love of tattoos, k-pop, skulls, moths, bees, Gengar, and otters.

When she is not writing, she can be found in her craft room making custom tumblers, watching C- or K-Dramas, or curled up with a good book and a cup of coffee.

Also by Whitney L. Spradling

The Obsidian Artifacts

The Obsidian Sword

The Obsidian Crown

The Cursed Realms

Of Flames and Curses

Of Smoke and Betrayal

Of Embers and Rising

Fates

These Dangerous Fates

These Deadly Dreams

These Wicked Desires

These Wondrous Moments: A Fates Novella

Standalones

Those We Couldn't Burn

The Last Dragon of Oz

More by Midnight Tide Publishing

See the full catalog at:

www.midnighttidepublishing.com

***

Heat Of Seas by DeAnna Hill

SOME ARE LED BY DESIRE.

After the mysterious death of the kingdom's queen ushers in a deadly plague, Carnaxa, Princess of Antalis, is promised to a rival kingdom. As ancient prophecies unfold, not only is Carnaxa in danger, but the fate of her kingdom as well.

Meanwhile, Anara, a gift of sorts and nothing more, was taken from her homeland. She didn't realize giving her heart away would keep her emotionally shackled, mirroring the physical chains she wore.

OTHERS ARE LED BY DUTY.

Captain Thylas has guarded Carnaxa since the day he washed ashore. When he's asked to accompany her to marry another, he finds himself torn between serving his kingdom and the desires of his heart.

Ereon, the Prince of Shaston, was raised in blood and battle. Faced with an uncompromising demand, he must choose between his birthright and his destiny.

WHEN DESIRE AND DUTY CLASH, LEGENDS ARE MADE.

Beyond the Iron Gate by M. A. Brown

A Pennies Worth of Dread Novella

"You shouldn't give your name so freely to monsters in the dark."

Beyond The Iron Gate is an eerie, dark winter Little Red Riding Hood retelling.